LAURA HOLTZ

WARM TRANSFER

COLUMBUS, OHIO

Warm Transfer
Published by Gatekeeper Press
2167 Stringtown Rd, Suite 109
Columbus, OH 43123-2989
www.GatekeeperPress.com

ISBN: 9781642371376

Printed in the United States of America

Grateful acknowledgement is made to Shari, Jon and Spencer Vegosen, and to Marcia Nickow PsyD, CADC.

Book Design by GKS Creative, Nashville

To Katherine, William and Henry, with love
To my family and friends, with gratitude

To the victims of abuse, with hope

Caitlin,
Happy Summer
Reading!

Leslie Holtz

"Who knows? Perhaps your love will make me forget
all I do not wish to remember."

ALEXANDER DUMAS
The Count of Monte Cristo

CHAPTER

1

Tamsen Peel had nothing to declare. She handed the stone-faced customs agent her blue-and-white form 6059B and waited unassumingly while he swept an apathetic gaze from her white canvas sneakers to her diamond stud earrings, lingering briefly just below the neckline of her sweater, causing her to adjust the position of a small tote bag carrying souvenirs for her children. There was no reason to feel nervous, yet she held her breath as the man rested his eyes on the Louis Vuitton roller bag that sat by her side like an obedient Labrador. Indeed, the bag likely cost more than the agent made in a month, but it had been a first anniversary gift from Victor, nothing she would have ever bought for herself, and aside from this weekend trip to London, it had only seen the inside of an overhead bin once in fourteen years.

"You're fine," the agent said flatly, nodding his head dismissively to the left, indicating that he was finished with her.

Fine. Given her fresh dusting of face powder, brushed-through thick dark hair, and a couple anti-redness drops in each eye, she could understand why her outward appearance might fool someone. The reality was, Tamsen was most definitely not fine. The only thing she sought from her time away from Victor was clarity. The answer to the Big Question: to remain in or to leave her marriage. She'd hoped her favorite city would give her the headspace for an answer, maybe even a sign—stay or go. She came back no clearer than when she had left.

It had been a light trip for shopping, nothing like her first return to London in her late twenties when her career in publishing peaked, and for the first and only time in her life, she had felt she made enough money to reward herself with several indulgent designer outfits and a fabulous pair of shoes. Even then, she had restrained her spending. Growing up, her father had frowned upon excess, often citing the Great Irish Famine to remind Tamsen that conspicuous consumption was a slap in the face of her ancestors.

With the exception of a Beatles t-shirt for Theo and a cotton Liberty London floral print skirt for Charlotte, Tamsen had acquired only a box of Harrods chocolate chip shortbread, a favorite of hers during her junior year college abroad, and a few small miscellaneous treats for the kids. She had also splurged for several varieties of soy waxed candles from a stand in Old Spitalfields Market, the same ones her best friend Petra stocked in her monstrous house on Victoria Road. Mission fig clover, honey orange blossom, and lavender basil, they were on sale for forty euros and worth their weight. If only Tamsen could replicate the feeling of Petra and Erich's peaceful Kensington domain—bottle up the ease and calm of their breakfast table, resplendent with jars of oozy strawberry preserves and flaky butter croissants. The magic of Erich's adoration for his wife, demonstrated as he gently squeezed the muscle tension from Petra's sore shoulders while she reviewed her morning emails—it seemed divine.

London had felt comfortingly familiar after all these years, and with the exception of her significantly upgraded accommodations and a Starbucks on every corner, Tamsen and Petra—now the Senior

Vice President of Ms Majestic Cosmetics company—happily found their old stomping grounds to be uncorrupted by the passing decades. Twenty years had evaporated quickly, yet their rare time together face to face never suffered because of the miles between them. Had Tamsen's husband allowed it, she might have tried to make a solo trip abroad an annual event, but given the fractured state of their marriage, she had no idea when she might get away again.

Victor agreed to Tamsen's London jaunt for one reason only—he wanted her to convince Petra to hire his advertising agency, Summers & Peel, for Ms Majestic's next big campaign. Ms Majestic, which dominated the women-with-skin-of-color market segment in Europe, was about to take the US by storm. Tamsen's job, at which she deliberately failed, was to grease the wheels for Summers & Peel. Petra blamed Victor for Tamsen's lack of visits, but Tamsen had her own reservations about being away from their son, Theo, for anything more than a day. Since Theo's diagnosis of epilepsy at the age of three, Tamsen had been entirely committed to his wellness.

She'd worried for months before the trip. Eleven-year-old Charlotte was an enthusiastic supporter of anything that helped control her brother's seizures. When she learned Theo was not allowed sugar, she threw her own secret candy stash from her backpack into the kitchen waste bin and instructed her friends never to tempt Theo with a cookie or a cereal bar. Theo's main source of calories was fat: organic butter, avocado, and heathy oils. Their dietician had been very specific about the amount of protein and carbohydrates Theo should consume, and even though Victor and their babysitter, Aneta, understood the importance of maintaining Theo's dietary protocol, Tamsen had left pink and green neon Post-it Notes all over the kitchen prior to her departure. Policing Theo's diet and activities had become second nature to Tamsen, but she knew that no one had the insight nor the concern to watch over him like she did. She had desperately needed to get away, but it would be an incredible relief to find him unscathed.

Once she'd arrived in London, however, Tamsen felt exhilarated by the sensation of being untethered, even if the feeling was short-lived. She had barely adjusted to the time change before she had to say goodbye to her guest room overlooking Erich's courtyard herb garden and savor one last brandy at her beloved Spaniards Inn, imagining the poet, John Keats, on the barstool beside her, twirling his pen between elegant fingers and thoughtfully curating the words to express his longing to escape his tortured world and follow the song of an enchanting nightingale. Tamsen made no apologies for being an insufferable literature geek. The Brontës, Dickens, Hardy, Austen, Eliot—these immortals were the authors in her bedroom bookcase; their voices were never more alive than when she was in London.

This year, Tamsen had been unable to read the classics. She was unable to read anything of substance, for that matter, with the exception of a book by a renowned family therapist, entitled *Separation: Sparing the Child*. Concentration was a lost aptitude. These days, she was lucky to make it through a Crate & Barrel catalog.

Tamsen walked toward the electronic doors that separated the jetlagged international travelers and all their baggage from waiting friends, sons, daughters, and parents. On the other side, Victor would be waiting, and Tamsen felt the prickling chill of goosebumps when she contemplated the penance to which he would subject her for taking time away. Her memory of their late summer altercation was still an open wound.

It had been his birthday, and though the novelty horoscope card she had purchased at the drugstore confirmed that the Leo male could be unpredictable and controlling, she was blindsided by the cruelty he'd displayed that evening after she'd prepared his favorite meal: salmon tartare with dill and capers, coq au vin, and chocolate ganache with raspberry coulis for dessert. Victor had complained for months, calling her an absentee wife, accusing her of having had a sexual lobotomy, so she had surprised him at bedtime wearing a La Perla ensemble he'd gotten her as a Valentine's Day present when they were first married, a coquettish bustier with matching garter belt, fishnet stockings, and crotchless panties. The getup had made her feel uncomfortable, anxious, and vulnerable—but at least she was trying. She had dimmed the lights in the master suite and lit several candles. After cuing a playlist entitled "Classical Libido," she had leaned provocatively inside the doorway with one hand on her hip and the other extended up, steadying herself in the highest pair of stilettos she owned. She had heard him advancing up the stairs and she licked her lips. When he had rounded the corner, he saw her and stopped, his eyes sweeping the length of her near-naked body. He leaned his head to one side and then the other. His neck cracked.

"Those shoes make you look like a whore," he said, and then he turned and walked away.

The next morning, Tamsen had told him she was moving to The Talisman.

Several days passed before Tamsen understood what had set Victor off—what she had done to merit his punishing words. She had said something at dinner about how terrific Theo's nineteen-year-old assistant tennis coach was—how smart he seemed and how handsome he was. Theo had seemed really drawn to the young man and Tamsen had suggested that maybe the coach could babysit some time. She should have known not to be so free with compliments, especially for a good-looking man. Tamsen wondered, if Victor had been so jealous and vicious when they met, would she have married him? His insults and the control he exerted had come later too. Theo's epilepsy caused his face and arms to twitch uncontrollably. She sometimes wondered if Victor had a brain affliction that cause him to become cold and harsh.

A serviceman's desert camouflage duffle bag nudged Tamsen as he hurried toward the exit, waking Tamsen up from the discomforting memory.

"Pardon me, Miss," he said at the same time the infrared sensor above spotted him. The milky glass doors whirred as they separated.

It was nice to be called Miss. It sounded respectful, and much more flattering than Ma'am. Tamsen glanced to the side at a sign that told her: "YOU ARE LEAVING A SECURE AREA. NO RE-ENTRY PERMITTED."

In front of the doors stood men with good posture holding white boards with names printed in black marker, a middle-aged couple with a child and three heart-shaped Mylar balloons, and a wrinkled grandmother wearing an American flag tunic and carrying a fistful of ink-fed fuchsia grocery store carnations. This was the movie scene, the one where the weary wife spots her expectant husband in the sea of excited eyes, mindlessly drops her belongings by her sides, and rushes to him, hurling her loving arms around his neck, kissing him while their children watch with a mixture of pride and embarrassment. But there would be no such reunion for Tamsen and Victor. Not today, not ever. The mere idea of his hand on her skin now repulsed her. She flexed her cheeks and exposed her teeth. She could muster a fake a smile. She could do that for her kids' sake.

Theo's voice caught Tamsen's attention. He was hard to miss, jumping up and down, yelling, "Mommy! Mommy!" with his sandy curls pouring out from beneath his Cubs baseball cap. Charlotte was there too, and although her lips were pursed tightly together, she couldn't suppress her welling tears that confessed to Tamsen how much her daughter had missed her.

Victor loomed behind them, all six-feet-four of him emanating a snapping force field of intensity. He held up a piece of paper with Tamsen's maiden name, "Kinney," written hastily with indigo Sharpie. "I love where you come from," he used to say about her South Side Chicago roots, so different from his own Gold Coast childhood. She used to believe him, until he lied in their interview with the membership committee of an exclusive golf club, telling them Tamsen was born and raised in the exclusive suburb of Brookhurst.

"Welcome home," Victor said. Tamsen ignored the salutation and bent down to embrace Theo, who continued to bounce as she hugged him.

"Do we need to find you a restroom?" Tamsen asked playfully, reaching out an arm to gather Charlotte in close.

"Did you see Daddy's sign?" Charlotte asked hopefully. It was her subtle way of trying to encourage some loving interaction between her parents.

"I did. So thoughtful," Tamsen managed, digging into her purse to avoid Victor's cool stare. She, too, had been a perceptive young girl, but she never would have attempted to defuse the tension in her own parents' marriage. The youngest and only female of four children, Tamsen's big brothers had little tolerance for sensitivity and she often had to stifle her feelings, burying them shamefully in the lumpy poly-fill pillows with which her brothers smacked her when she reported them for stealing cigarettes from the priest's office drawer at St. Christina's Parish. Charlotte was a sympathetic creature and her emotional intelligence had an almost a clairvoyant quality. The day Tamsen and Victor broke the news of their separation to the children, Theo was silent, but Charlotte, despite assurances that the time apart was a trial, responded calmly, "Please let me keep my bedroom, at least for a while."

Victor crumpled his sign and tossed it in a trashcan near the luggage carts. He navigated them past a series of backlit screen advertisements illustrating Windy City Bank, Ameriquik Car Rental, and Mobile Yo cellular service.

"How was the trip? Did you speak to Petra?" he asked. If Petra were promoted again, which was all but certain, she would have a say in every major marketing decision the company made. The blood in the water for Victor was Petra's influence when it came to which ad agency would be awarded the cosmetic giant's US business.

"Are you kidding?" Tamsen pretended she didn't know what he was getting at. "All we did was talk," Tamsen said as she slipped her passport back into its pebbled red leather cover.

Victor pointed to the screens. "This is fertile ground for a Ms Majestic ad," he said. Tamsen bristled at the suggestion—as if women with skin of color were found only in the international terminal. She held her tongue. She wanted to preserve the exuberant mood of her arrival. Disagreement with Victor would simply lead to an argument.

"Did you bring me a present?" Theo asked, reaching under his cap to scratch his head.

"Maybe," Tamsen toyed. She reached into her tote bag and handed her little man a compact zipper case of business-class amenities from the airplane. She knew Theo would love the sleep mask and earplugs.

"Yes!" he exclaimed, grabbing the case from her hands.

"Aaaand," Tamsen said, dipping into her bag with wide eyes, "Pork cracklings!" It was nearly impossible to find a treat that was suitable for Theo, but Tamsen had scored when she came across the traditional British snack in the Heathrow duty-free.

"Are cracklings the same as Cheetos?" Theo asked as they made their way out of the packed terminal.

"No," Victor said, glaring at Tamsen, "They are literally fried pig skin."

"Here, Theo," Charlotte laughed, handing Theo her bag, "you can have mine."

Charlotte, always the giver. She would gladly relinquish any possession if it made her brother happy. Tamsen leaned in and opened her tote just enough to reveal to her daughter a milk chocolate Toblerone bar she'd purchased in duty-free. They would sneak a bit later on after Theo went to bed.

Tamsen grabbed an espresso at the kiosk near baggage claim and hoped the caffeine would carry her through the rest of the afternoon. She needed to be alert. Their new family arrangement was uncertain territory for all of them and Tamsen wanted to navigate the volatile waters with care. The separation book warned that, most of all, Charlotte and Theo needed to know that none of this was their fault—that fighting or tension in front of the kids could only lead to difficulty at school and feelings of helplessness and abandonment.

Victor wordlessly pulled the Louis Vuitton out to the parking lot. Impatient to get home, Tamsen scanned the aisle of bumpers looking for the familiar black BMW sedan. Victor would not have taken the Boxster; there was barely enough room in the back for one person, let alone two kids and a suitcase. Charlotte grabbed her mother's hand and skipped a step.

"Daddy has a surprise," she said.

Victor pinched the key fob he was holding, evoking a chirp from a shiny dark blue Mercedes G-Class SUV. The chrome AMG letters on the back told Tamsen this was a serious, albeit gorgeous, purchase. It was unmistakably her husband's car. He had already transferred his vanity plate from the family four-door. It read VICTOR, and, as he liked to remind her, "It means I always win."

"Here we are," he said. Tamsen blinked, startled by this new acquisition and trying to process the motivation behind such an extravagant and untimely splurge. His BMW sedan was less than a year old, and though Victor owed her no explanation, she found this upgrade audacious considering the present state of affairs. To Tamsen, a trial separation meant that they should both self-regulate when it came to spending money. She was determined to demonstrate that their time in marital purgatory was not a frivolous sabbatical. Tamsen herself had given up her weekly nail appointment and even switched to Pantene from her pricey salon conditioner. Sure, Victor could afford a new luxury car, but Tamsen was well aware that he would view the slightest excess on her part as extraneous and retaliatory and make her suffer for it.

"Daddy's new car is so cool, Mom," Charlotte beamed, searching Tamsen's face for any sign of approval. It broke Tamsen's heart that the girl had misread Victor's act of buying a new car as an attempt to win Tamsen back.

"And there are buttons everywhere, and a TV right behind Daddy's seat," Theo added.

"Well, then I'm definitely sitting in the back with you guys," Tamsen said, engaging a door that practically opened itself. She was relieved that the bells and whistles of the backseat provided her an excuse to sit some place other than the front passenger side.

The line to leave the parking lot was backed up at least thirty cars deep. Bright orange cones and yellow tape directed drivers toward one functioning credit card machine at the exit. Theo's body writhed as he twisted the bill of his cap. After fifteen minutes, he'd lost interest in the Mercedes' amenities, and instead he began grinding his scalp against his seat the way a bear does against a tree when it has an itch. Any sort of repetitive behaviors demonstrated by Theo set off an instinctive alarm in Tamsen's head. His myoclonic seizures involved quick repetitive tics, followed by an abrupt loss of muscle control. This time, however, she could observe that his epilepsy wasn't to blame. Theo's fingers moved with purpose to the nape of his neck and he fervently scratched, checking under his fingernails for evidence of a culprit. She'd seen this behavior before, last summer, just after day camp at the Rink and Racket Club had ended.

"Did you go to the batting cages while I was away?" she asked.

"We did. The day you left for London," Victor replied, drumming his fingers on the steering wheel. "Theo, tell your Mom how you clocked one at fifty."

"You wore their plastic helmet, didn't you, bud?" Tamsen asked.

"So?" Theo replied. Tamsen scooted toward her daughter.

"Victor, put the car in park. Charlotte, why don't you hop out and take shotgun," she said.

"I want to be by you," Charlotte said, dropping her head against Tamsen's arm.

"You need to move," Tamsen commanded urgently.

"Why?"

"Because your brother has lice."

Charlotte, who was otherwise fiercely protective of Theo, contorted her face in a manner Tamsen had only seen in Snapchat filters. Victor threw the car into park. Charlotte threw her hands to her head and shrieked, casting open the rear door and dashing to sit up front beside Victor.

"Disgusting!" she cried. "Daddy, I told you to bring Theo's batting helmet from home, remember?" Charlotte insisted. "Everyone knows the ones at the batting cages are lice factories," she said, echoing something Tamsen once said. Charlotte gathered her long, thick dark hair into side a pony tail, tucking it into her t-shirt as added protection.

"Calm down," Victor urged, fumbling with the controls on the slick dashboard touchscreen.

Tamsen felt a phantom creeping sensation across her own head. "I still have some special shampoo," Tamsen said. She plucked a rubber band from her wallet and tied her own hair up into a tight ballet bun.

"What stinks?" Theo asked.

"Probably your lice," Charlotte replied.

"It's fresh asphalt," Tamsen replied. "They're paving, that's why we're down to one lane." Theo pressed his nose against the window to get a glimpse of the roller machine, which inched its heavy drum across a black ribbon of steamy surface.

"What's ashphalt?" Theo asked.

"It's the sticky gravel they use for roads," Victor answered. "It's actually pronounced as-phalt, but where your mom grew up, they say ash-phalt."

"What else do they say wrong where you grew up, Mom?" Theo asked.

"Just because something is different, doesn't make it wrong," Tamsen replied gently. "Victor," she continued, "your new car has music, I assume."

They listened to a classical satellite station until the minute they arrived at their elegant brownstone on Astor Street. Tamsen escorted Theo to the master shower, where she bathed his head in antiseptic-smelling lice treatment. She then sat him on a counter stool and dragged a metal-pronged lice comb through his wet hair. In an uncharacteristic show of support, Victor offered to pick up carryout Chinese while Tamsen took up arms against the scourge of zealous blood suckers. She was too busy sanitizing every bed sheet, garment, and plush toy with which Theo had come into contact to ponder what Victor might ask of her in exchange for the dinner run.

The jump of the six-hour difference between Chicago and London bore down on her. Her own scalp continued to tickle, and although it was unlikely she had contracted lice herself, Tamsen decided to book an online appointment with Louse Calls, a business established by an entrepreneurial college dropout who decided that there was money to be made off of wealthy families who could afford professional debugging. The best thing about Louse Calls, of course, was that they came to you—discreet and thorough, and booked through an app.

Victor's travel schedule had placed a terrible strain on their marriage, but in light of the separation, it was an unlikely convenience. Their "birds-nesting" arrangement, recommended by the child psychologist Tamsen secretly consulted, allowed the children to stay put, regardless of which parent was "on duty." When Victor was in town, generally two or three nights a week, Tamsen moved to The Talisman, a simple hotel located between the brownstone and the children's private school. While Victor was away, Tamsen stayed in the house. Just seeing the California King in their master bedroom made her terribly uneasy, so she'd taken up residence in the guest suite adjacent to Theo's room. Being near Theo gave her peace. Being back in Chicago gave her anxiety.

Tamsen heard the front door shut. Victor had dropped off the bag of steaming broccoli chicken, collected a few articles of clothing, and was out the door without a word. By text, he told Tamsen he would be back in town next week. He also asked her to assemble gift baskets for an important upcoming Summers & Peel client dinner. *So that's why he got the takeout,* Tamsen realized.

◆ ◆ ◆

"How much longer?" Theo pleaded, his penny loafers dangling above the Tibetan rug in the formal dining room. Tamsen folded a *Chicago Scene* magazine over her thigh. She and Charlotte had both checked out, bug-free.

"Hang in there, Theo. We want to make sure they get out anything I missed." Tamsen was trying to avoid the overuse of the words "lice" or "louse" because Theo was a parrot. The more he knew about his affliction, the more likely he was to discuss his condition with a classmate at The Dexter School, where he was already perceived as strange due to the seizures he'd had in front of his kindergarten class the year before. The children understood Theo's condition, and they weren't unkind, but he was often left off of invites for playdates and birthday parties. Theo was already painfully shy at school; the last thing Tamsen wanted was her son being labeled unclean or contagious. Both kids were going through enough already, and she was determined to spare Charlotte and him any further distress.

Harlow, the twenty-year-old working on Theo's comb-out, moved with surgical precision, swiping and wiping the metal-toothed instrument deftly between sections of hair and a damp white washcloth that sat on the bar cart Tamsen had wheeled in from Victor's study. The girl had perfect, crease-free skin and a naturally plump lower lip. There was something androgynous about her. Perhaps it was the absence of makeup or the way she concealed every inch of her hair beneath a knit Chicago Bears hat.

"Lice are fascinating critters," Harlow pronounced. "A female can lay ten eggs a day and once the babies hatch, they start their own families."

Harlow possessed all the hallmarks Tamsen had read of the millennial generation—the casual confidence, the arm tattoo, the air of knowing everything about everything, and in this particular case, the subject of mastery was entomology. It was as if the girl were the host of a hipster YouTube channel on the topic of lice.

"The mommy lays her egg close to your head where it's nice and toasty and then she glues the egg to your hair shaft with this sort of cement-like stuff that comes out of her bottom," Harlow continued. Tamsen was too intimidated by the conviction in the girl's discourse to ask her to shut up; clearly, Harlow took her vocation very seriously. Instead, Tamsen opened the oversized society magazine, desperately conjuring a visual distraction that might exterminate the image of a bug squeezing sticky eggs from its bum. But the biology lecture continued. "And lice don't like the sunshine—they're most active at night, while you're sleeping." Thanks for the detail, Tamsen thought.

Tamsen shoved the magazine under her son's nose. "Look, Theo," she brightly interrupted, pointing to the Fetes & Philanthropy page, "it's a picture of Uncle Digby and Aunt Hilly at the museum gala last month."

They weren't actually relatives; Digby Summers was Victor's business partner, and Hilly was Tamsen's closest friend by default. Hilly managed to show up in *Chicago Scene* quite regularly. Not only did she attend every high-profile fund raiser, she also happened to photograph exceptionally well. Hilly once told Tamsen that she practiced her stock faces in the mirror. There were three smiles: the wide and toothy, the serene and dreamy, and Tamsen's personal favorite, the eyes closed, mouth open like a fly catcher. Hilly had insisted the poses made her look younger, and that since she had introduced the fly catcher to her repertoire, editors had bumped up the number of published shots of her by at least ten percent.

Theo turned his head to look at the photo, disrupting the tech's rhythm and ruining the fastidious part she had carved into his wet hair.

Harlow sighed heavily and put her hands on her hips as Theo stared at the photo for a moment. "What is she laughing about?" he asked.

"Uncle Dig probably said something funny," Tamsen replied, knowing full well that Hilly no longer laughed at Digby's jokes.

Unimpressed, Theo turned his gaze downward to his small hands folded tightly against the crunchy black smock. The technician adjusted her protective Bears cap and resumed her methodical combing and wiping.

"This makes three nits for you, big guy," she claimed victoriously, holding the comb up toward the light. "Your mom did a pretty good job—better than most novices."

Before Theo could ask the girl to define "nit," Tamsen interjected. "Do you think we should cut his hair?"

"Nooooo," Theo whined.

"Naw, don't do that," Harlow concurred. "Theo looks legit rock 'n roll with his long hair."

The edges of Theo's mouth curled up. It was the first smile Tamsen had seen since the pork cracklings.

"I want to be in a rock band," Theo said, raising his chin.

"Tight," the girl replied, gently repositioning his head forward with both her hands. "You tear up the axe, or you more of a sticks guy?"

Theo wasn't tracking with her, but he sat up straight and gave her the enthusiastic answer she was looking for: "I'm going to get a guitar."

In an impulsive moment before she left for London, Tamsen had promised Theo a new guitar, but she still had not figured out how to finesse the purchase with Victor. Victor didn't think the guitar qualified as a musical instrument. He wanted both their children to play classical instruments like the violin or piano. He barely blinked to spend $275,000 on a custom wood-veneer concert model Fazioli piano for Charlotte, despite the fact that their daughter could barely see over the keys, refusing to "skimp" on a lesser brand. Furthermore, he said they had plenty of space for a full-size grand piano—even if the custom bay window needed to be taken out for the instrument to be hoisted into the front room.

"I met a guitar teacher on OkCupid," the technician mused, spraying Theo's hair with a tea tree oil finishing mist. "He was really more of cello player, I guess, but he quit and switched to guitar."

"Why would anyone quit the cello?" Tamsen asked.

"Emo sounds better on guitar. He liked all those depressed bands." She looked at Tamsen. "You know, emo, right? Angsty, emotional stuff."

The word cello had hooked her, so she probed further. "Does your friend teach guitar at a college?" Tamsen asked hopefully.

"Nope, he's indie all the way. He teaches a lot of Gold Coast kids," she said, noticing the ring on Tamsen's left hand.

Tamsen slid the *Chicago Scene* over her wedding ring. She was still self-conscious about the top-heavy emerald cut Victor had given her when they got engaged. The stone was objectively breathtaking, but it was also obscenely large. In an act of revolt, she pried the ring desperately over her bony knuckle the first night of their separation. Without it, she had felt dishonest, naked. She was still married. She had told Victor she was open to "working on things."

"Do you mind giving me the cellist's number?" Tamsen asked.

"Sure, but don't say I didn't warn you about him," Harlow said, dunking the lice comb into a jar of blue disinfectant.

"What do you mean? Is he okay with kids?" she asked, suddenly worried.

The girl laughed and snapped off her latex gloves. "Yeah, he's cool. He's just different."

"Thanks," Tamsen said. She was a little curious, but mostly elated that fortune and the lice fates had smiled upon her with a cellist–guitar player's contact information. Victor would never approve of lessons taught by some grungy, bearded musician who wore ratty black concert t-shirts and bad man jewelry, but she knew she could sell him on a trained cellist. In her decade of reissuing classic titles for Beau Monde Publishing, Tamsen had learned that packaging was everything. Slap a modern cover with a zippy font on *Jane Eyre*, and voilà—she was once again the toast of the book-loving town. Theo's rock and roll dreams were going to come true and Victor would have what he demanded—a professional cellist to teach his son.

"You're a new man, Theo," Harlow said. She patted down her pockets and fished out a Louse Calls business card, scribbling the cellist's name and number on the back before tugging off the knit cap, revealing gorgeous waves of shoulder-length toffee-blonde hair. She handed Tamsen the card and said, "Tell Whit I say hey."

"Am I really getting lessons?" Theo shouted. Tamsen nodded. Theo whooped, then leapt from the chair and wrapped his arms tightly around her hips. She could see the yet-unchanged September leaves twirling on the branches outside the bay window. It was one of those times she relished, knowing the arms that clung to her would not always think it was acceptable to so openly demonstrate unrestrained affection toward his mother, and feeling, for just one isolated moment, that everything in their world was entirely normal.

Tamsen slid a knife through the tough rind of an avocado, twisting the two hemispheres of the fruit to reveal the creamy meat inside. Charlotte turned on the Sonos system from an iPad mounted to the wall and *Separation: Sparing the Child* began to reverberate from the kitchen speakers. "The worst thing a parent can do," dictated a renowned psychiatrist, "is to speak ill of the other parent. Children associate themselves with both parents very deeply . . ."

Theo scrunched his nose. "What is this?" he asked disdainfully as Tamsen dove for the iPad.

"Grown-up stuff," she answered, switching from the audiobook to Charlotte's current playlist, Pop Chart Feels. Tamsen's pulse returned to its baseline and Demi Lovato came on, belting a power ballad about rising up.

"Ew! Change it," commanded Theo. "I hate her."

"We don't say 'hate,' Theo," Charlotte scolded.

"Sorry," he said softly.

"I like Demi Lovato," Tamsen said, mashing the avocado with salt and lemon. "She tells girls to be strong. Besides, it's Charlotte's turn to pick the dinner music."

Tamsen heard the familiar chime of an incoming call and saw the iPad screen light up with Victor's name and photo. Women found him handsome—his tidy brown haircut, the angularity of his cheekbones, and the cleft in his chin once captivated her as well. Now when she saw him, the shiny façade couldn't obscure the shadows.

"Daddy's calling," Charlotte said, coddling the device as she folded her legs comfortably beneath her on the slipcovered sofa.

Victor was hard on Tamsen, but he never apologized because, he told her, it was her behavior that triggered his admonishments. He felt it necessary to remind her of times like the Lake Michigan dinner cruise where she laughed too loudly when one of Victor's clients told an off-color joke, or the incident at Victor's niece's wedding when Tamsen joined the dance circle without him.

There was one occasion that stood out to Tamsen—Theo's uncharacteristically mischievous behavior at the annual Rink and Racket Club summer social. Theo deliberately dropped a glob of homemade slime into the coleslaw on the "make your own Chicago hot dog" buffet. It was the first time Tamsen could identify that she had done absolutely nothing wrong—the misdemeanor was entirely out of her control—yet Victor had led her to where they would be out of club members' earshot and then blasted her for being a "back seat parent," telling her, "no one here thinks you have control of your kids." He demanded that Tamsen "get busy" and fish the slime from the bowl, which she did to avoid the escalation of his anger. But upon their return to the brownstone, she told him she couldn't take it. She begged for couples counseling, but Victor derided the idea, saying therapy was "a scam" and that he wasn't the one with the problem.

Victor's parents had had a very difficult marriage. His mother, a public school teacher before marrying Victor's father, developed severe agoraphobia and Victor had terrible shame surrounding her inability to parent. He often spoke of how his mother never set foot inside his grade school and how her notable absence from his Little League games and soccer matches caused him years of profound embarrassment. Ultimately, they divorced, but Victor's father provided her a generous settlement, which included their family home—something he'd told Tamsen recently that he did not think his mother deserved. But it was Victor's cold words about his mother that preoccupied Tamsen: "She was lucky to be married to my father," he'd said a week or so after she'd initiated the separation. "If she had been my wife, I would have buried my assets so deep, she would have needed an ocean drill to find them."

His hard-heartedness prompted Tamsen's secret practice of stockpiling cash. Her technique was a variation on a ritual she had learned from her mother, who kept a steel-toed boot filled with "just in case" money—small bills and change—at the back of her closet on West 113th Street. For months, Tamsen had accumulated money and gift cards, stashing them away in a small monetary reserve she'd begun to build for Theo, Charlotte, and herself. She called the clandestine backup "The Fountain Fund" because she stored it in a dry electrical compartment behind the catch basin of her magnificent copper and slate garden fountain. The amount was laughable. To date, it was a whopping $1,865, not even enough to get them through a couple of weeks. She tried to siphon more but Victor monitored their joint checking account closely.

Lately, Tamsen reminisced about the days she received a paycheck: her name printed on security paper with company logo. Those gloriously free times when she spent money as she pleased with accountability beginning and ending with only herself, times when tangible validation was delivered by Phyllis from accounting, without fail, every Friday at 3:00 p.m. Most of Tamsen's female cohorts had married and had children, but unlike her, they had kept their jobs. Now, her former colleagues were scattered all over the world, running global accounts for huge clients. They had been promoted to directors, vice presidents, and beyond.

In the background, Tamsen could hear every word of Victor and Charlotte's chat. She reached over to squeeze Theo's hand three times; it was their silent code for "I love you."

"I still need to give you your meds," she told Theo softly.

"Yeah," he said, pinching a tiny LEGO block into place on the vehicle he was assembling.

Victor probed about Charlotte's day. "Did you win the figure skating competition?" he asked her.

"I got second because Emma went for the axel. She was in last place, Daddy, and she landed it perfectly."

"This is a very important lesson, so I want you to listen carefully. Always beware the guy in last place," Victor said. He was speaking to her as if she were an Olympic athlete, when, in fact, she only skated for fun, participating in little competitions at the Rink and Racket.

"But, she was last," Charlotte insisted.

"I understand that, but when people are down, they have nothing to lose. That's when they are the most formidable," he said in a dark tone for effect.

"What is formidable?" Charlotte asked.

"It means dangerous," he replied.

Tamsen was relieved the kids spent most of their free time with her. She did not regret her choice to leave her career to raise the children. Theo's condition revealed itself when he was three, and managing a full year of neurologist appointments and specialized tests was all-consuming; she would have had to quit anyway. Nevertheless, while she craved financial freedom, she was keenly aware that her decreasing market value compounded with each passing day. As a middle-aged housewife, all she had to offer was the ability to secure her kids a spot at the city's most exclusive summer camp, score Bulls tickets for a silent auction, and bake the finest nut-free, dairy-free, gluten-free brownies any first-grader could possibly imagine. When it came to designing invitations and table décor for a themed dinner, Tamsen tapped into her project management skills, a vestige from career days past. Where other volunteers wavered in their ability to deliver, Tamsen valiantly came through—consistently. In philanthropic society circles, she had the dubious honor of being known as Chicago's most dependable workhorse.

Tamsen deftly maneuvered a paring knife, transforming a farmer's market radish into a rosebud garnish. While she appeared engrossed in dinner prep, she continued to eavesdrop on every word of Victor's conversation with Charlotte.

"I made a popsicle stick dream catcher with Mom's dental floss," Charlotte said. So, that's where it went, Tamsen thought. "And I got to feed the hamsters in the science lab today. Can we get one, Daddy?" she begged.

"Charlotte," Victor said, "you know I'm allergic."

Tamsen was concerned about Charlotte's recently heightened tenderness toward Victor. She suspected Charlotte desperately wanted to protect her hero from the pain of the separation, and Tamsen wanted to protect Charlotte from the burden of parenting her wounded father. Tonight, in her sweet lavender fleece pajamas and fuzzy socks, she looked more like her six-year-old self than the tweenager she had become.

"Did you eat dinner yet, Daddy?" Charlotte asked.

"Soon, gumdrop, and I promise to finish everything on my plate," Victor teased. Tamsen's stomach turned. She could hear the jangle of ice cubes against glass and Victor paused to take a sip of his scotch. "Are you with Aneta tonight?"

A mercurial despair washed over Tamsen. Victor was fishing for intel and using Charlotte as his operative. Tamsen had spoken directly to Victor about avoiding this offense, even highlighting the quote in the separation book, "Do not make your children your unknowing intermediaries. If you have a question about what your spouse is doing, then ask your spouse directly. Your children are not your spies." Nevertheless, Victor had a proclivity toward manipulation and he enjoyed coaxing information from the children, quietly leading them into offering up any detail he wanted to know.

"Mom's in the kitchen," Charlotte chirped. "Should I get her?"

"No, darling." Now he spoke louder, making certain Tamsen could hear. "Just let her know that Pappy's airline miles were deposited into my frequent flyer account today."

Theo had let Charlotte do all the talking until this point, but upon hearing Pappy's name, he looked up from his LEGO set and chimed in, "But Pappy died."

"Yes, but before Pappy went to heaven, he flew on a lot of airplanes," Victor said.

Tamsen dropped the knife on the floor with a bang and it spun like a hazardous top. Indeed, Tamsen's father, Cormac, had flown close to a million miles in his lifetime. Any un-redeemed frequent flier points in his account were his sole legacy, his promise to her alone as a gift.

Cormac had had a small business that sold conveyor systems to manufacturing facilities all over the country. He never retired, not because he loved his job, but rather because his work ethic was rooted in a deep fear of losing everything to a bad economy, a natural disaster, or an alien invasion. Tamsen could recall countless lectures Cormac had delivered to her older brothers as they grew: "The business is two breaths from going under. If the Japanese lower their prices again, the business will suffer, and we will have to sell the house. Orders are down this quarter, looks like no presents this Christmas." And, of course, there was his favorite scare tactic: "No one saw the Black Death coming, either."

Scarcity was the Kinney mindset and poverty loomed over Tamsen's head like the dark skies of Galway. While her brothers were slated to inherit the conveyor-business albatross, Cormac made it clear that his daughter's promise of security lie in her beauty and her ability to marry well. After college, Tamsen sat her father down and broached the subject of joining the family enterprise. She tried to convince him that she had a degree now, and as much to offer as the boys—none of whom had graduated Phi Beta Kappa, as she had. Cormac laughed and told her she should go out and find a lawyer or some other professional who could keep her comfortable. Years later, with the Kinney boys working alongside their father, Cormac's prophesies came true and the business did go bust. Victor offered some help, but Cormac was too proud to accept. He preferred bankruptcy over a bailout. When Cormac lost his battle with leukemia, there was virtually nothing left. Her brothers pilfered the over-leveraged house in Greenview while Tamsen's only share of the estate was her father's trove of airline miles—all 675,000 of them.

"I miss you, Daddy," Tamsen heard Charlotte say. Please come home soon."

"You know it, baby," he said as the two of them enacted their farewell salutation: two fingers kissed twice, a double fist-pound on the chest, a self-hug and then a phantom double high-five. Tamsen exhaled, relieved that Theo hadn't chimed in to reveal the story of his new guitar. But before Charlotte could press the red button to disconnect, Theo thrust himself back into the dialogue.

"Daddy, wait!" He scrambled to the sofa, tripping over a Rubbermaid storage bin and sending a rainbow of LEGO blocks skidding across the walnut floor. "Mom got me a guitar and I'm getting lessons!"

In the silence, it was as if Tamsen could hear the muscles tighten over Victor's cleft chin—like she could see his ears draw back on his head, ever so slightly, in disapproval.

"Your mom and I will discuss all this when I get home, big guy." His voice was low and chilly.

The children were silent. Theo rubbed his nose with the back of his hand and Charlotte pulled a throw pillow into her lap, clutching it while she stared at the ground.

Victor's voice was normal again. "Char, don't forget to tell Mommy that I got the frequent flyer miles, okay."

"Okay, Daddy. Goodnight." Charlotte said, and she ended the call.

During the bedtime ritual, adrenaline coursed through Tamsen's body. She wrestled Theo through the bath-teeth-brushing-and-bed sequence, and she tucked in Charlotte with a book light and the latest tween fiction best seller. As soon as their rooms were quiet, Tamsen rushed to the computer and frantically logged in to her online airline mileage account, searching the website to verify the mis-transfer of her inheritance.

A live chat bubble appeared on the screen, asking Tamsen if she needed assistance. She pushed an errant swath of hair behind her ear and scrambled to enter her dilemma into the comment box: "My father died and bequeathed me his frequent flyer miles. You mistakenly put them into my husband's account."

She waited as the words *Agent typing . . .* appeared in the chat bubble. *Hi, Tamsen. Thank you for contacting us. We would like to assist you with this matter, but you will need to contact our mileage desk and speak to a representative during normal business hours 8:00 a.m.-9:00 p.m., Monday through Friday.*

Tamsen's knees bounced together under the desk. She feared the longer the miles sat in Victor's account, the less likely she would be able to reclaim them. She tapped furiously: *Is there anyone who could assist me right now? They are my miles and you transferred them to my husband, from whom I am separated.* She waited a moment, fearing she had revealed too much personal information to a complete stranger. No, she thought, *it's relevant that we are separated.* She typed on, *Please help!*

There was a pause and then *Agent typing . . .* appeared again.

Charlotte wandered into the family room, holding her dreamcatcher and blowing the tissue paper feathers so they spun as she walked.

"Do you really think these things can catch dreams? I mean, why would you want to catch a dream anyway? Catching a nightmare would be so much more useful."

"I completely agree," Tamsen said, watching the computer screen. "But you have school tomorrow and you should be in bed."

"Can I have some of the Toblerone?" Charlotte asked. Then she noticed the dialogue on the monitor. "What are you doing?"

Tamsen had the fearful notion that if Charlotte knew there was a problem, she would go to Victor about the situation and that Victor might then hide the miles or maybe even redeem them.

"It's too late for chocolate. I'll sneak it to you at breakfast," Tamsen said.

"But, Mom . . ." Charlotte insisted.

"Charlotte, bed. Please."

Charlotte sighed dramatically and turned to go. "I'm not even tired," she said as she headed up the stairs.

Tamsen looked back at the conversation on the screen: *I'm sorry, I have checked with my supervisor and you will need to call the mileage desk for further assistance.* Tamsen exited the chat without a salutation. She picked up her phone and dialed.

The line rang through to an automated customer service menu and the robotic operator began her litany of mechanical numeric cues. Tamsen punched the numbers as commanded and assumed her place in the virtual queue, which promised a brief hold of under five minutes. Then, finally, a human.

"How can I help you?"

Tamsen attempted a lighthearted tone as she recounted the story of her deceased father and his fortune of airline miles, and how, after months of back and forth, the airline had agreed to transfer the miles to her. She then implored the agent to remove the miles from Victor's account and rightly deposit them into hers. There was a long pause and Tamsen could hear the rapid clicking of fingernails on a keyboard. She drew in a breath. This was going to work out.

"I'm sorry, Mrs. Peel, but once the miles are deposited, there is a fee to withdraw them."

"But you guys were supposed to put the miles in MY account, not my husband's," she pleaded.

"I understand," the woman calmly responded. "It looks like Mr. Peel is a Zenith Preferred flyer with us."

Tamsen lost it. "And how is that even relevant?" she snapped.

The woman on the other end softened. "Our Zenith customers have access to a special customer-service line. I am going to get you to a supervisor at the Zenith desk, so you can explain to her what happened."

Tamsen exhaled, "Thank you."

As the call was released to customer service limbo, Tamsen recognized the familiar airline theme song. She heard the repetitive tinny loop stop abruptly as a beep interrupted the music—her screen said it was an incoming call from a local 312 number. She hesitated. Perhaps it was Theo's new teacher. What if something happened at school? Tamsen clicked over.

"Hello?"

"Hi," the voice was smooth and pleasant. "This is Whit. I'm returning your call about the guitar lessons."

Tamsen instantly regretted picking up. "I'm sorry, but I'm on hold and it's important. I'll call you back in a bit."

With that she toggled the call button on her phone. There was no tinny jingle, just silence.

"Hello?" she said.

"Hello?" Whit's smooth voice echoed.

Tamsen hit the toggle button again and listened. No corporate theme song.

"Hello?" she appealed anxiously.

"Still me," said the soft, masculine voice.

Tamsen's head dropped in defeat. It was now 8:58 p.m. and there was no time to re-initiate a call through the automaton customer service center. The miles would remain in her husband's account tonight. To the Victor go the spoils, she thought. She fingered the stack of retail catalogs in her mail pile, feeling sorry for herself.

"I lost my call," she said.

"I'm so sorry," he started. "I didn't know it was a bad time."

"No," she interjected. "It's not your fault. I shouldn't have picked up."

"I can call back tomorrow," he said with regret. Tamsen could sense he was ill at ease. She changed her tone.

"It's fine. Let's chat now while you have me," she said. "I understand you are a teacher and that you also play the cello?"

"Well, yes and no—I don't play the cello, but I do teach guitar."

"Where's your studio space?" she asked.

"Uh," he stammered. "I don't have a studio right now, but I can come to you if that works."

"It's perfect, actually," she said. Anything to cut down on the non-stop shuttling she did every day.

"I should probably meet your child, your son, before we lock in."

"Okay," Tamsen replied. "Let's meet." She had failed to secure the frequent flier miles, but at least her day would end productively:

a retaliatory strike against Victor for commandeering the miles. As a victory, she knew it would be short-lived. Victor would find a way to punish her for interviewing the guitar-playing cellist. He'd accuse her of dumbing down the children, cheapening them with popular music, the trash of her youth. Or worse.

"Uh, one more thing," Whit said with apologetic hesitation. "It's $50 for a half hour."

Tamsen looked at the computer screen, which displayed the status of her account: *Balance: 1,520 miles*

"Fine," Tamsen confirmed. "Can you come Tuesday?"

CHAPTER

2

In October, when the leaves on the resident sugar maples were at peak foliage, the Women's Social Club of Chicago held a gala at the Great Lakes Botanic Garden called the Harvest Moon Ball. It was the WSC's largest philanthropic endeavor, sponsoring Mothers Trust Foundation, whose goal was to provide immediate financial assistance to low-income children in times of crisis. When Hilly originally suggested that Tamsen join the WSC, Tamsen thought her membership would help Victor and reflect well on their family. She'd missed the purposefulness she'd felt working at Beau Monde and joining a charitable cause had made her feel like she was putting her station of privilege to good use.

Ultimately, however, her membership and tireless volunteering became less about others' view of her and more about the satisfaction of seeing her work translate into funds to help local kids in distress. Something about brainstorming a concept, executing ideas, and finally seeing the result in hard, tangible aid partially satisfied the constant inner ache, which Tamsen attributed to the lack within in her marriage.

Tamsen hoped to be invited by the Board to chair the biennial Harvest Moon endeavor. She fantasized about one day creating an apprenticeship program for immigrant mothers. After all, there was no organization in Chicago with more access to influential people, company executives, and employment opportunities. Chairing the Harvest Moon Ball for the WSC would give Tamsen a platform from which to sell the Board on her idea.

The past four years, Tamsen had been invited to shoulder considerable responsibility for the Harvest Moon Ball, which was an encouraging sign. If her deliverables lived up to expectation, perhaps next year the Board would consider her a worthy candidate for an actual chairwoman spot.

Tamsen saw Jacqueline Cole enter the stately dining room like a dark sorceress, gliding more than walking, as if she were delivered by conveyor belt. Her blonde hair usually fell around her face in blunt fresh layers, but today she wore it tucked tightly behind her ears. Tamsen had named Jacqueline's set "the Socialati," an exclusive and impenetrable coterie of women who were widely regarded as the very top of the social hierarchy in Chicago. They seldom flew commercial, their nannies signed non-disclosure agreements, and not one of them could operate a gas pump, even if her child's prep school admission depended on it. Jacqueline was queen of the Socialati.

Jacqueline paused at a table of six women who were seated in front of a vast picture window that faced Michigan Avenue. These women were the WSC elders, veteran members of the Board of Directors. Jacqueline uncoiled her arm and set her French-manicured hand on the shoulder of Cybill Hinton, the esteemed WSC president and the youngest of the senior women. When Cybill did not turn, Jacqueline seemed to think better of the gesture and recoiled, lightly touching the back of Cybill's chair instead. With the exception of one woman, Edith Knox, the old guard set down their soup spoons while Jacqueline campaigned. She was a vulture in red lipstick, circling overhead, waiting to dive into the first board chair vacated by one of the aging matrons. Today, however, the geriatrics displayed good color and high spirits.

Tamsen had collected and organized a three-inch binder of magazine tear sheets, fabric samples, and band résumés to review with this year's two Harvest Moon Ball chairwomen—her friend, Hilly Summers, and her very definitely not-friend, Jacqueline. Both Jacqueline and Hilly were Tamsen's age, but Jacqueline, like Victor, was bred, born, and raised in the Gold Coast to a prominent family, with bloodlines as pure as Al Capone's bootlegged gin and minds as narrow as the spaces that separated the zeros in their net worth.

Hilly and Tamsen, on the other hand, grew up in what Jacqueline would consider an Irish slum. Hilly, known to Tamsen as Hilaria Bozokowski during their twelve years at St. Christina Catholic School, clawed her way out of poverty and into the back seat of Digby Summers' cherry red BMW coupe after meeting him outside a U2 concert at Soldier Field. The girls lost touch after senior year and reconnected on a city sidewalk one evening in their late twenties when Digby, in a black cashmere overcoat and Burberry scarf, was escorting the breathtaking Hilly to opening night at the Lyric Opera. Setting Tamsen up with Victor Peel was Hilly's idea.

Tamsen had been skeptical of Victor at first. There was a quality about him that she found intimidating, but Hilly assuaged her apprehension. After all, her husband had known Victor since freshman year at Dartmouth, and Digby would never go into business with someone who wasn't a superstar. Tamsen immediately recognized Victor's impeccable manners. While Digby could be boisterous, Victor had a polished gentility about him—he made Tamsen feel special by rising when she got up from a table, and by giving up his suitcoat when she was chilly. The two men shared tremendous ambition and impressive marketing acumen, but Digby had a dynamic charisma and was always better with people. He was especially impressive to women. It was rumored that his lack of filter inside the office landed him in an occasional legal squall, but Victor had been vague when Tamsen once asked him about it.

The friends were in business only two short years before banking their first ten million dollars, and by the time Hilly and Digby introduced Tamsen to Victor, Summers & Peel was an outright advertising empire. On their first date, they had gone to dinner at a restaurant where there were no prices on the menu and servers draped your napkin in your lap for you. Tamsen had found Victor a bit intense. She understood from the publishing world that it took a type-A behavior to advance, but Victor made her nervous with his fancy gold cufflinks and the way he didn't make eye contact with the waiter when he asked for his Manhattan to be remade with French vermouth and not Italian, with an orange-peel garnish and not with a cherry.

Victor's charm, his sweetness, was revealed to Tamsen when he introduced her to his little brother—not a brother in the familial sense, but a boy named Shane who lived in a housing project and whom Victor had taken under his wing as part of a mentoring program for young executives and at-risk youth. Victor brought Tamsen along on a "field trip" with Shane to the Chicago Public Library, where Shane was to research influential African-American writers. It was a day she never forgot—Tamsen, Shane, and Victor, sitting for hours on the floor in the stacks, thumbing through volumes on James Baldwin, Frederick Douglass, Langston Hughes, and W.E.B. DuBois, whispering and communing over literature while eating an entire jumbo bag of peanut M&Ms. Tamsen had taken a course on black female authors in college and she reverently discussed her favorites with Shane: Toni Morrison, Alice Waters, Gwendolyn Brooks, and Maya Angelou.

Victor shocked her when he quoted Angelou to then twelve-year-old Shane. "I've learned that people will forget what you said, people will forget what you did, but people will never forget how you made them feel." On that day, they made Shane feel inspired and Victor made Tamsen feel like she'd found the one.

It was providence that Hilly and Tamsen would become pregnant with their daughters the same year, and it was a foregone conclusion that little Charlotte Peel and little Astrid Summers would gain certain admission to the most prestigious school in Chicago, The Dexter School. After all, their fathers were legacies and big donations always followed big names.

"I don't get it," snarled Jacqueline as she held her hand to block her view of the mock centerpiece. "Why would you put milkweed and tree branches in a flower arrangement?"

"They're cattails," Tamsen corrected.

The night before, Tamsen had lost track of time doting over a tall birch bark-wrapped vessel and positioned brittle fall elements alongside jewel-toned roses, graceful French tulips, and fragrant hyacinth. It was 3:00 a.m. before she had put down the glue gun, shut the curtains, and gone bleary-eyed to bed.

"Won't they leak sap or something?" postulated Hilly, attempting to harmlessly concur with Jacqueline. This was the fourth meeting on the topic of centerpieces and the sixth design Jacqueline had rejected.

"I like the variation of texture," Tamsen said. "Plus, we need height on the table since you decided in favor of votive candles over the tapers."

"Well, as far as I'm concerned, milkweed grows in the swamp and that is where it belongs." Jacqueline's expression reminded Tamsen of the face Charlotte made the time she bit into wasabi, thinking it was guacamole.

"It's a harvest theme, Jacqueline. When you consider the big picture, this centerpiece makes perfect sense."

"The big picture?" Jacqueline snuffed. "The big picture is that little old lady drinking tomato bisque through a 24-karat gold straw." Jacqueline nodded toward Edith Knox. "That dusty sourpuss is the only person I care about impressing. She will make or break this fundraiser, Tamsen, and if we can't milk the old heifer for at least twice what she gave last time, your hunter-gatherer arts and crafts experiment will be to blame."

The WSC depended on Mrs. Knox's generosity—her contributions kept the Woman's Social Club at the top of *Chicago Scene's* list of the most generous organizations. It was not enough, however, to simply make the list; the objective of each year's chairwomen was to exceed previous years' monetary success, and this year, Jacqueline had raised the bar. Her mission was to prove herself the unrivaled might behind the highest-grossing fundraiser the WSC had ever staged. Jacqueline resolved to establish a contribution threshold no future chairwoman could possibly surpass with one ultimate goal in mind—not to help the charity, but rather to secure herself a future spot on the Board of Directors of the Women's Social Club.

Tamsen watched Edith Knox, the elderly philanthropist and life-long member of the WSC, as her trembling left hand steadied a straw to her lips. Her boiled-wool Chanel jacket practically swallowed her tiny frame, but she was anything but frail. There was strength and purpose in the way she slammed down her coffee cup and picked the bacon out of her bibb lettuce salad, unapologetically feeding the salty bits to the Havanese named Dog who was nestled in her lap. She wore her tight bun of jet-black hair high on her head and always adorned it with some sort of tasteful ornament: an antique pin, velvet ribbon or, on fancy occasions, a Tahitian black pearl comb. It was widely known that Edith had taken ballet classes with Audrey Hepburn when they were teenagers in Amsterdam. Though unclear whether the two remained lifelong friends, Edith undertook emulating the actress' humanitarian deeds, traveling abroad during much of her life to support efforts for the welfare of children.

Some months ago, Edith had suffered a stroke, and Jaqueline was frantic over the certainty of the elderly woman's donation for the Harvest Moon Ball. Edith's generosity had been capricious in recent years. She'd gained a reputation for withholding money for bizarre reasons, rescinding a capital contribution to the local animal shelter because they wouldn't feature Dog in their annual Hot Mutts calendar. There was also an account of her momentarily refusing to pay out her commitment to the Contemporary Art Museum upon hearing a rumor that the museum's director had reduced the senior citizens' discount in the museum gift shop by one percent.

"I'm not saying we abandon flowers. I just think the dried cattails have a really unique, organic look," Tamsen pressed, laying out a canary-colored napkin with a chocolate-brown ikat pattern. "See that? They work really well with the linens."

Jacqueline's lips were closed tight as her tongue rolled slowly across the gum line, creating a bulge over her lower teeth. She squinted into space as if she were telepathically summoning her broomstick, then she turned her penetrating scowl to Tamsen.

"We can do better," she hissed, closing the snap on her alligator clutch and rising to leave.

"You'll think of something, Tam," Hilly assured Tamsen, giving her a gutless sympathy shrug.

As Hilly ascended the social ladder, Tamsen noticed that her allegiance wavered the higher she advanced. It didn't bother Tamsen that Hilly was the consummate suck-up. Someday, though, Tamsen suspected Hilly would find herself on the receiving end of Jacqueline's maleficence. The sad thing was, Hilly would never even notice she'd been eating a poisonous apple until it was too late.

Jacqueline summoned their server with a wave of her glossy French manicure and a flick of her forked tail. "I'm through here, Miguel. *Por favor* have the valet bring up my Aston Martin."

Tamsen watched as Jacqueline dragged her eyes up and down the waiter's backside as he briskly walked away. Jacqueline's moneyed husband, Stephan, had a remarkably fine physique for a man in his early sixties, although he was extraordinarily tall. Stephan was a falconer, a collector of antique plumb bobs, and he was famously successful for buying up most of a west side neighborhood in 2009, then banking hundreds of millions when he sold it all in 2013. Stephan was also really, really boring.

Tamsen cleared her throat and mustered all the self-assurance she could feign. "Jacqueline, I'm telling the florist to move ahead with this arrangement."

Again, Jacqueline's lower lip protruded as her tongue pushed it forward. She glowered at Tamsen with icy detachment. Tamsen felt needles under her armpits as microbeads of perspiration pushed through her pores. She could sense Edith Knox's eyes on them.

"Perhaps the unraveling of your marriage is impeding your ability to follow direction," Jacqueline snarled. So she had heard about Tamsen and Victor. "You need to put a smile on your face and do your job. If you can't, then you will be replaced. We're not here to accommodate your whimsy, Tamsen. I'm in charge and I am telling you if you don't pull together a decent centerpiece, I'll find someone else who will."

Then, like magic, the muscles in Jacqueline's face shifted, and with the same detachment Tamsen had observed in Victor when he had cast her from his mind, the woman's entire aura returned to a neutral state of indifference. She smiled perfunctorily, turned on her Lanvin heels, and glided from the dining room, her signature scent of 24 Faubourg perfume dissipating in her wake as she made her exit.

Tamsen turned to Hilly, worried the damp spots under her arms were visible. Her face burned, and she could hear her own heartbeat pounding in her ears.

"Thanks for backing me up," Tamsen said sarcastically to Hilly as she dabbed her damp palms with her napkin.

"Who cares," Hilly said dismissively. "It's just the centerpiece. We love the rest of your ideas. The invitations look great." Tamsen shook her head. The fact that Hilly kept referring to her alliance with Jacqueline by dropping the pronoun "we" was annoying.

Tamsen saw Cybill Hinton making her rounds from table to table. Cybill was a retired Cook County judge in her early sixties and there wasn't a woman in the WSC who didn't respect her, if even from afar. She was a composed orator, and when you spoke to her she listened with a focus that told you her mind was registering every word exchanged. Tamsen didn't know her well, but Hilly had managed to position herself in Cybill's distant social periphery because they shared the same Pilates instructor.

"Ladies," Cybill said, the shawl collar of her blouse rising stately behind the short hair on the back of her neck. "I trust preparations for the gala are nearly completed."

"Just tying up some loose ends at this point," Hilly said. Cybill reached out and touched one of the cattails.

"These remind me of the pond behind my grandfather's farm. They're edible in the spring, you know," she said. "Very inventive arrangement." Tamsen wouldn't dare gloat. Cybill was highly perceptive, and it was enough just to bask in the small compliment.

"All Tamsen," Hilly said. Just as Tamsen was thinking how it was surprising Hilly didn't somehow deflect credit to Jacqueline, Hilly went on. "You know, Jacqueline is just such a great manager. I couldn't ask for a better co-chair."

"Indeed," Cybill said. "You two are a good team." She wished them a pleasant afternoon and drifted away with courteous aplomb.

Tamsen's phone pinged her a reminder about Charlotte's next private figure skating lesson. Hilly leaned in, discreetly attempting to see the message.

"Tam, I don't mean to pry, but how are things with you and Vic?"

Tamsen exhaled. "They're fine." Tamsen knew full well the rumor mill was running at capacity with the news.

"I wasn't going to bring it up, but Astrid mentioned something at dinner the other night." There was a pause as Hilly turned up the level of reverence in her voice. "Charlotte told Astrid you guys are separated."

"We are," Tamsen replied. "But I don't want to make a big deal of it. We told the kids and the most important thing is that they don't think the situation is their fault."

Hilly gasped, "Well of course it's not their fault, poor babies. How is Theo taking it?"

"I'm keeping a close eye on him, but he seems to be okay so far," Tamsen said.

Hilly wrapped her soft fingers around Tamsen's wrist. "Sweetie, I didn't know you guys were in a bad place. Why didn't you come to me?" she asked.

Hilly wasn't mean-spirited, but Tamsen knew she was incapable of keeping a secret, even at the expense of a childhood friend. Hilly would spend the gossip like cash burning a hole in her $80,000 crocodile Birkin bag.

"Like I said, it's a family matter," Tamsen said.

"But what is your state of mind?" Hilly said, tightening her grip. "Everyone is wondering. I mean, you guys are our golden couple."

The golden couple. Until this point, Tamsen had not considered the effect the news of the separation would have on their inner circle; she had been completely preoccupied with the well-being of her children. Tamsen's hands fluttered to the white gold Cartier Tank watch she wore on the same hand as her wedding ring. The idea flashed in her mind that it would likely fetch a mighty sum at the pawn shop on Wabash.

"Look, whatever Victor and I are dealing with, we can take care of it. I just want the kids to feel secure," Tamsen said. Her mind flew to the section of *Separation: Sparing the Child* where the psychiatrist suggested that parents allow their kids to discuss the situation at home with friends in their own time, when they felt comfortable. "I am glad Charlotte was able to confide in Astrid," she added.

Hilly lowered her voice, "Did Victor move out?"

"No, well, sort of, but not really. We are trying this thing called birds-nesting."

Hilly made a high "hmmm" sound in her throat.

Tamsen clarified, "Victor and I alternate time at the house and the kids get to stay put; Victor and I come and go, but Charlotte and Theo get to sleep in their own beds every night."

The pitch in Hilly's voice was the same she'd have if she just learned of an exciting new limited edition Bogner ski jacket. "I have never heard of such a thing. I suppose it makes sense."

"The schedule is pretty loose, given Victor's travel," Tamsen downplayed.

"It all sounds very . . ." Hilly paused. "Evolved. I just hope you're staying at the Four Seasons."

"No, Victor's got a corporate apartment and I stay at The Talisman over on Chestnut when he's at the house."

Hilly looked mortified. "You mean that extended-stay place next to the dry cleaners?" If a hotel didn't cost north of $600 per night,

Hilly wouldn't stop there for a glass of water. "The Talisman is a flea bag, Tam."

Tamsen thought about her room at The Talisman. It was painted in a dull beige eggshell finish. The bedspread was quilted, with a geometric tan and brown pattern with a pilling taupe-ish pink throw at the foot. Opposite the bed, Tamsen stored her clothes in a circa-1976 armoire that also housed a television. Thankfully, the carpeting and mattress were relatively new and the room had a minibar with a tiny fridge outside the bathroom. The one complaint Tamsen had was the artwork above the bed—an oversized 1940s poster of an orange bearded Chicago World's Fair clown named Abie, who looked less like a circus performer and more like a chortling pervert.

"It's really not that bad. The room is clean and it's not like I spend a lot of time there," Tamsen said. False: the nights she spent there might have been only a couple per week, but they seemed eternal. She knew she could have done better, but she didn't want to burn through money unnecessarily. Plus, her choice put her on Victor's good side, showing him that she was being somewhat budget-conscious.

Hilly shook her Birkin bag and the muffled sound of pills rattled from within. "You need something to help you sleep?" she asked.

"No," Tamsen said. Pills were not her friend.

Tamsen had never been an insomniac, but things were stressful. Meditation and breathing exercises hadn't helped her much, but a dreadlocked guy at the market had given her some lavender oil to try. Lately, she had been lying awake listening to the feral street cats whining, wondering how it happened that she was alone in a budget hotel room less than a mile from where her children slept in their beds, staring into the blackness with no lighthouse by which to navigate and no map to tell her what turn to take. Perhaps not having a destination was the problem. After all, you can't program a

GPS to take you someplace when you don't know where you're going. Her room at the Talisman became the incubator for horror and guilt about the impact the separation was having on Charlotte and Theo, the gripping fear of being indigent, and anxiety over the manner in which Victor would punish her if she resolved to end their marriage. Tamsen would fall into nightmares sometime around 2:00 a.m. and awaken again at 3:00 a.m. to the revving of garbage trucks and the banging of dumpsters under her window.

"You know you could always stay with us," Hilly offered. "The coach house has been empty since our lusty housekeeper got knocked up and moved back to the Philippines."

"That's really generous of you," Tamsen said. "But Victor and I agreed not to impose on friends." The truth was, Victor never wanted the separation in the first place and he had very specifically told her he would gladly pay for a hotel before allowing her to openly stay with anyone they knew.

Hilly lowered her voice. "Did Victor cheat?" she asked in earnest. Tamsen had not anticipated such a direct question. Hilly usually lighted over troublesome topics. She reminded Tamsen of the 1950s housewives on those ubiquitous cocktail napkins. Did Tamsen suspect Victor was messing around behind her back? Of course. But she had no proof and she didn't have access to the funds necessary to hire a P.I. The problems in their marriage stemmed from something subtler, a toxicity that she couldn't name. It was insidious and devastating, but it was also elusive and Tamsen struggled to put a label on it.

"We didn't split up because someone was cheating." She watched the tension leave Hilly's face and she understood why her friend needed to know whether Victor had been unfaithful. When seemingly happy pairs break up, everyone wants to find a reason, a smoking gun. It's like hearing about a fatal car accident: if you can pin down a cause, then you have a fairly decent shot at measuring the likelihood that such a tragedy could happen to you.

"We just have some things to sort out," Tamsen said.

"Well, that's a good thing," Hilly said in the way a runner-up might say "Congratulations" to a newly crowned Miss America. Hilly would leave the lunch without knowing if the driver had been drinking, or if the car had some critical manufacturing defect, or if the perilous road conditions caused by inclement weather led to the fatality.

"I still think you should be staying at the Four Seasons. Hell, I'd separate if I could move in there: fabulous bar, room service, spa. But you know me and Digby, we've got too much stuff to ever get divorced."

Tamsen shuddered at the sound of the word.

"I mean, can you imagine? Between the Aspen house and the place in West Palm. And who would get the sailboat? I'm lucky he still puts up with me, with all the shopping I do." Hilly caressed her handbag and laughed with affectation, suggesting to Tamsen that someone must be listening nearby, but they were alone at the coat check. Not even the attendant was at her post.

"It's just a separation, Hilly," Tamsen clarified, although she knew the statistic from the book: 80% of couples who separate never move back in together.

"Of course," Hilly said. "Give him a couple weeks and he'll want you back."

Tamsen opened her mouth to reply that Victor did want her back, that it was Tamsen who asked for the separation, but she reconsidered. Let Hilly and the Socialati draw their own conclusions about who left whom. The truth behind her split from Victor wouldn't change, even if the swirling stories and lurid speculation did.

"You know you can call me any time," Hilly said as she puckered and moved in close for a hug and air kisses. Her lips lingered close to

Tamsen's ear and she said in a hushed tone, "We're South Side sisters, right?" This was the first time in years Hilly had openly acknowledged their humble beginnings.

"South Side," Tamsen concurred, but Hilly had turned away, her fingers already swiping away at the screen on her phone.

The next morning, Tamsen stood in the couple's laundry room tucking into a hanging bag an incredible Nina Ricci dress she had purchased at Bertrand's the year before, for a trip to Nevis that she and Victor had later canceled. She reached for the tag and turned the thick embossed stock over in her hand to see the amount: $2,200. Paying full price was an extreme rarity for Tamsen, but the romantic yellow dress had been love at first sight. She ran her hand over the intricate lace bodice. Though her breath was still taken away by the beauty of the design, she could never bring herself to wear it. It was too good for any summer charity event and too extraordinary for a birthday luncheon; she had been saving it for the perfect moment, and that moment had arrived. The dress would provide a huge infusion to The Fountain Fund, and parting with it translated to money of her own—cash she'd have, should Victor turn on her.

Tamsen bought all her clothes the way her mother did: on sale. Combing the "reduced" racks and finding a special designer dress, a stylish skirt, or even a pair of hip name-brand jeans gave Tamsen the feeling she had beaten the system. Besides, she had been indoctrinated by her father to think most luxury goods were a complete rip-off. Over the years Tamsen's taste in fashion had become increasingly more expensive, but she remained relatively frugal. The clerks at the most exclusive Oak Street boutiques knew her by name and they always called her first, just before markdowns, so she could take advantage of the sales.

Tamsen closed the zipper on the hanging bag and set it on the foyer credenza under a Laura Letinsky photograph. She looked up at the still life depicting a partially-eaten melon, a used paper napkin, and a haphazard set of spoons on a dirty white dinner plate. The scene was imperfect. It was messy, just like her life, and although she stopped short of using the "D word" in her head, Tamsen couldn't help but think that if she and Victor permanently split up, she would want this piece of artwork.

Tamsen popped the trunk on her glacier-white Audi. It was Victor's choice—he liked the safety rating for the children, and as long as she didn't have to engage in a blurry negotiating process where she'd end up paying more than necessary, she was happy to have it. She did wonder what she could get for her top-of-the-line model if she traded it for a smaller, entry-level version.

She had scored with a metered spot a half-block from Bertrand's and she took out the hanging bag, yanking it taut to make it appear extra-fresh. She was uncertain about such a belated return, but she was a decent client and the dress was certainly pristine.

Michael, the familiar Bertrand's security guard, gave Tamsen a reverent bow as he opened the towering glass door. "So nice to see you again," he said as he gestured for her to enter.

"Gorgeous outside, Mrs. Peel," Amy from behind the fine jewelry counter exclaimed.

"I'm loving your Balenciaga top handle, Tamsen," chimed Luke from behind a handbag display. Tamsen had picked it up two years earlier on pre-sale.

"It's a classic," Tamsen replied as she breezed past.

By the time she reached the fourth floor, word had already traveled to upstairs that Tamsen Peel was in the house. Lisa, her favorite associate, stood at the ready with a hot beverage and pistachio biscotti in hand.

"Good afternoon, Mrs. Peel," she said as she handed over an espresso. "How lovely to see you."

"You're so sweet, Lisa. Caffeine is exactly what I need after the day I've been having." She took the cup and handed Lisa a shopping bag in exchange. "I just need to return this Nina Ricci piece."

"Oh," replied the woman as her cheerful disposition dissipated. "Was there something wrong with it?"

"No," Tamsen said. "I just never wore it." Lisa picked the garment out of the bag with a limp wrist and removed it from the tissue Tamsen had used to wrap it.

"This is from last spring's collection," Lisa said.

"I'll just take cash for it," Tamsen said casually.

"I'm not sure what I can do for you." She bit her lip while she inspected the receipt. "It went on final mark down a year ago and we shipped out any remaining pieces."

A mother Tamsen recognized from The Dexter School stepped from the elevator and waved.

"Lisa," Tamsen lowered her voice. "I have been a very good customer. I have spent lord knows how much money here. Are you telling me there is really nothing you can do for me?"

"Mrs. Peel, if it were still on the floor we could definitely try," she said as she gingerly rewrapped the dress.

"Why don't you just give me the sale price for it?" Tamsen suggested.

Lisa went to the register and typed feverishly into the terminal while Tamsen eyed the gorgeous new fall merchandise. The girl shook her head. "Bertrand's really does value your business, but your receipt says it's been over a year and a half—the dress isn't even in our system."

Lisa handed Tamsen the shopping bag and gave a slight shrug of her shoulders. "If it's any consolation, you're going to look beyond fabulous when you wear it. Women coveted this dress when we had it in stock," she offered.

Tamsen's face was flushed with embarrassment. A year and a half. She felt foolish for even asking. But something Lisa said gave Tamsen an idea—the consignment shop on Armitage. She and her girlfriends used to browse there and at other thrift stores during high school. They would save their babysitting money and take the brown line to Armitage on Saturdays, stopping in the Loop at Mitchell's where they ate Milk Duds in the long waiting line and shared monster stacks of fluffy buttermilk pancakes. Thrift shopping was like treasure hunting in those days and Tamsen always wondered what could possibly make a woman who could afford such exquisite clothing relinquish such luxurious brand names for pennies on the dollar, when the items were in such perfect condition. Now she understood.

The moment she arrived home, Tamsen stripped off her Proenza Schouler luncheon uniform and pulled on a pair of stretchy yoga pants and the favorite oversized gray sweater she'd had since college. With her hair pulled into a loose ponytail, she headed directly to the back deck. Passing the kitchen en route, she paused to check on the sous-vide lamb chops that bubbled on the cooktop while Aneta tossed a salad of kale, romaine, and pine nuts. Charlotte helped by setting the table.

"Let's add some queso fresco to that tonight, Aneta," Tamsen suggested. "And if you want to take some home for yourself and Pawel, please feel free."

"Theo is downstairs playing," Aneta said. "Should I call him up?"

"No," Tamsen said. "I just need thirty minutes to dig in the dirt, then I'll sear the lamb."

"What's for dessert?" asked Charlotte.

"Anything Theo can eat," she replied. "But we can share a bowl of ice cream while he's in the bath tonight," she whispered.

The bluestone patio was a place of solace for Tamsen. It was there she'd assembled a group of treasured garden relics procured in her travels abroad when she was still independent. It was an homage to her wanderlust. A Balinese teak work table with intricate carvings held a trio of hand-painted Peruvian terra cotta pots containing carefully manicured bonsai trees, and a garland of small hammered Tibetan bells draped from end to end. They pinged sweetly in the evening when the easterly lake winds kicked up. On the lower shelf of the table sat a shallow French laundry basket whose wooden handles had long been stripped of their lacquer finish and whose wire was just beginning to rust. In it, she kept all her gardening tools: a spade, a pair of rubber gloves, a bag of potting soil, and a small hand rake. She had rescued the piece from a trash bin behind an apartment building in the 4th arrondissement when she had passed through Paris on a publishing boondoggle.

But of all the treasures, Tamsen's most beloved was a weathered statue of Ganesha, remover of all obstacles. She kept it near the foot of the fountain where it stood guard near the utility access panel, behind which Tamsen hid a Ziploc storage bag containing her secret stash of money and gift cards. My precious Fountain Fund, she thought.

Tamsen pressed her fingertips against the panel to ensure it was snug in its place while the soothing cascade of water slid down the cleft black slab and into the recirculation pool below. A sudden gust of September wind sent a disposable green plastic planter into a furious spin, scudding it across the patio and littering soil in its wake. Tamsen fumbled a rust-colored mum, sliding it gently into place beside a giant head of cabbage and a crimson sweet potato vine. The landscapers could have easily done this job, but the transformation of the faded summer pots into bursting fall arrangements was a ritual Tamsen relished—one she especially needed now.

She wiped her nose against the back of her muslin glove and then stood back to assess her installation. It was all about balance, scale, size, color, and texture. Fall offered so many alternatives for embellishments: speckled corn cobs, pumpkins, milkweed pods, and even the recently denounced cattails. Tamsen found herself in a daydream of aesthetic possibilities when the sudden chime of the doorbell encroached on her thoughts.

"Mom, there's a man here for you," Charlotte said through the screen.

It took Tamsen a moment to register who may be at the door. The cellist, she remembered, looking down at her Smith & Hawken resin clogs, caked in mud. "Send him back."

"Who is he?" Charlotte asked, twisting her mouth.

"He's here for Theo. Ask him if he wants anything to drink," Tamsen replied.

Tamsen checked her phone; there was a text from Victor saying he'd be home at 8:00 p.m., in time to tuck in the children. Today was a mutually agreed-upon changeover day and Victor was planning to move into the house through Saturday. The passing of the domestic baton would not be an easy one tonight, and the thought of seeing Victor caused an uncomfortable itch of adrenaline under the surface of Tamsen's skin. He would want answers: How much longer did she need? When would their lives return to normal? Why was she destroying him like this?

"I'm Whit."

She looked up from her phone. He was tall, probably six-foot-two or -three, and he had dark brown hair that that bent up at his ears and the top of his collar. He took his hand from the pocket of what appeared to be a Members Only jacket and extended it toward her. Tamsen hesitated and then pulled off her gardening glove, feeling the warmth of his firm grip against her palm. The wind stopped blowing for a moment as if the world had paused to inhale.

"Sorry about the mess," she said unselfconsciously. "I was just finishing up out here."

The wind kicked up again, swirling an empty bag of potting soil and Whit quickly sidestepped to capture it beneath his foot. "Let me help you," he said, reaching down.

Tamsen collected the plastic cabbage head containers and flipped the switch on the back of the fountain to shut it off. The gusts were causing the water to splash from its copper trough. Whit thrust the trash into a recycle bag and then reached for a nearby broom.

"You don't have to do that," Tamsen insisted. No one had ever offered to lend a hand with the garden, let alone to clean up. Tamsen did most things solo. Victor barely noticed when she decorated the boxwoods with twinkle lights every Christmas and he was certainly nowhere to be seen when it was twenty below in January and time for her to take them down. Tamsen recalled a podcast where some self-help guru was extolling the benefits of marital teamwork and its ability to strengthen interpersonal bonds. Unfortunately, with Victor, life was an individual event.

Tamsen watched as Whit reached to touch an overhead vine. He caressed the wide leaf between his thumb and forefinger as if its surface had a message for him written in Braille. Maybe this was why Harlow thought he was peculiar.

"I could forget I lived in the city if I had a yard like this," he said.

"It's hardly a yard," Tamsen replied. "But it's an escape, that's for sure."

"This is an espalier, isn't it?" he asked walking to the tree on the north wall.

For five years, Tamsen worked to train the espalier to flatten and for the first time, someone actually noticed its existence. "I found it at a nursery in Michigan. I had to rent a pickup and drive four hours to a farm in the middle of nowhere—"

"But it was totally worth it," Whit said, finishing her sentence. "Do you use the apples?" he asked.

She was dumbfounded; not even the women who had spent hours at her catered garden parties had shown the remotest interest in her flowers, let alone this incredible tree she had transplanted, nurtured, pruned and preened. Whit pressed his palm against one of the pliable branches, gingerly tucking an errant tendril into place. There was a raw unedited inquisitiveness about him and she resisted the euphoric urge to sit this person down at her umbrella table and subject him to a TED Talk on the joys of urban horticulture.

"This is the first season it's produced enough fruit for much of anything," she said, turning one of the unripe apples carefully so that its stem wouldn't release. She tried to temper her enthusiasm. "I haven't decided whether I want to do an apple sauce or a pie," she continued.

"Mmm, you can't go wrong with apple pie," he said.

Tamsen laughed. "The cellist votes pie."

The corners of Whit's mouth crept down and he shifted his hands back into his pockets, turning his back to her. He shook his head and Tamsen could sense that she was suddenly at risk of losing her shot at finding a guitar teacher Victor might just be willing to tolerate.

Tamsen had an acute radar when it came to sensing a misstep and suddenly the alarm in her head began to buzz loudly. A familiar constricting around her chest, the same fearful confusion she often experienced with Victor, squeezed her lungs. The magical spell of Whit's enchanting curiosity was broken. Perhaps she was being overly sensitive, but she knew his abrupt withdrawal wasn't in her imagination—more evidence that he was different.

"We should go in so you can meet Theo," Tamsen said.

The basement looked like a toy store that had barely survived a tornado. When all the books were neatly stacked on their shelves and every puzzle piece, train track, miniature farm animal, and wheeled vehicle was placed neatly into its designated bin, the playroom was passable. But this afternoon, Tamsen was ashamed of the extra effort Theo had put into obliterating Aneta's efforts at organization.

"It's not usually this messy," she said.

Whit followed behind Tamsen as she navigated around the landmines of trucks and blocks to a nylon pop-up fort. They could hear Theo role playing inside.

"Knock, knock," Tamsen interrupted. "Come on out, Theo. I want you to meet somebody." The fort shifted, and Theo emerged holding two figures: A G.I. Joe that was once Victor's and one of Charlotte's old Ken dolls. "This is Whit—he teaches guitar."

"Hi," Theo said, quickly casting off the dolls.

"Hey, Theo," Whit said, holding his left fist toward the boy. "Whatup, man?"

Theo reciprocated with a return left fist bump. "Yo, whatup?"

"Alright! You a southpaw too?" Whit mused.

"He sure is," Tamsen replied.

Whit ignored her, keeping his focus on Theo. "I understand you like rock, is that right?"

"I want to be in a band."

"Theo's dad took him to a concert at Ravinia this summer," Tamsen offered as clarification.

"Who'd you see in concert?" Whit asked, still refusing to acknowledge that it was Tamsen doing the answering.

"UB40," Theo said.

"Legit," he responded.

Tamsen found it interesting how Whit lapsed into dude-speak when he was talking to Theo, while he had been much more formal with her. This cool approach would resonate with Theo, but Tamsen knew it wouldn't play well with Victor, who was very traditional regarding his views on the manner in which children should speak to adults. Even their closest friends were never addressed by the children using first names. It was always Mr. and Mrs., or, in the case of the Summers, Aunt and Uncle.

Charlotte stepped cautiously down the stairs fixing her gaze on the mug of steaming hot liquid in her hands and gripping it tightly in a dish towel. Tamsen saw that she had changed her outfit from ten minutes earlier. Her wavy sable hair was brushed, and she was wearing a pale pink lip gloss that matched the new Brandy Melville sweater Tamsen had bought her.

"What do you have there, sweetheart?" Tamsen asked, tiptoeing toward her daughter, hoping to circumvent a spill.

"Charlotte!" Theo scolded. "Daddy says no eating or drinking in the playroom." Charlotte's bare foot came down on an upturned Hotwheel. She yelped and lost her balance. Half the brown liquid and a flurry of wet brown tea leaves sloshed from the mug onto the carpet. Tamsen quickly swept the cup from her daughter's hands.

"Char, did you forget to use a strainer?" Tamsen asked, looking at the swampy sediment on the floor.

Charlotte's face flushed red. "What's a strainer?"

Whit looked at Charlotte and then at Tamsen. "I never strain my tea. I have a friend in Shanghai who swears it tastes way better this way." He took the mug from Tamsen and, with a loud slurp, he drew in a giant sip. "Delicious," he added with a funny face that exposed chunks of brown tea leaves between his teeth.

The children looked at each other and began to giggle.

"What's so funny?" he asked, as if he were oblivious. His teeth were full of tea leaves and Theo and Charlotte laughed wildly.

Tamsen smiled. She couldn't recall the last time she herself had been able to surrender to hilarity, the kind of convulsive laughter that took on a life of its own. Maybe she was too grown up for that kind of joy, or perhaps she had simply become too self-conscious to let go.

"Do you have a guitar yet, Theo?" Whit asked after taking a moment in the powder room mirror to clear his teeth.

"He does," Tamsen interjected. "I got him a Martin Dreadnought Junior. They're putting strings on it, but I can pick it up by the end of the week."

Whit's expression flattened and Tamsen wished she had let Theo answer the question. She didn't want to appear to be one of those helicopter moms, but she wanted Whit to know she took his musicianship seriously, and that her investment in an $800 Martin guitar for Theo was a symbol of her commitment.

"We can still return it if you think he should play something else," she said.

His jaw tightened. He was even more handsome when he looked stern. "As long as it's not the adult size, it'll do the job."

She walked Whit to the door calculating the most diplomatic way to ask him for details of his professional background. It wasn't a question of if, but rather when Victor would interrogate her about the cellist's resume.

"Is that a Miró?" he asked of a painting that hung above the limestone fireplace.

"Yes," Tamsen said, "I love surrealism." In art, at least. Not so much in her life with Victor, the experience of always feeling she'd done something wrong.

"This is an unbelievable instrument," Whit remarked of the concert piano in the bay window. "I've only played one Fazioli, and that was in Munich—do you mind?" he asked, hovering his fingertips above the keys.

"Please," she said. "Charlotte studies with the Metzger School."

He fluttered his fingers across the piano and closed his eyes, playing something intricate and sweet from memory. Charlotte spied from around the corner. He finished and thanked Tamsen again.

"Did you study music in Europe?" Tamsen asked.

"Not exactly," he replied, reaching for his pockets.

"How long have you played guitar?" she pressed.

"I suppose I was about Theo's age when I started messing around on guitar. It definitely wasn't on a Martin, though," he said.

"The woman who gave us your number—she's the one who said you play cello, which is why I reached out." Tamsen said.

Whit withdrew one hand from a pocket, burying his fingers in the front of his thick dark hair. He stood still for a moment, his weight on one foot, and then sighed deeply, raising his eyes.

"Mrs. Peel, I think your kids are great, but this isn't going to work out for me."

Tamsen stepped back, holding up her hands. "Wait, you misunderstand," she insisted. "I don't care about the cello. It's just that Theo's father can be difficult."

"I understand, Mrs. Peel," he said. "Certain people can give their kids experiences that are," he hesitated, "extraordinary, but I'm just a regular guy who teaches guitar."

"Which is perfect," Tamsen insisted, wishing they had arranged their meeting at a park or a coffee shop and not at her twelve-million-dollar home. "It's just that Victor wants Theo to play something traditional like violin or French horn. At least if I say you're a classically trained cellist, I have a shot at convincing Victor that Theo's guitar lessons will lead to bigger things, even if they don't."

Whit shook his head and his eyes went vacant. "Bigger things."

"Please, can we just give it a try?" she pleaded, wishing Whit could understand what this meant for a kid like her son. She checked over her shoulder that Charlotte was gone. "You are exactly what Theo needs."

Whit opened the door and he thanked her for the tea and she watched him as he unlocked his rickety ten-speed bike from their towering black iron fence. She didn't want him to go. She wanted him to help her cover the roses for the winter. She wanted him to know where she came from and that this grand house and the rare Fazioli didn't define her. But it was too late. To him, these things probably already defined her.

She reached for the button to buzz open the front gate when Theo rushed out the open door.

"Whit, I made you something," he said, holding out a non-descript LEGO creation.

"Whoa," Whit exclaimed. "Tell me about this, buddy," he said as if the lump of blocks was the most captivating invention he'd had ever seen.

"It's a zombie laser shooter," Theo replied.

"Well, duh," Whit responded as he turned the item over in his hands.

"Do you like laser tag, Theo?" he asked.

Tamsen held her breath. She and Theo had role-played scenarios like this many times.

"I never play laser tag," Theo replied. Tamsen hoped Whit would ask something more about Theo's invention.

"You would love it," Whit said enthusiastically.

"It's not that I never have played laser tag," Theo clarified. "It's that I'm not allowed to play it."

Whit didn't try to hide his distain. He gave Tamsen a chilly side glance and she could practically hear his thoughts: these over achieving, uptight, pretentious parents won't let their kid have any real fun.

"I have Doose Syndrome and the doctor says sometimes I get thunderstorms in my brain."

The muscles in Whit's face softened and he steadied his bike against the fence. "Thunderstorms, huh?"

"Yeah. I don't watch a lot of TV either."

"You're not missing much, pal, believe me," Whit assured him. He bent down in front of Theo on one knee. "I know a little about thunderstorms and brains."

"Yeah?" said Theo.

"Yup," Whit replied, nodding and tussling the boy's hair. "You must be a genius if you've got thunder and lightning in there."

Tamsen felt proud that her son had shamelessly divulged his condition to this stranger. She herself seldom volunteered information about Theo's diagnosis because she wanted him to be seen as a regular boy.

Whit handed Theo the laser shooter. "You hang on to this, Theo," he urged.

Theo put his hand on Whit's arm. "No, I want you to take it. You can give it back to me at our guitar lesson."

Whit paused and looked at Tamsen. "I insist, comrade," Whit said. "I could never leave you unprepared for the zombie apocalypse."

3

The clock on the microwave read 9:33 p.m. Theo and Charlotte were asleep and Tamsen's roller bag stood by the front door, at the ready for the changing of the guard. The kitchen gleamed and Tamsen had wiped up any trace of the spilled tea in the basement. She looked at her phone: still no text from Victor. She dialed him again, and again she was bounced to voicemail. Tamsen opened the Sub-Zero and began mechanically organizing the bottles of salad dressing, soy sauce, and mayo in the door by height, her mind landing on every possible reason for Victor's failure to come home—a conference call, a spontaneous dinner meeting, an accident.

He always took a black car; those were safe, right? A funeral for Victor would be well-attended, a Socialati blockbuster event, and Digby would insist on delivering the eulogy since he knew Victor best. Tamsen let out a soft laugh. As if anyone knew the real Victor. She thought she heard the sound of footsteps upstairs and she held still for a second. No, there was nothing but the bathroom fan outside Charlotte's bedroom. With the fleeting thought of her pure-hearted daughter, Tamsen silently admonished herself for entertaining the prospect of Victor being dead.

Then came the foreboding jangle of keys outside the front door and Tamsen's heart rate surged. She tucked her hair behind her ears nervously, picked up a dish rag, and scanned the marble kitchen counter for a spot she hadn't already wiped. The door eased open and Victor stepped into the foyer. He quietly slid off his suit coat and then methodically held it at arm's length, smoothing nonexistent wrinkles before laying it over the bannister at the foot of the front staircase. He didn't perform his typical ritual of loosening his silk Ferragamo tie or removing his black wingtips and leaving them by the door. Rather, he stepped into the dim glow of the crystal chandelier and raised his wrists, first the right, then the left, to reveal the silver and black onyx cufflinks he turned once, then again. Tamsen felt the atmosphere around her thin. He didn't need to utter a word; when she saw his face in the dim light, the way his skin tightened around his mouth, she knew she had done something very, very wrong.

Her brain went into hyperdrive, ticking through the past several days, taking rapid inventory of all the events that could have triggered Victor's wrath. The lice: unlikely, the kids knew to keep news of the outbreak on the down-low. Her meeting at the Women's Social Club: not a possibility, there had been nothing remarkable about her lunch to discuss the Harvest Moon event. The new guitar: yes, this had to be it. She must have misjudged the degree to which Victor objected to Theo taking lessons.

For a split second, she envisioned herself bypassing the confrontation by rushing past Victor and running as fast as she could out the front door. It was a liberating fantasy, but not remotely possible given her fear of certain retaliation. He might change the locks and accuse her of abandoning Theo and Charlotte. Or . . . Tamsen truly believed that Victor was even capable, with enough provocation, of inflicting physical harm. She needed to deal with this situation, to gain the upper hand by once again facing him, appeasing him. She took a deep breath in and repeated a mantra in her head before joining Victor in the living room: *Do this to get through this.*

She left an arm's length distance between them, but he stepped in close to her. She felt his warm bourbon breath touch her face, and watched his dry lips curl back, his eyes seared in fury.

Tamsen recalled a taxidermy timberwolf she always had to avoid when she visited the Field Museum with young Charlotte. It was the "mean dog," the one that always made Charlotte cry, suspended in a predatory stance only seconds before it tore into the throat of a helpless wounded deer.

Victor appeared larger in the soft light, his unforgiving dark eyes drawn into their familiar slits. She swallowed, attempting to ingest her dread and act normally, as if she had done nothing wrong. Somewhere along the way, "wrong" became inexplicably subjective and Tamsen's default mode began to track with Victor's warped point of view that she was guilty until proven innocent, or guilty until he decided that he had disciplined her adequately. Years of the same routine had conditioned her to respond with the same fear and the same defense; her way of coping was to handle him, to manage him the way a bomb squad deals with a hot explosive.

She delicately began her attempt to defuse the ticking device. "It's late."

No response.

"The guitar I found for Theo is a really nice one. The sales guy actually played a classical piece for us in the store. I think it was Haydn."

Victor was silent.

"I know you don't want Theo playing guitar, but I found this teacher who is actually an accomplished cellist. Maybe if Theo starts with guitar, we can transition him to—"

"Stop trying to manipulate me."

"Victor, I—"

"You know what you did," he interrupted.

"I'm sorry, but Theo wanted a guitar so badly."

"I don't give a FUCK about the guitar."

The kids would hear him. She was off-track. What did he want her to say? Her heart raced. There was no air. She needed to cut a wire, but which one? *Do this to get through this. Do this to get through this.*

"Hilly and Jacqueline and I met to discuss the fundraiser," she explained, keeping her voice quiet and steady.

"So, Jacqueline was there too?" he rumbled.

"Part of the time, then I stayed and talked to Hilly."

"Got nice and personal?"

"Victor, she already knew about our situation."

"Our situation?" he sneered.

"Charlotte told Astrid," Tamsen could tell by his pursed lips that she was getting warmer. Tick, tick, tick. "We knew that might happen."

"Don't use the kids as a shield," Victor spat.

She needed to redirect. "I told Hilly we were working some things out."

Victor inhaled deeply. He raised his voice again. "What else did you tell her, Tamsen?"

"Please," she implored. "The kids are sleeping."

He glared, a disturbing half-smirk revealing how he relished her discomfort. "What did you tell her?"

His fingers twitched by his sides, the way a cowboy's did in old movies, movies with holsters, spinning six-shooters, and duels.

"Nothing, I swear." He was going to wake the children. The ticking, she had to stop the ticking. The separation book said to avoid exposing the children to arguments. "Nothing bad," she pleaded.

Even louder yet, "What did you say?"

Tamsen quivered, expecting Charlotte to pad down the stairs any second now. She desperately tried to recall the details of her conversation with Hilly, but her neurons were firing too fast. Tick, tick, tick, tick, tick. She looked beyond Victor. Past the piano and the bannister, her eyes coming to rest on her wheeled suitcase—and then it struck her. She knew which wire to cut.

"I told Hilly we were nesting," she blurted.

Victor's mouth was pinched, but the way his brow softened told Tamsen that she had made the right move.

"I did. I explained how it was best for the kids." She gushed on. "I said you were staying in a corporate apartment, that you were traveling a lot, and that I was at The Talisman a few nights a week. I told her how the children were our primary focus and that they got to sleep in their own beds." Total transparent honesty would disarm him. She wouldn't leave out a single detail, she had to make sure she covered it all.

"Do you think it's anyone's business where I sleep?" he hissed, his voice returning to a level that wouldn't disturb the children. "Now the entire company is going to know about this arrangement."

"You're right," she said. "I shouldn't have gone there," she quickly agreed.

He raised his arms. "How's this all going to look to my clients?"

"I'm sorry."

"You better be sorry. Do you actually believe any of those women care about you?" he huffed. "They don't even like you."

His statement was a roundhouse to her abdomen. She wanted to cry but she wouldn't.

"Hilly seemed to really respect how hard we're trying to keep the kids in the house. I told her how important you thought it was for them to feel safe." Inside, Tamsen was wailing.

"You do not discuss my marriage," he barked in staccato.

"I know. I'm sorry," Tamsen said.

Victor kicked off his shoes and tugged sharply on his Windsor knot, then he unbuttoned his collar. Tamsen's panic gave way to despair and she stood frozen in place, waiting for the all-clear. Victor walked slowly to the bar and took out a lowball. He poured himself a whisky from one of his vintage decanters and took a gulp. He dropped his head side-to-side until Tamsen heard a crack as his neck released in a quick jerk. He turned to face her. His expression was neutral.

Tamsen steadied herself against the back of their coral mohair settee, soothing herself with knowledge that the episode was ended and soon enough she would be away from him. The adrenaline in her bloodstream began to dissipate until she could feel herself returning to normal.

"I told Digby you would be at the closing dinner Friday night," Victor said evenly.

Tamsen seldom attended the lavish client dinners thrown by Summers & Peel, but under the circumstances, she most definitely did not plan to attend this one. "I'll have the gift baskets done in time, and I can drop them off, but I won't be there. Besides, I'm driving carpool that evening for figure skating."

"The reason George Woodley hired us is because Summers & Peel reflects Thunderchicken's same core values: God and family. Aneta can carpool the girls. Digby agrees, the Thunderchicken execs are all flying up from Alabama and they're bringing their wives. It would look bad if I showed up alone."

"Aneta isn't comfortable with that kind of responsibility," Tamsen replied.

"Do you have any idea how many hundreds of millions of advertising dollars they spend with us?" he said, with an urgency in his voice that hinted at his desperation. "We need Woodley to feel good about

Summers & Peel—not like he's dealing with a bunch of flakes who've lapsed into some frivolous midlife crisis." Victor's lips momentarily formed into a familiar tight line, but quickly morphed into a sickly-sweet smile veiling his aggression. "It's really great that you signed up Theo for guitar lessons, but what you need to appreciate, Tamsen, is that the money I earn from companies like Thunderchicken makes it possible for you to stay home every day, doing paint-by-numbers or whatever it is that fills your time. My money also makes it possible to buy expensive guitars and to pay the losers you employ to poison our son with rock music."

She knew what he was saying, but she wanted to hear it from his mouth. "What's your point?" she asked.

"I will allow Theo to take guitar lessons, and you will be at the Thunderchicken dinner."

Ute Tanaka Salon occupied the second-floor space of a sleek, modern four-story building on Oak Street. The small oasis was named for the parents of the salon's forty-two-year-old owner, Yasutaka Tanaka, who had long abandoned his Japanese given name in favor of something more western: Clay. His mother, Ute, was a German model who met Clay's father while he was stationed in Heidelberg. Anybody who was anyone was trying to get into Clay's chair for their cut and color, and at $450 per sitting. Although she had tempered her spending elsewhere, Tamsen refused to give up this indulgence. Plus, Clay was Tamsen's dearest friend in Chicago. She wouldn't think of bringing her business any place else.

Clay's salon was small and exclusive, with only two black leather swivel chairs for cuts and color positioned in front of oversized black lacquer mirrors propped against a graphite gray wall. The floors were dark brown Brazilian walnut, with a stain that complemented the large carved wood desk near the entry. He had a small seating enclave with a deep navy sofa near the check-in desk, where a waiting patron could sip expensive water or Moët & Chandon while they leafed through coffee-table books on art and culture. Black and white photographs of male nudes hung tastefully throughout the space, along with antique prints of traditional Japanese kimonos. Clay always kept an oversized Baccarat bowl of Caramel Cream Bulls Eyes candies on the Jonathan Adler coffee table. He said they reminded him of growing up in a provincial southern Illinois town where the only culture they had was a 7-Eleven and ballroom dancing at the VFW hall. Beside it sat a leather-bound photo album containing prints of Clay and his older brother, Mirko, who lived in California.

Tamsen was shocked at how gaunt her face looked in the reflection of Clay's mirror. She traced the hollows below her cheek bones with her fingertips.

"Is this one of those vanity mirrors?" she asked.

"I wasn't going to say anything, but you look like you're not eating."

"I eat," she said. "It's stress."

"Why don't we have Kiki grab you a sandwich, or maybe some chicken soup," he suggested, nodding a directive toward his assistant with the pink hair.

"Thanks, no appetite."

Clay raised his orange, blue, and yellow tattooed arms, gently letting his hands come to rest on her shoulders. He looked at Tamsen with the same sincerity he did before telling her that he had broken up with Mr. Wrong or that he'd met another Mr. Maybe. She'd been seeing Clay since she made her first paycheck at Beau Monde and his price for a color and a cut was a mere $80, still a huge splurge for her twenty-two-year-old tresses. Clay and Tamsen had come up together and their journey to the top of their professional games had bound them for life. She trusted him with all her secrets and he trusted her with his.

"When are you going to leave that fiend, Tam?"

"We're separated."

"Really leave him," he said, shaking his head. "This marriage is not good for you." He ran the brush through her hair and held it up, pulling off strands and letting them drop to the floor. "Look at this, now you're losing your hair."

"It's not that simple. We have kids."

"And you think Theo and Charlotte are better off with a mom who looks like she's on an air diet?" he said. "Kids are smart; they can feel the tension in the house. It's like when elephants sense a tsunami and they head for high ground."

"I read an entire chapter of Harry Potter to Theo and Charlotte last night and I couldn't tell you the first thing about it. I even used a British accent, but I wasn't there. I was in my head the entire time. God, I'm a terrible mother."

"Stop it. You know that's not true. Those kids adore you."

"They deserve better," she said, looking at her drawn reflection.

"*Und wenn sie nicht gestorben sind, dann leben sie noch heute*," Clay recited. "That is how the Germans say, 'They lived happily ever after.' The direct English translation is, 'And if they are not dead, then today they are still living.'"

It took a minute for Tamsen to process Clay's observation. "That's how they end their fairy tales?" Tamsen asked.

"Ja," Clay answered with a sweet lilt in his voice.

"So, what you're telling me is you don't believe in happy endings."

"Ja, again," he said. He bent close to her ear, meeting her stare in the mirror. "Isn't it time you saw somebody? A therapist?"

"I'm fine," she answered, fighting the urge to cry.

"Tamsen, I know you don't think you need help, but as your friend, I am telling you, you need help," he said emphatically.

Tamsen felt a burning as tears began to surge. She held her eyes open because if she blinked, the liquid pain would surely spill out onto her cheeks. When she had cried publicly as a child, her brothers had condemned her mercilessly. They made up a chant, "Blubber Tam, Uncle Sam, crying like a baby lamb," when she broke her arm falling from a tree on the Fourth of July. And they shouted it in unison at recess, "Blubber Tam, Uncle Sam, crying like a baby lamb," when she couldn't contain her tears at school the day her guinea pig died. "Quit being a baby," they told her. She loved the way Clay's tiny salon felt like a safe zone, far away from the Kinney boys and their cruelty. Nevertheless, she'd become very adept at swallowing her anguish. Clay gave her shoulders a pinch.

"When Jasper and I split up, I was a mess. Remember that? How I didn't eat or sleep for days? How if I wasn't doing hair, I was rolled up in a ball in the back room with all the dirty gowns?"

Tamsen laughed, choking back her emotion. "That's revisionist history, Clay. You were curled up with that cute barista on the leather pullout in your break room."

"True, but I was still a disaster and I got a lot better a lot quicker when I found my therapist."

"That's because you started sleeping with him."

"Fair enough," Clay said as he spun the chair around and bent down to face her, nose-to-nose. "But it's already bad, and it can get a lot worse. Victor is not a nice person."

"I have you," Tamsen whimpered, taking a tissue from Kiki and wiping her nose.

"You have me to tell you when you look like hell. You have me for glasses of your husband's expensive wine when he's on the road. You even have me to watch your rugrats when that entitled babysitter of yours asks for a paid vacation."

"Aneta is not entitled. And me. Yes, poor me with my Astor Street house and my kids at Dexter, while I get a $450 haircut."

"Whatever. You need a shrink who can give you oars to stay on course, and a lifejacket, so that when the raging sea of domestic conflict dumps your ass, you don't get sucked down to the cold murky depths."

"That's an awfully violent metaphor, don't you think? Maybe there's a treasure in the murky depths."

"There's a treasure, all right, but you're gonna need all your strength to drag it to the surface."

Clay reached into the pocket of his vinyl utility apron and pulled out a business card.

"Call this woman," he insisted, handing it to her. "I have a client who swears by her. She specializes in all that female stuff."

Tamsen looked at the pink vellum stock. "Female stuff" was not printed on the card. Instead, there was a name in dark plum calligraphy: Fariah Valentine, LCSW.

"She's not a real doctor. She can't even prescribe meds."

Clay let out a loud "Ha!" and spun Tamsen back around to face the mirror. "We both know how well you tolerate drugs."

Tamsen cringed. Her mind flashed to last New Year's Eve and the annual bash at the Yacht Club. Everyone had looked forward to the decadent event with its mouthwatering food, glittering decorations, and impressive turnout. That New Year's there would be no celebration, which was fine, because the party no longer held luster for Tamsen. Its significance was now the disquieting memory of the first and only time she had taken a prescription sleep aid—a decision that had resulted in choppy recollections, a scalding headache, and a fearful sensation she could not quite grasp with Victor. Probably his ceaseless ire.

Tamsen unzipped her over-stuffed wallet, and tried, unsuccessfully, to find a tiny bit of space in which she could slide the therapist's card. As Clay applied the dye that would cover her first gray hairs, she began prying at the thick brick of gift cards that were lodged between the leather slits: Nordstrom, Whole Foods, Target, Best Buy, Amazon, iTunes, Costco, and more.

"I really need to get organized," she said.

Tamsen hastily shoved the open wallet into her handbag, spilling a cascade of plastic cards to the floor.

"Dammit," she said.

"Are you counterfeiting gift cards in your spare time? Cuz if so, I want in on that action," Clay said. He delicately plucked one of her acquisitions from the floor and blew off the black hair trimming that clung to it. "Why are you carrying these things around?"

Tamsen eyed the Starbucks card in Clay's hand. She had loaded it using the family charge card and was prepared if Victor called her out—$100 for a teacher gift, she'd say.

"You know how it is with Christmas," Tamsen said. "Nobody wants presents anymore. Everyone wants gift cards: housekeepers, babysitters, hair stylists . . ." She took the Whole Foods card from Clay's hand as Kiki gathered the others that had tumbled beneath the styling chair.

He raised an eyebrow and stopped working. "That Starbucks card has fireworks on it. Seems to me someone started her holiday shopping early this year."

"Can't be too prepared," Tamsen returned, unable to look him in the eye.

"Call the therapist, Tam," he insisted. "And for Christ's sake, get yourself a safe deposit box."

When Tamsen checked her phone, there were three missed calls and one message from the school. Thankfully, the voicemail started with the qualifier, "This is not an emergency." It was Theo's teacher: "Call us at your earliest convenience."

Tamsen pulled up the school's number swiftly, her pulse accelerating with the memory of Theo's seizure in PE last year when a fast-moving kickball knocked him in the head.

"Theo dictated a story today to one of our upper-class volunteers and I thought it was important for me to read it you," Ms. Ellison explained with clipped East Coast matter-of-factness.

"Of course," Tamsen concurred.

"The cue today was, 'name an object you cannot live without,'" she explained.

"Okay," Tamsen replied expectantly, thinking of Theo's obsession with a threadbare stuffed turtle he had named Brian, after their handyman.

Ms. Ellison cleared her throat. "'I got a new guitar and it is my favorite thing because I am going to take guitar lessons and I am going to play it so good that my mom won't leave.'"

When she heard these tragic words, Tamsen's heart, awash in guilt, split wide open. How had she failed so terribly that her son feared that she would abandon him?

"Was there anything else?" she asked. "About me? About Theo's father?"

"No, that was it. As I told Victor when we spoke earlier, Theo is obviously feeling a great deal of stress due to the situation at home. I was going to wait until our parent-teacher conference, but I thought it was best to alert you immediately, so you could help Theo manage his feelings around your separation from Victor."

Tamsen balked. The teacher had already spoken to Victor. "Theo hasn't expressed anything to me at all," Tamsen said. "I thought he was doing okay."

"Mrs. Peel, kids at Theo's age feel responsible when their parents split up. They actually take the blame because if they accept a role in the breakup of the marriage, then they wrongly believe they can actually fix it. Assure Theo you love him—that he had nothing to do with your decision to separate from your husband." Ms. Ellison sounded like she was reading a page from *Separation: Sparing the Child*. "When I spoke to Victor, he asked me to put together a reading list for him—books on the effects of divorce on children, coping strategies, you know, basic stuff."

Since when had the two of them been on a first name basis?

"Would you like me to send it to you as well?" Ms. Ellison asked.

Tamsen felt a mounting pressure in her head. "Thanks, but I'm good. Let me know if anything else comes up."

"Any time, Mrs. Peel," Ms. Ellison assured her. "That's why I'm here."

"Please, Ms. Ellison," Tamsen said. "Call me Tamsen."

Business functions at the Summers' always followed the same trajectory. The evening started with very stiff conversation about "the campaign" and then, sometime after the drinks kicked in, everyone lowered their guard and became marginally tolerable. Still, there was always an air of formality to these things and Tamsen suspected that the tone of the night would be governed by the uptight nature of the Thunderchicken executives rather than the amount of whiskey being poured.

Hilly and Digby's penthouse co-op in the Gold Coast was perfectly appointed. The home had been featured in the fine design issue of *Design Digest*, a fact that was critical to Hilly's identity and one that she regularly worked into conversation. Everything, from the Jim Thompson Floriental silk draperies to the velvet throw pillows coordinated in complimentary yellow, green, and blue pastels, reminded Tamsen of the butter mints her grandmother used to give her after mass. Hilly's aesthetic was traditional, mimicking the taste of the women who appeared in *The Chicago Ancestral Register*, a catalog of the original moneyed Chicago families. Tamsen was fairly certain every piece of furniture Digby and Hilly owned was crafted before women's suffrage. The stormy Turner landscape over the carved statuary marble fireplace was an original, and the walnut Chippendale dining chairs surrounding the claw-footed mahogany game table had been re-upholstered with needlepoint seats, displaying the likeness of each of the six cats the Summers had owned.

Tamsen arrived early to the party with the intention of assembling the gift baskets onsite. She didn't want them to be crushed in transit and she figured Hilly might need a hand with setup. She made several trips up the elevator with the doorman before all the party favors were ready to be bundled in the oversized nests Tamsen had handwoven from corkscrew willow branches. She spread the loot on the desk in Digby's paneled library and went to work, carefully arranging them on a bed of brown crinkle-cut craft paper.

"Come look at the dining room!" Hilly squealed, grabbing Tamsen by the arm and leading her to where the table was meticulously set for twelve. A young woman in her twenties wearing a purple bubble dress with matching tights and stylish short black boots breezed in, holding a clipboard and a long utility lighter.

"I suggest we wait until just before dinner is served to light the candles," she chirped.

"This is Madison," Hilly said as the young woman zealously extended her hand. "She's with Flare Events—only the best caterer and party planners in the city."

"I've heard the name," Tamsen replied. Leave it to Hilly to overkill a dinner party for twelve by hiring the biggest event company in Chicago.

"Madison had this great idea to do upscale fast food for our dinner tonight." Hilly clapped her hands together. "I mean, so original! Right?! Even the servers are dressed up for the theme." Hilly motioned toward the bartender, who passed through the dining room wearing a familiar-looking uniform, an apron, and a paper hat.

Tamsen nodded her approval. She didn't have the heart to tell Hilly that the "dressed-up version of lowbrow food" concept was about as fresh as sack races at a company picnic.

"What's on the menu?" Tamsen asked, noticing the mustard-yellow napkins and bright red ceramic dinner plates.

"Gourmet beef sliders wrapped in parchment with a side of rosemary duck fat French fries, served in these cute cardboard box thingies," Madison answered holding up a red carton.

"Burgers?" asked Tamsen. Hilly couldn't possibly be this easily seduced by a novice.

"They're Kobe beef, with caramelized onions," Hilly added.

"And don't forget the special sauce!" Madison added.

"We're doing side salads too," Hilly explained. "And hand-held sour cherry pies for dessert." A whirring noise could be heard coming from the kitchen.

"That must be the milkshakes!" Madison exclaimed. "I'll get you ladies a sample," she said, disappearing through the butler's pantry.

Tamsen looked at the spread and all she saw were the missed

opportunities—so many chances to create a sense of camaraderie between Summers & Peel and this client, who had never even been to Chicago.

She looked up. Why hadn't Madison done anything about the lighting? Even strings of bistro bulbs dipping from the ceiling would have made the sterile dining room seem more like an intimate café and less like the Oval Office. The menu could have been vibrant and eclectic, an ethnic mélange showcasing Chicago neighborhood specialties like roast lamb and flaming saganaki cheese from Greektown, or butter chicken from the Devon corridor. At least Tamsen had included a special certificate in each basket for an overnight home delivery of a jumbo Lou Malnati's deep-dish pizza.

Tamsen frantically plucked the dinner plates from the white table cloth. "Get me your Bernardaud," she said to Hilly. "A dozen place settings."

"What are you doing?" Hilly asked, taking one of the plates and replacing it from behind her.

Tamsen spun around. "Do you know the name of the company we are honoring tonight?"

"It's Thunderchicken, of course," Hilly laughed nervously.

"And what do they do, Hilly?"

"They sell fast food?"

"That's right, they sell turkey, not burgers and fries like their number one competitor," Tamsen said firmly.

Hilly scrunched her brow as much as her Botox would permit. "But the table looks so great. Madison thought of every last detail."

Tamsen picked up one of the yellow napkins and held it next to the red dinner plate. "This detail plus this detail equals complete disregard for the fact that these colors represent Thunderchicken's competitor."

Hilly gasped, "I didn't even think about that . . ."

"The Bernardaud," Tamsen ordered.

"Oh, no!" Hilly said, rushing to the China cabinet. "What do we do about the food?" She was entering full panic mode. "Jesus Christ, Digby is going to be furious."

"Given the client, you're going to want to leave the Jesus Christ out of this, unless you're singing a hymn."

"God, you're so right," Hilly conceded, not even recognizing she'd spoken profanely again.

Tamsen's gears began to turn and she could feel herself entering The Zone. The opportunity to avert a potential PR disaster for Summers & Peel was secondary to the thrill of the creative challenge Tamsen was facing. Her heart raced, and she was giddy with ideas. "I'll talk to the chef. Just promise me you haven't hired a red-headed clown for the entertainment," Tamsen said.

Madison appeared in the doorway holding two paper cups with striped straws. "Vanilla milkshakes!"

Tamsen gritted her teeth. "Madison, change of plans."

With the table finally set and the menu completely reworked, Tamsen stood, martini in hand, in front of Digby's pride and joy: a sixteenth-century Francis I French Renaissance sideboard that he had bought for just under a million at Sotheby's. Hilly liked to tell guests that it was one of three in the world and the only one that wasn't part of a museum collection. The piece was empirically hideous, and no one was allowed to touch it, so Tamsen wasn't surprised when Hilly rejected her suggestion that they use the sideboard to display the Thunderchicken deal gifts. Neil Nevin, Victor's Chief Financial Officer, walked up beside her, wearing his traditional Scottish kilt. Neil liked Tamsen, and the feeling was mutual. He reminded her of her father on her father's best days, a spark in his eye that belied his stiff, reserved manner. He nodded devilishly toward the elaborately carved piece.

"What is the point of an object that cannot exercise its purpose?" he asked, looking sideways at Tamsen.

Tamsen raised her glass. "Here's to pointless treasures and all they will never be."

Neil was a notoriously private man. He was socially uncomfortable unless he was discussing his golf game, movies, or Scottish plaids. He collected tartan kilts and nice cars like Victor collected country clubs. A graduate of the Scottish Air Force Academy, Neil had somehow gained entrance into the very exclusive Thornberry Links. It was the elusive crown jewel in Victor's menagerie of memberships, and Tamsen was convinced Victor's determination to secure a sponsorship at Thornberry was the sole reason he'd hired Neil.

"Hello, my darling," Victor said, ambushing Tamsen with a kiss. "I would like you to meet George Woodley, CEO of Thunderchicken." Tamsen wiped her mouth where Victor had left his saliva and took a swig of her martini to cleanse her lips.

Neil cleared his throat and smacked George Woodley squarely between his scapula in an uncharacteristically manly gesture. "Congratulations, Maestro, on a very profitable summer campaign."

"Where's your lovely lady this evening, Neil?" George asked in an accent thick as sawmill gravy. "We've spent so much time crunching numbers for the media buy, she probably thinks we're an item." George laughed heartily at his own joke and Neil's fair complexion turned pink.

"I'm solo this evening," Neil said, looking down at his spats.

A timely server swooped in with a tray. "Caramelized onion tart-elette, anyone?"

Tamsen was relieved by the arrival of Russell Kupiac, also known as Koop. Koop was the effusive creative force on the Thunderchicken account. He oversaw all video production for the fast food chain—and he was irrefutably brilliant. Victor, who'd plucked the young director from graduate film school, called Koop his "golden boy." He had the ability to turn television commercials about the Thunderchicken cheddar grits into sublime cinematic ambrosia, and his YouTube ads for the Thunderchicken Gobble Grande Texmex sandwich had more views than the latest Rihanna video.

"Come here, you big visionary," George Woodley said as he embraced the thickset Koop. "I can't tell you how many calls we are getting on the Little Drumsticks kid meal spots. Sales are up 25% and it's only been a week!"

"I believe in the quality of your product, George, but I believe in wholesome family values most of all, and good old-fashioned American values are driving this entire process," Koop said. He knew how to play the game.

"Well, we could not be happier," George gushed.

The guests advanced into the living room where the wait staff, now dressed in the Summers & Peel t-shirts Tamsen had customized for the gift baskets, floated among the attendees, passing duck fat potato rillettes and Kobe beef canapés. The repurposing of tonight's dinner ingredients was coming off flawlessly.

"Now, Hilly, I'll be doin' the blessing tonight," Tamsen overheard George's wife, Eleanor, say. It was time to get some air.

Tamsen stole away from the group onto the expansive balcony, slipping out of the red lacquer-soled designer shoes she'd unearthed at a sample sale and easing back into a plush chaise overlooking Lakeshore Drive and Oak Street Beach. She watched a slow serpent of taillights creep north along the water and its quicker twin of bright headlights wind its way toward the city. Lake Michigan glistened under the waning moon and Tamsen closed her eyes, wishing she could open them and be someplace else, snuggled up under a big blanket on the sofa with Theo and Charlotte watching *Animal Planet* or reruns of *The Voice*.

She heard the sliding door open and felt Victor standing behind her.

He pulled a chair up beside her, his demeanor soft. "We're getting ready to sit down to dinner," he said. He took her hand and kissed it. She yanked it back.

"How dare you kiss me," she fumed. "We're separated."

"I love you. And you're still my wife." He stood and moved to the railing, leaning with his back against it, looking at Tamsen the way Charlotte looked at kittens when they visited Petco. It was with the knowledge they wouldn't be taking one home, but with just enough faith to still believe it might happen someday. Tamsen fantasized about the rail giving way. Her torment over in an instant.

"When are you going to stop?" he asked. "When can we be a normal couple, a family?"

Had he forgotten the vile name he called her that night she dressed up for him? How he humiliated her? She couldn't have answered him if she wanted to. The space created by their separation was supposed to illuminate a solution, but instead, here they were, three months in, and the same patterns that were habituated during their years of marriage continued. Why couldn't she make a move? Maybe Clay was right; maybe she did need to see someone.

"I just don't know yet," Tamsen conceded.

"Well, you'd better figure it out, because you're the one with the problem and it's fucking up our kids."

He was referring to the scribing incident at school. The words stung like the fiery strangle of a jellyfish tentacle. She hoped Victor couldn't see the pain she likely wore in her face, so she looked out at the lake, unable to make out the line between the water and the sky. It was bad enough that she had disrupted the flow of their daily life; it was worse yet that she couldn't see a resolution on the horizon.

"You understand that I want you back, but you can't expect me to be celibate, Tamsen," Victor said, staring at her legs. She sat up straight and slid her feet into her shoes.

"Celibate," she repeated softly, shaking her head. They were in the center of a Category 5 marital fiasco—sex was the farthest thing from her mind.

"I don't want you to be surprised when one of your so-called friends sees me out with another woman," he said. She knew this was his way of telling her had started dating, or at least begun looking for someone to satisfy his appetite.

Hilly poked her head out the balcony door. "Get in here, you two. George is going crazy! He can't get over the entrée—Thunderchicken dark-meat turkey roulade with rosemary-infused sour-cherry filling and vanilla foam. He called it, 'Thunderthighs.' He wants to put it on the menu!"

It was Monday afternoon and never was Tamsen so happy to see her children as she was after three nights at The Talisman. She sat at the kitchen table with them after school, nibbling string cheese and relishing every story of who got into trouble, which teacher had freaked out, and what they planned to wear in the Halloween parade this year. Her phone pinged. It was a text from Whit.

Does tomorrow still work?

Tamsen felt a huge burden lifted. Thinking they would never see Whit again, she had already called the Old Town School of Folk Music to try to find Theo a teacher, but the only person they had available was a sixty-year-old woman who played folk and wore overalls in her profile picture.

Yes! 5:00?

See you then.

Tamsen gathered the kids in her bed after dinner and, though she made a conscious effort to focus on the Mad Libs they did together, she was dogged by an ever-present unease, the sensation that she couldn't get enough oxygen. No matter how hard she breathed in, she could not fill her lungs; it was if they were operating at half-capacity and the strain to fill them left every burning muscle in her neck so tense she was certain it might snap. The irony that she now slept in the guest suite did not escape her. She was a visitor, present but not a member. No longer did she operate as an integral part of a unit; she was an incapacitated appendage, dragging her behind her host. While Tamsen fed off the unconditional love of her children, the heavy guilt she carried overwhelmed her, even in moments like these. Flanked by two little warm bodies under her covers, she was able to experience a small trace of security, but somehow their roles were convoluted and now she had become reliant on them, just as much as they depended on her.

Tuesday came and Tamsen anticipated Whit's arrival. She gave Aneta the afternoon off because the ratio of three adults and two children in the house overwhelmed her. It was true, she needed help now and then, especially with the nearing of the Harvest Ball. But her separation from Victor had made Tamsen realize how she found having additional people in the house oppressive at times. She remembered her life before all the help, the simplicity and peace of fewer bodies.

Her phone pinged, and Whit's name appeared on her phone. He was due in less than an hour and she feared he was texting to cancel.

Ok if I bring a treat for kids?

She relaxed.

Theo is on a special diet. No carbs, no sugar.
Ah keto
Yes, I am impressed that you are familiar.
I tried it once . . . lasted till lunch

When Whit arrived promptly at 4:55 p.m., he appeared at the door carrying a brown paper bag and his guitar case strapped to his back.

"Hi," he said smiling. She over looked over his shoulder at his sad green bike, now locked to the front gate. It was a relic, with its logo half-rubbed off and a rusted patch where the frame had been welded together some time around 1975. The original curved handlebars had been stripped of their tape and were now bare silver.

"Okay that I locked up to your fence?" he asked.

"Of course," she replied. "But the gate locks so you're probably safe just leaving it." Even if it had been left in the parkway, she couldn't imagine anybody wanting to steal something so rickety.

"Force of habit," he replied casually, taking off his Bern helmet and roughing up his flattened hair.

"I had a Schwinn once," Tamsen mused. "It was bright blue with a black seat."

"Cool," Whit replied.

"I even named it."

Whit stopped and crinkled his nose. "Really?"

"Well, I was eight and liked to pretend 'Misty' was a horse and not just a three-speed." They walked into the kitchen.

"Nice," he replied. "I like to pretend Edmond Dantès is a retired Tour de France winner that I rescued from the jaws of a recycling furnace."

"You named your bike after a Dumas character?" Tamsen couldn't believe it— the cellist was also a reader.

"*The Count of Monte Cristo,*" he replied gallantly. "Killer book."

She hadn't read it since she oversaw its reissue back at the Beau Monde, but she recalled enough to know it was rich in themes of justice and revenge. Edmond Dantès was wrongfully accused of a crime and imprisoned for fourteen years. After escaping, he avenged those who had done him wrong under his new identity. He called himself The Count of Monte Cristo.

"I love all the classics," Tamsen said, her mood rising. "Majored in English a hundred years ago." It occurred to her that Whit was the first person in years who spoke about reading actual literature, not the variety of cotton-candy fiction discussed over cosmos at her former book club, in which the protagonist was either a vampiress or an oversexed cat lady. "You would love the lecture series they're doing at the new Reader's Museum called Seduction and Revenge. They're hosting a wine event next week."

"Not really my scene," Whit said with a slight frown.

Tamsen dialed back her enthusiasm. "Oh, it's no big deal, really. Super casual."

"I'm not an expert. Actually, *The Count of Monte Cristo* is the only classic I've read since college. It was my dad's favorite. He used to quote it all the time," he said. "*Life is a storm, my young friend. You will bask in the sunlight one moment, be shattered on the rocks the next. What makes you a man is what you do when that storm comes.*" He looked down at his shoes.

Tamsen pushed her hair behind her ears. She didn't know how to reply. It was a quote charged with wisdom. She tried to burn it into her memory while still trying to listen to Whit. She was grateful that Theo bounced in, carrying his Martin.

"Hey, man," Whit said, handing Theo the bakery bag. "These are for you and Charlotte." Theo accepted the offering, but looked at Tamsen for permission. Whit continued, "Almond flour, butter, stevia, cacao nibs, and eye of newt. They're from a shop near my place."

"Cuddle Cakes!" Tamsen said. "We love that place." It was the only game in town for ketogenic baked goods. Tamsen was always careful to lock her car doors when she dropped in there to buy keto treats.

An hour passed and Tamsen could hear Whit and her son from the basement. They were engaged in serious dialogue about the anatomy of a guitar. After Whit briefed Theo in proper posture, he introduced him to a simple D chord and told him to practice his strumming technique with a pick Whit had gifted him. The music gave way to the sound of Whit and Theo playing a round of ping-pong. They eventually made their way upstairs and Tamsen was pleased by the apparent connection between Theo and his new mentor.

"We had an excellent lesson and this guy," he said, putting his hand on Theo's head, "is well on his way to a Grammy for Best New Artist."

"Rock on," Theo said, making a hand gesture that Tamsen thought meant hang ten.

"Rock on, man," Whit echoed, making the hand sign back, as Theo disappeared.

Whit scooped up his helmet and put it on, leaving the straps to dangle along his face. His jaw was square and sharp, and masculine stubble was beginning to emerge across his beard line. His cheekbones were high with distinct hollows below, and his brow was subtly pronounced in a way that gave his expression a look of forceful concentration. She noticed a mark in his earlobe and she wondered if he had once worn an earring. Tamsen got a second piercing in secondary school and her father called her a "Gardiner Street gutter slag"—Irish slang for prostitute.

"By any chance does your fancy coffee maker dispense hot water?" Whit asked, eyeing a tower of built-ins on the kitchen wall. He held up his dented travel Thermos.

"It does," replied Tamsen.

"Mind if I make some tea?" Whit asked.

"Not at all," she said. He shook an envelope of loose leaves into his stainless steel vessel.

"This kitchen is bigger than my apartment," he said, admiring the appliances. "Correction, your refrigerator is bigger than my apartment."

"We used to entertain a lot," she rationalized. "I barely fill half of it now." This was partially true; she had cut the number of groceries she bought by a third, while maintaining her typical grocery bill by getting cash back for the difference.

The nozzle on the water dispenser sputtered twice and then a stream of steaming water filled the metal container, releasing an aroma that smelled like compost. Tamsen turned her head from the odor.

"It's the Valerian root," Whit said. "Tastes better than it smells."

"That's a relief," Tamsen said, screwing the top back on.

"You should try it," Whit suggested. Tamsen watched him, crouched on the floor, a pick held in his teeth, as he lowered his weathered guitar into its soft case and drew the zipper around the hourglass shape. His offer of a sip from his cup seemed to breach an implicit line between unfamiliarity and friendship. She was at least fifteen years his senior. Maybe she was reading too much into his suggestion. Or maybe she needed to loosen up. Tamsen watched as a ribbon of steam rose from a small hole in the top and she lifted the cup to place her lips to the spot where he would put his.

"Here," Whit said, handing her a small tin of dried herbs. She jerked the cup away from her mouth before he could see she was about to drink from it, and she abruptly handed the beverage back to him. She examined the herbs through the clear top. Her face burned. She couldn't believe she had allowed herself to read into his invitation.

"Valerian root tea. Thank you," she said, stifling her embarrassment.

Tamsen's handbag sat on the counter and she reached for it quickly, reminding herself that the cellist was only teaching as a means of income and not to become her new pal. Now, even more than the days on West 113th Street, when Cormac would have the kids pool their meager summer earnings to put toward future college expenses, she could relate to the urgent desire to amass even the smallest reserve.

She opened her wallet, once again pregnant with gift cards, and she was surprised to find it otherwise devoid of cash. "Oh, my gosh, Whit, I forgot to go to the bank," she said. "But I can write you a check, if that's okay."

He drew air in between his clenched teeth and exhaled a sigh. "I'm actually on my way to Guitar Center to pick up a new amp. It's been on layaway and I'm down to the last payment."

Layaway. She opened the junk drawer, hoping that perhaps Victor had stuffed some bills inside, which he often did when he returned from a business convention. Unfortunately, the only cash within a hundred-foot radius was hidden on the back patio. Leaving Whit to go outside and extract the money from her Fountain Fund was absolutely not an option. It pained her, but Tamsen knew her only immediate option was to relinquish a newly acquired $200 prepaid debit card.

"Here," she said, extending it, "they'll take this at the music store."

He looked at the gold card like it was foreign currency, turning it over and back.

"I've never used one of these," he said. "Are you sure it will work?" As if she was trying to swindle him.

"It's a debit card with money on it," she said, trying to suppress her annoyance. Based on her designer kitchen, the expensive musical instruments, and the Miró he so admired, Tamsen knew there was no way Whit could possibly comprehend what a $200 debit card represented to her. If things ever escalated with Victor, he would choke her off using the only leverage he truly had—finances. She saw this play out like an inferno behind her eyelids at four in the morning when she lay awake at The Talisman. He would cancel every credit card, freeze their accounts, and deny her any means to support herself.

"I'm so sorry," she said. "I'll have cash for you next week."

"Okay," he replied, pulling the guitar case onto his back.

"There's a lot going on around here," she said, folding her arms around herself tightly. "And I haven't been myself for a while."

He pushed the card into his pocket and blinked with his with sincere eyes.

"I completely understand," he replied. "I know how that feels."

4

The sound of wrenching metal as Victor drove his blue Mercedes SUV through the garage door at full speed jolted Tamsen awake with a heaving gasp. She urgently scanned her surroundings with bewilderment. Beige walls. Armoire from the 70s. As the mental fog cleared, she realized it wasn't actually the SUV that caused her to lurch forward, her brain yet lagging in another realm of consciousness, but rather the Chicago Department of Streets and Sanitation garbage truck body-slamming six dumpsters beneath her hotel window.

Tamsen flopped back onto the springy mattress, the wild sanitarium grin of Abie the clown and the red digits on the clock radio corroborating that she was at The Talisman. The paperback copy of *The Count of Monte Cristo* she had finished the night before lay partially under her pillow. It was barely light out, but the horror of the nightmare she had conjured prevented her from returning to sleep. She went down to the lobby without brushing her teeth.

"I'm sorry, Mrs. Peel, but we're filled to capacity," Ron, the front desk manager said as his corpulent fingers tapped the filthy keys of a dated computer. "I honestly don't have anything else in our extended-stay category until after Christmas. I'd be happy to put your name on a wait list, though."

"Can you speak to the city?" Tamsen implored. "I mean, how are they allowed to make so much noise when people are obviously sleeping?" The phone on the front desk began to ring.

"It's Chicago," he said, as if this were meant to explain everything. "There is only so much we can do." With that, he held up his index finger and picked up the incoming call. "Front desk, this is Ron."

A woman in her forties wearing the customary high-necked pale-green Talisman blouse set three large coffee carafes on a buffet near the hotel entrance. Tamsen waited for her to finish arranging sugar packets in a fan formation.

"We have earplugs, if that would help," the woman said, standing back to admire the sugar packet art. Her nametag read "Nicole" and Tamsen was surprised, given the woman's age, that the title on her badge read "Trainee." She had obviously been eavesdropping on Tamsen's dead-end conversation with Ron.

"I could use a sleep mask too," Tamsen said.

"Sorry?" Nicole replied.

"I have to wake up every morning to the sight of a demented clown," Tamsen declared. "The irony is, I left my husband and moved into this place to avoid that very sight."

Nicole laughed lightly. "He's in all the second-floor rooms. We have a different painting for every level. There's the Chicago River on three, and four has the Merchandise Mart."

Tamsen pumped herself a cup of coffee. "Let me guess, the lion sculptures in front of the Art Institute on five and the Picasso at Daley Plaza on six."

"Actually, my favorite one is on six, the Old Water Tower," Nicole said as she placed a handful of stirrers in a paper cup. "As landmarks go, she is one tough babe."

Tamsen considered the building with its limestone spire and

castellated corners. "I like the Old Water Tower too," she agreed.

"Nicole, I need you over here," Ron summoned from the desk.

Nicole handed Tamsen a small napkin. "She watched the entire city burn down around her, and she's still standing."

The drive up Sheridan Road to the campus of her alma mater took Tamsen thirty-two minutes. A college friend had told her that the music school at Northwestern was an excellent place to hire musical talent, and the objective today was to line up a few performers for the Harvest Moon Ball. She parked on the top level of the lakefront garage and sat in her car like a voyeur, watching a wiry coed with a man bun lug a sousaphone up the path that led to the new home of the university's Bienen School of Music. The modern building looked like an angular glass space station, a far cry from the five-story painted white brick music building with the mansard roof she recalled from her own college days.

Two girls, one wearing a boho dress with tights and the other in a black biker jacket and pink flannel pants, took syncopated steps toward the music building. They stopped before they parted and shared a brief farewell kiss. Tamsen gazed down at her practical pumps and the navy St. John suit she had owned for sixteen years. She looked like an outsider—she wasn't even hip enough to be mistaken for a professor, but something about being back on campus made her feel young and adventuresome again. It wasn't long ago that she, too, was hustling across campus, rushing to make it to a discussion group or hauling her overstuffed backpack to a lecture. Time had crumpled behind her, and at some point, she realized she could measure her life in decades: her childhood, the young adult period, her working phase, and the recent decade of raising a family. The "you are here" dot on her life's timeline, however, was in some obscure realm whose characterization had not yet come into focus. In six short years, however, she would be moving Charlotte into her freshman dorm room and perhaps only then would she be able to label this abstruse stretch of time.

"You really only need three of us, ma'am. Especially if they're going to mic the instruments," the assistant professor explained to Tamsen as the undergrads tuned up for their rehearsal. "Any more than that and it will feel like a concert, not like background music."

The stage in Galvin Recital Hall was set against an immense glass curtain of floor-to-ceiling windows, revealing a live backdrop of Lake Michigan and the Chicago skyline. The view was spellbinding and the grandeur of the hall made even the musicians' warm-up exercises sound like symphonic compositions. Tamsen knew these kids would impress at the gala.

Tamsen agreed. "Are you sure the trio is okay with volunteering on a Saturday night?" she asked, knowing that many of the students had paid weekend gigs.

"Totally," he replied. "These guys are happy to give back and they're stoked to jam for charity in exchange for a free meal." He leaned in, "Of course, they always appreciate a tip."

"I'll take care of them," Tamsen said. A few hundred dollars was nothing compared to the thousands the committee had shelled out in past years.

"Andre, here, on piano, will be your point of contact. Becca plays double bass, and Paulie is your guy on drums."

Tamsen couldn't believe her luck. She was able to find unbelievably talented musicians who actually wanted to contribute their skills. For the first time ever, the music budget for the Harvest Moon Ball could go directly toward helping kids through Mothers Trust Foundation. This would definitely bode well for Tamsen's shot at chairing the next

Harvest Moon event. She would not call Jacqueline yet, but Tamsen could hardly wait to see the look on her face when she announced that she had procured pro bono talent for the evening.

South campus was home to the university's dozen or so sorority houses, as well as Willard, the residential college Tamsen called home during her time as a student. Willard was a huge blonde limestone residential college with an arched doorway and a small outdoor patio where Tamsen recalled spending countless hours deconstructing poems and sipping her trademark Bartles & Jaymes Fuzzy Navel wine cooler. There was always a day in March when the brutal winter weather broke for twenty-four hours and a handful of Evans Scholars would appear shirtless on the adjacent lawn to toss around a Frisbee.

Tamsen stood outside the old building and contemplated sneaking in, but she decided she liked her memory of the mismatched upholstered swivel chairs, the tired pool room, and the utilitarian cafeteria in the basement. An alumni email showed photographs of a complete transformation, including a fitness center and state-of-the-art collaboration room, but no matter how many upgrades Willard had received, she preferred the blissful nostalgia of her memory.

"Tamsen Kinney." She was startled to hear her maiden name in a man's New York accent. "What are you doing up here?" the voice continued.

She turned and recognized a former colleague, Josh Blum, whose diminutive stature was in no way representative of his tenacity in business. Josh was incredibly smart and likeable. He had discovered countless new authors in his heyday, and he rose quickly up the ranks. But he had sharp elbows and Tamsen had always known to keep him at an arm's length.

"Josh!" she said, noticing his worn and fitted burgundy Henley jeans. "You look so cool." His current fashion was a far cry from the days when he wouldn't be caught dead in anything but a Brooks Brothers suit and tie.

"Yeah, gotta project the right image to get the best kids," he said.

"You're recruiting?" she asked.

"First-round interviews start today," he replied. "I do it for kicks."

"How do I get on your list?" she replied, half-joking. The idea of returning to the workforce terrified her, but she'd often thought about how it would feel to be part of a company again.

He huffed. "If you have a 4.0 in Snapchat, a quarter of a million Instagram followers, and a blog, you're hired," he said.

Tamsen's lungs deflated. She had an Instagram account, but she had only posted a few photos. She mostly followed NoCrumbsLeft, a passionate local cook who introduced Tamsen to Theo's favorite dish, Heroine Chicken. She loved the stories NoCrumbsLeft posted simply for the woman behind the burgeoning business—a middle-aged mom who redefined herself based entirely on what she loved to do.

"So, what you're saying is I'm old," Tamsen said.

"Not old, just obsolete," he retorted.

"Ouch," she laughed. But it was true. Publishing was largely digital now, and her skills were no longer in high demand. It was that simple.

"It's a good thing most people still love the feeling of a book in their hands," he said.

"There's no substitute," Tamsen agreed.

"The only reason I have a job is because nothing can replace my years in the trenches. If you and I could harness half of these kids' cybertise, it would be world domination." He handed Tamsen his business card, which now boasted the title of "Managing Director," and told her how he and his wife would love to see her at their daughter's bat mitzvah. "It's still a couple years out, but my wife is already scouting venues."

He was as ambitious as ever, and he had a big heart, but Tamsen still had to bend down to hug him goodbye.

The airline was "experiencing unusually heavy call volume," so Tamsen entered her ten-digit cellphone number and secured her spot in the American Advantage callback queue. The matter of Cormac's misdirected miles was keeping her up at night, especially since she had been reading up on the many ways to cash in on her award points. Her thorough Google search on the matter unearthed a website that would "legally" pay her cash for her miles. If that option proved shady, she took great comfort in the notion that she and the kids could afford to escape from Victor at a moment's notice on flights to anywhere in the world.

Tamsen checked to make sure her ringer was on and the volume was all the way up before setting down her phone and going back to work on Charlotte's fortune-teller Halloween costume. A year ago, Victor found out that Tamsen used the Dessin Fournir dining table as her crafting surface and he half-jokingly threatened to cancel her Michael's card. She'd only once had a close call with some acrylic paint and since then she had used heavy canvas dropcloths to protect both the table and the Persian rug beneath it. She finished hot-gluing some shiny gold medallions to Charlotte's silky purple skirt when it occurred to her that she could use the extra pieces to embellish the table number cards for the Harvest Moon Ball.

The doorbell interrupted her creative flow. She wasn't expecting anyone until after 3:00 p.m., so perhaps it was UPS with an early delivery of the extra green cotton gauze she'd ordered online for Theo's swamp creature costume. Tamsen wiped her hands on her skinny jeans and checked the wall for the iPad security camera feed.

"Hey." Whit stood outside the gate wearing Ray Ban wayfarers, his shiny black cycling helmet, and a light down vest. He straddled his bike. "I'm just dropping off your gift card."

Tamsen buzzed the gate. "Come in," she yelled from the doorway. "Just leave your bike—believe me, nobody's gonna take it."

The gate shut behind him and he proceeded to unhinge the U-lock mounted to his cross bar, securely fastening Edmond Dantès to the iron bars.

He shoved his hands in his pockets as he climbed the front stairs. "It's the only bike I've got."

"I just meant it would be safe here behind the security gate," Tamsen said, embarrassed.

"It's okay," Whit replied.

Tamsen could tell he was uncomfortable. "I didn't mean to offend Edmond Dantès—we both know how the Count carries a grudge."

"You've revisited *The Count of Monte Cristo*, then?" he asked.

"I was reading Dumas when you were reading Dr. Seuss," she said. He started to kick off his scuffed sneakers.

"You can leave them on," Tamsen told him. "Would you like some tea? I have Gun Powder Green, Peach Paradise, Earl Grey, Chamomile, and Oolong." Tamsen had driven to Andersonville to visit an artisanal tea shop she read about on thrillist.com.

"Oolong, please," he said, lifting the canister to smell the fragrant leaves. "Are the kids home?"

"They're at school till 3:00 p.m. and then Aneta is taking them to tennis at the Rink and Racket." She felt she needed to justify the reason she was home and not sitting in the pickup line at school. "I'm waiting for the landscaper. He's supposed to shut off the irrigation."

"Here's your card," Whit said. "There's $150 left on it."

Tamsen took the gold card from him. She was secretly relieved to have it back, and the fact that Whit had appeared on her doorstep was a welcome distraction.

"It's nice for October, let's go outside," she said, opening the door to the patio.

Whit spotted Theo's guitar and song charts beside the sectional. "Somebody's been practicing."

"I think he wants to impress you," Tamsen said. Whit scooped up the Martin and followed her outside. As she cranked open a tall cantilever umbrella, her cellphone rang in her front pocket. An 800 number—it was the airline. "I need to take this," she said. She was surprised when he jumped up and took the crank for her.

A robot asked Tamsen the requisite questions confirming her identity, then she heard the voice of an actual human being. She paced, explaining the story of the displaced 675,000 miles to the customer service agent. Whit sat down and blew gently on the steamy surface of his tea. He lifted Theo's small guitar to his lap and began to seduce a delicate tune from the little instrument. He played softly, with his chin bent toward his chest, his eyes closed.

"Mrs. Peel," the agent explained, "I apologize for this inconvenience, but I need to elevate this matter to a specialist."

A specialist was good. "I appreciate it," Tamsen said.

"Please hold for a moment," the agent requested.

Tamsen breathed deeply as Whit's fingers ambled over the soothing strings of the Martin, the satiny chords rising over the gurgle of the fountain. There was something about the way he cradled the instrument, something in the meter of the music, that exposed a vulnerability in him. She was so transported by his melody that it took her a moment to register the cold silence at the other end of the line.

"Hello? Hello?" Tamsen repeated. She felt panic and frustration rising in her chest.

Whit raised his head and opened his eyes.

"Is anyone there?" Tamsen asked.

She consciously tempered her reaction because she didn't want Whit to see the desperation she felt. Her shoulders dropped.

"You need a warm transfer," he said as his fingers crawled up the neck of the guitar.

She was confused. Was he referring to her phone call?

He continued to play as the delicate notes lightened the gravity around her. "It's when a person stays on the line with you during the call transfer, you know, to make sure you don't get disconnected."

"I didn't realize that was a thing," Tamsen said.

"I sometimes volunteer at a suicide hotline," he said. "Pretty important to make sure those people get where they need to go."

"Yeah," Tamsen said. Seeing him play with such effortless calm, she understood how he might connect with someone who had lost their sense of purpose. "It's really noble, your doing that sort of work."

"My dad took his own life," he said, not looking up. "I can't bring him back, but when I'm able to, I like to try and help."

She clamped her teeth down on the inside of her cheek so she wouldn't cry. Tamsen was struck by the pain this experience must have caused him. She wondered how much it shaped his sometimes-sudden mood shifts, his decision to leave classical music.

"Hey," Whit said, nodding toward the irrigation timer. "I'm pretty sure I can disconnect that." He set the guitar down and pulled out his phone, tapping rapidly on the glass.

"I think you need a compressor to clear the hoses," Tamsen said. She wasn't very mechanical, but that was only because she didn't need to be.

"No," he confirmed. "The internet says the hoses are fine—no need to clear them. You just to drain the water from the drip heads and unscrew the mechanism. And don't forget to shut off the master valve to this spigot before winter." As he tightened the sillcock that fed the fountain and the irrigation, the hypnotizing trickle tapered off until the last of the circulating water emptied down into the fountain's catch basin. Tamsen noticed the protruding veins in Whit's forearms as he torqued the timer loose, shaking from it any residual water. He reached down to empty the trough where The Fountain Fund was hidden.

"Don't touch that!" Tamsen snapped, grabbing a hold of his hand and pulling it back before he could disengage the vessel. He looked up at her sharply.

"I'm sorry," she gasped. "That was so out of line."

He stepped back, his eyes cast down, holding up his hands.

Tamsen swept her hands to her heart. "I'm mortified," she said.

"Don't worry about it," he replied.

"I . . . It's just . . .the fountain is so temperamental."

"Yeah, I wouldn't want to break it."

"No," she insisted. "That's not what I meant."

"I should go." He stuffed his hands in his pockets and sidestepped her, making a move toward the door.

"Wait," she said, raising her voice.

He stopped and stared at her. The urban breeze carried a faint smell roasted cocoa beans.

"Please don't leave." She picked up the small lefty guitar and held it out like a peace offering. His hardened expression searched her face. "Just play a little longer?" she asked, desperate to say how much she needed his company. He didn't break her gaze for what felt like minutes, then he reached out and took the instrument.

Whit sat down on the hearth of the outdoor fireplace and began to maneuver his thumb over the strings with delicate purpose, finding a groove that ambled like a lullaby and saturated the fall air with a calming timbre. Tamsen resumed her work, moving from planter to planter, unscrewing the tops from the watering spikes and knocking out drops of water onto the bluestone. She glanced over her shoulder and saw that his eyes were closed again.

Maybe it was the bewitching quality of the music, or perhaps his youth that disarmed her, but Tamsen knew Whit was safe. In recent years, her wide social circle had grown tighter and tighter until she discovered that she trusted almost no one with her most honest thoughts. Yet here was a person tied neither to her past nor to her future, and in this anonymity, she knew she could divulge everything to him—that her life was flawed and that she felt unbearably isolated, and how a fight to the death duel between relief and guilt was constantly and exhaustingly at play behind the perfect façade she struggled to project.

"You're distracted," he said.

She glanced at him. How would he feel if he knew she was thinking about him?

"You've just watered your jade plant with my Oolong," he said.

Her face was hot. "It's an old Chinese gardening secret," she joked.

"Is that right?" he replied, a smile curling the corners of his mouth.

She undid the safety on her gardening shears. "I'm confused. And disappointed, I suppose."

"You're distracted by thoughts of being confused and disappointed." He strummed with extra zeal as he said the words "confused" and "disappointed."

"Exactly," she laughed lightly.

"Well, at least you have a sense of humor about it. When that goes, you're in deep shit."

"Trust me, I'm in shit quicksand."

He became serious and the tune he played wandered in minor chords.

"Theo told me you and his father are separated."

"I'm glad he's open about it," Tamsen said. She wanted to tell him more, but she didn't. She didn't trust herself not to go too far. "Is Whit your real name?" she asked.

"My surname is Whitman. My name is actually Kyle."

"Kyle. Does anyone call you that?"

"My mother does, but that's only because she called my father Whit."

Whit began plucking each string and twisting the tuning keys, one by one. Tamsen stopped clipping.

"I'm so sorry," she said. "Losing your dad must have been really hard on your family."

"He had pretty severe depression. There were a lot of rough patches."

Tamsen hoped he would go on, but he was done speaking about it. He shut his eyes and elevated the tempo of the piece he was playing, taking the music on a discordant tangent.

"Is this some sort of Bob Dylan, Hootie and the Blowfish mashup?" she asked, nipping a dead tendril on a climbing hydrangea.

"I'm going to pretend you didn't just put those artists in the same sentence," he joked. "How's this?"

Tamsen watched him inhale deeply. His shoulders moved, and the forward curvature of his long torso cupped the guitar. She noticed his dry, nubby fingertips—how the nails looked like those of a nervous thirteen-year-old, bitten to their limit. He lured a song from the guitar that was round and full and romantic and although she couldn't name it, it was familiar to her. It became impossible, if not impolite, to continue pretending to garden. Tamsen set down the clippers and curled her legs beneath her on a weathered teak lounge. She leaned back her head and succumbed to the urge to close her eyes. Her mind uncoupled from the worry that spun incessantly in her brain until there was nothing but Whit and his song. When he brought the tune to an end, she raised her head and he did not try to conceal that he had been watching her.

"Thank you for that," was all she could manage, and she felt stupid because it was hardly enough.

"My pleasure," he said.

He passed her the guitar, grazing her skin as she reached for the instrument. She watched him carefully, searching his reflective expression for a tell, trying to understand whether the touch carried more, or if it was simply a gesture of solidarity. She settled on the latter.

Tamsen raced to the printer's shop. She was cutting close to her Wednesday 10:00 a.m. deadline for the Harvest Moon auction booklet. Traffic in Lincoln Park was uncharacteristically bad, given all that the roadwork crews were attempting to complete before winter. When she finally arrived for her parent-teacher conference at Dexter School, the always-amiable security guard waved Tamsen past the mandatory sign-in book, knowing by the way she burst in that she was in a hurry. She fumbled through a sea of uniformed second graders waiting in line at the drinking fountain, then bolted down the hall toward the school's atrium. Yarn and coat-hanger mobiles designed with primary-colored crayons and wax paper fluttered and twisted on the ceiling as she hurriedly passed, checking her watch to determine exactly how late she was running. Ten on the dot, she was fine.

The door to Theo's classroom was shut, but the scene Tamsen observed through the sidelight stopped her from knocking. It was Victor, sitting in a bright green miniature children's chair, his knees practically at his chin, leaning over to accept an embrace from Theo's petite first-grade teacher. Ms. Ellison lightly patted Victor's back and Tamsen swallowed the bile that rose in her throat. Victor would now be adding

Miss Child Psychology Expert to his list of allies, thereby contaminating all the school faculty against her. There was no point in making a subtle entrance, so Tamsen opened the door abruptly, wanting Ms. Ellison to know she had witnessed the special parent/teacher moment, and that she knew on which side Ms. Ellison's allegiance fell.

"Hello, Mrs. Peel," the teacher said, her hands fluttering to the ladybug charm on her necklace. "Victor didn't think you were going to make it, so we got started a little early."

"I thought you were in Seattle till Friday, Victor," Tamsen said. He didn't make eye contact while he shuffled some of Theo's papers on the squatty table.

"We were just discussing Theo's academic progress," Ms. Ellison chirped.

"Really?" Tamsen said, pulling up a vibrant yellow munchkin chair.

"Kimberly says Theo's keeping up," Victor said. Tamsen felt his eyes moving all over her.

"Yes," chimed Ms. Ellison. "I have been monitoring him quite closely. With his Doose Syndrome, I like to keep vigilant track of Theo's cognitive development. The long-term outcome for kids with Theo's condition is highly variable."

No, duh, Tamsen thought. Now she was a neuro specialist? They were really getting a bang for their $35,000 per year tuition.

"Kimberly feels Theo really needs support right now," Victor said.

"That's right, not academically, but emotionally," Ms. Ellison said. "I'd like Theo to start seeing the school counselor, you know, now that you've moved out." Given Victor's vehement position on therapy, Tamsen was shocked he'd agreed to this.

"We are birds-nesting, I'm sure you've heard of it," Tamsen told her.

"Victor explained that to me," Ms. Ellison said. "So great, really."

"It's all about the children," Victor added.

"Which brings us to Victor's other great idea, a homestay for Roscoe," the teacher beamed.

"What?" Tamsen glared at Victor.

"The ball python," they said in unison, as if Tamsen wasn't already aware. She looked toward the windowsill, where petri dishes with damp paper towels and beans sat under a sign that read "Day 5 Cotyledon," next to the "Germination Station," where there were three glass terrariums and a bird cage.

Victor continued, "Kimberly agreed it would lower Theo's stress level if we took Roscoe home with us for a couple weeks."

"Pet therapy can help the entire family, not just Theo. It harnesses the human-animal bond that brings us closer to our innate kindness," Kimberly said, rising to collect the reptile's terrarium.

Tamsen had a terrible aversion to snakes and she didn't have to look at Victor to know he was wholeheartedly satisfied. She might have resisted the pet homestay, but she had to be very careful not to alienate Theo's teacher. Not only did Kimberly author Theo's quarterly report card, she also had the power to assign him to one of three teachers for the following year. Tamsen needed to stay on her good side so that Theo would be placed in the best possible class.

"Could we take the rabbit home instead?" Tamsen asked politely, knowing something with fur would irritate Victor's allergies.

"Coco has conjunctivitis," Ms. Ellison replied.

Victor pouted his lower lip, "Poor Coco."

In the hallway, Kimberly handed Tamsen the glass box and a small shopping bag containing some sort of light bulb apparatus.

"Roscoe is easy to care for," she assured Tamsen. "Just make sure you keep the lid on the aquarium." There would be no threat of the snake escaping. Tamsen would Super Glue the lid shut if she had to.

"They sell his food at Petco," Victor added. "Pre-killed rodents."

As they made their way down the main hallway, Victor walked silently, two steps ahead. Tamsen looked beyond him, moving as quickly toward the exit as possible. Out of nowhere, Oliver Putnum, a perpetually jovial school board member and formidable divorce lawyer, appeared in their path. He and Tamsen had an excellent rapport; they had been room parents together when Charlotte and Oliver's son were in kindergarten.

"Roscoe!" Oliver said, clapping his hands together delightedly. "We love this guy! He's a rescue snake, you know." He lifted the lid and put his hand into the terrarium to pet the creature, who coiled on contact.

"Really?" Tamsen replied. "I didn't know there was such a thing."

"He was on his way to becoming a wallet, if you can believe it. Or probably a pair of your new shoes, Tamsen." He laughed heartily, looking down at her fake snakeskin pumps. Given Victor's income, Tamsen could fool nearly anybody into thinking her imitations were the real deal.

"Ball python is so last season," she replied, glancing at Victor. His eyes narrowed, then he turned to engage Oliver in a discussion around the skeet shooting season at The Lakeshore Hunt Club. Tamsen stared blankly at Roscoe while a symphony of basketballs pounded erratically from the adjacent gymnasium. Her mind escaped to Whit and what he might be doing at this moment; maybe he was playing his guitar or tinkering with his decrepit bike.

After disengaging from Oliver, the two passed security. The desk had a large bottle of hand sanitizer, and had Tamsen not been carrying Roscoe, she certainly would have helped herself to a generous blob of the disinfecting goo.

"You made it on time, after all?" the kindly security guard said.

"Thanks for bending the rules," she replied. She was grateful she was able to skate in without signing the visitors' book. Victor helped himself to the sanitizer.

"I know you," he said. "I never forget the pretty ones." Tamsen smiled at the guard. He was nearing retirement and she heard he had lost his wife over the summer. His creased face brightened.

Victor followed Tamsen outside. He waited for a teacher to cross under the brass plaque displaying the school motto, "Your Future Begins Now," and then he checked behind him to make sure they were alone.

"That's a tight skirt," he hissed between his teeth. Tamsen's skin prickled.

"I had a meeting at the printer this morning," she countered, though excuses were pointless. She'd learned it mattered very little what she was wearing, a bathrobe with flip flops or jeans and clogs, even the most modest attire would elicit Victor's criticism when he'd been set off. Still, she wished in this moment that she had chosen to wear trousers to the conference and not a skirt.

"You want to blow the security guy?" he spat. "School guards do it for you, Tamsen?" She flinched when he said her name out loud.

"Stop," she whispered, wanting to let the glass tank slip from her grip so it would shatter into a thousand pieces. She wished someone, anyone, could see this Victor, this monster with his inimitable brand of torture. No one would believe it. It was unfathomable even to Tamsen. In her head, a level voice articulated the appalling truth: Charlotte and Theo have a father who speaks to their mother this way.

"I can drop the snake off at the house," she offered with hollow affect. It was Victor's night with the children. She suddenly wanted Theo to have Roscoe there.

"Tamsen," Victor said, lowering his voice as a sandwich delivery guy rode past on his bike. "You know I love you, but sometimes your behavior is just so inappropriate."

Tamsen was standing but she felt leveled. She was inert. She watched as he turned and hailed a passing cab, climbing into the backseat without looking at her as the car pulled away. She could no longer sense the weight of the terrarium. She did not register the laughter of the primary school children on the playground, and she never noticed Charlotte waving furiously from the window of her classroom across the street.

After a minute, or some indeterminate stretch of time, she opened the hatch on her Audi and gently slid Roscoe next to a box of Summers & Peel pullovers she had designed for the company's Chicago Marathon team. She climbed into her car and mechanically fished through her purse for her wallet, bursting again with precious gift cards. There, wedged between $25 Sephora and $50 Toys"R"Us, was a card that she finally needed to redeem. Tamsen took out her phone and dialed the therapist.

CHAPTER

5

Tamsen stood on the threshold of a red brick industrial building in the West Loop, scrolling through an alphabetical list of names on the intercom: Taylor, Thompson, Upton, and finally Valentine. Inside, she walked by a drinking fountain where a man with sunken eyes lifted his head and wiped a dribble of water from the corner of his mouth. His hair hadn't seen a comb in days and he looked like he'd been up all night in his rumpled gray suit—definitely a person who fit the profile of someone needing therapy. Tamsen wondered if she, too, wore the tell-tale signs.

Suite 404 was at the end of a long corridor, where an old oak door bore a brass placard with the names of four LCSW professionals below an etching of a lotus flower with the words "The Devi Group" emblazed above it. The door shut with a heavy click behind her and she was greeted by a whooshing sound blasted from a white noise machine plugged into a corner outlet.

The walls in the waiting room were painted light taupe and had coves for flickering battery-powered candles. There were three lithographs depicting Sanskrit messages against a mystic starry background and an artificial palm plant in the corner. Tamsen took a seat in one of the seven chairs that were arranged in an L shape around a Live Edge wood coffee table. She tried to put the $300 per hour cost of the counseling session, for which she would need to pay cherished cash, out of her mind. She couldn't claim the session on insurance, nor could she pay for it with a credit card, for fear Victor might find out she was getting professional help. If he knew she was speaking to someone about her distress in their marriage, he would bully her mercilessly—but only after he'd finished berating her for having mental problems and wasting his money.

In her initial call to Fariah Valentine the day before, Tamsen had left the therapist an embarrassingly long voicemail about Victor and her marriage. She thought if she dumped out the history, they could move straight into solutions. God, she thought, she'd provided examples, specific quotes. She used the word "whore." The therapist likely thought she was crazy.

A sign with the caption "You can't start the next chapter of your life if you keep reading the last one" was propped behind the Nespresso machine that sat atop a small refreshment table. Please let this woman be more than a new age cliché, Tamsen thought. She decided to brew herself a beverage—might as well get something extra, given the cost of this extravagance.

One of the three doors off the waiting area opened and a young woman with a splotchy face and a crossbody purse walked out, grasping a tissue in one fist and her cellphone in the other. Tamsen felt a knot tighten in her stomach. Her brothers would have a field day knowing she was here. She silently pledged that she would not cry, no matter how hard Fariah Valentine pushed her. Several minutes dragged by and the door opened again.

"Tamsen?" a middle-aged woman said in a low, raspy voice. "Please come in."

Fariah Valentine was average height. She had rounded edges like the biblical Delilah from a Rubens painting Tamsen always admired on her visits to the National Gallery. Her hips were wide, and her chest was more than a pair of breasts. She possessed a full-on bosom, one from a bawdy sailor song—the sort of ample haven into which babies liked to bury their faces.

Fariah relaxed into a supple, brown leather wingback chair that had an antique indigo Fulani wedding blanket draped over the back. She crossed her fleshy bare legs and initiated with typical getting acquainted language, asking about children and what Tamsen did with her time.

"Tell me how you're faring?" the therapist asked.

"I'm holding up all right," Tamsen replied. "But I'm stuck. That's why I'm here."

"How long has it been going on?" Fariah inquired.

"Sorry?" Tamsen wasn't sure to what exactly the woman was referring.

"The man you described in your thirteen-minute message; the man who calls you a whore and who is unalterably opposed to couples therapy—how long has he been treating you this way?"

Tamsen noticed Fariah's shoes. They were four-inch Jimmy Choo, the ones she had her eye on a year ago with a wide ankle strap that looked like a collar. Shoes Victor would have hated because, he would say, they made Tamsen look like she was working the pole at a strip club. Fariah didn't look like a stripper—she looked like a goddess, a woman Tamsen would want to have a drink with.

"Years," Tamsen said. "To varying degrees." She petted the cream-colored chenille loveseat, watching the color change from darker to light as she moved her hand with and against the grain.

"Go on," Fariah responded.

"It's like I've been . . . targeted. I don't know." Fariah let Tamsen's words hang in space.

The therapist probed, "Tell me what it looks like to be his target."

Tamsen sighed. "It's more how I feel when he ignores me. When I do something wrong he shuts me out. He won't talk to me for days—literally days, unless it's absolutely necessary like, 'where are the car keys?'" Tamsen struggled to make herself sound legitimate. "My marriage feels like a vacuum. He doesn't hear me. I feel like I'm subhuman."

Fariah waited.

"But he's fine with everyone else," Tamsen added.

"Victor is everyone's friend but yours," she finally said.

"No, that's not it," Tamsen replied. "I'm his only friend. He has a lot of acquaintances, but he's not close to anybody but me."

"Close," Fariah repeated.

"He doesn't trust anyone. He's always said that. I'm really the only person who he can depend on. I'm the only one he's ever really let in."

"How does that make you feel, that you're the only one?"

Tamsen considered the question. "I like that he needs me, I guess. Aren't wives supposed to support their husbands?"

"Support is very important," Fariah concurred. "But you're Victor's only real friend—how does it make you feel when he belittles you?"

Tamsen couldn't put it into words. When she talked about her husband, it was as if she were experiencing his rejection in real time: the urgency, the desperation she felt when she tried to connect with him—when she tried to justify herself. She pulled off her red J. Crew puffer coat and looked toward the window. She wanted to crack it open. "It's hard to explain—I feel like I'm going crazy."

Fariah leaned forward. "You feel like there is something wrong with you?"

"Yes," Tamsen concurred.

"Anything in particular spur his emotional abuse?" Fariah asked.

Abuse. The word was jarring. "I just don't know why he does it, why he ignores me sometimes," Tamsen said. "He starves me. And then I grovel for some crumb of acknowledgement." She looked at Fariah hard. "I'm a good mother to our children. I'm a good wife."

"You're a wonderful mother and a good wife to Victor," Fariah echoed. She flexed her foot. "I can hear how excruciating this is for you."

Tamsen's hand went to her neck. She coughed. Her throat was dry.

Fariah continued. "Abusers want to manage what you say, whom you befriend, and how you dress." Tamsen recalled sitting beside Victor at an advertising honors dinner, where Victor hissed at her between his teeth that she'd won the "slutty award" for wearing a stunning backless dress. Fariah went on. "They want to isolate you."

The fourth button on the therapist's pink silk charmeuse blouse fought hard to hold on, and her suede skirt crept slightly up her thighs. Fariah was what Tamsen's father would have referred to as a sexpot. She went on.

"The abuser wants you to submit. He makes you his employee. The abuser is unpredictable, and his episodic verbal attacks leave you feeling confused and ashamed. But the silence, the deprivation—that is the abuser's secret weapon. There's even a name for it. It's called withholding."

Abuser. Every time the word formed across Fariah's heart-shaped mouth, Tamsen felt like the therapist was speaking of someone else. Victor had a mean streak and he was nasty, but the harsh label sat on the surface of her consciousness like a bead of water on waxed cotton.

Fariah fell silent, her folded hands resting easy like a sleeping cat in her lap; she gazed at Tamsen warmly. Tamsen wondered where this talk of "abuse" was all headed and how much time they had left.

"How can you classify someone you've never met?" Tamsen asked.

"Your husband is an archetype. He is essentially playing out a prescribed role characteristic of anyone who engages in the emotional or verbal assault of another, usually their child or their partner, in an attempt to control their victim through nonphysical violence. Of course, the aggression can certainly escalate to the physical realm, and often does."

"He's never hit me." Fariah tilted her head and dipped her chin. Tamsen crossed her arms tightly. She watched a squirrel dodge across a telephone wire outside and she conjured the experience at Dexter where Victor made the disgusting suggestion about giving the security guard a blow job. "Sometimes it feels like I've been hit."

Had Victor struck her, it would have hurt less. The degradation she experienced burned for days after such an event.

Fariah raised an eyebrow. "Where did you go just then?"

Tamsen looked down. The pattern in the carpet reminded her of an abnormal EKG. The silence felt exceptionally long. She could hear the whooshing from beneath the door.

"It's like I'm down on the ground and he's got a boot on my throat, and it feels like I am trapped beneath his foot."

"Mmm," was the sound that came from the therapist's chest. "Are you the abuser's only target?"

"He's never gone after the kids."

Fariah took a sip from her "Just Breathe" mug. It had a coffee-stained hairline crack in the side.

"Can you accept that you are in an abusive marriage, Tamsen?" Fariah asked.

"That sounds extreme."

"To call it abuse?"

"You can call it that," Tamsen replied.

"But you're not prepared to?" Fariah suggested.

Tamsen hesitated. Where were the words to describe her feelings? She scoured her brain. "It's comforting when you say it."

"Comforting when I call it abuse?" the therapist asked.

Tamsen swallowed hard before speaking again. "I guess I feel relieved that I'm not insane, that there is some recognition of how awful it is."

Fariah leaned forward, her gilded Buddha medallion swinging out from her cleavage. She smiled tenderly. "I'm a mental health professional. You're not insane."

Tamsen shifted in her seat and struggled to collect her thoughts. "I keep thinking somehow I can make him understand."

"Understand?" Fariah asked.

"He had a rough childhood," Tamsen said. "His mother spent most of her time locked in her bedroom. Agoraphobia. He was bullied because of it. The kids called him an orphan."

Fariah took another slow sip from her mug, peering over the brim at Tamsen.

"Was there substance abuse?" the therapist asked.

"Victor called her a junkie once, but I'm not sure. He doesn't like to discuss her."

"Does Victor drink? Take drugs?"

Tamsen knew Victor did not have a drinking problem, and he despised medication. He wouldn't even allow her to give the kids ibuprofen unless the pediatrician insisted. "No, there's nothing like that. I just . . ."

"You, what?" Fariah asked.

"I just want him to know that we're on the same team," Tamsen said.

"That you're on his side," Fariah replied.

"I just don't get why he hates me so much."

Fariah shook her head. "Victor doesn't hate you. He hates women."

The statement rumbled with unsettling magnitude. He hates women. Tamsen reached for the arm of the plush loveseat as if it would steady her disquieted thoughts. Misogyny. She wanted to reject the notion.

Fariah watched her closely. "Why are you here?" she asked.

"I don't know what to do anymore," Tamsen said, staring at the charcoal drawing on Fariah's wall. It was the scales of Libra, the sun and the moon balancing on either side.

"Therapy is your last resort?" Fariah asked.

"Leaving is the last resort," Tamsen said.

"Are you willing to stay in an abusive relationship?" Fariah asked.

"I have two children."

"Two young children," Fariah replied as she etched a circle in the air with the pointed toe of her Jimmy Choo, "who will model the manner in which you give and receive love? And punishment?"

"Theo and Charlotte are not exposed to Victor's episodes," Tamsen insisted.

"They haven't seen this side of him, or how it affects you?" she asked.

"I do think the separation is affecting them. That's why I can't justify ending it," Tamsen said.

"You can't divorce the abuser? Is that what you mean?"

Why did Fariah keep peppering in that word? "Can someone like Victor change?" Tamsen asked.

Fariah sighed. She unfurled her legs, then crossed them again with the opposite on top.

"You have come to me, Tamsen. I want to stay focused on you." She reached for her pendant and moved it slowly back and forth along the track of its chain. "We all have something I like to call a tolerable limit. As long as another, a friend or a partner, stays below our threshold of abuse, below the level we think we deserve, we will remain in that relationship. But when that person crosses our line of tolerable limit, exceeding that which we believe we deserve, the relationship ends."

Tamsen thought for a moment. "Do you think I've reached that place?"

Fariah smiled and Tamsen thought she read compassion between the crinkles that appeared at the outer corners of the woman's eyes. "Only you know the answer to that question."

Tamsen leafed through three days' worth of mail, separating out the catalogs and pizza delivery fliers from the envelopes Victor had left behind. Since he managed all the banking, nothing material was ever addressed in Tamsen's name. However, this afternoon, the mailman had dropped off a curious-looking envelope that carried only a *Mrs.* salutation and looked intriguingly official. Tamsen dug her thumb beneath the flap, tearing open the paper, and pulled out the motherlode: payment from the consignment shop on Armitage. They had sold the lace Nina Ricci dress for $1800 and she got half. In a flash, The Fountain Fund became $900 richer. Meals for a month, gas for the Audi, or holiday gifts for the kids next year—Victor would never even know she'd received the windfall.

She folded the check and gingerly placed it in the back pocket of her True Religion cords, plotting its safe storage for after the kids went to bed. She grabbed four plates from the cabinet. Whit was in the basement teaching Theo, and she hoped he would stay for dinner. Tamsen set out cloth napkins and candles before slipping into the powder room to add a few strokes of bronzer. She thought it always made her look a few years younger, or at least a little less exhausted.

"Mom, Theo is wearing his Swamp Thing costume and Halloween's not until Saturday," Charlotte complained.

"It's okay," Tamsen replied.

"It's embarrassing," Charlotte insisted.

Tamsen wiped her hands on a striped dishtowel and pulled Charlotte in for a hug. "I promise you, Whit doesn't think it's weird. He probably thinks it's awesome."

"Mommy, I don't want to go trick or treating with just Daddy. I want you to come. It's a tradition."

Tamsen felt the familiar clench of emotional distress. "Not this year, love. I'll help get you ready for your school parade on Friday, though, and you can wear some of my costume jewelry, if you'd like." Tamsen sat on the cushy sofa, patting the spot beside her.

"It's not the same," Charlotte sighed.

The crushing anvil of guilt pressed down, trapping Tamsen under its invisible weight. It was moments like this in which she could actually feel a separate part of herself beginning to relent, to finally surrender and call off the ordeal to which she was subjecting her children.

Charlotte grabbed the turban sitting beside her crystal ball prop. "You promised you'd teach me how to read fortunes, remember?"

The smell of sage and butter wafted through the air and the sound of Theo and Whit's chord progressions emanated from the playroom. There was something wonderfully comforting about having Whit in the house. Tamsen realized that she had been running scenarios of him through her brain since he'd texted that he'd be by this afternoon: Whit wrestling with Theo on the playroom floor, Whit remarking about the elaborately carved pumpkins she'd crafted for the doorstep, Whit staying long after she tucked the kids in, just because neither of them had anything else to do.

"Come on," Tamsen said, forcing her mind off these scenes. She thought of the images she had first had of a life with Victor. Fantasies could be dangerous. "Put your turban on and I'll teach you how to read palms before dinner. You can practice on Theo and Whit."

Tamsen didn't recall much about fortune-telling, just the things that stood out from a weekend trip years ago, when she and Victor encountered a palmist at a summer street fair in New Orleans. She had searched online for some additional tips and collected just enough insight to give Charlotte's act some "legitimacy."

After the lesson, Theo burst in, his little arms outstretched and his green gauze dripping down. "I want dinner!" he growled.

Whit followed behind, combing his hair back with his fingers. Tamsen noticed that he wore a thick rubber band as a bracelet. He looked down at his feet and dully scratched his unshaven chin.

"All set," he said, tugging at the tail of his untucked flannel shirt. The hollows of his eyes had shadows as if he hadn't slept in days. Tamsen found it strange that he didn't remark about Theo's costume, something she thought he would typically find wildly funny.

"Whit, do you want me to read your palm?" Charlotte asked.

Whit looked at Tamsen and she could clearly see the apathy in his weary expression. Charlotte reached out for his hand.

"How about some tea first," Tamsen offered as she pulled the steeping spoon from a drawer.

Charlotte lifted Whit's leaden arm. "I can't stay," he said.

"We're having a big turkey and cauliflower disguised as mashed potatoes," Tamsen said, attempting to entice him.

Charlotte peeled back Whit's fingers and stared at his palm. "This is your heart line; it tells whether you will fall in love with someone. If it is deep, you will fall deeply in love, and if it is light, well, then…" she laughed nervously. "Not so much. But yours is deep, so you're good." Tamsen smiled and Charlotte blushed. He had never mentioned a girlfriend and it had actually never occurred to Tamsen that he might be involved with someone.

Whit shifted his weight against the wall. Tamsen noticed his running shoe was untied and that he wasn't wearing socks.

Charlotte continued, "If you make a fist like this . . ." Whit complied. "Then I can see how many children you are going to have. One, two, three, four, five. Five children."

Whit raised his eyebrows and feigned interest. "I better get a second job."

She brought his hand closer to her face and squinted. "Your life line is supposed to be here, but you don't really have one," Charlotte said, perplexed.

Whit pulled his hand from her. "Yeah, no life. That pretty much nails it." He made no attempt at seeming amused and they all stood still. Charlotte's cheeks turned scarlet and she glanced at Tamsen the way she did from the ice when she failed at a jump during lessons.

"Mom, I'm going to sign up for the talent show." Theo said in his Swamp Thing voice. "Whit is teaching me a secret song." This was extraordinary news. Theo usually cowered from attention—Ms. Ellison said he seldom raised his hand. The fact that he was thinking of performing for his classmates was an epic step.

Theo grabbed a dinner plate from the table, turning it like a steering wheel, and rushed around the kitchen island. Whit pulled on his winter coat. Tamsen noticed a tear under the arm.

"I'll walk you out," Tamsen said as she quickly wrapped a piece of homemade stevia-sweetened lemon cheesecake in aluminum foil.

Charlotte gave her mother a perplexed shrug at her failed attempt at revealing Whit's future. Indeed, Charlotte's plan to connect with Whit fell short, but Tamsen was surprised at how disappointed she, too, was that Whit declined her dinner invitation. She had even brined the turkey breast in her pathetic hotel room the night before so it would be extra juicy.

At the door, Tamsen squeezed Whit's arm warmly. His biceps were firm. "Is everything okay?" she asked. He didn't move. There was an emptiness in his expression and the corners of his mouth relaxed down into an involuntary frown. His mind was clearly elsewhere.

"I'll be fine," he answered without making eye contact.

"Anything I can do?" Tamsen asked.

Whit huffed. "No." He paused for a moment as if he were deliberating with himself, then he looked at her intently. "I get this way," he said.

Tamsen knew by the force of his stare that he was sending her a message: don't take it personally—there's nothing you can do about it.

"Okay," she said softly. "Take this," she offered, extending the foil-covered treat. "Homemade sorta cheesecake. It's sugar-free."

"Sorta thanks," he managed. "Do you mind?" He turned his back to her and she faced his beat-up knapsack.

As she unzipped the largest compartment and nestled the foiled treat between a binder and a paperback music booklet, she saw a prescription bottle in the mesh side pouch. She felt ashamed for looking. Lithium. She zipped up the backpack and turned him around to face her.

The thought of another week passing before she would see him again swelled into something like loss. Being around Whit was different. It felt good—even if he didn't. She could see his agony in his halfhearted motions. She could read the pain in the dark crescents under his eyes. She wanted to help him.

"I am going to a masquerade party at Sidebar with a few friends," she blurted. "You should come, if you don't have plans."

"In Boystown?" he asked dully.

"Yeah, my gay friends like to think they own Halloween," she replied.

"Sounds fun," he said with zero enthusiasm. The pall over him lingered. Maybe she had gone too far—inviting him to something without the kids. "Maybe," he said. She instantly regretted asking him.

He opened the door, which was seized by a blast of cold air, ripping the knob from his hand and sending the massive slab of mahogany back on its hinges, slamming into the adjacent wall with a powerful bang that startled them both.

"I'm such an idiot." He stepped over the threshold and rushed down the steps to his bike.

Tamsen flipped her wet head forward to twist her hair into a towel. The Charlie's Angels group costume had been Clay's idea and he had promised to style her tonight; they were going as Kelly and Bosley. Tamsen had ravaged her closet at home and found a retro-looking pair of flair-bottom pants and a dated-looking silk blouse with billowy cuffed sleeves and a collar that tied into a big bow. She laid the pieces out on the hotel bed, removing the spread first, as her mother had always instructed her to do when she traveled on business. "You never know what sort of disgusting thing is on the bedspread," her mother always said.

Of course, she was talking about excrement or semen.

Tamsen had picked up some dramatic false eyelashes at the drug store and was tapping them into place with a Q-tip when she heard Clay at her door.

"Trick or treat, sexy?!" Tamsen hurried to let him in, but when she saw what he was wearing she knew there had been some sort of miscommunication.

"I thought I was Kelly," she said to the man who stood before her, wearing a long chestnut wig with feathered bangs and a 1970s knee-length skirt with a button-down satin blouse.

"It's Halloween. Why would I dress as the man?" he asked, strutting in with a garment bag.

"Of course, my bad," she replied.

"Not to worry," Clay said, tossing his things on the bed.

"You brought me a suit?" she asked.

". . .including white dress shirt, tie, and shoes," he said. He held up an old-fashioned desktop phone speaker. "If we're going to be legit we need a Charlie too." Then Clay reached into his bag of tricks and pulled out a men's toupee. "Let's get to work on your hair. And you're going to need to take off those eyelashes immediately."

Clay sat her down in the hotel room desk chair and began to work her hair into a low and tight chignon bun. He then stretched a nude wig net over her head, concealing most of her natural tresses. Finally, he slipped the Bosley hair into place, securing the ridiculous synthetic mop. Tamsen got dressed while Clay re-adhered one of his fake pink fingernails.

"This suit is way too big," Tamsen said about the two-piece pinstriped sack that hung from her slim figure.

"It's perfect," Clay said. He took one of the decorative bolster pillows from the bed and stuffed it under her shirt, securing it in the tuck of her pants. Clay insisted he fill in her eyebrows so that she'd look more masculine, producing a makeup case from his leather satchel.

"Don't turn me into Frieda Kahlo," she said, puckering her lips.

"Can we talk about this depressing hotel room?" he asked. "Who's the decorator, Hannibal Lecter? I mean, that painting, come on."

"I should cover it, shouldn't I?" she asked.

"In lighter fluid," Clay replied.

Tamsen turned to where Abie the clown hung, but the disturbing portrait had disappeared. The creepy image was gone. An oil painting of the Old Chicago Water Tower hung in its place.

"I love it," Tamsen said. She thought of Nicole, the trainee from the lobby coffee station. "An entire city burned down around her, and that babe is still standing."

"Hold still," Clay demanded as he smudged a five o'clock shadow over Tamsen's chin. She ducked into the bathroom to see the final result.

In the bright lights of the vanity mirror, her reflection was striking—a woman with another identity. The male alter ego she saw in the mirror would have a few cocktails—maybe more than just a few—and dance until his feet were covered in blisters. But the real Tamsen, the mother, the wife, should be elsewhere tonight—on a tree-lined urban street, skipping up sidewalks and clambering up grand limestone steps, with an eager Swamp Thing and a gypsy fortune teller. In their heated pursuit of full-size candy bars, her children had probably forgotten that something was missing from their trick or treat ritual this year; tomorrow morning, when Charlotte was sluggish from her sugar binge and Theo crawled out of bed to re-tell accounts of the spookiest decorations, they would both long for Tamsen and feel sad because, because of circumstances not under their control, and for reasons they couldn't comprehend, their mother was absent. Tamsen grasped the vanity and leaned over the sink, waiting for overdue tears to drop into the clean white porcelain basin. But the tears didn't come, only the shame.

"We don't have all night, Boz," beckoned Clay. She could be in her pajamas in three minutes flat, her face scrubbed clean, watching *A Room with a View* on her laptop.

"Coming," she answered.

Sidebar was an immense gay club with three dance floors, a stage, a DJ booth, and gilded cages displaying male dancers in sequined leotards suspended from the ceiling. Clay led Tamsen by the hand as the rest of their squad, Sabrina and Jill, followed in tow. The group navigated past Black Panther, Harley Quinn, Tarzan, and a cluster of shirtless lumberjacks. Tamsen shut her eyes to give them a brief rest from the flashing green laser lights that deflected off a huge turning disco ball. She was less than enthused about being there, but the crowd was euphoric. Her thoughts were on Charlotte, who was likely in her jammies now, sitting on her bed, sorting the spoils of trick or treating into piles of favorable and unfavorable confections.

A sea witch wearing pasty makeup and purple glitter on her eyelids bumped into Tamsen, offering her Molly in a dark gravelly voice.

"Ignore the dealers in drag, Bosley," Sabrina yelled in his character's firm feminine voice. He put his hand on the fake gun tucked into his flared jeans. "We can't allow them to derail Charlie's mission for us."

"That's right, Sabrina," Jill said with the toss of his Farrah Fawcett wig. "There's a cash prize for the winners tonight." Now they had Tamsen's attention.

It was difficult to hear anything over the melodic chaos of bass, laughter, and the Scissor Sisters. Sabrina did her best to explain to Tamsen in sign language and shouts that the costume contest judges were anonymous and would be walking around the club scoring everyone on originality, quality, and likeness.

"It is very important that you don't break character," Jill said with her trademark breathy voice. "You need to exude Bosley until the prizes are awarded."

Sabrina pointed to a clearing on the dance floor and the entourage of four began their act, a freestyle dance that periodically resolved into a pose where all three of the angels assumed the iconic "hands as guns" stance. Tamsen didn't anticipate having to contribute much, since Bosley only played a supporting role in the real show, but when her comrades formed a dance circle around her, the two vodka gimlets she'd already sucked down fueled her groove. A remix of Diana Ross' "Love Hangover" blasted from the DJ booth and a surge of something resembling happiness washed over Tamsen from beneath the pillow-stuffed suit. A cowboy in a G-string and a skeleton wearing little more than body paint began to chant her name, "Bosley, Bosley!" Maybe they'd actually win the cash prize and the night would pay for itself. Tamsen was perspiring profusely, but she figured Boz was a sweat machine himself, so the moisture on her face was probably serving the act. She caught her breath and a skinny twenty-something Robin handed her what appeared to be a cosmo.

"Great moves, Bosley," Robin said. "Love you, love the show."

"Oh, no, no, no you don't, Boy Wonder," Kelly said, pushing Robin's drink away and splashing pink liquid on his utility belt. "We do not accept a drink from a rando stranger unless we watch the bartender make it." Jill, who was Clay's Taiwanese friend, Huang, in real life, turned to Tamsen. "Bosley, would you be a dear and buy me a margarita? I need to hit the little ladies' room."

Tamsen reached into her pants pocket for the debit card Whit had returned to her. She fished out her driver's license and the $5 that was left after she paid the $35 cover, but the debit card was gone. She scanned the floor around them.

"What's wrong?" Jill shouted.

"I lost my card, Huang," Tamsen returned. "I must have dropped it at the bar."

Jill jutted out a hip and tossed back his sexy sun streaked hair, "Who is Huang? Stay in character!"

Tamsen trolled the club for the prepaid debit card on which at least a hundred dollars remained. Kelly pressed another gimlet into Bosley's hand, tapping his wrist to indicate the costume judging would soon commence. She should have brought the family credit card as a backup, but Victor regularly monitored where and when she was spending his money—Halloween in Boystown was so far outside the lines of what constituted "appropriate behavior," Tamsen couldn't even fathom what he'd do if Sidebar appeared on their statement. He'd probably start with a litany of insults aimed at her gay friends, followed by a slam involving her ability to parent being compromised by her lack of good judgment, then culminating in a slur about her being frigid. He might finally hit her.

She found the bartender who had served her earlier. He was difficult to miss with the phoenix tattoo across his entire torso and the bunny-ears headband he wore.

"Have you seen a gold debit card?" she hollered at the top of her lungs. He shook his head dismissively. The music pounded in her ears and she covered them, resting her elbows on the six inches of unoccupied bar in front of her. The air inside the club had become stifling and the loss of the money squashed the thrill of her earlier lack of inhibitions like a bug on a dance floor. She felt the pressure of a gentle hand on her upper arm and for a split second her mind went to Whit, but when she turned she saw a Scotsman who wore a towering black bearskin hat with a proud red feather plume. He was holding a set of bagpipes and wearing a kilt.

"Neil!" She was happy to see a familiar face, but she wasn't exactly sure whether she should amp up her surprise to find him in a gay club. He certainly was not out at work. Summers & Peel liked to think of itself as an open-minded and tolerant firm, but they were not very warm to anything that deviated from straight, white, and male. Apparently, Neil checked only two of those three boxes.

"I don't suppose you're here with your husband," Neil said.

"All clear," she replied, the liquor making her unusually candid.

"So, we agree to be discreet about our tryst?" Neil asked.

"What happens in Boystown . . ." Tamsen slurred.

"You need to drink water," he said in his Scottish brogue.

"I bet it's tough to dance with bagpipes," she said. "And that headdress."

The pillow on her stomach was cumbersome and sticky. Tamsen was ready to abandon the Charlie's Angels charade and go rogue, but Sabrina motioned furiously from across the bar to her that it was award time.

"I don't dance," Neil said. "But everyone loves a bloke in a skirt." He wished her luck with the costume contest, although he confessed he thought she was dressed as Winston Churchill.

By the time the DJ summoned the group costume finalists to the stage, Tamsen was fairly certain her five o'clock shadow and her bushy eyebrows had melted off. Kelly stood next to her on the stage evaluating the two other group costume finalists: The Seven Deadly Sins and five legendary female Olympic figure skaters: Tonya Harding, Nancy Kerrigan, Michelle Kwan, Tara Lipinski, and Kristi Yamaguchi.

Sabrina surveyed the crowd from the stage as the judges argued with six of the Seven Deadly Sins. Word had it that one of them had taken his role to heart and was passed out on the men's room floor.

"Isn't that the guy who offered you a drink?" Sabrina asked, pointing toward Robin, who held a clipboard.

"Holy roofies, Batman!" Jill exclaimed. "Robin is a judge."

"You were polite to him, right, Kelly?" Sabrina asked, irritated.

"Don't worry," Kelly said. "I'm about to lock in our victory." With that, Kelly unsnapped his conservative mid-calf skirt, letting it drop to his ankles. The DJ queued the "Charlie's Angels" theme song and Kelly slowly and demurely unbuttoned his silky blouse, revealing his perfect six-pack and the Kelly character's recognizable white bikini. The audience went wild with whoops and whistles.

As the uproar mellowed, Robin shooed the Deadly Sins off the stage and spoke into a hand-held mic: "Regrettably, the Seven Deadly

Sins are disqualified because Sloth was Gluttonous." The crowd cheered and Robin looked pleased with himself for the clever remark. "So," he continued, "the winner of this year's Sidebar costume contest in the group category is . . ." Kelly squeezed Bosley's hand as Robin drew in a dramatic breath. At once, the Olympic theme song began to blare from the club speakers.

The crowd erupted simultaneously in boos and cheers. While her fellow champion figure skaters raised their gold medals and waved to the crowd, Tonya Harding accepted a two-foot-tall trophy—a fake gold victory chalice filled with green jungle juice, and an envelope of cash that Tamsen very badly needed. Robin sauntered across the stage to where Bosley and the Charlie's Angels stood. He stopped in front of Kelly.

"This is a customized, fully operational utility belt you spilled that drink on."

Clay, breaking character, snarled back. "You know our costumes are better. They didn't even include Dorothy Hamill, let alone Peggy Fleming." Tamsen thought Clay had a valid point, but she was more disappointed about not winning the $500 prize than she was about the integrity of anyone's costume.

Huang chimed in. "My Pomeranian looks more like Tonya Harding than that wannabe disaster."

"Here's your consolation prize, Bosley," Robin said, handing Tamsen four drink coupons. "Better luck next year."

Tamsen was relieved the competition was over. She was staving off pangs of exhaustion, and for the first time ever, the thought of her bed at The Talisman was appealing.

From the stage, Clay scanned the crowd of dancing men. "All these queens and not one prince," he sighed.

"I thought you didn't believe in fairy-tale endings," Tamsen said.

"And yet, I can't stop reading them." Clay grasped her hand—someone had hooked his attention. "Well, hel-lo, Zorro," he said, adjusting his bikini top.

Tamsen followed his sightline to a tall masked figure wearing a high-collared shirt and a black velvet cape with a gold chain clasp at the neck. She could barely make out his eyes in the frenetic laser light chaos, and for a moment she thought she might be imagining it. But the mouth on the masculine character bent into a wry smile—and she knew.

"That isn't Zorro. That's The Count of Monte Cristo."

CHAPTER

6

The Count glided through the horde of colorfully adorned figures toward the stage, barely fazed by the frenzied commotion around him and unconscious of the painted faces that turned admiringly to behold his imposing physique as he passed. Tamsen moved her hand to her mouth, wondering whether she had somehow conjured this magnificent creature out of thin air, whether he was a mirage of her own artifice, or maybe a gimlet-induced fantasy that would melt into the backdrop of heaving bodies if she blinked. So she didn't—she just stared as he approached.

Whit. The fatigue that consumed her moments before vaporized and she felt a warm surge of adrenaline quicken her heartrate. Though Whit's face was half-concealed, his eyes pierced through the holes of the black mask; they looked like lustrous amber stones tonight. She couldn't have stifled the exhilaration he evoked even if she tried. She was suddenly giddy and spellbound, stirred by a charm that she guessed Whit wasn't even aware he possessed. Tamsen forgot the blister that had puffed up between her heel and Clay's leather shoe as an involuntary laugh escaped her. The Count stopped in front of the stage, bowed reverently, and lifted a white gloved hand.

"Care to dance, Sir?" he said with exaggerated ceremony.

He led her to the fringe of the crowded floor and turned her as "Family Affair" by Mary J. Blige segued into something by Kesha. Whit appeared much taller than the men around them, and though he swayed with an economy of motion, she could tell he had rhythm. Elbows, arms, tentacles, and tails flailed to the bass beat, yet in this mob they were alone, completely unknown to the watching world, and it occurred to Tamsen that the only heterosexual male in the club, The Count of Monte Cristo, had come tonight to be with her.

They danced for two more songs, until Whit moved his velvet cape off his shoulders and Tamsen could clearly see the skin of his chest through his sweat-drenched cotton shirt. She pretended not to notice Whit's obviously defined pecs, but when a nearby wicked witch brazenly cat-called him, Tamsen decided it was time to cool down. She motioned Whit toward the bar. He nodded, taking her hand commandingly. He navigated past a lip-locked gladiator and a guy dressed as a lion, but her focus was tuned solely to the sensation of her fingers in his sticky grasp.

Whit passed Tamsen a handkerchief he pulled from his back pocket and asked the bartender for two ice waters. He leaned toward Tamsen's ear, "Do you want a drink?"

"I'm okay," she hollered back, dabbing the moisture on the back of her neck. He thirstily guzzled his water and she watched as he emptied his cup, his Adam's apple rising and falling insatiably with every gulp. He noticed her looking and smiled skeptically.

"What?" he said.

"Nothing," she mouthed back. Even if she had wanted to say something clever, there was no point—the crowd had swelled, singing "Born this Way" at unhealthy decibels.

Whit pointed to Clay, who waved from the packed spiral staircase to the second floor. Clay put on his best perplexed diva expression and waggled his finger between her and Whit. She responded with an okay signal. Clay blew her a kiss and held up his phone, sign language for "goodbye, have fun, text me all the details."

Tamsen's stomach churned and she realized that all she'd eaten in the last twenty-four hours was a dry lemon poppy-seed mini-muffin from the complimentary Talisman coffee bar. "Do you want to get some food?" she yelled.

"What?" Whit asked, lowering his ear to her lips so close she could feel the tips of his sweaty curls brush her face.

"Food," she answered loudly.

"Yes," he yelled, before chugging his second glass of water and planting the empty glass on the bar. He pulled on his cape and grabbed her hand.

The night air was pleasant for October and it was a relief to step out onto the street where costumed revelers staggered by, yammering about which bar they should hit next. Tamsen's ears adjusted to the relative quiet, still buzzing from the hours she'd spent in the alternative universe of the club. She dug in her jacket pocket for her phone, seeing a string of text alerts from Clay, and one from Victor. Her husband's name was a jolt of electric reality.

As Whit unlocked beat-up Edmond Dantès beside her, Tamsen tapped the screen and opened Victor's message which contained three photos. The first shot was taken on the front steps of the brownstone where Charlotte and Theo posed in front of a bounteous fall display Tamsen had arranged with mums, kale, gourds, a gigantic pumpkin, and an assortment of festive bats and spiders. The second photo was an after-dark group shot. The children were huddled in a pack, holding out the loot they'd collected. Tamsen recognized Oliver Putnum's son in the foreground. The kids had never trick-or-treated with the Putnums before, and Tamsen shook off the gnawing discomfort she felt knowing that Victor had infiltrated yet another new friend group. The last photo was a selfie with Victor sandwiched between Charlotte and Theo at the kitchen table, Theo eating the cacao coconut treats Tamsen had made specially for him. Victor captioned it, "Wish you were here."

"Tamsen!"

A familiar Scottish accent called her back from the melancholy into which she was beginning to slide. Neil stood at the curb, holding open the door of his vintage red Jaguar coupe for a man in aviators and a pilot-style leather jacket. She felt self-conscious. Neil had seen her with Whit, and although there was nothing inherently wrong with the two of them socializing, still she feared Victor might punish her if he learned of their friendship. He could forbid Theo from taking guitar. He could make her fire Whit.

Neil took his place in the driver's seat and through the front windshield they locked eyes. She watched as he lifted his index finger to his lips and Tamsen gestured back the same, sealing their pact of silence.

Whit yanked off his wristband and offered it to her. "For your scrapbook," he joked.

"Where to?" she asked, pulling up a ride app on her phone.

"How do you feel about falafel?" he asked.

"It's almost 2:00 a.m.," she said, still a little drunk. "Where are we going to find falafel?"

"Are you kidding?" he replied. "You can get falafel around the clock in Chicago. There's a spot in my neighborhood."

She slid her phone back into her jacket pocket. "You want me to get on the back of your bike?"

"You're probably going to need to lose the belly," he teased, handing her his bike helmet.

"Exactly, I'm going to push your fixie over its load capacity."

"You need to start appreciating Edmond Dantès," he joked.

She laughed in return, eyeing the narrow hard plastic saddle. "I just don't think he's built for a woman."

Whit swung his cape over his arm and walked to her. He untucked her white shirt and slid the pillow out, wedging it between his knees as he cinched her belt tightly. Then he straddled Edmond Dantès, holding the pillow in place for a comfortable seat. "The falafel express is leaving, lady. Get on or go home."

Tamsen reached up and took out the hairpins that secured her Bosley toupee, unfastening her tight bun and liberating her hair, which tumbled freely over her shoulders. She pulled on the helmet and it immediately slid back and off to the side. "How big is your head?"

Whit laughed. "I have an unusually large cranium, characteristic of sperm whales and extraterrestrials."

Tamsen stood on one of the pedals for support, held Whit by the shoulders, and lifted herself onto the seat. Her toes dangled above the pavement and her legs swung forward as he maneuvered the bike over the curb with a lurch that nearly knocked her off. She shrieked and grabbed hold of him. His torso bobbed up and down as he pulled into the bike lane, gaining momentum.

Together they sped west, passing the leather specialist Tamsen used for the knock-off quilted Chanel handbag to which Charlotte had taken a permanent marker, as well as the meat market where Victor stood in line every Thanksgiving to purchase an organic free-range bird. It felt invigorating to experience the city streets at night without the armor of steel and glass protecting them. She had a bike of her own in the garage, but she hadn't taken it out since her wedding, not because she lost interest in riding but because Victor said it wasn't safe. "Anybody who chooses to ride their bike on Chicago streets deserves to be mowed down by a bimbo on her phone."

Tonight, she was glad to disregard her husband's condemnation. With each pump of Whit's legs, Tamsen swayed back and forth. She was conscious cargo, aware of the flexion in his obliques as he pedaled, the softness of his heavy velvet cape, and the faint smell of fabric softener and sweat that trailed him. She didn't feel like herself—she was someone new and daring. As they made a wide left onto Damen Avenue, with all its bright storefront signs, Whit gently squeezed the moaning brakes and came to a stop in front of a tiny dive that was packed with chattering taxi drivers and Halloween revelers.

They were led to a four-top in the corner. Tamsen was pleased when Whit selected the seat beside her and not the one facing, but she told herself it was because he probably just wanted a better view of the clientele.

Whit poured himself a glass of water from a waiting carafe.

"You're very dehydrating," Whit said, wiping his mouth on the back of his cuff.

"I've never been told that before," she laughed.

"Well, it's not a compliment, Tamsen," he joked, taking one last drink. He set down his cup exhaling with relief.

It was the second time she had heard him say her name. "I drank way too much tonight," she said.

"Are you one of those lonely housewives who gets into the wine by noon, and by dinner, you've friended three high school boyfriends?"

"Lately, I suppose," she said, opening the laminated menu. "But that's only because liquor is cheaper than therapy."

"That all depends on the liquor," he retorted.

It occurred to Tamsen that she had a scant $5 dollars in her pocket.

They would have to go Dutch. How embarrassing. She pretended to be interested in the menu, checking the prices that corresponded with the unappetizing photos beside each description.

"Don't look at the pictures," Whit said. "You'll lose your appetite."

Too late, she thought to herself. Not only was she broke, but Tamsen didn't even feel like eating now. She had Whit all to her secret Bosley self, in a tiny falafel restaurant on a side of town where no one but the butcher would ever recognize her.

"Ready?" the server asked impatiently, his head darting from table to busy table.

"A small hummus," Tamsen said, having noticed it was only $3.

Whit raised an eyebrow. "And I would like the Supreme Meat Combo with a side of tabbouleh, please. You can have some of mine," he said to Tamsen.

The server didn't look up. He snapped his fingers, barking something in Lebanese to a bus boy and wigwagged his hand toward a dirty table.

"Whit," she said. "Can I ask you something?"

"Sure," he said.

"Why did you leave the Philharmonic?"

Whit groaned and leaned back in his chair. Tamsen reached out and touched his forearm, glad again that he picked the seat beside her.

"Your playing was so amazing last week on the patio, I had to search you."

"You kids and your cyber stalking," he teased, but his expression was pained.

"There was a video of you performing "Gabriel's Oboe," and Whit, it took my breath away. It was masterful."

"Stop," he laughed, annoyed. "A tone-deaf orangutan could play that piece and it would sound beautiful."

"Seriously, why did you quit?"

"Are you sure you want to ruin a perfectly nice evening talking about me and my issues?"

"I'll tell you mine, if you tell me yours."

"Is that how this is going to go?" Whit said as the server dropped a plate of pita bread, iceberg lettuce and hummus where Tamsen was sitting and a slurry of lamb, chicken, and beef over dill rice in front of Whit.

"Could we get some hot sauce, please?" Whit asked, and the server disappeared. He unrolled his utensils from the white paper napkin, then he shifted in his seat, squaring his shoulders to her. "I haven't talked about this with anybody. No one outside my family, anyway." He paused. "And maybe a few overpaid medical professionals."

She waited as Whit smoothed his napkin slowly and methodically. He drew in a breath, and looked at her carefully, as if he were gauging her reaction before he'd provide the stimulus. "After I graduated Julliard, I moved back home and played for the the Philharmonic for a couple of years. When a spot opened up for me in Vienna, I couldn't pass it up. I packed up all my things and moved to Austria. I wanted to travel, see Europe and Asia. It was a huge opportunity."

He turned to face forward, looking ahead like he was narrating a silent movie. "The buildup to my departure was really frenetic. I had two weeks before I was leaving and I remember feeling super ecstatic, and I had all these ideas for compositions—and I wanted to get them down all at once. Then, when I got over there, I was trying to keep it together, but I wasn't sleeping much. It got to the point where I literally didn't sleep for days. I would go out on these long walks without money or a phone. I just wandered, thinking about music—I'd start at the Opera House and meander up and down Kartnerstrasse, feeding off this ridiculous energy.

"I had ideas and they were flying through my brain at an absurd rate, it was constant. And scary. These thoughts would come into my head about how my music was supernatural—how it could communicate with people, not in the normal way, not even in an egotistical artist way." Whit's hands were moving, his fingertips tracing opposite circles on either side of his plate. "And this is where it gets really weird. I mean, I actually believed I was sending telepathic messages. Whatever I wanted to communicate, from 'you left your garage door open' to 'please don't snap your gum during my solo'—all I needed to do was take the stage and lift my bow and my telepathic powers would kick in." He shook his head, running his fingers through his thick dark hair. The tears suspended inside the brim of his eyes held on. "Insane," he said. "Literally."

The waiter approached tentatively, disdainfully eyeballing the food that still sat on their table, untouched.

"We're fine here," Tamsen said firmly, sending the message to the man that he need not return until summoned.

Whit continued, the pace of his speech gaining agitated momentum. "I started having more hallucinations. It was bad. I could see bends of color flying off the orchestra's instruments in some sort of rainbow animation. And then one night, in front of 1700 people, who had all paid good money to hear Bach's "Cello Suite Number 1," I had a complete psychotic break. Just like that, in the motherland of Sigmund Freud, I snapped. I laid down my cello, stood up on my chair and I started pulling off my clothes. All my clothes." Whit's voice trembled as he stared fiercely toward the center of the table. "The conductor and a big guy from the woodwinds section grabbed me before my pants were down, thank God. The ambulance got me to the psychiatric hospital, my mom flew over and waited for three weeks until I was released. End of cello career, end of story." He looked at the plate of food and raised his fork. "Baked kofta, anyone?"

"Whit, I'm . . ." she wanted to express her empathy, but he cut her off abruptly, raising his hand as he swallowed a bite of food.

"Nope, nope, nope. No, 'I'm sorry.' No, 'you poor thing' or any of that other bullshit, just tell me how fucked up your marriage is and we can get on with our nice meal."

Two cabbies at the next table stopped conversing and stared, seeming captivated by the scene: young man, older woman, profanities, and lots of shawarma.

Whit plunged his fork into the meat combo. "You're up, sweetheart."

Tamsen looked down into her lap. She had shredded her paper napkin. It was true, her problems couldn't touch Whit's.

Whit looked up, his mouth full of food and his eyes searing. "I'm waiting."

She badly needed a glass of wine, but she didn't want to drive up the bill.

"I don't really know where to start," she began.

"Just lay it on me."

"Well, I graduated from college and landed at a killer publishing house. Worked my way up to Senior VP, fell in love, got pregnant, quit killer job, had babies, husband became controlling, husband called me terrible things, acted crazy, and now we're separated. The great American story," Tamsen said.

Whit didn't look up from his plate. "Stupid head?" he said.

Tamsen felt herself shrinking. "What?"

"Names, you said he called you names—so, like what?" He chewed defiantly, with his mouth open.

She wrestled back the tightening sensation in the back of her throat. She thought of her brothers and summoned the track of their voices in her head: *Pull it together, Tamsen. You had better not cry.*

"Poopy pants?" Whit laughed. He turned to her. "Come on, full disclosure."

"I don't want to say," she managed, struggling to steady her voice.

He took a bite of food, pieces of rice falling from the edges of his mouth onto the table. "I gave you the details of my mental breakdown and you don't want to say?"

She shook her head and opened her mouth to speak, but a gasp came out and her body heaved forward. She covered her face behind her fists. "It's too humiliating."

Whit set down his knife and fork and urgently slid his chair close to hers. "I'm so sorry, Tamsen, you don't have to say. I was trying to be funny. It's my defense mechanism."

The server approached, and Whit snarled at him, putting a protective arm around her. "Can we get some wine over here?"

Tamsen held up her hand, making an effort to compose herself. Whit gave her a handkerchief and she dabbed her eyes, certain there had to be tears, but they were dry. She felt stunned by the overwhelming sense of hopelessness her half-hearted admission to Whit had evoked. It was different from when she had discussed things with Fariah. What Fariah thought didn't matter; what Whit thought did.

He sat close beside her, his face drawn with sympathy, and set his hand on her back with measured platonic pressure.

"I am so sorry." He ran his hand through his hair. "I'm such an asshole!"

"I asked for it," she said. This was all her doing.

"No," he said.

The server set the glass of wine on the table, glaring at Whit with displeasure before handing him the check. "The wine is on those guys," he motioned to the cabbies who were putting on their coats.

Tamsen moved to pull the $5 from her jacket and it wasn't there.

She only felt the open tear at the bottom of the pocket's satin lining. Still, she didn't care now that she couldn't cover her part of the dinner.

Whit was silent, but his hand stroked her back lightly. She dipped a corner of pita in the hummus, forming tiny peaks in the viscous dip; she felt hurt, but she was probably being overly sensitive. She didn't want Whit to go away—she needed him to know she wasn't angry. She needed to restore them back to where they started the evening.

She raised the wineglass. "Here's to you for picking up the tab."

"Here's to manic episodes and shitty husbands," he added. "Cheers, we're both fucked."

She lowered her voice, "I promise, I am through talking about a certain stringed instrument."

He lowered his in response. "And I will do my very best to never again be such an insensitive dick."

She gently set her hand on his heart. "Had I known you used this kind of language, I wouldn't have hired you to teach my son guitar."

He lifted her hand from his chest and drew it to his mouth, kissing it lightly. "Had I known you were going to stick me with the dinner bill, I would have asked for a signing bonus."

It was Veteran's Day and the children were off from school. Thankfully, Aneta was able to work, so Tamsen could attend the final luncheon meeting for the Harvest Moon Ball. Theo had fallen off his skateboard that morning and bumped his head on the sidewalk. His seizures were under control, but Tamsen wasn't going to take any chances. She dashed Theo to the pediatrician for a quick concussion check, and as soon as he got the green light, she dropped him at home, and sped downtown.

When Tamsen arrived at the Women's Social Club, Hilly and Jacqueline were deep in discussion with Fred, the director of the Botanic Garden. The subject: the valet situation and the debate surrounding the preferential treatment of high-end luxury automobiles. Jacqueline thought the more expensive vehicles should be kept up front versus in the vast lot adjacent to the main building.

"Last time, we were allowed to select ten cars to be kept in the circle drive," Jacqueline declared. "We gave the valet advanced notice on who would be driving a Bugatti, Ferrari, and so forth, and they gladly staged these cars in full view."

"It's a fire code issue, Ms. Cole. The Botanic Garden Board specifically asked that we park every car, regardless of make or model, in the main lot to clear the way in case of an emergency."

"The automobiles to which I am referring send a message to our donors about the stature of our attendees. There is no question that the presence of the cars elevates the event," she insisted stridently.

Fred drummed his fingers anxiously. "It's out of the question. I simply cannot allow it this year."

Weaving through the white table-clothed grand dining room was Edith Knox, pushed in her wheelchair by her devoted, yet seldom seen son, John. He was objectively handsome, but his most striking quality was his posture, erect and proud as if he'd been in the Navy. He was dressed impeccably in a dark gray suit and French blue shirt, and his carriage was dignified and certain without coming across as pretentious. Tamsen had been introduced on a number of occasions and she was impressed. He always met her eyes with deep contact and remembered her first and last name. She knew from Hilly that he lived on the North Shore with his very private wife, who was rumored to be a Baroness, and that he managed the family's worldwide luxury brand conglomerate, which was started by his great grandfather, Earnest Knox, back around the turn of the century. Victor estimated they were worth $24.9 billion dollars. Tamsen hated that she knew this information—she didn't see people like Jacqueline and her husband did, in terms of their possessions, as numbers.

John also oversaw the Knox Family Foundation. However, despite her old age and rumored senility, Edith was known to have ultimate say which charities were the glad recipients of the Knox's generosity. Her reputation as a renegade philanthropist was based on Edith's mercurial favoritism; one year she directed all their money to a hurricane relief fund, and the following year she divided her generosity between Mothers Trust Foundation and the comfort animal alliance, Fur Good. The latter organization was headquartered downtown and had a new pet hotel retreat and spa, conceived by Edith along with celebrity designer and fellow Havanese enthusiast, Kevin Sobin.

"Excuse us, please," John smiled at Tamsen as he accidentally bumped her with his mother's wheelchair.

"John!" Jacqueline practically leapt out of her seat. "Are we going to see you and your incomparable mother at our gala this weekend?"

"We're planning to attend," he said evenly.

"Excellent. Will you have a chauffeur, or will you be driving the Rolls?" she droned.

"I haven't given it any thought," he replied.

Edith Knox raised her hand from the wheelchair. "Johnny, since that woman is speaking to you as if I'm not present, please tell her about your father. Two terms in Korea . . . two."

"Mrs. Knox, don't you agree it would be best to have your Rolls-Royce up front by the door? Wouldn't that make it easier for you?" Jacqueline suggested.

"Oh, yes," chimed Hilly, who had to get a word in.

Edith's head moved jerkily toward Jacqueline and John quickly repositioned the chair so that his mother didn't have to strain her neck. "Why are you talking about cars?" Edith shouted. "It's Veteran's Day. Show a little respect for the people who put their lives on the line for this country."

"Both my father and my grandfather served," John said, out of deference to his mother.

"That's right," Edith barked, now pointing at Tamsen, "and they were fine and noble Americans."

"I'm sure they were, Mrs. Knox," said Tamsen.

Edith waved her hand again, motioning John onward. He obliged, bidding the group a good lunch.

Jacqueline turned to Fred. "I can't believe that corroded old bat is the key to my success. Her white Rolls-Royce is as hideous as that hairy mole on her pointy chin, but people love her and if I don't see it parked directly in front of the entrance to the Harvest Moon Ball on Saturday night, you better believe I will unleash a swarm of aphids on the Botanic Garden, the likes of which you have never seen."

Tamsen reached for her ice water and thought of Whit, in his Halloween costume, guzzling water at the gay bar.

"What are you smiling at?" Jacqueline asked.

Tamsen lowered her face toward her bag and checked her phone. She had texted Whit a photo that morning of the crinkled handkerchief she found in the pocket of her Bosley suit, asking whether she should launder it before returning it or if he preferred it as a wrinkled token of their Halloween bond. She didn't like the anxious sensation she felt when she saw that he had not replied, but it was only lunchtime and, given his age, he probably wasn't even waking up until now.

Jacqueline lightly tapped a fork to her wine glass as the maître d' escorted a young woman carrying an orange, nubuck leather Coach portfolio to the table.

"Attention, everybody, there is someone I would like you to meet."

Tamsen thought the girl looked familiar but couldn't place her.

"This is Madison. She graduated from Heatherington, my alma mater, and she now works for Flare Events, the premier party planning company in the city, if not the country."

Tamsen widened her eyes at Hilly. This girl was the architect of the ill-conceived, hamburger-themed, Summers & Peel Thunderchicken dinner.

"Madison found me through the alumni network about three months ago and, well, suffice it to say that my dearest friends have been giving her rave reviews," Jacqueline boasted.

"Oh my god, Jacqueline, that is so nice of you to say," Madison beamed.

"Good event coordinators are tough to find," Fred chimed in.

"Sit down, Madison," Jacqueline commanded. "There is an empty seat next to Tamsen."

"No way!" Madison squeaked when she saw Tamsen. "From Thunderchicken! You were so amazing."

Tamsen wanted to hate Madison, but the girl was actually quite nice. It wasn't Madison's fault that her bosses threw a novice into a corporate party that was way over her head.

Jacqueline continued. "When Madison mentioned she had landed at Flare and was looking for new clients, I thought, what perfect timing! You see, Madison, now that I have all but wrapped up the Harvest Moon Ball, we are looking ahead to the gala two years out and we are in desperate need of creative assistance."

Hilly cleared her throat and shot Tamsen an apologetic smile, trying energetically to distance herself from Jacqueline's decision to undermine Tamsen's certain spot in the chairwomanship succession.

"Excuse me, Jacqueline, but are you suggesting we hire an outside firm to handle the next fundraiser?" Tamsen asked.

"Event planning is all Flare does," she replied.

"It's true," piped in Madison, in her adult voice. "We offer our clients a full array of services starting at the nebular stage, through the critical planning phase, and ending in massive, fully actualized stellar experience."

"Are we talking about a party here, or the Big Bang?" Tamsen interjected.

Madison laughed, "I know, it sounds a little cheesy, but Flare really does handle every detail in the creation of your event universe."

Hilly retained her neutrality and asked her first intelligent question of the day. "Is there an extra cost to use your company?" Jacqueline rolled her eyes so hard Tamsen could practically hear them rumble in their sockets.

Madison handed everyone at the table a custom, bounded, color brochure. "This is a breakdown of our services as well as a sample contract. Cost is something I like to address right up front—that and the inclusion rider we've recently added to all our contracts."

Brava, Tamsen thought. She was all for a company that recognized the importance of race and gender diversity. Still, Flare's presentation was dubious.

Jacqueline moved the pages of the proposal. Her extremely rare, four-karat green marquis diamond caught the light and Tamsen mused at the irony of its fancy color, created by Earth's naturally occurring radiation. Instead of focusing on the numbers, Jacqueline was craning to see which other high-net-worth individuals had populated the WSC dining room since she sat down. "This looks entirely doable to me," she said.

"I'm not sure the budget for the next Harvest Moon can shoulder a $45,000 retainer, due upon engagement," Tamsen pointed out.

Madison interjected, "The $45,000 covers all initial concept meet-
ings, creative fee for the overall theme, and any of my time, excluding
hours dedicated to the procurement of décor, entertainment, and of
course, food and beverage."

"And, correct me if I'm wrong, Madison, but all services are à la
carte and subject to both an hourly rate and a 25% commission. In other
words, beyond the $45,000, everything from the cost of the venue to
the foil-wrapped truffles at each place setting is on a pay-as-you-go basis,
subject to both a percentage fee and an hourly charge."

"Boom," Madison said matter-of-factly.

Tamsen ran the numbers in her head and determined that an event the
size of the Harvest Moon Ball could cost the WSC half a million easily,
meaning Flare would reap a staggering profit of $100,000 for one event.

"We usually work with a steering committee. Would that be you?"
Madison asked Tamsen.

"Hilly and I will work with the Board of Directors to select the
next chairwomen, Madison," Jacqueline said. "Tamsen has been great
help in the past, but with you on the job, she'll be free to focus on the
situation with her family."

So, Tamsen thought, word of the separation was out.

Tamsen held up the brochure. "Jacqueline, I don't understand what
all this is about."

"It's about cattails, Tamsen. Cattails."

"Table arrangements aside, the Board of the Women's Social Club
will want to see your numbers, and my mental math suggests you'll be
paying Flare six digits to do the heavy lifting."

"Whoa," Fred blurted. "Tamsen comes much cheaper."

"The purpose of the ball is to raise every penny we can for charity,"
Tamsen said. It was distasteful to her that anyone could gouge them
in good conscience.

"We can steal from the money we raise at the ball to pay for Flare," Jacqueline proposed. "Mothers Trust can keep whatever's left—it would be so worth it." Jacqueline didn't care about the next ball—in fact, she might even be devising an incantation to sabotage it. She just needed the current Harvest Moon Ball to break all the records.

Tamsen tilted her head, addressing Jacqueline. "You're quoted in *Chicago Scene* as saying, what were the exact words? Oh, yes…'the WSC donates 100% of all charitable contributions directly to Mothers Trust Foundation,'" Tamsen said.

Jacqueline was silent and Tamsen supposed she was trying to shapeshift into a flying monkey. "You really think you can manage a gala with all the upheaval in your life right now, Tamsen?" she asked. Tamsen's cheeks burned. Fred and Hilly were silent.

"I always manage," Tamsen said.

"Madison," Jacqueline said. "Thank you for your time and your professionalism. We will look forward to finding funds to work with Flare—some other time." She then tucked her forked tongue behind her bottom lip and turned her attention to the second page of the proposal, a list of Flare's "Immediate Action" items.

"Tamsen, Flare was prepared to provide me a list of things next week. Since you'll be picking up the slack until we officially name the chairwomen for the next Harvest Moon Ball, I'll need to see a vision board with three theme options, a budget, the initial targets for the live auction, and a few concepts for the invitation." She gracefully lifted her gaze, her mouth in a thin smile as she stared Tamsen down.

"You know, Fred," Jacqueline purred. "You're right. Tamsen is cheap."

CHAPTER

7

The afternoon of the Harvest Moon Ball, Charlotte and Tamsen stood in Tamsen's custom-paneled closet and shopped for a gown. The dress they selected couldn't be a repeat from prior years' Harvest Ball events, nor could it be something Tamsen had recently worn to another charity event. "People keep track of these things, and there will be photographers," Victor had told her last year when she appeared in a dress she was trying to repurpose two weekends in a row. The point was irrelevant these days, because it had been nearly six months since Tamsen had attended anything besides a school play or Book Fair at Dexter. They narrowed it down to a floor-length navy blue evening gown with a wide skirt, or a slinky claret-colored column gown with a high front slit.

Tamsen stepped into the claret dress and Charlotte zipped her up from behind. Tamsen spun around. "What do you think?"

"The other one looks like a tent, but it has pockets, which is cool," Charlotte said. She stood back, her chin in her hand, and studied Tamsen in the fitted gown. Her expression showed a hint of disapproval. "This one's going to fly open and people will see . . ." Her eyes grew wide. ". . . Up your skirt. Maybe you should wear shorts underneath like I do on PE day," Charlotte resolved.

Shorts would have been a game-changer had girls worn them under their jumpers when she was in school. Tamsen's first-grade Catholic school nemesis, a boy with a buzz cut named Scotty, flew into her mind. She batted away the memory of how he had bullied her, constantly lifting her skirt and exposing her white cotton Carter's. Tamsen amused herself by imagining how her therapist, Fariah Valentine, would hit pay dirt if she delved into Tamsen's grade school days, her penny-pinching family, and all the other experiences that landed her in her present situation. Fariah would wear the claret dress.

Tamsen pulled Charlotte into a hug, grateful her daughter never had to fend off a Scotty of her own. "I'm not planning to do any cartwheels tonight, at least not in the literal sense," Tamsen said. "So, I think it's more a question of which dress makes me feel good."

"How can a dress make you feel good?" Charlotte asked.

Tamsen considered the question, then she heard the front door open.

"Daddy!" Charlotte said, darting out to greet him. Victor had agreed to stay with the children for movie night while Tamsen attended the ball. He had undergone an emergency root canal that afternoon and was miserably numb, which worked out beautifully for Tamsen. She looked at herself in the three-way mirror. The claret fit her perfectly; its cool, silky fabric was liquid against her skin. She heard Victor's footsteps on the hardwood downstairs. She checked her watch; he was an hour early. Her mind was made up without a second thought—she'd wear the blue. Tamsen slipped out of the claret gown, letting it slide over her thighs and calves into a pool on the carpet. She texted Clay.

SOS. Get here ASAP.

Tamsen picked up her jeans from the carpet and the proceeds of the consignment check she had cashed that morning tumbled out of the front pocket: a wad of hundred-dollar bills secured with one of Charlotte's sparkly hair ties. Tamsen looked at the roll of bills, ready to be deposited into her hiding place. But hearing Victor's voice bellowing from the living room below, she knew she couldn't put the cash into the fountain with him in the house; she needed to find another spot for it quickly.

She thrust the money into the pocket of the billowy blue dress and took her jewelry from the open safe, then stepped into the attached master bedroom. The lights were on behind the glass-paned doors of the millwork that ran the length of the wall, adjacent to where Tamsen used to sleep. This expanse of tabac-stained cabinetry was home to Tamsen's treasured library and several sterling-silver picture frames that housed the 5" x 7" milestones in her and Victor's marriage: the spot near North Pond where Victor proposed, the windy day of their wedding reception, infant Charlotte swaddled in a pink flannel hospital blanket, and Theo putching in the bath. The neatly-packed shelves contained all of Tamsen's favorite books—everything from the classics she'd studied in college, whose pages were molting from their spines, to the autobiographies she'd read in her late twenties and the how-to guides for pregnancy and child rearing she'd collected when they started their family.

She switched off the bookcase lights and touched the wooden post of the California King, resplendent with fluffy goose-down pillows and sublime Anichini linens. She and Victor used to call this bed their private island, but when Tamsen looked at it now, all she could think was how she dreaded ever having to lie beside Victor again. She felt a tightening in her lowermost abdomen, near her pelvic bone. It was a dull ache—her internist hadn't been concerned because it came and went and wasn't extraordinarily painful. Tamsen knew that if she and Victor reconciled, the matter of sex would be foremost on Victor's agenda. The book on separation had dedicated a late chapter to "Rekindling Your Mojo," but Tamsen couldn't bring herself to get past anything beyond the sections about the children's well-being.

Tamsen's mind flashed to the day she and Victor met with the priest who would marry them before the ceremony at St. Christina's. They had laughed afterward about the statements he'd asked them to initial. Most were expected: "I will not be unfaithful, I will live according to the Bible," and so on. But on the ride home that day, Tamsen had remarked to Victor about how archaic it had felt to have to put her initials beside the statement, "I will not deny him." Tamsen assumed Victor was asked to initial the same proclamation on his inventory, but apparently, what they came to jokingly call the "tenth-and-a-half commandment" or "the duty-sex clause," was only on the form for women. As the years went by, and their sex life slowly lost its luster, Victor invoked this mandate in jest whenever Tamsen gave him signs that she was exhausted from a day with a colicky Theo, or that she wasn't feeling well because she'd caught Charlotte's cold, or when she was simply not in the mood because of some barb he had thrown her way. Victor never acknowledged that their duty-sex joke had lost its punchline.

"Are those real diamonds?" Theo asked of her necklace with exaggerated volume as he rummaged through the basket of approved snacks at the back of the walk-in pantry. He was listening to Whit's playlist with her headphones while the cluck, cluck of a ping-pong ball sounded from the basement where Victor and Charlotte were facing off.

"This diamond was made in a laboratory, not mined from the ground," she said, touching the pendant on her neck. "I think it's just as pretty, but it cost a lot less," she added. She didn't elaborate about the pear-shaped diamond drop earrings Victor had gotten her as a wedding present. They were exquisitely clear and colorless, but Tamsen had always felt like she'd needed a bodyguard with her when she wore them. She'd never have known their value if Victor hadn't sent her to have them insured.

Theo drizzled pumpkin seeds like a trail of breadcrumbs from his fist as he made his way to the puzzle he was assembling on the coffee table. Tamsen darted into the pantry, her heels giving her the extra five inches she needed to reach the airtight storage vessels on the second-highest shelf. Hearing Victor's and Charlotte's voices approaching, Tamsen popped open the top of the ceramic flour canister and dropped in the wad of cash, closing it quickly and sliding it back into place beside the baking powder and sugar before Victor rounded the corner. She turned back to him, pretending to straighten canned goods into orderly rows. He stood in the doorway; she could feel his mass blocking her exit.

"A little overdressed for a stock girl, don't you think?" he asked good-naturedly.

She chuckled mildly, trying to keep him in the happy zone. "I'm waiting for Clay to pick me up."

"Ah," he said with the lilt of sardonic humor. "You're taking your eunuch to the party."

Victor wasn't homophobic—his college roommate had come out freshman year and they were still close friends. Victor just didn't like her friendship with Clay. Tamsen fought the urge to lash back in Clay's defense, but she couldn't afford to set Victor off, not right before the gala.

"Clay knows all the women; he does their color," she said evenly.

He stepped closer as she reached up aimlessly for a box of cereal. "Here, let me give you a hand with that," he insisted. Victor was never this solicitous; Tamsen knew something was up. "I was thinking maybe we should go out for dinner one of these nights," he suggested.

Tamsen shook the cereal box nervously, as if she actually cared that it was nearly empty. She needed to get him out of the pantry and away from the money.

"Come on, Tam. I read the separation book you gave me. We're supposed to go on a date."

There was something strikingly unnatural about her husband, standing in the pantry, asking his bejeweled wife out on a date. Maybe it was the excessive cologne he wore, or how the wrinkles in his forehead looked particularly prominent, but Tamsen sensed he was straining to convey his desperate wish for things to return to normal—his unique brand of normal in which love and loathing constantly battled for the upper hand.

"Maybe in the next few weeks," she said cautiously. "Let me get through the gala first."

His mouth drew into a tight line, foreshadowing a mood swing. She knew it was time to break for the door.

"I need to see if Clay is out front," she said, escaping past him, her wide skirt brushing his leg. Victor followed close behind.

"I've been thinking about all the work you do on these benefits. How much time it takes you away from the kids."

Tamsen clamped her mouth closed and checked the live front-door camera feed on the iPad monitor.

He went on, "None of those social climbers appreciate you. You're nothing but slave labor doing their grunt work."

Tamsen walked to where Theo did his puzzle and kissed him on the head, reminding herself that her children loved her unconditionally.

"Seriously, they must think you are the biggest sucker for raising your hand every time you kill yourself to put on one of these stupid events."

"The kids who don't have winter coats, or even a decent pair of boots, don't think these events are stupid," she said, her limbs suddenly feeling heavier.

"That's right," he said. "Keep telling yourself about all the good you're doing for the children." His ears slid slightly back, and his lips tightened.

"I'm late," she said. Her voice was shaky.

"You think you're invaluable—like they can't replace you? Well, make no mistake, anybody could fill those $900 shoes—they just don't want to."

Tamsen's designer shoes were from an outlet mall near the airport. She paid $72.99 for them, less than a tenth of their original price, because several of the gem embellishments on the toe had fallen off. She herself had restored the decorations using stones she found at a craft store, but let everyone else think otherwise. The shoes were the least of the illusions in her repertoire.

"Daddy!" Charlotte called as she bounded into the kitchen. Tamsen watched Victor's sinister squint dissolve in an instant. Theo pulled off his headphones, eager to hear what his sister was so enthusiastic about. "Daddy, can Madeline come over after dinner?" she asked, speaking of the sixteen-year-old neighbor girl whom Charlotte idolized.

"She's in high school. Doesn't she have a party to go to or something?" Victor asked, clearly disappointed by Charlotte's enthusiasm.

"She wants to show me how to make cut-out cookies," Charlotte replied.

The equivalent of a ten-amp shock radiated through Tamsen's body. They'd need the flour.

"Yes!" Theo cheered.

Victor took a sip of water through the side of his mouth that wasn't numb, catching a trickle down his chin. "If that's how you guys want to spend your Saturday night," he said.

Tamsen grabbed her red satin purse from the kitchen island. What if Victor found the money? She felt the uncomfortable sting of sweat in her armpits, and the rushing in her ears began to amplify. "I have to go, guys." She turned to Victor. "Walk me to the door," she said.

As they moved toward the front foyer, her heart palpitated while she tried to think of a plan.

"You're right, we should go on a date," Tamsen said. "Let me know what night works best for you." The suggestion would surprise and calm Victor's ego and buy her a precious minute.

Victor unlocked the door, opening it slowly.

Outside, Clay rolled down the window of his double-parked Range Rover. "Hey, Victor," he waved. Tamsen made her move.

"My shawl," she said, finally coming up with an excuse to run back inside. She hurried past the Fazioli and the Miró and gathered her huge dress in her arms as she raced up the marble staircase, snatching whatever wrap was closest to the front of her closet. She bolted down the back stairwell to the kitchen and rushed into the pantry, seizing the flour canister with both hands and then prying it open, rescuing the wad of cash and shoving it into the pocket of the swishing satin dress.

Victor was in the street speaking to Clay through the window. He hurried to the passenger side, intercepting Tamsen before she reached the car.

He didn't offer to open the car door for her, so she made a move for the handle.

"Wait," he said. Victor leered at the pocket that concealed the cash. Tamsen realized in horror that it was now dusted in flour. His fingertips brushed away a swath of white powder and he smirked. "If I didn't know you better, I'd think that was coke," he said.

"I put some of the cookie ingredients on the counter for the kids," she said.

"Well," he said. "Clean yourself up in the car—you look like a mess."

The entrance to the Botanic Garden had been transformed. Tamsen had created an immersive autumn experience that began at the point where guests dropped off their cars with the valet, under the grand *porte-cochère*. Just as she had specified, the crews suspended twisted willow vines with orange and red dried oak leaves over an arched frame, leading from the main entrance to the atrium, where cocktails would be served in just under an hour. Tamsen herself had spent three days, glue gun in hand, assisting with the assembly of the entryway because she wanted to make sure her idea was executed according to her sketches.

"You have outdone yourself this year," Fred said as he escorted Clay and her inside. "I don't think the entrance has ever looked this beautiful. The work you did in the atrium is spectacular. I took a photo of it for a bridezilla we're working with."

They continued into the atrium space, where high-top tables were dressed in full-length dark chocolate-colored organza, tied at mid-pedestal with thick flaxen twine. The sun had not yet set, and the dramatic full-ceiling skylight revealed a cloudless twilight sky. Tamsen had worked with the crew on a canopy of sunflower garland and grapevines, integrated with strings of pinpoint white lights, which gathered at a center point and then loosely tented across the expanse of the room.

"People don't usually decorate the skylight," Fred remarked.

Clay chimed in, looking up. "Why would you? The view is so gorgeous."

"The impact of the skylight is diminished when it's dark outside," Tamsen said. "But our pin lights make the space more intimate—wait till it's dark, they look like constellations."

"I always knew you'd do something about the glass ceiling," Clay said with a wink.

Hilly appeared in a jade, stretch silk crepe dress, her arms urgently outstretched toward Clay.

"It's Narciso Rodriguez," Hilly said. "I wanted my hair down, but Jacqueline says it makes my neck look short," she whined.

"Did you tell her she's Satan?" Clay asked, admiring his buffed fingernails.

"She's been looking for you, Tamsen. Something about the band," Hilly said.

Pleasing Jacqueline was akin to satisfying Victor. You had to accept that you would always fall short of her expectations. Maybe the college musicians were too young, or maybe they weren't wearing the right shoes. Who knew what Jacqueline might have found to criticize. She tried to focus on Fred's praise and not the dull-edged sword Jacqueline was about to plunge into her side.

Tamsen and Fred walked beneath an arbor-covered pathway where knee-high candle lanterns illuminated the short walk to the dining room. Tamsen had taken a risk with a quiet background recording of a soft breeze rustling autumn leaves to give the passage an enchanted fall feeling. Jacqueline had resisted the idea and only gave it a reluctant go-ahead when Tamsen insisted the sound machine could be turned off if Jacqueline wasn't happy with the effect.

Emerging from the passage, the tunnel opened up to the grand ballroom, adorned with oversized antique brass lanterns suspended over each table, casting a romantic light over the scene. Each table was draped in iridescent pomegranate taffeta and carefully set with gold chargers and delicate crystal glassware: water, red wine, white wine, and dessert wine. The jewel-toned ikat napkins added visual interest to the tables, and the centerpieces tied the scheme together with texture and seasonal sophistication.

"Hilly, what happened to the cattails?" Tamsen asked. "I cut down them down to one per arrangement to appease Jacqueline."

"She pulled them out. I tried to stop her, but, you know . . ." Hilly's words trailed off. She flitted her hand in the air. She must have taken something for her nerves.

Tamsen surveyed the room. Even without the cattails, the look was exactly what she wanted, and she felt a great sense of accomplishment; the aesthetic could not have been better.

Fred lifted one of the brown birch votive holders. "It's unfortunate no one will know how you used the brown birch trees we lost in the storm for these."

"Tamsen," she heard Jacqueline's shrill voice. "Did you not get my texts?"

"I haven't checked," Tamsen said, dipping her hand into her dress pocket for her phone.

"Where is your band?" Jacqueline demanded. Tamsen's eyes went to the corner of the room, where a stage with a baby grand piano had been set up for the jazz trio. "The guests will be arriving any minute and we have no music."

Tamsen scrolled through her contacts for Andre's number. She didn't even know his last name.

Jacqueline continued her rant. "If there's no music, there's no ambiance, which means no drinking—and if people don't drink, they won't bid. And do you know what happens if people don't bid? This fundraiser is ruined."

"I told them 5:00. Maybe they got lost."

"Maybe you gave them the wrong date," Jacqueline snapped back. "Did you reconfirm with them this morning?"

Tamsen looked down at her phone. "No," she said.

"I can't handle your amateur moves right now," Jacqueline barked back. "Fix it."

Tamsen tried Andre again. This time, he picked up on the fifth ring. It sounded like he had a bad cold.

"Tamsen who?" he asked, sniffling.

"The Women's Social Club? The Botanic Garden? You're playing tonight," she said.

"Oh, yeah. Tamsen."

"Where are you guys?"

"Uh, didn't Becca call you?"

"Who's Becca?" she said.

"My girlfriend. Standing bass."

"No one called," Tamsen said with a tremor in her voice.

"Actually, she's my ex-girlfriend."

"Where are you?" Tamsen pressed. She was feeling short of breath.

"We broke up this morning."

"I need you at the Botanic Garden right now," Tamsen demanded.

"It was a bad scene. She was screwing the saxophonist, so . . ."

"Andre!" Tamsen yelled, then she glanced behind her to make sure no one had heard.

"Sorry. You might be able to get a hold of Paulie," he offered.

"You mean the drummer? What am I supposed to do with a drummer?" she pled.

"He plays French horn too," Andre said.

"I am not calling Paulie. You call Paulie, and you tell him to get over here now."

Tamsen's blood pressure ticked higher. Maybe Fred had a list of local bands. Who was she kidding? A last-minute band available on the North Shore ten minutes from start time? She considered a DJ, but she knew it would be impossible to find anyone at all at this hour.

Jacqueline stood at the podium, checking the sound system. She looked like an overdressed fitness instructor with her wireless mic that wrapped around the back of her head. She stared daggers at

Tamsen—thrusting her tongue behind her lip. In her red dress, with hair pulled into a severe bun, she really did resemble Satan.

Jacqueline stormed toward her. "Did you fix it?" she fumed loudly over the PA.

"I've got it under control. I just need to keep everybody in the atrium for an extra half-hour."

"You're joking, right?" Jacqueline lashed.

"We can sell more raffle tickets."

Jacqueline became unhinged. "I will not change my schedule to accommodate your ineptitude," she raged. "You will go down for this, Tamsen. Where the hell is Fred?"

Tamsen was past the point of panic. She was sensationless. For once, Jacqueline was right. The entire night was in jeopardy because of Tamsen's bungle. She looked at the baby grand on the stage and racked her brain for the name of a pianist. Then she thought of the Fazioli. Of course, she couldn't believe it didn't occur to her sooner. She dialed his number.

"Whit," she said, "I need a huge favor."

Tamsen circulated among the well-heeled crowd, stopping to prime the individuals she knew were most likely to bid on some of the live auction items: a week-long stay at a private villa in Tuscany, a ski in—ski out vacation house in Aspen, Bulls season tickets for four, and an exquisite diamond and ruby pendant necklace generously donated by Graff. She managed to avoid Jacqueline, but Jacqueline's dull husband, Stephan, was omnipresent tonight. At first, she thought she was imagining it, but every time she turned around, Stephan, with his underbite and long earlobes, was there. Tamsen even made a concerted effort to shake him by hiding behind Digby, but he was always nearby, glancing her way and then pretending to be riveted by the view of the fire extinguisher behind her.

Tamsen's entire body felt effervescent—not because of the flowing champagne, but because Whit was about to step into her world. The excitement of showing his fresh eyes the magnificent Harvest Moon Ball she had created made her feel a lighthearted anticipation, which she related to other thrilling firsts: first date, first trip to London, first apartment. She hovered near the entrance, and when the taxi dropped him and his guitar at the door, she felt like her life boat had just been deployed.

"Cocktail hour is almost over," she said to him as she swiftly led him through the sea of extravagant haute couture. "I hate to throw you in cold, but there's no time to warm up."

She saw him lift his hand to cover his grin—she knew he was amused by her naiveté. She gave him a playful elbow in the side. Of course, he didn't need to warm up.

Whit didn't turn his head to admire even one of the stunning Socialati. His eyes were fixed on Tamsen and the blue dress that trailed behind her as she hurried him toward the small stage, where Paulie was liberating his instrument from its case. As they neared the bandstand, she reached her fingertips to the nape of her neck and righted the shining synthetic stone. Whit was her precious jewel—he was the real thing.

"Meet your bandmate," Tamsen said. "He's the sole representative from the jazz combo I hired. Please feel free to play the piano, guitar, horns, drums, spoons, washboard, whatever you two need to do to fill this room with lovely dinner music."

Whit extended an amiable hand. "Let's jam." With that, he looked at Tamsen reassuringly and whispered, "Don't worry. I got this."

She exhaled. She knew he did.

Tamsen shot off a quick text to Charlotte, who promptly responded with a selfie of herself and Madeline holding up a ball of dough. She located her table number and draped napkins over the backs of two chairs, ensuring Clay and herself an unobstructed view of Whit during dinner.

"Change of plans," Hilly said, replacing Tamsen's napkin to the table. "Jacqueline moved you and Clay to number thirty-two, near the door. She said we needed someone at the back who had a view of the entire room 'in case something comes up.'" Then she leaned in and uttered the last words Tamsen expected to hear. "Hey, Victor just walked in."

The room became one of those spinning carnival rides where people stick to the walls of a whirling centrifuge and then the floor drops away. Tamsen felt a commensurate wave of nausea. Why was he here? Who was with the children?

Hilly nodded to where Victor was standing, dressed in his tux, and speaking to John Knox, probably trying to sell him on Summers & Peel and their recent mention in *The Atlas Rankings* as "the next North American advertising superpower."

Tamsen swayed involuntarily and Clay braced her with his arm.

"Don't let him ruin this for you," he said.

The ballroom was a mass of commotion as partygoers tried to find their assigned tables, and Victor used the chaos as an excuse to throw himself into the path of any heavy hitter he wanted to pursue. Tamsen watched him move from chair to chair, like a seasoned politician, reintroducing himself to acquaintances for whom he previously had no use, as well as those he formerly claimed to loathe. This was her event and he was doing all he could to eclipse her.

Victor slithered up beside Tamsen, popping a blue cheese–stuffed olive into the good side of his mouth. "How long did it take you to collect all that kindling?" Victor said, referring to the arbor. "Shame it'll all be in the dumpster tomorrow morning." Then he chuckled without cracking a smile, "You know I'm kidding."

"What happened to watching a movie with the kids?" she said.

"Madeline's there. Plus, I wanted to see what the mother of my children has been doing all these months," he said. He set his lips over the edge of the thin martini glass and slurped. "To see what she's been up to."

Victor's menacing words caused Tamsen to quake. She fought the urge to look toward the stage, afraid of catching Whit's eye while she was speaking to her husband. She needed to keep the two men in separate compartments of her life; she didn't want to corrupt the giddiness she felt when Whit stared back at her with the anguish she felt in the presence of Victor.

Digby gave Victor a slap on the back. "Saw you talking to Knox. You lock in a pitch for us?"

"Working on it. He's tough—loyal to their current agency," Victor said.

Digby looked at Tamsen and let out a long whistle. "You look stunning tonight, Tam. You guys are at our table, right?"

"Clay and I have been relocated," she replied.

"Jacqueline made room for me, but I'm out after soup and salad," Victor said. "Parenting first, parties second." He leered at Tamsen, pursing his lips. It was another swipe. Nevertheless, Tamsen felt a swell of relief that Victor had given himself a curfew.

Tamsen wandered among the tables, making sure there were no seating crises or misplaced salad forks. She cleared a chair for Mrs. Knox, who looked ancient, almost a caricature, in long, black satin gloves pulled up over her emaciated, wrinkled arms and a cap-sleeve black gown that concealed her feet. She wore a small tiara in her up-do.

Around her neck she wore an immense, triple-strand pearl necklace that was joined in the front with a diamond brooch, the weight of which Tamsen imagined could snap the elderly woman's head from her body.

John Knox pushed his mother's wheelchair to her place at the table and Jacqueline materialized from Dante's eighth level of hell. "Lovely to see you tonight, Mrs. Knox," Jacqueline droned.

"Yes, no thanks to a garish Bentley that was blocking the wheelchair access in front. Who thought parking their car at the entrance was a good idea?" she said, peering at Jacqueline through her clouded lenses.

Tamsen would have ordinarily relished the glorious moment Mrs. Knox eviscerated her nemesis, but instead, her attention was focused on Whit, playing with his eyes closed and gamboling his fingers up and down the neck of his guitar. She thought of how he might look while asleep—probably much like he did now, minus the instrument and the tux. A server tapped a small xylophone and circulated among the tables, indicating that dinner was about to commence.

Tamsen waited for the artists to finish their unconventional version of Pachelbel's "Canon in D," and as Whit stepped from the stage, she grasped his arm. "You saved me," she said.

"I almost didn't come," he laughed. "I wasn't sure I could do it." Tamsen understood. This was the first time Whit had played in front of an audience since the Vienna episode. She squeezed his hand.

Paulie set down his horn. "Man, you are incredible," he said to his new bandmate. "How long you been playing?"

"Just long enough to pull this off," Whit said.

Tamsen noticed that Whit's tie was askew, so she reached up and straightened it. The outside edge of her pinky grazed the skin beneath his chin and she quickly shook off the notion that he might have perceived the contact as deliberate. "I've arranged dinner for you two, but I need you back here when we start dessert," she told them. "I hope you like beef tenderloin."

"Beats dorm food," Paulie replied.

"And falafel," Tamsen returned, shooting Whit a furtive smile.

If the dining room had nosebleed seats, then Tamsen and Clay were in them.

"She exiled me because of the band," Tamsen said, stirring her spiced pumpkin soup with crème fraiche and celery root.

"She's just nuts and jealous of you, T.," Clay replied.

"But she's the chairwoman. I'm just a minion."

Clay chuckled, "You can't possibly be naïve enough to believe this is only about the ball." Tamsen looked at him quizzically over her spoon. He sighed. "Her husband cannot keep his eyes off you tonight."

Tamsen groaned, passing a basket of cheddar brioche to the stranger beside her. "I know."

The meal was incredible. Tamsen had requested the freshest seasonal vegetables, allowing the chef to procure whatever he thought looked best at market the day before. He chose a crab and corn pudding amuse-bouche. For the salad course, Tamsen requested something with snap, so the chef prepared a butter lettuce salad with crispy prosciutto, tart dried cherries, and a pear vinaigrette. The best part of the salad course, however, was Victor's departure. She made sure to avoid his glances as he left the dining room, glad-handing anyone and everyone on his way out.

Cooking tenderloin for four hundred guests was not an easy trick, but Tamsen thought her filet was perfect, juicy and tender with a sprig of parsley and a dollop of herb butter melted across the top. She sampled a taste of Clay's vegetarian risotto with English peas and mushroom, but only because he insisted. The fact was, she had no appetite. Her nerves were frayed from Jacqueline and then Victor, but with Whit present, Tamsen could concentrate on little else. She existed that night only to catch his eye again and again; she merely endured the in-between.

Paulie and Whit returned to the stage just while the dinner plates were being cleared. As Whit slung his guitar across his body, Tamsen watched John Knox rise from his seat and wheel his mother close to the stage. Edith raised her claw-shaped hand, knobby with arthritis and spotted with age, and motioned to Whit. His face was tranquil as he knelt next to the wheelchair, listening to the old woman speak, then he nodded and returned to his stool.

It took only four notes for Tamsen to recognize the tune. It was "Moon River" from *Breakfast at Tiffany's*. Mrs. Knox swayed, crowing the lyrics like an anthem, but stumbling on the line about two drifters. Paulie joined in with the French horn and Whit began to sing, his voice resonating with velvety depth. The din of chatter yielded to a low hum as Edith Knox warbled the final note, and everyone clapped as Whit and Paulie finished the song.

With outstretched arms, Mrs. Knox signaled Whit to come close. He bent down to shake her hand and she embraced him. Tamsen watched them converse, wondering what the old woman could be saying. Whit gestured to where Tamsen was sitting. Whatever the venerable matriarch told him next caused Whit's face to fall. Tamsen observed them talking for a minute more, and as her wheelchair pulled away, Whit looked at Mrs. Knox intently, his brows bound tightly together. She raised her crippled hand in a stiff farewell and John wrapped her shoulders in a black mink stole.

"Zorro is quite the hit tonight, Tam," Clay said.

"Yes," she answered, noticing the approaching wheelchair.

"Tamsen?" the old woman cawed.

"Are you leaving, Mrs. Knox?" Tamsen asked.

"I have traveled the world: Amsterdam, St. Petersburg, Beijing. I have heard every orchestra from Boston to Vienna, and I never forget a prodigy."

"I'm so glad you were able to join us tonight," Tamsen beamed. She was pleased Mrs. Knox had made a connection with Whit, not because it guaranteed a hefty donation, but because it validated Tamsen's own recognition of Whit's extraordinary ability.

"Enjoy his talent while you have him, dear," she said, clutching Tamsen's hand. "You and I both know he is meant for nobler arenas."

It was a peculiar choice of words. Tamsen looked deep into Edith Knox's cataracted eyes. Behind the drooping creped lids, Tamsen thought she saw a glint of prescience, the kind reserved for the sooth-sayers of Shakespeare's tragedies.

"Thank you for a beautiful evening," John said to her. "You always throw the best parties."

"I appreciate that, John," she answered, stunned that he was aware she had any role. They left, and she turned to Clay.

"Did you?"

"You know Mrs. Knox is my client. John just happened to be sitting there when she asked me who was in charge," Clay said innocently.

"But I'm not chairing," she insisted.

"She didn't ask me who was chairing. She asked who arranged all of this," he said.

When the live auction was announced, Whit and Paulie packed up their equipment and cleared the stage for the auctioneer. Tamsen watched Hilly and Jacqueline, primed with fresh coats of powder and lipstick, make their way to the front. Tamsen knew the routine. The two women would gush about how they were so grateful for all the support, for the large sum they could give to Mothers Trust. There would be a blanket acknowledgement of "everyone who helped make this possible," they would thank their respective husbands, and fake bow to the applause.

Tamsen felt the wad of cash in her pocket. She didn't want to part with the money, but she had to offer the two musicians a little something for their time tonight. She hoped the gala budget would reimburse her for the tips the musicians deserved. She snuck out of the dining room in search of Whit, hoping to intercept him before he headed back into the city. He wasn't anywhere near the entrance or the coat check, nor had the valet seen him leave. Exhausted, Tamsen leaned back against the wall beside the drinking fountain and reached for her phone. She sensed a figure coming around the corner. It was Stephan Cole. He must have followed her out.

"I thought I was the only one who escaped the perfunctory speech," he said, stopping close enough that she could smell his breath mint.

"Looks like we both dodged that bull . . . et," she replied. She almost let something else slip, but she didn't care enough to be that honest with Stephan.

His long arms dangled down his sides and his eager hairy fingers fluttered, tapping below the hem of his jacket. "Tamsen, I'm not sure whether you noticed, but I have been wanting to talk to you all night."

"Is something wrong?" she asked, knowing full well there was not.

"I've heard some news about you and Victor and I want to tell you that I'm sorry about your separation."

Tamsen felt desperate to find Whit. "Don't be sorry," she said. "We're working things out."

"I hope so," he said, wetting his thin lips with his whitish tongue. It occurred to Tamsen that not only did Stephan resemble Abraham Lincoln, but that he also shared the dead president's gawkiness. His attempt to be smooth was almost laughable, far too ridiculous to ever be considered threatening.

He started to lumber toward her just as Whit emerged from the restroom, but before Tamsen could realize what was happening,

Stephan's body was practically touching hers. To make the encounter more confounding, Stephan awkwardly reached to brush a stray eyelash of Tamsen's cheek. Whit froze for a breath, as if not moving would make him invisible, then his eyes shot to the carpet and she felt a whirl of air move as he walked quickly past.

"Whit, wait," Tamsen shouted after him. He ignored her. "How are you getting home—let me arrange a car," she called.

"I'm an adult," he said as he walked out the door. "I'm quite adept at figuring things out for myself."

Tamsen stood there, dazed. Stephan cleared the phlegm from his throat, searching Tamsen's face for a reciprocal scrap of admiration. Jacqueline's voice rose over the applause in the background, telling the crowd how much she loved each and every one of them. Tamsen wanted to chase after Whit and assure him that Stephan's advance was uninvited. Was it even possible that he felt jealous? Maybe Whit just wanted to flee the strange world of privilege she inhabited; it was more likely he just felt embarrassed to walk in on what he thought was an intimate moment. Tamsen needed to explain. Even if he didn't care, she did. When he showed up for Theo's lesson, she could clear things up. She would attempt to defend herself—and she hoped, she prayed, he would believe her.

CHAPTER

8

It had been eight days and Tamsen had not seen Whit. She sat on the chenille pink rug in Charlotte's room, flanked by piles of girl clothes. There was a mound of garments for the Salvation Army, and another containing stained and damaged clothes for the trash. The closet doors were open wide, revealing hangers of beautiful apparel Tamsen had curated for weekdays, Sunday school, summer afternoons, snowy days, and play dates. Cubbies of shoes and sandals, ranging from well-worn to barely-seen-pavement, begged to be purged to make room for her daughter's next generation of larger, more mature footwear.

She turned over a pair of Prada ballet flats to inspect them for size. A sticker was still adhered to the sole: $280 with a red slash mark and a secondary price of $140. What had she been thinking? Prada made impeccable things, but for Charlotte? These days, Tamsen regretted any spending spree, wishing instead she'd started saving money sooner. Perhaps the consignment place would accept girl's clothes, or what if she started a store on eBay? Charlotte had talked about doing that for her Dolls Like Me collection.

Stacked beside Tamsen were several carefully folded mounds, two years' worth of folded heirloom-quality items, including three

Portuguese cotton pin-tuck dresses, and a soft knit poncho Astrid had given Charlotte for her birthday two years ago. These were destined for a keepsake bin, one that Tamsen had steadily been filling since Charlotte was a baby. It was bittersweet—the years of dressing Charlotte in sweet little girl outfits were part of the past; her tween had turned an inevitable corner and now preferred stretch pants to skirts and comfy tunics to sweater sets.

With the Harvest Moon Ball behind her, Tamsen had hours of empty time every week. She needed to stay in motion, to channel her anxiety and distract herself from the stress that roiled her consciousness. She was still searching for a sign, some signal from the cosmos that leaving her marriage was the right action to take. Or not. Closets, bathroom cabinets, the garage—she attacked everything and anything in an effort to drag herself out of the irresolution crevasse that split her life into two sides—stay or go.

Tamsen switched on Charlotte's Bluetooth speaker and searched her music app for something that would move her. Dvořák, "Cello Concerto in B minor" popped up at the top of the list. She checked her notifications. Still nothing from Whit. He had canceled his lesson with Theo the week before, saying something had come up. With Thanksgiving around the corner, she worried it would be December before she could finally see him and clear up the incident with Stephan. She wanted him to know her for the person she was, not to be perceived as the type of woman who was enjoying stolen moments with another woman's husband. And, of course, there was Theo. Since starting lessons with Whit, he'd seemed happier and more self-confident. He barely set down his Martin, practicing guitar every day—alluding to the talent show at Dexter he and Whit and been working toward.

She argued with herself about whether to text Whit, for her own sake and for Theo's. There was really no harm in reaching out. They'd shared Halloween falafel. They were friends, after all.

The last time I saw you I was fighting off an unsolicited advance. Time for therapeutic tea and/or guitar lesson before Tgiving?

She hit enter and waited, hoping for the immediate gratification of three dots. She stared at the screen another minute before resuming the tedious chore of sorting.

The heat kicked on and the warm draft from the overhead vent stirred the tissue feathers of Charlotte's dreamcatcher. Suspended from the ceiling, the gossamer papers spun around and around over themselves in monotonous loops while Tamsen shook the creases from a yellow rain slicker she had bought when Charlotte was eight. She reached into the pocket and found a wilted note Victor must have put in Charlotte's lunchbox two years before. She opened it, ignoring the twinge of hesitation that fluttered in her chest. "My sweet Char," he wrote. "Know that as you read this I am thinking of you. You are a star. Love, your favorite Daddy." If he weren't a good father, it would make things so much easier.

The doorbell rang, startling Tamsen. She extracted herself from the mess on the floor and jogged to the security camera. The camera feed showed a mass of craft paper, obviously cloaking an immense floral arrangement, and a pair of legs. Tamsen smiled and her heart felt light. Whit. She'd summoned him with her thoughts. She quickly dotted her lips with Charlotte's sheer lip balm and fluffed her hair with her fingers before she opened the door. The figure turned to profile. Her mouth went dry. It was Victor.

"Toscanini roses for Tamsen Kinney Peel," he quipped, a whirl of early lake effect snow encircling his feet.

She shivered. The same roses that she had selected for her bridal bouquet. Cautionary yellow lights blinked in her subconscious. Do not get caught alone in the house with Victor.

"Looks like an entire rosebush."

"You gonna make me stand out here in the blizzard?" he asked.

The warning lights turned red. "I'm cleaning out closets," she said, shifting from one leg to the other.

Victor elbowed the door, pushing it open so he could pass. He crossed the threshold and set the arrangement on the foyer credenza. "I wanted to do this right, ask you out on a proper date," he said.

Now the red lights screamed. She zipped her hoodie up to her chin. With no one else in the house, Victor would suggest an afternoon romp, make-up sex. She wiped her lip balm off on the back of her hand.

"I called in a favor and got us a table at Linear Saturday night."

Tamsen agonized at the prospect. A twelve-course, four-hour degustation menu with emulsified foie gras, carrot-granita palate cleansers, and disgusting scallop-infused espuma.

"I'm with the kids," she said.

"I talked to Aneta," he replied. "Jesus, Tamsen, it's freezing," he said. He put his palm on the door and slammed it closed.

She looked around the foyer, which was now as cold as a meat locker. She was alone with Victor for the first time since January 1st, and this afternoon not even her children were in the house to act as a mitigating presence.

"No," Tamsen said, her voice shaking. She didn't even think about it, the word just tumbled out.

Tamsen's windpipe pinched in her throat. She labored for air, wanting to flee. She tried to calm herself, but the fuse was lit.

"No?" Victor repeated.

Tamsen's heart pounded. "I told them we'd go bowling," she lied. "The book says not to change plans last minute." Something was happening to her—she was having a vision of the bedroom bookcase. It was like a dream, but not. She was overtired. She pinched the bridge of her nose.

Victor's eyes narrowed into slits. "How convenient," he said. "Then let's go out on Sunday night, or Monday, how about Tuesday?"

Tamsen gripped the door handle. It was cold to the touch. She was being irrational, she could at least pacify him with dinner.

"I'll check," she managed, inhaling. The bookcase disappeared.

"What kind of game are you playing?" he lashed. She watched the menacing signs emerge: mouth tight, eyes narrow, jaw tightened. The punishing mask he wore was at full potency.

"Is there ever going to be a time?" he demanded.

"There's just so much going on with the holidays," she muttered, crossing her arms. "I want to give the kids my full attention."

Victor sucked air from the back of his throat and it sounded like the ocean. Tamsen watched his lower ribs expand, and as he expelled the breath he ticked his head to the side, cracking his neck with a dreadful smirk.

Tamsen jerked as her phone began to vibrate, the chorus of "Bohemian Rhapsody" blaring from the pocket of her hoodie. It was Petra's ringtone. She must be calling from the UK. In this moment, Queen sounded like a choir of angels.

"Petra got promoted," Tamsen blurted, disclosing to Victor the early announcement she had gotten via text the day before. She could see her hands visibly shaking when she pulled out her phone to answer it on speaker, so her rescuer would be with them both in the echoing space.

"Congratulations, hotshot," Tamsen said, her voice trembling. "I have Victor here."

"When are we going to work together, Petra?" Victor said into the phone. He stepped back and glared at Tamsen.

"I'm on my way to Heathrow, you guys. I have a meeting in Chicago."

"I'll clear my calendar," Victor said. She could feel his scowl locked on her.

"Not this time, love, but I do owe your wife dinner," Petra laughed. "We made a bet about my career trajectory and she won."

"She is a clever one," Victor said.

Tamsen needed to keep Petra on the phone as long as possible. Maybe Victor would grow tired of their typical discussion topics, revolving around new women's fiction, art exhibitions, and their favorite romantic comedies. Victor gestured with his arms, a sign for Tamsen to talk him up.

"Now that you're in charge maybe you can work on product placement in some big films," Tamsen suggested.

"For sure—and then we'll walk the red carpet together for Ms Majestic!" Petra mused. Victor was not smiling.

"Summers & Peel negotiates product placement all the time. It's only one of our many services," he interjected.

"Anyway, I have to make another call. Tam, I'll text you when I land."

They hung up. Victor took a step toward the door and Tamsen immediately opened it, relieved to have earth, air, and sun in the space with them. He turned to her as he stepped out. "Get me a meeting with her. It's the least you can do."

Despite the responsibilities of her new position, Petra looked fresh and energized. Her ebony skin had not aged since the women were undergraduates. Only a couple of gray hairs betrayed her age—Petra could still beat most teenagers to the finish line in a triathlon. The best friends sat at their favorite intimate city bar, Bardot. They silenced their cell phones and banished them to their designer handbags, minimizing distractions for their cherished girl time. The acoustics of the silver- and white-flocked wallpaper and plush velvet drapes dampened their voices to a mere murmur.

"How is Erich?" Tamsen asked. Petra had sent Tamsen a selfie from a London hospital after Erich's hip replacement three weeks ago.

"Erich is a pain in the arse," Petra replied endearingly. "I swear that man is milking this surgery for everything it's worth. He hasn't left the house in ten days."

"Doesn't he need physical therapy?" Tamsen asked.

"The PT makes house calls and Erich has the kinetic exercise machine set up in the family room, so he can watch football while he's rehabbing."

Tamsen laughed. "He's a sportscaster, Pet, he needs to stay in the game."

"He's in the game all right—his eyes on the television and his fist in a bowl of crisps. What about Victor? Has he flown a million miles this year?"

The mention of flight miles reminded Tamsen of her airline points. She had emailed through the airline's website, but the automated response had not made good on its promise to get back to her. She made a mental note to hound them again tomorrow. She would sleep so much better when those miles were secured as part of her Fountain Fund. The miles were the cornerstone of her portfolio.

"He's okay," Tamsen said, drawing in a breath. It was time. Victor didn't want her sharing their secrets, but she had to confide in Petra. "Victor and I are separated," she managed, washing the words down with a swig of Grey Goose.

"What?" Petra said, her jaw slacking in complete disbelief. She reached out and grabbed Tamsen by the arm.

"I'm sorry that I didn't say anything in London," Tamsen said.

"How long?" Petra asked.

"Months," Tamsen confessed.

"Why didn't you tell me?" Petra asked.

Tamsen noticed Petra's gold lioness brooch; it reminded her of the ones Madeleine Albright always wore. "You're running a billion-dollar business. I didn't want to burden you with my nonsense."

"This from the woman who interrupted my board meeting when George Michael died." The bartender discreetly plucked up their empty martini glasses. "We'll each have another," Petra said. "Pour heavy."

"My pleasure, Dr. Robbins," he replied, with a slight bow.

Petra searched Tamsen's face for more. "Talk to me, Tam," she said.

Tamsen fought to contain her rising despair. "Why does this feel like a confession?" she said.

"I'm not here to judge," Petra returned.

"I try to do everything he asks, but I still keep messing up."

"Did you have an affair?"

Tamsen shook her head and laughed lightly. "It's nothing like that." She paused, wanting to use the word Fariah used for Victor, but Tamsen was still unconvinced of its accuracy.

"With Victor, everything can be going along fine, until all of a sudden, it's not. He just gets angry with me for insignificant things and then he forces me apologize. 'Say you're sorry, Tamsen. Say it—say it!'"

Tamsen's hands were shaking and she shifted on the barstool, trying to find a comfortable posture. Petra slid her drink aside and gathered Tamsen's hands between her palms. "For what are you apologizing?"

"I don't even know half the time; I just say it, so he'll stop . . ."

A seldom-seen deep vertical line appeared between Petra's eyebrows. "Stop what?"

Tamsen didn't even know how to finish the sentence. Shutting me out? Saying horrible things? Calling me a whore? She thought of the adage her brothers used to recite, "Sticks and stones may break my bones but names will never hurt me."

"Victor has a vicious streak," Tamsen confessed.

"Is he violent with you?" Petra asked.

"With words. And silence."

"What can I do for you? You must be so overwhelmed."

"No one would ever believe it. Everyone loves Victor. Victor is the best dad, he's handsome, he's funny, he's the smartest guy at the firm. No one could imagine someone so wonderful could be so cruel. Yet, here I am." She held out her arms. "Beaten without scratches, or bruises, or any evidence at all. Sometimes I wish he'd hit me because then at least I'd have something to show for it."

"You need to have something to show for his psychological abuse? Then you'd be able to rationalize leaving him? His robbing you of your dignity isn't enough?" Petra asked.

"My kids, Pet," Tamsen beseeched. "And where would we go? What would I do to take care of them?" The bartender dropped the top of a martini shaker into his small sink with a clang. "No man is perfect. Except Erich."

Petra sighed. "Do you know the story of the frog and boiling water?" she asked.

"No," Tamsen answered.

"When you put a frog in a pot of boiling water, it will jump out, straight away. But if you put the frog in a pot of tepid water, and slowly raise the temperature, the frog will acclimate and remain until it boils to death."

"You think I'm the frog?" Tamsen asked.

"You're a good mother, Tam, and when you're happy, those kids feel strong and they feel safe. Doing right by yourself is doing right by Theo and Charlotte."

Dread circulated in her veins at the thought of leaving Victor— Tamsen pulled her wool coat off the back of the barstool and covered her shoulders. "I just don't know what he'd do if I ended it."

"Look at me," Petra said. "You have nothing to be ashamed of. You are not the one with the problem. Victor is."

"That's what my therapist says."

"Thank God you are seeing a therapist. I hope it's a woman."

"It is."

Tamsen's head hung. The conversation had depleted her. Petra opened her handbag and pulled out her phone.

"You're violating our no screens pact," said Tamsen, reaching for her own device.

"I'm sorry," Petra said. "There's a huge deal happening, and I need to make sure I don't miss anything critical."

"Can you tell me about it?" Tamsen asked, reaching for her own phone to check notifications.

"Let's just say, if it happens, your husband is going to soil his knickers."

Tamsen looked at her texts and her heart jumped—Whit had replied. *In Boston. Let's hang after TG.*

The dark ether that loomed over her conversation with Petra evaporated. Tamsen tore into the bread basket, heaping a generous smear of salted butter across a lavash cracker.

"Do you have any money set aside?" Petra asked.

"Almost thirty-five hundred dollars," Tamsen said, counting the gift cards in the total.

Petra shot her a look. "Seriously? I spend that on groceries for a dinner party. What about a solicitor? A lawyer?"

"I'm not ready for that," replied Tamsen.

"If you leave a man like Victor, he will not be kind. The man knows more about financial loopholes than most of this country's politicians, and that stunt he pulled when he bought the California agency and then dumped everyone except the production department—he's heartless." Petra leaned in. "Promise me you'll speak to an attorney."

Tamsen thought of Oliver Putnum. "Yes," she said.

"Are you getting out? Dates? Reckless Christmas parties?"

Tamsen huffed, "I haven't been invited to one holiday party—Victor is the one with the money, so he's still on everyone's list."

"Well, it's awful but I understand why," she said.

"I'm that much of a pariah since we're separated?" Tamsen asked.

"You're a threat."

"A woman who's made no money of her own in years, has no career, and whose marriage is dissolving. Look out, everybody, Tamsen's on the loose!"

"You are a smart, creative woman," Petra said. "Remember when you resigned from Beau Monde? They would have done anything to keep you."

Tamsen winced with a pang of regret. Abandoning her career was a mistake; when she turned in her keycard to human resources over a decade ago, she also handed Victor the only power she ever felt she had.

"I could never have worked, Pet—Theo needed me." In her head, Tamsen pictured the neurology department waiting room at Children's Hospital, and the collection of books and *Highlights* magazines she and Theo had read and reread a thousand times. It had been 322 days since Theo's last seizure and being jobless was worth every single one of them.

"Do yourself a favor—check out your options. You could get back into the workforce, you know." Petra took the last swallow of her martini.

"Easy for you to say, you're fearless."

Petra tossed back her head and laughed. "Don't be fooled, my friend, I am terrified every single day, and thank God, because if I weren't afraid, I'd be complacent."

"I've been out of the game too long," Tamsen said.

"I understand how you feel, but the only true antidote to fear is courage. It's not because I don't have fear that I am successful, it's because I act despite it. I am fearful, but I am braveful."

Tamsen bunched her nose. "I'm pretty sure braveful isn't a word." Tamsen lifted her glass for a sip, but it was empty. She stared at the bottom and they both burst out laughing.

Tamsen's brain was awash in vodka. While Petra texted her driver, Tamsen imagined herself between the sheets with Whit, feeling shielded in the envelope of his body, safe for just a while from Victor's tyranny and the oppressive burden of her dilemma. She wondered whether she was worthy of that much comfort.

At midnight, beneath an awning that flapped in the merciless Chicago wind, the best friends waited for their cars. Petra pulled Tamsen into a tight embrace as a huge black SUV with tinted rear windows pulled into the valet lane. The winter air was soberingly crisp, and the tinsel snowflakes that hung from each lamppost twirled furiously.

"You know I think you can help yourself," Petra said. "But if you need anything at all, there is nothing I wouldn't do for you."

Tamsen kissed her cheeks the way Europeans do. "Thanks for listening."

"Always," Petra whispered, and then she climbed into the waiting car. Tamsen watched it round the corner onto Michigan Avenue, frosty exhaust evaporating behind as it disappeared. She laughed out loud thinking that, in some alternate universe, that might have been her.

Theo's aquarium gurgled, and the tank light cast a luminous glow across his rocket-ships-and-planets duvet. The home visit with Roscoe the snake accomplished very little aside from stinking up Theo's room and further whetting his appetite for a pet. Tamsen agreed he could have fish, as long as he kept the tank clean and fed the happy creatures as prescribed. He had yet to clean the gravel or scrape the sides of the fish tank.

Tamsen knelt beside his bed as he slept, snoring softly. He was a boy now, but she could still see in him the face of the defenseless infant she brought home prematurely and cradled protectively at late-night feedings. She recalled how he would doze in her arms, his expressions shifting from grimace to smile, his tiny lips puckering and then relaxing in a ritual sequence before he fell into a deep contented sleep. She grazed his forehead with a kiss and he snuggled deeper into his downy nest.

Tamsen expected Charlotte to be up. Lately, it was rare for her daughter to fall asleep without a parent in the house, and since the separation, the faithful Aneta ceased to be an adequate substitute.

"Hi, Mom," Charlotte said as Tamsen entered with a mug of tepid chamomile tea. "Is that for me?"

"Yep," replied Tamsen. "And I brought you a shortbread cookie, too."

"Ugh," she said, putting her hands on her stomach. "No more food. Dad got this thing called a kringle at the Hollydaze Festival and I couldn't stop eating it, it was so good."

Tamsen laughed, "I love kringle—it's a Danish pastry."

"Theo said it looked like a toilet seat," she replied.

"Did you have a good time tonight?" Tamsen asked.

"It was super crowded." Charlotte took a sip of the tea.

"I'm sure," agreed Tamsen. "Did you ice skate?"

"Dad said the line was too long, but he got us a quick pass for Santa's Snow Castle."

"Is that a roller coaster, like the Matterhorn?"

"It was sort of a haunted house, but Christmas themed."

"Sounds cool," Tamsen said. "But not very scary."

Charlotte pulled lint from her blanket and then rolled it into a tiny ball. She shifted back and forth under her covers, diverting her attention to the ceiling while pulling the sheets up under her nose the way she did the time she was caught shredding her pop-up books with a pair of nail scissors.

"Mom," she said, her blue eyes wide and her long lashes skyward. "Something happened in the Santa Castle."

A release of panic chemicals ripped through Tamsen's body. She sat on the edge of the bed and forced a steady voice.

"What happened, sweetheart?" she managed, smoothing Charlotte's silky hair.

"One of the elves called me a bad name."

"In the Santa Castle?" Tamsen asked.

"Yeah."

"A boy elf?"

"He was older, like, high school or college maybe," Charlotte answered.

"What did he call you?" Charlotte's mouth was still concealed. Tamsen gave her time.

"I can't say the word."

"You can tell me, honey." Tamsen was reminded of the separation book, which encouraged parents to simply listen without judgment.

"An ugly . . ." Charlotte paused, ". . . starts with an S."

Tamsen's mind was a search engine. "A snot?"

Charlotte's eyes were glassy and Tamsen recognized the expression as one of her own. The innocent girl blinked, and tears of shame spilled down her temples. "He called me an ugly slut."

Tamsen clenched her fists and counted to three, blood pounding in her head. She reached down and held her daughter. "Baby," she said, rocking her now. "I know it feels terrible, but you need to know you did nothing to deserve that. That word is disgusting, and that young man was inappropriate. He should lose his job."

"Daddy said sometimes boys call you a name because they really like you," Charlotte sniffled.

It was everything Tamsen could do not to curse. She dug her fingernails deep into her palms. "I'm glad you told him what happened, sweetheart. What else did Daddy do?"

Tamsen braced herself for the answer.

On the ninth time she called his cell phone, Victor finally picked up. In the background, Tamsen could hear animated conversations and the raucous laughter of inebriated men and women. She figured Victor was trolling the swanky singles hangout, Sabre Lounge, probably trying to close the deal with a strumpet who was impressed when he pulled up in his fancy ride.

"Everything okay? I'm in the middle of something," he said, annoyed. Surely, she had torn him from a scintillating discussion on Kant's critique of pure reason or Fermi's theory of beta decay.

"I'm calling about the elf," Tamsen said pointedly.

"I can't really talk right now," he replied.

"An elf at Hollydaze Festival called our daughter an ugly slut."

Tamsen could hear Victor's hand muffle the mic as he spoke to his floozy du jour.

"Did you file a report?" she asked in a loud, enunciated staccato.

"There were literally a hundred elves in that castle," Victor said. "They were all dressed the same, pointy hats and wigs, and they had makeup on."

"But she told you what happened, right? You knew she was upset," Tamsen insisted.

"I talked to her about it."

"When a boy calls a girl a slut it means he likes her?" Tamsen said.

"I was trying to make her feel better. Defuse things. If I knew which guy called her that, I would have killed him."

"You didn't need to murder anyone, Victor. What you did need to do was show your daughter that men are not allowed to speak to her that way. Have you filed an incident report, or should I?" Tamsen asked.

She wanted to reach through the phone and choke him. The trouble was, of all people, Victor didn't get it—he would never get it. "Charlotte needs to know she has done nothing to deserve this kind of verbal assault."

"I agree completely," he said.

Rage swelled in her chest. "You agree?" Hypocrite, she thought. "Then show her by doing something the fuck about it."

Tamsen hung up on him.

Hollydaze Fest was a tradition for Victor and the kids. The 170,000-square-foot indoor carnival boasted mini-golf, giant slides, and a holiday carousel sponsored by The Hinton Family Trust. Tamsen knew Cybill was on the North Pier Guild and they were friendly enough for Tamsen to reach out; at least Cybill could connect Tamsen to the person in charge of the Santa Castle.

The last time she'd seen the spiral-bound WSC directory it was near the computer off the kitchen. Tamsen rifled through the surrounding drawers but came up empty-handed. The book had to be in Victor's home office, a space he often kept secured so that the kids wouldn't play inside when he was away. She always used a mini-screwdriver to pop the lock, so she grabbed one from the junk drawer and stormed to the third level. The screwdriver slipped in easily and Tamsen felt a huge relief with the click of the release, but when she pushed against the door, it wouldn't budge. She stopped cold. Above the handle was a new fixture. Victor had installed a deadbolt.

CHAPTER

9

Victor's office had never been off-limits to Tamsen; she was in and out of there at least twice a week, and he knew she needed access to the kids' immunization records and birth certificates, not to mention all the supplies that the office housed: printer paper, ink, pens, and pencils. Maybe she'd damaged the lock's inner machinations by using the mini-screwdriver, forcing Victor to add a different method to secure the space. She jangled the knob and stared at the newly-drilled deadbolt. An unfamiliar sort of fear welled in her chest. Behind the office door were all the bank statements, files of financial documents, records he kept for insurance purposes, and any legal document they had signed since their wedding. Something besides the lock had changed—Victor was onto her.

Tamsen felt the prick of paranoia at the back of her neck. Had he finally recognized her ambivalence, realized there was a possibility they would not work things out, not reconcile? Victor worked like a light switch—on or off. With him, a person was in or out. Once out, a person became an enemy, and Victor would begin his advance. He would protect the thing he loved almost as much as their children: his money.

It was late and the house was dark, and even though she had a precise mental ledger that told her the exact balance of The Fountain Fund, she needed to check on the money the way new parents hover over the bassinet to make sure their sleeping infant is really breathing.

Tamsen tiptoed into the freezing night, sensing the grit of the heated bluestone pavers beneath her bare feet. She carefully dislodged the fountain's copper trough and fished out the gallon Ziploc Freezer Bag, heavy with months of steady fortification. The tiny colored Christmas lights that hung from the eaves of the mansion next door switched off. Tamsen stiffened. The lights were on a timer, she thought. Even if they weren't, the neighbors couldn't see into her garden. Still, she should probably consider a new hiding place—a safe deposit box, like Clay had suggested, or a bank account even—one she could open without Victor's knowledge.

When Tamsen worked for Beau Monde, holiday time brought the promise of an annual Christmas bonus. The checks would be handed out after lunch on a Friday in early December, and everyone would drop what they were doing and head for the bar at The Peninsula to celebrate. That feeling of accomplishment, of reward, was a thing of her past. But here in the glow of the Christmas tree lights, Tamsen felt for the briefest moment, even though she'd scavenged and scrounged for every cent, that she was the beneficiary of a hard-earned dividend.

She looked up from her treasure laid out on the table and saw the stockings dangling from the garland-adorned mantle. Charlotte had helped Tamsen tack up every beautiful holiday card they'd received since Thanksgiving, each one of the unique tidings placed in a frame around the marble fireplace surround. Tamsen stared at the images of family friends in coordinated outfits, their staged candids depicting open-mouthed laughter and perfectly-coiffed hair. Some of the photo cards had been professionally shot in black and white—portraits of sweet children with their faithful pets, biding Christmas cheer, good health, and prosperity. The popular greeting card picture this season was definitely the ubiquitous synchronized family jump, where everyone leapt with elation while the camera captured them suspended in midair.

Tamsen recalled the Peel Christmas card from last December. Victor had set up his tripod and a timer so the four of them could pose in front of their thirteen-foot tree. They must have spent an hour trying to nail the perfect shot, one in which Theo wasn't making a funny face or Tamsen's eyes weren't shut. There would be no holiday card this year. Tamsen just couldn't muster the energy to pretend all was merry and bright.

She inhaled the faint scent of cut Douglas fir wafting from the tree, its limbs sagging with the weight of mercury glass ornaments and strings of popcorn and cranberries. She surveyed her store of money—her Christmas bonus. Victor was mounting his offense, but Tamsen's Fountain Fund was growing by the day: thirteen $100 bills, twenty-three fifties, forty-eight twenties, twenty-nine tens, fourteen fives, and $3,475 in gift cards.

Tamsen stood in the small library at the Talisman. It was more of a glorified business center, with its 1994 fax machine and a dusty computer monitor. She replaced a volume of Longfellow poems she'd snatched from the hotel's paltry collection of paperback books. Aside from *The Count of Monte Cristo*, she still hadn't picked up a piece of fiction that was longer than an *Us Weekly* article, but poetry was bite-size and she could still manage to make it through several stanzas without being derailed by sadness. Poetry knew heartache; poetry could sympathize.

Tamsen noticed Nicole across the lobby.

"You've graduated," Tamsen remarked to the woman, who no longer wore the stigmatic trainee badge on her nametag. "Congratulations."

"I qualify for a free Christmas honey ham," Nicole said. "Which is great because I don't cook."

Ron had delegated to Nicole the unenviable job of slop mopper; she was stationed near the revolving door to wipe the floor of filthy slush as holiday sale chasers tromped in and out of the lobby with bulging shopping bags. It was the Festival of Lights weekend and The Talisman was buzzing with suburban celebrants in parkas who migrated into the city for sales and for the eternal line to sit in the lap of Macy's Santa Claus. The Macy's Santa had a real beard and a legitimate beer belly, giving him a leg up on the imposters in neighboring State Street department stores.

Tamsen watched Nicole sling the mop back and forth across the terrazzo entry. Nicole's taut arms protruded from the short sleeves of her uniform, arms that would have been the envy of the Socialati, who tirelessly pursued deltoids sculpted like perfect teardrops. Tamsen thought of Nicole's chipped nail polish and home dye job, similar to traits Tamsen had borne in her twenties until Beau Monde allowed her to splurge on her appearance.

"Do you live in the city, Nicole?" Tamsen asked.

"I moved back to the West Side so I could be closer to my sister," Nicole said. "She's going to watch my kids over break, so I'm hoping Ron will give me some extra hours."

"How many children do you have?"

"Three girls," Nicole said, her cheeks forming two small apples as she grinned, "eight, nine, and eleven."

Ron wobbled to where Nicole was cleaning. His tie was the only thing that made him look managerial; otherwise Tamsen imagined him on a threadbare sofa watching porn on VHS, his wire frame eyeglasses sliding down his sweaty nose.

"Break time, Nikki," Ron said, looking down at his gold-plated Timex. "Take thirty."

"Okay, I'll check the restrooms first," Nicole replied.

"Nah," Ron said. "I'll get one of my girls in housekeeping to do that." His chubby fingers plucked a candy cane from the lobby Christmas tree. Nicole's potential was completely lost on Ron. What a waste, Tamsen thought.

A chirp sounded from deep in her handbag and Tamsen fished out her iPhone. Whit.

Holiday thing at Garfield Park Conservatory Tuesday—interested?

Tamsen didn't expect the overture, so she attributed her instant nervousness to surprise, but the truth was she had been hoping Whit would reach out for days.

She was on the conservatory's mailing list and knew it was kicking off its holiday flower show early in the week. Ordinarily, Tamsen wouldn't have gone out of her way to see the exhibit, but now it was on the top of her to-do list. She thought of how to respond to Whit's message—not too zealous, but with tempered eagerness.

Yes!

Tamsen's hotel room smelled of fresh grapefruit, a successful result of the oil infuser Tamsen had stationed by the phone on her nightstand, beside an eight-by-ten frame of Theo and Charlotte petting a goat at the children's zoo. With a shot of fresh optimism born of Whit's text, Tamsen punched the speaker button on the landline and dialed the 800 number for the airline customer service desk.

After the requisite call center gymnastics, a pleasant-sounding woman who said her name was Constance asked Tamsen how she could help.

"My miles were misdirected into my husband's account," Tamsen explained, detecting the rapid tapping of computer keys in the background.

"Yes," the woman replied. "I can see the history here and it appears you have not yet submitted the required affidavit to initiate further action."

"You really must be kidding," she fumed. The hotel felt sweltering and Tamsen stormed to the thermostat to shut it off.

"There's nothing we can do until we have the affidavit and also a death certificate," the woman said.

"Could you please put a supervisor on?"

"I am the Zenith level supervisor."

Tamsen rested her forehead in her palm. "Why didn't the last person I spoke to, or the person before that, or the chat android you guys have working for you, tell me about these documents months ago?" She paced the room. "We're not talking about a one-way ticket to Detroit, we are talking about a huge number of miles here—675,000 miles, enough to fly me and my kids around the world three times."

"I understand that, but unless we have the proper documentation in hand, we are unable to process your request."

"You don't understand. This is my inheritance—the one thing my father left for me."

"I'm sorry, ma'am, but this is the protocol. Would you like me to provide the web address where you can find the affidavit? I can email it or fax it if you'd like."

"Yes. Yes to it all." Tamsen pulled the desk drawer open and it roared. She pulled out a green pen with words *The Talisman* written in gold. "Just, please, one last time, tell me EXACTLY what it is that I need to do here. And then I want your name, your full name."

"Of course," the woman said.

Fariah Valentine's waiting room had all the best magazines—the ones Tamsen could never bring home without Victor's scorn. He told her she had an "appetite for trash" the time she picked up a celebrity magazine from the hospital gift shop when Theo was undergoing tests. Now she voraciously leafed the pages of a glossy entertainment magazine, skipping past a blurb about how the stars lose weight before awards shows and a human interest story regarding a man who'd claimed to have bred a red-nosed reindeer. The headline in the centerfold caught Tamsen's attention: *Leda Sparrow: Putting the Over the Hill Back on Top*. She had to read on. The article chronicled the astounding success stories of women who had been inspired by Sparrow at her Flight to Financial Freedom seminars. Women who'd stayed home to raise their kids. Women making seven figures after being out of the workforce for years. Momtrepreneurs. Sparrow's workshops popped up in the margin on Facebook and Tamsen had occasionally seen her billboards on the expressway. Sparrow's message to women, Hilly had once joked, was an opiate for washed-up, middle-class simpletons. Tamsen quickly tore out the article, replacing the magazine on the expensive coffee table before Fariah summoned her in for another pointless round of therapeutic Q&A.

"I just want my children to be okay and I want Victor to quit being so nasty to me," Tamsen repeated for the twelfth time. The truth was, Tamsen was aggravated with Fariah Valentine. For what this woman was charging, Tamsen expected results.

Fariah rose from the wingback chair, tugged down her clingy, rayon dress, and sauntered in her bedazzled Balenciaga ankle boots to her desk. She opened the small bone inlay wooden box that sat atop Don Miguel Ruiz's book *The Four Agreements* and a copy of Tolle's *The Power of*

Now. She handed Tamsen a refrigerator magnet with a photo of Albert Einstein and the words: "Insanity: doing the same thing over and over and expecting different results."

"You say you want a different outcome—so, do you intend to change or do you expect the abuser to change?" Fariah asked.

"I think we've established that I'm not doing anything wrong," Tamsen snapped.

"You're not doing anything wrong," the therapist said gently. "But that doesn't mean you wouldn't benefit from change. Yet we continue to talk about Victor. Why? Why does he behave this way? Why does he treat you the way he does?"

"You're the one who said he hated women," Tamsen shot back.

Fariah had a way of curling only her lips while the upper half of her face remained perfectly expressionless, except for widening her eyes. It was a look that reminded Tamsen of the ventriloquist puppet her mother had picked up for her at a garage sale when she was nine years old.

Fariah's voice was level. "I'm feeling some anger toward me," she said.

"Look," Tamsen replied, digging her fingers into the arm of the sofa. "I need to know how to manage Victor. I can't let my kids grow up in a home without a father. It will compromise their healthy development. How are they supposed to navigate romantic relationships when they don't have two parents under the same roof as role models?"

"The children might do what we all do until some kind of intervention occurs—seek relationships that are familiar, relationships that are reflective of experiences we witness in childhood," Fariah said evenly.

"So, now what? We dissect my formative years and analyze my relationship with my father? I get to relive all the dysfunction of my hopscotch and bedwetting days, just to end up at square one?" Tamsen demanded.

"Is that what you'd like to do?" the therapist replied.

"I don't have time for that," Tamsen insisted. "We're at critical point, here, something needs to change." The image of Victor's dead-bolted office door flashed in her mind.

"Why would Victor change?" Fariah asked.

Tamsen sat, pulling a fuzz ball from the chunky blanket that hung over the back cushion.

The therapist inhaled deeply. "Tamsen, have you ever heard the term codependent?"

"Of course." She had heard about the spouses of alcoholics being codependent when they enable their partner's drinking.

"It's at play here, in your marriage."

"How?" Tamsen asked.

"The abuser's profound insecurity, his need to assert dominance, is met by your need for his attention, for communication with him, for his affection," Fariah explained. "It's a power-control dynamic."

"He's very controlling, it's true. But I wouldn't call Victor insecure."

"If your husband were secure, would he treat you this way?"

"No," Tamsen answered.

"And if you were secure, would you tolerate it?" Fariah asked.

"No."

"Do you see how Victor establishes dominance over you, and how you submit?" Fariah asked.

Tamsen felt like a whimpering dog groveling for even the slightest pat on the head when Victor ignored her. She had never thought of it as domination, but she could see it now, albeit vaguely. "So, how do I fix this? Because love certainly isn't enough," Tamsen asked.

"You want to fix Victor."

"Yes!" Tamsen's hands flew into the air. "Him—the situation."

"I can feel your struggle about leaving or continuing this relationship,"

Fariah said. "But you're trying to control the uncontrollable. Is Victor willing to take responsibility for his part?"

"We've discussed that my husband blames his behavior on me," Tamsen insisted, as if Fariah were unaware. "According to him, it's what I do that causes him to act the way he does."

"What do you tell yourself that you did?" Fariah asked. Tamsen seethed. How many times were they going to go over this? It felt as if she were gunning the engine of a car stuck in shit quicksand, while her therapist, in spikey heels and a push-up bra, tried to rock the vehicle out of its deepening trench. "What have you done, Tamsen?" the therapist repeated.

Tamsen raised the fringed bolster pillow beside her and slammed it down. Her therapist was no longer someone with whom Tamsen would want to have a drink.

"Nice expression of emotion," Fariah said.

Tamsen released the pillow, stretching her hand and coiling her fingers in the strap of her handbag. She was silent and Fariah was still, not even blinking when Tamsen finally met her gaze.

"What I did is, I chose Victor," Tamsen said. She could feel the veins in her neck bulging and her voice amplified. "I picked him. I walked down the aisle with someone I thought was my soul mate. I chose him. Then he turned into a monster and every day I am still there, married, choosing this. Every day we are together—again and again and again."

Tamsen felt something dislodge. Her own words resonated—there was logic in this realization and she felt as if a tire had caught hold and her vehicle had begun to advance from the sloppy rut.

"You chose to marry him, and you choose to stay in the relationship," Fariah said.

The thought suddenly seemed novel. "I tolerate it. I allow it."

Now Fariah smiled with her full face. "Why does Victor want to control you, Tamsen?"

"So that I won't leave."

Tamsen applied a swipe of hibiscus lip tint in her rear-view mirror. She looked out her window at the giant greenhouse off the parking lot. Garfield Park Conservatory: almost two acres of indoor landscaping. She scanned the rack for Edmond Dantès, but he wasn't there. Just a few snow-covered bikes that must have been left behind the day before. Maybe she should have offered Whit a lift. No, it was better that they meet here. She didn't want to make him feel like a kid in a carpool. She was excited that they were going to "hang out," whatever that meant.

The conservatory looked different on a Tuesday morning. Tamsen had visited it on so many occasions, but the majority of them at night and obligatory in nature. She'd always been so busy circulating among the Socialati, she never truly appreciated the conservatory's scale. It was a different place when it wasn't peppered with cocktail tables and packed with servers passing trays of canapés to the affluent party goers.

Three inches of fresh snow blanketed the park surrounding the immense glass building, yet the air inside felt thick and dewy, with the aroma of earthy flora. A pair of finches darted between the high steel support beams. Tamsen stood under a palm tree marked *Roystonea Regia* and closed her eyes, imagining she was on a steamy Caribbean beach with Charlotte and Theo, playing in the sand at the azure water's edge.

"Hey," Whit said, coming up from behind her, bundled in a ski coat and rubber snow boots.

She turned. His torso was engulfed in the jacket. He hugged her, pulling her body into the feather swell.

"Hi," she replied as she experienced the gentle pressure of his arms. She didn't want to let go first, so she hung on, appreciating the extra few seconds before he backed away to sneeze.

His nose was red from the cold and he sniffled as he unzipped. "I saw the Holiday Train," he said, his broad smile energized as he gave her the news.

"Is that like the Polar Express?" she asked.

"Oh my god," he said. "You don't know about the Holiday Train?" He put his gloved hands on her shoulders. "It's like spotting sasquatch."

"Really?" she said.

"Tamsen, have you ever even taken the L?"

"Yes."

"When?" he challenged.

"In college," she confessed.

"Every year, the city pimps out one train with these over-the-top Christmas decorations, only nobody knows where it's running." He took her by the elbow and steered her toward the coat check.

"Sounds festive," she said. His excitement was genuine and Tamsen was amused by his childlike obsession.

They piled their outerwear on the counter, but Whit kept his beanie on. Tamsen watched as a green-eyed redhead in a concert t-shirt handed him the claim ticket. "Don't lose this, now," she said with mock sternness, her obscenely-full eyelashes batting like Bambi.

"And don't lose that shirt," he replied admiringly.

She brightened. "You're an LCD fan?"

"Are you kidding, James Murphy is my man crush."

"Ripe!" the girl chimed with an unfamiliar word of agreement. "Did you see them at Lolla?" Tamsen knew enough to understand they were talking about Lollapalooza.

She had attended the festival once, when Victor took some clients to see Coldplay. Of course, the experience was never about the music, it was all about the schmoozing. She recalled looking out at the general admission crowd from the VIP seats and thinking, no band could possibly be worth standing in that sweaty throng of drunken teenagers.

"I caught them at Lolla, but their show at the Riv forever ago was so extra," he said. Forever ago. On a relative scale, that was probably four years back.

"Shut up! With Hot Chip?" the girl asked.

"You've probably heard Hot Chip, Tamsen," Whit remarked, trying to include her in the discussion. "They're British."

"They totally rock," said the girl as she reached under the counter, retrieving two tokens. "Here, you guys, two cappuccinos on me. The coffee's down by the holiday flower exhibit, but heads up, there's a wedding that starts soon, so . . ."

"Who gets married on a Tuesday?" Tamsen asked.

"Someone who wants a one life stand," the girl said, coyly shifting her gaze to Whit.

They walked away and Whit leaned in to whisper, "She's referring to a Hot Chip lyric." Tamsen felt like an outsider.

They strolled into the massive fern room where prehistoric fronds exploded their buoyant plumes from the soil. Overhead, a giant banyan tree dropped its vine tentacles, and exotic yellow and white orchids hung still from the nooks within the bark. Tamsen stopped and pointed to a particular stalk of blossoms.

"Those reddish ones are Sherry Baby Orchids. They smell amazing, like cherry and vanilla," she said.

Whit leaned carefully over the guardrail to take a close-up shot of the flower. Tamsen heard her phone ping, and she pulled it out, checking that the message wasn't from The Dexter School. It was the Sherry Baby image from Whit.

"Did you just send me flowers?" she asked.

"Close your eyes and bring the orchid photo to your nose," he said. She looked at him skeptically. "Trust me," he insisted. She closed her eyes and did as he told her.

She opened her eyes a crack and giggled at the absurdity of the scene. "No peeking," he scolded.

"Okay, okay," she said, holding the screen beneath her nostrils.

"Now take a long slow whiff," he told her.

"Cherries!" she said delightedly. "How did you do that?"

"Scented photos 2.0," he said. "It's an upgrade." He'd held his cherry ChapStick under her nose. He laughed and smeared it across his mouth, raising his eyebrows with a perfunctory lip smack.

They followed the gravel path leading to a great hall with a towering ellipse ceiling and Seussian powder-puff trees, whose cartoon blossoms dangled like ornaments from over-arching branches. The humidity felt like Florida in July. Whit pulled off his beanie and jammed it in his back pocket.

"Will Theo get to see you over holiday break?" Tamsen asked.

"I'm around for Christmas," he said.

"What about New Year's?"

"No plans," he replied. "Nobody to kiss when the ball drops."

"Maybe the coat check girl's free," Tamsen baited.

"Nah," he said with a tinge of heaviness. "Not really feeling the dating thing. Hard to find the right match when your background includes psychotic breakdown."

"Is that really part of your profile?" Tamsen asked. "Online dating just seems so contrived."

"Everybody does it, you know." He laughed. She read between the lines at his suggestion that her aversion to the idea was a generational thing. "And no, psychotic breakdown is not a profile question."

"I'm just saying it's easy to misrepresent yourself. I mean, there must be a lot of people who lie."

"I was suspicious of the woman who said she was a professional wrestler, had a PhD in physics, and modeled on the side for extra cash, but otherwise, there's really no upside to lying if you're looking for something serious."

"Did you meet your old girlfriend that way?"

Whit mused, "NPR junkie seeking Sunday mornings with Stroopwafels, Coltrane, and the *New York Times*."

Tamsen hated that she felt a little jealous. "Sounds like your soulmate," she replied.

"I picked Vienna and she retaliated with the East Coast and a Harvard Business School grad."

"Ouch," Tamsen said.

"No, completely justifiable. She was great, but our timing wasn't. I like to think I spared her from the Vienna meltdown."

Whit grazed the gravel path with the lug sole of his boot and plunged his hands into his pockets as he ducked to avoid the low hanging corkscrew willow branches that dripped down from above.

"How about you?" he asked, casting his eyes up toward a towering royal palm.

Tamsen spotted the small wedding party assembled in front of a colorful Moroccan tile fountain and surrounded by white poinsettias. The bride wore a modest white gown and a pillbox hat with a delicate veil that covered her face. She released her father's arm as she turned to face the groom in his dark suit; his posture was stiff, and his cheeks puffed out as he exhaled, like he had never beheld a more beautiful woman.

"I don't know," Tamsen said, stopping to look at the wedding party. "I used to be romantic, but now, when I see couples like that, I want to grab them, shake them, and yell, 'Run while you still have the chance!'"

"That's kinda dark, Tamsen."

"I know," she said. "But I can't help it."

"Believe it or not, sometimes it actually turns out okay," he said.

The bride and groom were exchanging vows before a friend—a woman wearing leather pants and an oversized cream sweater, who had probably gotten ordained online a week or two earlier.

"Do you promise to stand by each other's side during times of challenge, times of exultation, times of lack, and times of abundance? Do you promise to bless your children with love?" the officiate asked.

"That's all I want," Whit said, the corners of his mouth turned downward.

"You'll have it," she replied. He was so good with Theo; she knew he'd be an incredible father someday.

Whit stared at the bride and groom. "Not kids. I could never impose my crazy on a kid. Play genetic Russian roulette? No way."

Tamsen hooked his pinky in her own. Her youngest brother had struggled with alcoholism, but mental illness was not on the menu of afflictions at Chez Kinney. She thought of Theo and his epilepsy. She would never want her son to rule out children because he was fearful of passing along his disorder. The mere thought that her son would ever consider altering any of his dreams because of his Doose Syndrome was heartbreaking to her. She tugged Whit's pinky.

"Believe it or not, sometimes it all turns out okay," she said. "*He who has experienced the deepest grief is best able to experience supreme happiness.*"

Whit eyed her sideways. "The Count didn't have mental illness, he was in jail."

"Exactly," Tamsen said.

The officiate looked up from her notes and smiled. "Congratulations, I now pronounce you husband and wife. So, kiss already!"

Whit turned to face Tamsen and in a split second, his eyes asked for her permission. She took one step closer to him and, in an instant, his mouth was on hers. She sensed the pressure of his palm on the small of her back and she tasted the scant residue of cherry ChapStick on his lips. Her mind scrambled to process the sensations that bombarded her brain. This was really happening. He pulled back and looked into her face for a sign. She didn't blink. She stood on her toes, gripping his arms tightly, and hovered close enough for him to know he should continue.

Whit spun her around and guided her to an adjacent alcove. He took hold of her hips and backed her carefully into a wall beside an automated barista machine, pressing his body determinedly against hers. For an instant, she wondered if this was okay. Then she recalled the terms Victor had spelled out at the Thunderchicken dinner. He told her he intended to be with other women.

"Care for a cappuccino?" he said as he ravaged her neck.

"I'm good," Tamsen managed.

His hands were all over her, feeling from the soft indent of her waist to the contour of her cheekbone. She was giddy with the happy chemicals that broke the stalwart dams in her head, flooding her entire body. The oxytocin-induced trance that brought boys and girls together under grapevine trellises on snowy Tuesdays in December—this, she mused. This was the euphoric feeling that blinded people to the inevitable annihilation of romantic union and the ultimate devastation of the self.

The father of the groom rounded the corner, clearing his throat. "Just getting a hot beverage here, don't mind me," he said.

Whit walked Tamsen past the Persian Pool, a wide pond flanked by massive tropical plants and filled with white and orange Japanese koi that swam leisurely beneath sculptures of yellow concave glass. The translucent circles dotted the water, mimicking lily pads that formed a sculptural path that was intended to be admired and not to be traversed.

"Incredible, huh?" Tamsen said over the rush of an adjacent

waterfall. She had visited the exhibit in the early 2000s as part of an art history class, but she decided not to mention the fact. Whit would have been in grade school back then. Grade school.

"I love Dale Chihuly's work," Whit said. "I actually read someplace that he's bipolar."

"A renowned artist, a husband, a father," Tamsen reflected. "Not a bad thing to 'impose' on a family."

She smiled at Whit and reached into her bag to check her phone. Aneta would pick up Theo and Charlotte shortly, and she wanted to be home for dinner with them. At the same time, the euphoria of being with Whit fed a part of her that had been neglected and shadowed by her exhausting default modes, guilt and disappointment.

Outside in the parking lot, Whit gathered handfuls of snow and began lobbing them at Tamsen's coat. She laughed and retaliated by swiping his beanie and thrusting it into the pocket of her open shearling. Tamsen imagined what the critical Socialati would make of her child-like behavior, having a snowball fight in front of Garfield Park Conservatory with her son's guitar teacher. They would be aghast, but she didn't care. It was invigorating to kiss her handsome friend, and she was electrified by the anticipation of the indeterminate future.

The brakes of an approaching L train screeched.

"Whit," Tamsen shrieked, pointing over his shoulder. "Your sasquatch!"

He whirled around. There it was, on its trip back into the city. Two hundred and fifty tons of metal, enveloped in tiny blinking red and green lights bordering its windows and full-surface decals of ice skaters, snowmen, ornaments, and garland wrapped around the entirety of its cars. Whit grabbed her hand and they ran across the parking lot to catch it, up the icy steps of the station, and toward the automated turnstiles. Tamsen was so exhilarated that she barely noticed the burning in her lungs. Whit slid his ride card twice and the gate yielded as they bolted toward the platform.

"Wait!" Whit yelled as the doors began to close.

An expressionless elderly black man shifted his walker forward between the doors, drawing them to an abrupt halt and triggering the safety alarm. The doors re-opened, releasing the walker from their death grip, and Tamsen and Whit stumbled onto the train.

"I've been standing on that platform for two hours, freezing my ass off, waiting for this damned Christmas train. Hell, if I'm going to make a young man and his moth—" He stopped himself, noticing Whit, who swooped himself around the vertical handrail and planted his lips on Tamsen's.

"Well, all-righty then," he said with a chuckle, and shuffled toward an open seat. Tamsen took a step back, creating a bit of space between herself and Whit. She considered what she was wearing under her coat: sleek, black leather boots with burgundy, velvet jeggings and a white button-down blouse, and compared it to Whit's black t-shirt and jeans. She supposed she looked older simply by virtue of her outfit, but the old man's gaffe stung nonetheless. The train lurched forward, and Whit's arm circled tightly around Tamsen's waist.

"I hope you appreciate the magnitude of this experience . . . Mom," he said in a serious voice, his eyes crinkling at the edges as he grinned. He then leaned over to kiss her with exaggerated passion, softly groaning "Mom" and slurping for dramatic effect. It was funny the first time he said it, but Whit was getting carried away and she was glad when he stopped.

He broke free as "Blue Christmas" blared from the speakers above and Tamsen watched him snatch a water bottle from beside a young woman, hold it to his mouth like a mic, and sing loudly like Elvis Presley. Their fellow train riders exchanged awkward glances. He raised an arm and pivoted his leg inward, pretending to be the king himself, and Tamsen wondered if she should say something to distract him.

Thankfully, the conductor announced the next stop, his voice metallic and inaudible, and the train stopped to let on more passengers. When they started moving again, the tune changed. It was an elevator-style rendition of "White Christmas," and Whit gave Tamsen a meaningful nod.

Whit began singing again, his Bing Crosby voice elevating the quality of the poor recording. The old man joined in, revealing two missing front teeth and a surprisingly decent voice. They continued together in concert and Whit shifted to the seat beside him and they locked arms, bellowing the carol in harmony. The other commuters now watched in amusement, but if she hadn't spent the past couple hours with Whit, Tamsen would have thought he'd been drinking—he was so up.

She looked around the L car with its LED light strips and garish graphics of dreidels and holly, and at a CTA employee in a Santa hat passing around small striped paper cups of diluted hot cocoa. Tamsen reached into her pocket and pulled on Whit's beanie, eliciting from him a wide, approving smile. She tendered her agreement by lending her voice to the familiar last lines and Whit started laughing hysterically.

"You think I'm a bad singer," she said, faking a pout. He rose and hugged her close.

"It's okay, you can still be my roadie."

CHAPTER

1 0

Three dozen children in red gowns with dark green yokes and fluted sleeves mounted a dais at the far end of the ballroom of the Women's Social Club. It was the kick-off of the organization's annual family Gingerbread House Decorating Party. The musical director for the Robie Children's Choir waved his arms urgently, shepherding singers to their places in a crescent formation near a towering blue spruce that was gaudily adorned in oversized gold balls and flocked candy canes. Hilly's daughter Astrid led the charge, tripping on her hem as she forced her way to the front and center position of the stage. She puffed out her already-developing chest in a manner of self-possession only seen in children whose parents had convinced them that they alone were the center of the universe.

Hilly had spent the last fifteen minutes fussing relentlessly over Astrid's hair, wrestling a giant red bow higher and higher on the girl's blonde head until it sat securely at the top like a perky grosgrain crown. The bow was so large that the tall girl in pigtails standing behind Astrid was entirely blocked from view. Cybill Hinton, wearing a hunter-green Dior suit and patent pumps, welcomed the choir and the opening number commenced. Hilly bit the skin around her thumbnail, leaning in to Tamsen.

"I should have gone with the black bow," Hilly whispered. "Do you think the red draws out her rosacea?"

Tamsen wanted to laugh. Rosacea, no. Acne, yes.

"She looks beautiful, Hilly," Tamsen said instead. "She's probably blushing because they put her next to Graham Wemmick." Tamsen saw Hilly press a tablet between her lips.

"Her future husband, if I have anything to say about it," interjected Digby about the handsome young heir to a construction fortune.

The choir began with "Ode to Joy," and Tamsen caught sight of Victor across the room, ducking out to take a call. An anxious pang pulled at her solar plexus; he worked constantly, but at least when they lived together, she could be with the kids while he was busy for hours on the phone. What would happen to them if she ever left him? She imagined Charlotte surfing the internet unattended and Theo snacking on something high in carbohydrates—something that would kick him into a seizure.

Tamsen pulled in a cleansing breath and pushed out her chest, consciously wiping those daydreams aside. She looked to where Charlotte was, sitting obediently on the floor with the other children, singing along quietly to the high, sweet refrain. Charlotte no longer believed in Santa Claus, but this year she almost too zealously played along with the tradition for Theo's sake. She anticipated the wonder that Christmas morning would bring, with her brother's staunch faith that a 350-pound man would actually squeeze down their narrow chimney and emerge over hot embers.

"If Santa could be real," Charlotte told her mother, "anything is possible." Even, Tamsen extrapolated, the reunion of her parents. The flames of Tamsen's guilt were stoked.

The choir's jaws slackened in unison with the long notes, their mouths in relaxed pouts while their eyes fixed on the director, whose arms flailed wildly to the music as he ardently over-enunciated each lyric. Hilly gloated, glancing between Astrid and Jacqueline, hoping to receive some sort of non-verbal acknowledgement from her friend regarding her daughter's superior vocal abilities. The irony was that Astrid was basically tone-deaf. Had it not been for the other vocalists drowning her out, Astrid's voice would have summoned every stray dog within a five-mile radius of Michigan Avenue.

After the third song, a sing-along rendition of "We Wish You a Merry Christmas," Cybill returned to the stage.

"Before the gingerbread decorating fun begins, I want to remind everyone to contribute to the tins being circulated by some of the young people. Of course, your dues cover all gratuities, but this tradition provides some of our part-time staff with a special Christmas bonus, so please be generous."

Tamsen checked her handbag, relieved to see she had remembered to tuck an envelope containing cash in the inside pocket. She'd sent Victor an email informing him of her proposed withdrawal of $1000 intended for the collection, which was split between the valet, the elevator attendant, and the coat check girls. Tamsen felt guilty holding back $500 for herself, but in this case, the money might serve her better than even a deposit into The Fountain Fund; it was enough to cover the cost of the women's employment workshop with Leda Sparrow.

She'd carried the article for Leda's workshop around with her since her first visit to Fariah's office. If Sparrow had indeed done what she claimed—changed the lives of thousands of women looking to reenter the workforce—then the workshop was worth investigating. After more than a decade of rearing children and "playing the role of Betty-bloody-Crocker," as Petra had once described stay-at-home motherhood, Tamsen had called the Flight to Financial Freedom 800 number. As a Christmas gift to herself, and as fulfillment of her promise to Petra to find the courage within, Tamsen was considering taking the one-day seminar, which would pass through Chicago on its winter tour. To hide her plans from Victor, Tamsen had the enrollment packet sent to The Talisman. The bundle of pre-seminar materials was bulging in her purse now. As soon as the gingerbread party wrapped up, she would get the kids home and bathed, and then dive in to begin availing herself of the wonders of Leda's Sparrow's expertise.

Cybill rotated through her last notecard at the podium. "Now, I invite Jacqueline Cole and Hilly Summers to give us a brief report on the success of our biennial Harvest Moon Ball."

Digby clapped harder than anyone in the room, shouting, "Woo, woo!" The pianist peppered the keys with an upbeat ditty as Hilly and Jacqueline approached the podium. "Check out the gams on my wife," Digby said, letting out a whistle.

Jacqueline's skinny flank edged Hilly away from the microphone.

"Thank you, Cybill. Edith Knox couldn't be here today as she has taken ill," she said. "But her generosity, which has been nothing less than epic, reminds us that this is, indeed, a season of giving. I worked very hard to get Mrs. Knox to finally agree to the substantial commitment that took the Harvest Moon Ball beyond anyone's wildest dreams and put us a half-million dollars over the amount raised at the last gala."

Digby cheered over the applause.

Jacqueline continued, "We all know Mrs. Knox demands perfection and she certainly held me to the highest standard."

She broke from her composed tone and the pitch of her voice modulated to something that sounded like Kermit the Frog. "We did have a little music snafu . . ." She laughed and returned to character. "Don't worry, responsible person, I won't name any names." A few newer members of the Socialati chuckled, bending to look Tamsen's way. Jacqueline had successfully enlisted them into her posse, but judging by their structured Chloé handbags, which were all the same design in varying colors and sizes, these novices had a lot to learn about the subtle art of individuality within conformity.

Jacqueline continued. "But that aside, I am eager to charge ahead into the new year with the momentum of Edith's generosity and the satisfaction of knowing I have delivered this astonishing gift for our charity, Mothers Trust Foundation."

Digby yelped, and the room erupted into an ovation. Tamsen fantasized that one of the choir boys would pull the fire alarm and activate the sprinkler system. Gooey gingerbread, sticky peppermint candy canes, and Jacqueline's thick foundation would melt into soupy pools on the floor. Hilly tugged at her earring, seemingly peeved that she had not been acknowledged, but wearing a painted smile, nonetheless. Tamsen wanted Hilly to lift her leg and drive her spiky Stewart Weitzman heel through the top of Jacqueline's foot. But as the children's choir began bellowing "It's Beginning to Look a lot Like Christmas," Hilly simply redirected her attention to Astrid and channeled her brief frustration into her wringing hands, while a heavy accordion room divider was drawn back, tripling the size of the ballroom.

Tamsen walked to her South Side sister. "Don't they know any neutral holiday songs?"

Hilly shook her head. "The only Jewish person here is Carole Maltzman O'Grady, and she's married to a Catholic."

"Everyone knows how hard you worked on the ball," Tamsen said, putting her arm around Hilly.

"Oh," Hilly waved her hand. "That was Jacqueline being Jacqueline."

"She couldn't have pulled it off without us."

"You know, you're right," Hilly answered, her voice wobbling. "I'm going to suggest more secular carols for next year, maybe 'Let It Snow.'"

The choir disbanded and children in their tweed sport coats and velvet dresses and tights scrambled to find a station along the length of the ballroom, where a hundred pre-assembled gingerbread houses were placed among plastic bowls of every candy imaginable: red hots, sugar-coated gum drops, red licorice whips, and tubes of thick white royal frosting. The elderly reverend from First Episcopal Church stood near the over-dressed Christmas tree and handed out Advent calendars. Tamsen saw a couple of Theo's brazen classmates in plaid pants duck behind a potted poinsettia bush to prematurely puncture all twenty-five perforated windows and stuff the Advent calendar chocolate bites into their swollen mouths. It was scold-worthy behavior, but her brothers used to do the same thing when Cormac brought holiday candy home.

Victor munched on a sugar cookie and hovered over Theo as the boy labored to compose his Christmas list at the Letters to Santa writing station. Both the children had told Tamsen what they wanted. Charlotte had requested a color change case for her iPhone and some scented colored pencils. Theo wanted a video game that Henry Kimball, the "cool" kid in Theo's class, boasted about. Tamsen researched the game and found it flagged on a parental website for gratuitous violence and extreme obscenities. He'd be getting a *Star Wars* LEGO set instead. Tamsen wondered whether her children's desire for their parents to live under the same roof had been a factor in their sparse wish lists. Her heart seized a bit when she considered the ways in which the children were collateral damage in this separation.

"Tamsen," Jacqueline said from across the table, swishing a glass of Dom Perignon and watching her nephew struggle to construct a marshmallow snowman. "We missed you at the Donoghues' party this weekend."

Tamsen blinked. She had been invited to the Donoghues' with Victor the past twelve years, but this holiday, no invitation. She'd heard rumors that Nancy Donoghue was recovering from knee surgery and told herself that perhaps she had not been ostracized, but that the party had simply been canceled. Nancy was one of the few genuinely kind women Tamsen knew through mutual WSC friends. Hers was the one party Tamsen would have looked forward to.

"It was fantastic, as usual," Jacqueline continued. "And from the looks of it, Victor had a smashing time."

Tamsen knew a dig. "I had a conflict," she replied. Tamsen forced a smile, placing a row of lemon drops across the roofline of Charlotte's gingerbread house. Tamsen didn't want to give Jacqueline the satisfaction of knowing the invitation had never arrived.

Jacqueline's eyes became hawkish as Tamsen felt a hand on her shoulder. It was Cybill.

"Tamsen, is this your daughter, Charlotte?"

Charlotte stood up and faced Cybill, extending her hand in the manner Tamsen had taught her. "Pleased to meet you," Charlotte said.

Since their conversation about the episode at the Hollydaze Festival, Cybill had gone out of her way to speak to Tamsen. She had approached her at brunch the weekend before, expressing honest appreciation for the hours Tamsen had spent wrapping gifts for the WSC toy drive.

Cybill ushered Tamsen aside. "I really appreciate the courage Charlotte displayed in coming forward with the incident involving the elf. I called a mandatory meeting where all current staff were notified they would be fired if any further report was made."

"Thank you so much, Cybill," Tamsen said, wanting to hug the woman, but knowing she wasn't the touchy-feely type.

"How is Charlotte?" Cybill asked, the pupils of her light gray eyes like pinheads.

"She knows I went to you about the matter, and I will tell her what you're doing to prevent it from happening again."

"Good," she said with her widest businesslike smile. "I'm working on adding more surveillance cameras, but we won't be online with those until next year."

Tamsen sensed that the incident struck a chord in Cybill, who emphasized how important it was for women to come forward with their experiences, and how much she admired mothers who set strong examples for their daughters. With the odds that well over half of women have been victims of harassment, Tamsen wanted to ask Cybill about her history, but held herself. If Cybill wanted to share her story, she would have done so.

Astrid walked up to where Tamsen was meticulously placing Necco wafers as shingles on the roof of Charlotte's house. Tweezers would have come in handy; she'd try to remember them for next year.

Astrid shook the change at the bottom of the tip collection tin. "Aunt Tamsen, would you like to make a donation to the help?" she asked.

Tamsen's fingers were coated in royal icing or she would have strung the girl by the bow. What sort of indoctrination had Digby and Hilly used that would give an eleven-year-old girl the idea that it was okay to call a service professional "the help"? Tamsen suspected it had something to do with Hilly's anger over their nanny, Angeline, getting pregnant and returning to her homeland.

"There's an envelope in my tote," Tamsen told Astrid. "You can be the help and get it for me."

Hilly walked up as Astrid reached under Charlotte's chair to open Tamsen's tote bag, rummaging through its main compartment. Suddenly, Tamsen gasped, feeling a stab of panic as she recalled the contents of her bag.

"Outside pocket!" she insisted, but it was too late. Astrid withdrew her hand and in it was the glossy seminar brochure with Leda Sparrow's smiling face against a background of flying money and a huge yellow headline that read, "You're On Your Way to Financial Freedom!"

"Isn't this the woman from the infomercial?" Astrid asked, holding up the document in plain sight.

Charlotte stopped decorating momentarily, glanced at the photo, and returned to her house. "Leda Sparrow. I heard Daddy call her an idiot." The two girls laughed. Tamsen's face burned. She braced herself as she looked up at Jacqueline, but instead of a satisfied smirk, Jacqueline's face was entirely blank. She picked a piece of lint off her nephew's blue blazer and took a sip of her bubbly as if she hadn't been paying a fleck of attention to the exchange.

"I'm on her mailing list or something," Tamsen dismissed.

"Our old nanny used to listen to her podcasts," Astrid chimed.

"That explains a lot," Hilly said under her breath as she snapped up the brochure and inspected it like it was contaminated.

Theo rushed up with Victor on his heels. "Can we go now?" Theo asked. Tamsen knew how difficult it was for Theo to be around all the sugary treats.

She grabbed the document from Hilly's hand and stuffed it back into her purse, but it was too late. Victor's cold stare said it all. He'd seen the brochure.

Victor tilted his head to the side and mimicked confusion. "You're not actually thinking about getting a job, are you, Tamsen?"

Hilly froze and three pairs of young eyes rose from the gingerbread houses to Victor as if they anticipated something explosive.

"I was reading about a seminar she's hosting," Tamsen said.

Victor continued, keeping his tone jovial enough to sound like he was teasing her. "You're nearly forty-five. Companies want young and hungry, not middle-aged and irrelevant."

Tamsen squeezed her fist, feeling her fingernails bite into her palm. She was paralyzed. She wanted to fire back, but she would never engage Victor in the children's presence. They were in a fragile place and the book on separation was very direct about parents always maintaining a civilized tone in their presence. Of course, Tamsen was also keenly aware of the backlash she'd suffer if she crossed Victor in public. Worse was that a small part of her knew Victor had a point. She'd been stupid to think someone like Leda Sparrow could reveal hidden potential or new possibilities to her.

"You know," Jacqueline said. "If you really want a job, Stephan always seems to be looking for a girl to do this and that."

Jacqueline's tone was shockingly non-confrontational, and if she didn't know better, Tamsen might have thought her adversary was being gracious. But Tamsen quickly chided herself for giving Jacqueline the benefit of the doubt. There was innuendo in Jacqueline's words and it wasn't far below the surface. Girls—to do this and that for Stephan.

Victor helped Theo with his pea coat. "I can't believe you got sucked in by that evangelical job coach," he said aside to Tamsen. "You have never had to work, and as long as we're still married, it's going to stay that way."

It was a threat. Tamsen felt like a beetle on its back, its legs thrashing for traction as Victor watched her flounder. He walked the children and her to the valet, and as Tamsen passed the lobby trash can, she reached into her tote bag for the seminar packet and dumped Leda's face in with the mound of dirty paper napkins, Starbucks cups, and half-eaten cupcakes.

Charlotte paced between the bay window and the formal powder room where she kept a hairbrush, checking her reflection in the foyer mirror each time she passed it.

"Mom," Charlotte said. "Whit's nine minutes late."

Tamsen looked at her watch. "He's walking from the L, sweetheart. Sometimes the trains run behind when it snows."

Charlotte joined her mother in the kitchen, where Tamsen was massaging lemon, peppercorn and garlic onto two butterflied birds. She had made fresh baba ganoush, one of Whit's favorites. He'd been joining them for Heroine Chicken after Theo's lesson.

"Whit's always on time," Charlotte said. "Except for when his bike lock froze, but he texted you, remember?"

Tamsen looked up from the seasonings. "Char, are you wearing my makeup?" she asked calmly, biting the inside of her cheek in an attempt not to laugh at the round, rosy blush marks that made Charlotte look more like Abie the Clown than her sweet girl.

"There's a twelve-year age difference between Jay-Z and Beyoncé," Charlotte said.

"You're beautiful without makeup," Tamsen remarked, thinking how she herself was trying to look younger for Whit while her daughter was doing the opposite.

Tamsen knew Charlotte's crush had intensified over the past several months; as her daughter's affection grew, so did the number of minutes she was spending to choose an outfit on guitar lesson days. Whit thought it was sweet, but his focus always remained faithfully on her son. Theo, who seldom asserted himself, continued to insist on a private space to practice the special song he was learning for the upcoming class talent show. Getting dedicated attention from Whit every week was paying off better than Tamsen had ever dreamed.

An hour later, Charlotte gave up waiting. "He's not coming," she huffed. "He would be here by now if he was."

"Were," Tamsen corrected. "Were coming." It was Tamsen who was now pulling back the sheer drape at the bay window looking for signs of the guitar teacher. Tamsen replayed their last encounter in her head, nervously wondering if she had somehow offended him. After the holiday train ride, they had returned to the conservatory parking lot where she'd left her car. He hopped in to warm up and they'd kissed until she needed to leave to meet the children. He'd wanted to take the train home, but she'd insisted on dropping him off at his apartment in Humboldt Park. While she drove, he'd held her hand, squeezing it spontaneously.

"I like you," he'd said, with his disarming squinty smile.

"And I like you, Whit," she told him, clinging to him in the warm car outside his building. "You are my something to look forward to."

Her words didn't seem to frighten him at the time, but perhaps he felt it was too much pressure to play any role in Tamsen's life. Maybe being something to her, as fragile as they both were, imposed upon him a sense of responsibility. Maybe she had come on too strong or too needy; maybe he didn't want to be her life raft.

After the children were tucked in, Tamsen propped herself up in bed with her laptop. She opened her text messages.

Everything okay?

She leafed through a Saks Fifth Avenue catalog, waiting for a reply, but there was nothing. She kept her phone beside her, checking it until midnight when she finally turned off her ringer, disappointed, and slid under the covers. For hours, she baited sleep by focusing on her breath, counting backward by threes from one hundred, and even doing a relaxation exercise she recalled the doctors suggesting for Theo during his tests.

It occurred to Tamsen that she was powerless against the cyclone in her mind; she knew nighttime amplified cataclysms that during the day were simply problems. She stared at the ceiling, her brain violently oscillating between thoughts of Whit: how his tongue felt when it skimmed her lower lip, how he kept his eyes open while he kissed her, and about what she might have done to scare him off. Maybe it was the tinge of jealousy over the girl and that band they were talking about, or the comment she made about relationships that he thought was dark. Why hadn't she heard from him in days? She slammed her palm against the bed, frustrated by her preoccupation with a younger man whom she had allowed to become the tether looped around her waist, keeping her from slipping into an abyss of hopelessness. At 4:00 a.m., she allowed herself one last look at her screen. Before turning the phone face down, she told herself that Whit might cast her off for wanting him too much, but he would never let Theo down—she would hear from him eventually.

The ping finally arrived at 6:00 a.m. Tamsen was already awake. To her inquiry as to whether he was well, he texted a one-word reply.

Yeah

Tea this week?

Sure

It was terse. Certainly not the playful, flirtatious interchange she'd hoped for. But it was something.

Christmas Eve morning was a bitter twenty degrees, and Tamsen was grateful that the bellman at The Talisman was waiting under the heat lamp at the curb to help her unload shopping bags. She and Victor had agreed that he would have the kids all day and tonight, and Tamsen would be at the brownstone at 6:00 a.m. to open gifts and stay the rest of the week. She glanced down at her Christmas Eve to-do list, which had become a necessity since her insomnia-induced fatigue had been short circuiting her memory.

Nicole clothes
Wrap gifts
Shower / call T&C
Whit
Clay?

She heard a series of horns blare behind her and watched in the rear-view mirror while a horse and carriage lingered, blocking traffic on Chestnut Street because the recalcitrant animal refused to pass a flashing barrier over an open manhole. The poor beast threw its head back again and again, pawing at the snowy ground against the driver's forward command. An assembly of pedestrians gathered like spectators, one of them gesturing to the carriage driver to come down and lead the horse around the obstacle. But the driver remained in his seat, tapping the animal's neck with a long whip and barking indistinguishable commands.

From around the corner, she saw a bike messenger wearing a black balaclava and ski goggles, his bag strapped tightly across his back. He was riding a bicycle with the fattest tires Tamsen had ever seen. She watched him navigate easily through the snow, pass the carriage, dismount, move the flashing barrier to the side, wave the horse-drawn vehicle by, and then replace the source of the animal's fright. The spectators gave a cheer and he raised his arms in victory before hopping back on the bike and riding off. She thought of Whit and rickety Edmond Dantès, its skinny tires worn and cracking. She would finally see him for tea later at a diner in his neighborhood.

Inside the lobby, Tamsen shivered, waiting for Nicole to finish making a dinner reservation at Fogo de Chão for a waiting couple.

"I have something for you," Nicole said, reaching under the laminate reception desk for a small bundle wrapped in gold tissue and tied with brown twine. "Merry Christmas, Mrs. Peel."

Tamsen carefully folded back the paper, revealing a cellophane-wrapped bag of granola clusters.

"They're paleo," she said.

Tamsen turned the package over, admiring the carefully-designed sticker with Nicole's monogram and a list of ingredients. No grains, no sugar. Even Theo could eat this.

"I thought you said you didn't cook."

"It's basically bird food, nothing much," Nicole replied. "I can bake pretty good."

Tamsen was suddenly embarrassed by what she had to offer Nicole: hand-me-downs. She could have thought of something more original.

"I have a few things for your girls," Tamsen said, gesturing to the shopping bags. "Things my daughter has outgrown."

Nicole's hands flew to her mouth and tears filled her eyes as she rounded the desk. She bent down and gingerly lifted a pile of sweaters from the closest bag.

"Can I?" she managed as she delicately peeked at each article. "These will fit Camila—Marisol is big-boned, so she can wear some of them, too. My baby, Beatriz, is only five, but she's growing real fast."

"There are shoes too, and some boots."

Nicole squealed and clapped her hands. Ron looked at her over the reading glasses that appeared to be cutting off the circulation in the tip of his nose.

"Prada? Are you kidding me?" Nicole asked, aghast at seeing the lovely ballet flats. "The American dream, right—my kids are already doing better than me!"

Tamsen's mind went to Charlotte and Theo and the abundance in their lives. Their material fortune had far exceeded that of Tamsen's own upbringing, but it was the wealth of opportunities only money could buy that set their prospects apart from Camila, Marisol, and Beatriz.

"You can't understand what these gifts mean, Mrs. Peel. My girls' daddy is out of the picture."

"That's really tough, Nicole." Tamsen could only empathize. Charlotte and Theo had a gilded launch pad: the best education possible and two parents who loved them and who should be living under the same roof to really guarantee them success as adults.

"It took a detached retina and restraining order, but he's out of the picture now."

"This paperwork isn't going to do itself, Nikki," Ron said, emerging from behind the desk, his stubby arms resting against his Humpty Dumpty torso.

"You're my Christmas angel," Nicole said, standing to embrace Tamsen. The hug was all the affirmation Tamsen needed to know she'd made the right choice to sacrifice the few hundred bucks the clothes would have fetched at consignment for a woman in need.

Tamsen tugged off the drab Talisman bedspread and let it rest in a heap on the floor. She'd asked housekeeping to take it away entirely, but they persistently made up the bed according to the cover photo on their website. Sitting on the edge of the mattress, she stared blankly out the window at the adjacent brick wall. Heavy footfalls echoed from the room overhead, reminding her that she was not at home. Home—the cozy place that smelled like spiced apples and crackling cedar, where she knew every creak and idiosyncrasy of the temperamental plumbing and all the hiding places her children would choose for games of Sardines.

She let her body flop back, her arms strewn at her sides. Her view shifted to the domed ceiling fixture that coffined a small moth, whose singed wings mimicked her own spread arms in silhouette through the milky glass. This was the last place she wanted to be, stagnant air smelling of veiled cigarette smoke and hand lotion, a leaky showerhead clogged with limescale, and nobody to snuggle under the covers for old

Tom and Jerry cartoons. Yet she had moved out. She had demanded this. Tamsen looked at her roller bag. It could all be over within thirty minutes. They could be a family for Christmas.

She turned her head to the Old Water Tower painting. The building survived because it was resilient, because it was made of material that could take the scorching heat and withstand the raging fire of 1871. Tamsen wished she was made of such tough stuff.

A room service cart rattled outside her door, its aluminum plate covers jangling until the noise stopped at a nearby room. She could hear a man's husky voice excuse the server. She imagined him in a bathrobe, protecting the identity of a forbidden rendezvous by refusing the server's invitation to set up a late brunch of Belgian waffles and scrambled eggs inside the room. She envisioned the man's contented lover reclined across the hotel sheets, her hair tousled and mascara smudged as the man poured her an effervescent glass of Asti Spumante.

Tamsen closed her eyes. She placed her fingertips at the crown of her head and ran them lightly over her eyes, skimming her eyelashes, feeling the creases in her lips and the round tip of her chin. She grazed her breasts slowly, drawing chills up her arms. Then she floated her hands over the soft tissue of her belly, down between her legs, and finally resting her hands on the tops of her thighs. A woman's voice laughed from down the hall. It had been eleven months since Tamsen had been touched. She wondered if Whit wanted her that way. She would not allow herself to hope. If he didn't, she couldn't handle the rejection.

Late morning was consumed with wrapping the last of the children's gifts on the hotel bed and reruns of reality TV in the background. Salacious shows had officially replaced classic literature as her pastime;

mindless television took a lot less energy to process and was a welcome anesthetic given that Tamsen wouldn't be with her babies on Christmas Eve. She pressed the off button on the remote. No matter how many times she'd disinfected the device, she still sensed germs and a sticky film when she touched it. Her mother had warned her many times when she traveled on business, "You know those men and their hotel pay movies." Gross.

Tamsen's phone flashed a text message banner: Clay urging her to attend his annual Christmas Eve party. She responded.

We'll see.

She showered and pulled on a pair of faded jeans with tall gray boots and a fitted blouse. Her hair was down and sleek and she'd pulled on a loose-knit beanie because she'd seen an attractive young woman wearing one on Oak Street and figured it was a current look. An article in a December fashion magazine touted the benefits of a revolutionary eye cream, suggesting it restored flawless skin by plumping epidermal cells with micro-peptides and something called Elastoyouth. Tamsen mocked herself for falling prey to the pitch; she knew from Victor's stories about the advertising industry that there was a fine line between illusion and scientific fact. She gently tapped the cream under her eyes—her own fine lines didn't care whether the claims were exaggerated. She wanted to look her best for Whit.

Tamsen's taxi pulled up at the corner near Keeler's coffee shop. When she got out, an adjacent mom and pop sporting goods storefront with a yellow door and a baby jogger in the window caught her eye. The sign in their window read "New Year's Markdowns Start Today!" Tamsen was early, so she decided to check out the sale. When she walked in, a tiny bell jangled and the owner greeted her though the large wad of chewing tobacco that bulged in his cheek.

"Last minute shopping?" he asked.

She was struck by how many tennis rackets, hockey sticks, and bicycles the owner had managed to cram into such a small space.

"Just looking," Tamsen said.

"We got an extra 10% off," he said, as if dangling an incentive would motivate her to buy the new pair of rollerblades in front of her. She moved on, admiring the vibrant selection of skateboard decks, one illustrated with a delicate geisha girl and another depicting a cat giving the finger.

Just when she'd decided she'd seen enough, something in the back corner caught her eye. It was perfect for Whit, and though she had planned to give him cash for Christmas, she knew this particular item would be extra special—much more personal than a card and money. The gift was more than the amount Victor would ever authorize, but she decided she could divert some cash from the Nina Ricci dress windfall toward the purchase. She realized it was risky to give Whit a Christmas present from her alone, but she would make it from the kids, a thank you for all he'd done for Theo.

Keeler's was at full throttle with their holiday decorations. Gaudy tinsel garlands draped from the ceiling and plastic decals of snowmen and Santa adorned the windows. A Christmas nativity scene made with Smurf figurines was erected on a bed of cotton near the hostess stand. Tamsen recognized Whit's parka from behind; his back faced the entrance and his shoulders sank forward. If she hadn't known better, she might have mistaken him for an old man hunching over a bowl of soup.

Tamsen's heartbeat quickened as she approached him. The nervous pit in her stomach felt reminiscent of when she used to stand up in front of the nuns to lead St. Christina classroom invocations. She didn't know what to expect from Whit tonight.

"Hi," she said, touching his shoulder as she pulled out the chair opposite him at the two-top. He stood up and hugged her without making eye contact, but the puffy skin under his eyes suggested he had been crying. His hair was damp as if he had just showered, and he smelled clean, like scented men's soap.

"I'm so sorry about yesterday," he whispered as they sat.

"You all right?" she asked. He had dark circles and a waxen pallor to his cheeks.

"I've been down," he said.

"It's okay," she assured him.

He leaned in and pressed his forehead against hers. "Thanks."

"Here's a menu for your friend," offered an emaciated server with earlobe gauges. "Just in case you're hungry."

Whit seemed to be mustering up the energy to speak. She grasped his cold hands, weaving her fingers between his.

"My doctor changed up my meds." He paused, licking his lips.

"You're having trouble with the new ones?" she asked, trying to see his eyes.

"This always happens," he said, shaking his head. "I should have warned you. I thought I could handle it, the transition." He stared at her directly now. "There's a reason for the absurd litany of side effects at the end of those pretty drug commercials."

"Tell me," she said.

"It's like your brain has been immersed in marshmallow cream so all your thoughts are slow and milky, and your mouth feels like you've been sucking on a crusted exhaust pipe."

Tamsen swallowed. "What can I do?"

"A foot massage would be nice," he said rhetorically.

She was so relieved he was cracking jokes. Hopefully his meds were stabilizing.

"You'll find the right balance."

"And if I don't, it's a buy one, get one—suicidal depression and a bare-chested interpretive dance in front of the Austrian royal family."

"Shit," she said. "At least you've got rhythm," she said, meeting his degree of levity.

Whit sat back in his chair. "The Count said, *There is neither happiness nor misery in the world; there is only the comparison of one state with another, nothing more.*"

"I love that quote," Tamsen said.

"When I'm medicated there is no comparison—there's just flat."

The waiter brought them tea and a basket of warm corn muffins. "Fresh from the oven, get 'em while they're free."

Whit grabbed one.

"Weight gain—another side effect compliments of the good folks at Drug Central," he said. She watched as he finished his bite and dabbed his mouth with a napkin. "I want to feel better so I can feel everything with you," he said.

Tamsen felt a tiny pinch in the inside corners of her eyes. She bit down on her cheeks and squeezed his hand. He stared at the glowing neon menorah in the Keeler's window. She reached into her handbag and pulled out her phone.

"Theo and Charlotte made something for you." She pulled up a video and handed the phone to Whit.

"A one, and a two, and a three . . ." Charlotte cued onscreen.

Whit watched as she sang, and Theo labored to keep up with the melody on his guitar.

"We wish you a Merry Whitmas, we wish you a Merry Whitmas."

He chuckled. "Charlotte got a little carried away with the eye shadow."

"We know that you'll really miss us, we will see you next year!"

"You have awesome kids, Tamsen," he said. "And thankfully, they didn't inherit your singing voice." His playful jabs continued—it was a good sign. "They were going to perform it for me yesterday, weren't they? And I completely blew them off." He slumped again. "I'm always letting people down."

"Not at all," Tamsen insisted, attempting to intercept a negative spiral. "They could never make it through a live performance; if you were there, Charlotte would need to comb her hair every other word."

Whit was silent for moment. He reached for a muffin and then withdrew his hand, changing his mind.

"You've made a huge impression on Theo. Even his teacher said something." Tamsen imagined how brilliant Whit would be in a conference with Ms. Ellison. She indulged in a brief fantasy where he replaced Victor as Theo's parent.

"I can't be what you're looking for, Tamsen," he said.

"What exactly do you think I'm looking for?" she asked, feeling him slip away.

"Undamaged. Ambitious. I don't know how my future looks," he said.

"I just like being with you," Tamsen said. She sensed him pulling back.

Whit went on. "We occupy spaces at two opposite ends of the universe."

"It's the same universe," she answered. "Besides, there are no certainties in life. We just have to do the best we can. Edmond Dantès knew it: *All human wisdom is contained in these two words—wait and hope.*"

"But you're so together, you have a real life, with leather interior and eight-hundred-thread-count sheets. I live in a studio apartment with patio furniture and a hot plate."

"It's the age difference, isn't it?" she asked, bracing herself for his answer.

He flexed his long fingers and she thought of them wrapped around the neck of a cello. She watched the muscles in his jaw tighten and he stared at her from under his dark, pronounced brow.

"Your age is irrelevant to me."

"My thread count is irrelevant," she replied. "I understand our circumstances are different, but I don't want us to be the same. The same is stifling."

"You're out of my league," he said.

"If you're uncomfortable with me because of my leather interior, that's on you. That's your judgment; it has no bearing on who I am or why I'm so enamored with you." She shocked herself with her candor.

They sat in silence, staring at one another.

"You're spending New Year's Eve with me," he said. "Drinks, dinner, the whole thing."

"On one condition," she said.

"Name it," he said.

Tamsen left a ten-dollar bill for the server and they walked outside. She took Whit by the hand and guided him around the corner.

"I will go anywhere with you on New Year's Eve," she said. "As long as we take this."

Locked to a frozen metal rack was a shiny, black fat-tire bike with a big red bow fastened to the handlebars.

"Merry Christmas, Whit."

CHAPTER

11

Tamsen made it to Clay's Christmas Eve dinner party before the entrees were out of the oven. She carried a bottle of Silkbush Viognier, and an assortment of signature bonbons from Veruca Chocolates. There was a yellow and black lacquered coat rack set up in Clay's ultra-modern foyer, with its gray tone on tone wallpaper and a slick, silver Nambe tray filled with giant gourmet candy canes centered on his entry table. Tamsen loved how everything Clay owned had a purpose. There was no clutter in his three-bedroom condo, just expensive Italian furniture, a stunning Lynn Davis iceberg photograph, a gelatin Mapplethorpe print of a poppy, and seamless custom built-in cabinetry.

Tamsen peeked into the living room. A couple in matching tweed vests were playing a duet on Clay's glossy upright piano. His Christmas tree was meticulously adorned with chocolate brown, bronze, and antique nickel-colored orbs. Quite a contrast to the Peel tree with its multitude of pom-poms, cardboard, and yarn ornaments handmade by Charlotte and Theo. Victor called dibs on Christmas Eve, but Tamsen would have Christmas Day and, even better, the kids to herself for the next six nights. She found comfort in anticipating the delicious morning they'd spend together with her kids tomorrow, unwrapping the surprises

Santa Claus had delivered and eating cheesy scrambled eggs in front of her own splendid tree.

Tamsen stepped into the kitchen and put her hands over Mirko's eyes from behind.

"Guess who," she said in the best low masculine tone she could muster.

"Not even my brother has such feminine hands," Mirko laughed, pulling her into a tight hug and lifting her feet from the floor.

Men in Burberry plaid dress shirts and tight-fitting Armani t-shirts milled around a seafood platter of crab claws and jumbo shrimp which ran half the length of the pure white Caesarstone-topped island. The real attraction, though, was not the spread of food, but an oyster shucker Clay had met on Scruff.

"He's a personal trainer and a model," Clay whispered to Tamsen, pulling her into a hug. "Merry Christmas to me."

"I've got someone under the mistletoe, too," she said without trying to suppress the glow she could feel herself exuding.

Clay snapped a glass of wine from a passing tray and handed it to her. "It's that boy from Halloween. The one in the cape."

"We have a New Year's date." She nursed the wine with tiny sips, wanting to avoid a hangover.

"Anything to wipe clean the memory of last year," he said. "Steer clear of Andrew and Sabastian—their grab bag gift is in capsule form."

Hearing Clay mention last December 31st evoked in Tamsen a writhing discomfort that was enough to dampen the buzz she'd had from seeing Whit just an hour ago in Keeler's with all its cheesy decorations. It was nearly one year since Tamsen confirmed she would never take another sleeping pill. Still, the memory of Victor's face the next morning when she woke up with a throbbing headache still haunted her. The way he sat on the edge of the bed, moving his head side to side, then jerking it to crack before leering over his shoulder at her, mocking her while he glowered with animal detachment and arrogant disgust.

Clay continued, "Whit's the perfect transition for you. Young . . . eager." He winked and nudged her with his elbow.

"Jill's here!" Tamsen said, spotting her Halloween Charlie's Angels comrade, Huang, across the kitchen. Tonight, Huang was dressed in holiday attire: tight designer jeans, green suede Gucci loafers, and a fitted angora Christmas sweater with a giant snowman on the front.

"Ugh, his bear can't hold his liquor," Clay said about the whiskered heavyweight Huang was dating.

"Where's Pepper?" Tamsen asked.

"She's grounded for eating a tube of Vaseline," Clay replied.

Tamsen grabbed a shrimp and snuck into Pepper's bedroom. She found the French bulldog with a red and emerald soft-cone collar around her neck, curled up in the center of a queen-sized bed with an umber velour duvet. Pepper approached Tamsen sheepishly, her tush swaying back and forth from beneath a doggie diaper. Tamsen scratched behind the pooch's ears. She snapped a photo for Theo and Charlotte—a selfie with Pepper's irresistible scrunched face, held cheek to cheek with Tamsen's own. Clay had elected not to spay Pepper and Tamsen wondered when he would finally breed her.

The pooch hopped to her hind legs, licking Tamsen's chin. Theo had begged for a puppy, but Victor had said even a "hypoallergenic" dog was out of the question. For just a flash of a second, Tamsen envisioned a cozy, three-bedroom Bucktown walkup, where she and the kids could walk a puppy of their own to the dog park by their favorite Italian ice stand. She recalled Clay saying that, given her rare lilac fawn color, he had paid north of $4,000 for Pepper. She and the kids would get a rescue dog, she thought, as she rubbed Pepper's pedigree belly. She quickly calculated the maintenance cost of the proposition: the shots, food, kennel stays, and training. Even with a rescue dog, the cost was too much, and she quickly disposed of the fantasy in her mental "wouldn't it be nice" pile.

◆ ◆ ◆

Tamsen washed the dog hair off her hands in the kitchen sink while Huang's date stood in front of the refrigerator, looking blankly into his beer and shifting from one foot to the other. Tamsen inched between him and Mirko to fill her glass at the bar faucet with Whit's favorite party drink, ice water. Mannheim Steamroller's Christmas album roared from Clay's holiday playlist.

"Are you one of those MILFs Clay hangs around with?" Huang's date slurred, drawing the attention of Mirko and a guest with a man bun. "Cuz' I would totally fuck you if I wasn't into guys."

Tamsen's brain had barely processed the man's words before Mirko grabbed his collar and slammed him into the adjacent wall, narrowly missing Clay's prized signed Keith Haring lithograph. Clay materialized out of nowhere, his mouth so close to the offender's face that Tamsen was sure Clay might bite him.

"Apologize, now!" Clay growled.

Tamsen was still registering her response. The boys were overreacting. There was a part of Tamsen that wanted to accept the backhanded compliment. He was gay, after all, so it wasn't like he was hitting on her.

"Apologize!" Mirko echoed. "This is a lady."

"I didn't mean anything. I'm sorry," the bear bumbled, wide-eyed.

Huang pushed his way to where the drama had unfolded, smacking his date across the face.

"Are you playing grab-ass again?" he scolded.

Clay glared at the culprit. "Show some respect for a woman."

The kitchen was quiet except for Barbra Streisand singing "My Favorite Things" while twenty pairs of eyes fixed on the bear, whose jowls hung as he looked at Tamsen, the altercation shocking him sober. She herself was startled by Mirko and Clay's response. Until they stepped in, she hadn't really considered that something all that inappropriate had occurred.

"I'm truly sorry," he said. Tamsen thought of the elf who had called Charlotte an ugly slut and she considered whether she would have excused this man's vulgarity if it had been directed at an adult Charlotte. She put her hand on Mirko's shoulder.

"Your mother raised you boys right."

Tamsen's television at The Talisman blared early coverage of the New Year's Eve party in Times Square while she spritzed her décolletage with a cinnamon-vanilla fragrance she'd bought on Amazon. She didn't want to apply anything heavy, but a magazine "study" she'd devoured in the waiting room at Fariah's office cited the fragrances men find most alluring. The scent of baked cinnamon buns topped the list. Even if her therapist wasn't able to help Tamsen fix her marriage, at the very least she'd indirectly given Tamsen all sorts of advice like how to "Buy the Best Bikini Bottoms for your Booty," which "Three Foods to Avoid if You Want a Flat Tummy," and "How to Hit the Big O Every Time."

For New Year's Eve, Tamsen was committed to casting off negative thoughts of Victor's next attack, of her persistent financial worries, and of her constant anxiety about the well-being of Theo and Charlotte. After a crazy week of gift opening, indoor rock climbing with the Socialati and their children, and a visit to the Zoo Lights Festival, the kids were safe, warm, and exhausted back at the brownstone. Tamsen had kept Victor at a distance, but she did cross paths with him long enough to overhear him telling Charlotte he'd bought ingredients for s'mores and that there would be sparklers and party favors if the kids could keep their eyes open till midnight.

Tamsen looked forward to her one night of relief, one night where she could remain completely in the moment with someone who didn't care about the brand name of her ski jacket, the number of charities to which she'd donated this holiday, and who wasn't going to criticize the tightness of her jeans or the heel height of her leather boots.

She pulled on a cream cashmere turtleneck sweater to go over a pair of suede Ralph Lauren pants that Hilly had outgrown when she was pregnant with Astrid. Then she brushed out her thick dark hair, which flowed luxuriously down her back. Whit's directive was to wear something warm, but no denim. He was arranging everything tonight, including drinks and dinner. But other than the dress code, he'd given no hints as to what was in store.

Tamsen grabbed a rubber band from the vanity and tucked it into her hip pouch, just in case it got windy on the back of the fat-tire bike. The anticipation of the night ahead made her cheeks glow. Tamsen pulled out a wad of cash from the hotel room safe. She felt each bill in her hand like a blackjack dealer. Five $50 bills. She didn't think she would need that much, but it was a big night and she wanted to be prepared if a decadent opportunity like a festive carriage ride down Michigan Avenue presented itself. She used to scoff at the suburbanites who overpaid for such tourist traps, but anything with Whit was fun, regardless.

Whit sat waiting in a broken easy chair in the lobby of the Talisman; the tufted seat actually rotated when Tamsen checked in more than four months earlier. The hotel certainly lived up to its average marks on TripAdvisor.com, with its second-rate fixtures and saggy lobby sofa cushions that were begging to be replaced.

"You look beautiful," Whit said, beaming. He was wearing black jeans that clung just enough to hint at the musculature of his glutes, and not too much that he looked like a TV sitcom character from the 1980s. Under his parka, he wore his tuxedo jacket and an unbuttoned white t-shirt with a Johnny Cash Folsom Prison mugshot decal and an undone bow tie that hung limply around his neck. He had a dark green canvas Herschel backpack with leather straps over his coat and there was a handled shopping bag on the floor beside him.

Tamsen sighed involuntarily when she saw him, which made her laugh aloud at herself. It was a relief to see Whit, a relief that he was happy again—happy in a stable way, not in a manic way.

Whit folded her in his nylon arms, kissing her intently.

"Where are we going first?" she asked.

"You know I'm not going to tell you," he said. Whit reached into the shopping bag and pulled out a brand-new, turquoise Bern bike helmet with a sticker of Bigfoot stuck to the side.

"A sasquatch!" Tamsen exclaimed.

"He reminds me of you," he said as he placed it on her head and fastened it into place under her chin.

"Wild and hairy?" she asked.

"You're not wild," he replied, laughing.

She sat in the saddle while he pedaled evenly over the packed snow. The ride was amazingly smooth, and she felt blissfully comfortable as he chauffeured her down Delaware.

"We need to come up with a name," Whit said above the street noise.

WARM TRANSFER | 237

"A name?" Tamsen asked.

Whit tapped the handlebar with his winter glove. "For the bike."

"How about Heathcliff?" Tamsen suggested. "Or Pip, or Mr. Darcy?"

They rode past the iconic John Hancock Center with its matte black crisscross exoskeleton. Tamsen loved the feel of Whit's hips under her hands as she squeezed him for balance and closeness. Whit pulled up onto the sidewalk.

"We're kicking off our New Year's Eve with a cocktail," he said as he unfastened her new helmet.

"The Pinnacle?" She dropped her head back as her eyes swept a new modern building from the mezzanine all the way to the top, where a band of red and green blinked around the perimeter of its uppermost floor. She knew how expensive The Pinnacle was and she also knew they were profoundly underdressed for the swanky bar. "I think it might be black tie up there tonight," she said gingerly.

He clamped the U-shaped bike lock into place. "And what does it look like I'm wearing?"

She laughed, embarrassed. "I'm sorry, we agreed this is your night."

"Thank you," he replied. "Now if you will follow my lead, we just might make it past security and enjoy one drink before they kick us to the curb."

They didn't enter through the main entrance, but rather through the rear service door, where an armed guard sat in front of a panel of small screens. The guard lit up when he saw her date.

"Well, if it isn't the ghost from New Year's past," the uniformed man joked.

"Dutch!" Whit said as he and the man engaged in a ritualistic handshake that ended in a side-five and a hug. "You got this place secure? Wouldn't want anything to happen to my pretty date, here."

"You better watch yourself, friend," he said. "I got eyes on you."

They waited for the building's secondary elevator in a cold hallway that reminded Tamsen of the boiler room at St. Christina's. Whit bounced nervously on the balls of his feet. Inside the lift cab, Tamsen's ears popped as they were propelled into the air. Whit moved close to her and kissed her again, holding his hand over a spot in the two-way mirror where there was obviously a watching camera.

The elevator came to a graceful, almost ceremonious halt at the ninety-seventh floor. But the scene revealed by the parting doors was not one Tamsen expected. Rather than the elegant and dimly-lit restaurant, the two stepped into a linoleum-tiled hallway with scuffed walls and florescent ceiling lights. The clanging of pans, the sizzle of a fryer, and the shouting of voices filled the space. Whit led her by the open kitchen. A handsome Latin server rushed past them, then stopped.

"*Hombre! Gusto verte!*"

"*Lo mismo*, Hector!" Whit replied.

It was beginning to occur to Tamsen that perhaps Whit had at one time been a fixture at the famous restaurant. She wondered if he'd bussed tables alongside Hector during college summers, or maybe he had been part of the wait staff.

Whit led her through a door marked *Quiet Beyond this Point* and, on the other side, was the answer to her question.

The warmly-lit room with its taupe carpet and supple white leather chairs had the reverence of a library and the low-key quiet of a day spa. Modern brass and crystal chandeliers hung low over small tables, and in the corner, a small coterie of musicians set up for their New Year's Eve gig. Whit escorted her to a spot close up, where a "reserved" plaque was perched in front of a bud vase holding a white rose and sprigs of pine. Before sitting down himself, he pulled out Tamsen's chair in a way that made her chest ache. She was remembering what it felt like to be valued.

An older brunette with slicked short hair and red lipstick set down two sparkling glasses of champagne.

"Welcome back, Whit. Compliments of Dutch," she said.

Whit tilted his glass and leaned toward Tamsen. "To what are we drinking? To our incredible liaison? To the forces that brought us together?"

"I hate to break the spell, but Theo's head lice brought us together," she said as she hooked her leg around his underneath the table. "That, and the girl with all the body art."

"Then I propose a toast to lice and to ink," he said. "And to the benevolent fates that sent me this improbable connection."

"To improbable connections," she said, touching the rim of her glass to his. Tamsen liked to think there were no random events—that every encounter had a purpose. Maybe it was just chance that had dropped Whit into her life at a such a desperate point, or perhaps there was a larger force with great designs at work.

Whit slid his chair back. "You need to see something," he said.

He took her hand and guided her across the bar. They wove between tables of couples cozied together, speaking intimately over small plates of rosemary almonds and Niçoise olives. He led her in front of the vast wall of windows to the west, an expanse of floor to ceiling glass, ninety-seven floors above the city. The only thing separating them from the icy, thin atmosphere at this confounding elevation was a transparent barrier that allowed them to glimpse not only the stars above, but the stars below. There were miles and miles of pinhead lights, some steady and others pulsing to an inaudible tempo.

"It looks like a circuit board," she said.

"It looks like a map," he replied.

"A map of what, though?" she asked. He paused a moment, looking out into the blackness toward the invisible horizon.

"A map of conceivable things," he said. "Of dreams and notions."

She understood, marveling at the human ingenuity that created everything they could see and beyond. "And potential realized," she added.

Whit took her hand and drew his face close to the glass, parting his lips. He exhaled a delicate cloud of vapor and, taking Tamsen's index finger, etched a heart into the fog. She watched his expression, trying to read something into the gesture, but his aspect was distant. He noticed he was being observed and his eyes twinkled like one of the lights on the ground, reflecting only her amusement and refusing to give up whatever resided in his head.

A tall man with angular features, whose scrubby head hung down as if he had spent a lifetime avoiding low ceilings, pressed his palm into Whit's shoulder. "I hate to interrupt this tête-à-tête, but we've got a deal, young man."

Whit turned and embraced the man. "Lenny," he said affectionately.

"You ready to impress your lovely lady?" the man asked.

At the piano, Whit shifted a standing microphone and tugged back his jacket cuffs. Lenny coddled an immense stand-up bass and two other band members, a sax player and percussionist, tweaked and tuned their instruments until Whit leaned back and mumbled directives. They all nodded, waiting for his count-in.

The waitress refreshed Tamsen's drink, but she didn't notice. Her attention was fixed on her date's nimble fingers and the way he closed his eyes while his piano riffs wove their color into the fabric of the improvised jazz melody. The sophisticated lounge patrons in their tuxedos and sequined dresses bobbed their heads to the rhythm, pausing their conversations to watch while Whit lost himself in soaring arpeggios and mesmerizing triads.

The waitress jarred Tamsen from her trance. "He's pretty amazing, huh?"

"He used to work here?" Tamsen asked.

"He played our weekend brunch for years. Started when he was, like, twelve. I've never seen him on piano."

Whit rose from the piano bench and turned the knobs on a small floor amp, then slung on an electric guitar and cued the drummer.

"He always does this song," the woman said about the distinct rhythm.

"Who is it?" Tamsen asked, loving the sultry groove and entrancing percussion. Whit's mouth was practically touching the mic as he sang.

"It's an old George McCrae tune," the server replied. Tamsen had never heard of him.

Tamsen was surprised by Whit's range and the falsetto he managed to hit with unwavering clarity. When the final soulful note diminished, and the audience whooped and applauded, Whit looked to her. His expression was inquiring, a soft smile with lifted eyebrows. It reminded Tamsen of the way Theo looked for her in the bleachers at the tennis club when he won a point at the end of a match. She nodded to Whit, pressing her palm to her chest, and joined the other patrons' eager applause as Lenny reverently acknowledged "our longtime friend, the incomparable Kyle Whitman."

Tamsen was dizzy from the champagne when they took the elevator to the first floor and exited again onto the street. They found the nameless fat tire bike locked up to a black painted rack near the parkway. The alcohol and proximity to Whit on the bike gave her a sense of infallibility, despite the fact that they were hydroplaning over icy streets. She wound her arms around Whit's waist and rested her helmet against his back, feeling his side muscles contract through his coat as he pedaled toward Superior to their next stop. They passed the Old Water Tower, decorated in Fraser fir garlands with strings of white lights. Massive holly and juniper wreaths hung on each of its enormous windows. The painting in her hotel room did not do it justice. Tamsen marveled at the yellow limestone, its thick clefts and bumps casting shadows across its stalwart façade, luminous in the wash of footlights.

"I have a painting of this building over my bed," Tamsen yelled over a blaring firetruck. The building showed no outward scars of the fire that had incinerated everything around it. "It's a fortress," she said out loud to herself.

Whit navigated his way around a taxi stand. "Where next?" Tamsen hollered.

"Sushi," he said, veering across four lanes toward Lake Michigan.

They got off the bike at Monroe Harbor and stood facing a landscape of white that dead-ended into the blackness of the horizon. With the city at their backs, everything was so still, unlike the Lite-Brite matrix they'd seen from the top of the Hancock. There was no distinction between the shore and the water. Weeks of wind and frigid temperatures had created a four-inch-thick base, and on top of that there was another three inches of freshly fallen powder.

Tamsen spied a glowing structure about a hundred yards out. "A tent?"

"C'mon," Whit coaxed, pushing the bike onto the white blanket toward the tent. "We have a 10:30 reservation."

Her instinct was an immediate refusal to budge, but she wanted to show him she wasn't afraid of cracking the surface and plunging into the thirty-eight-degree water, even though she was already shivering from the thought.

"How thick did you say this ice was?" she chattered, her breath dissipating in a wind gust.

"You have to trust me," he replied as they advanced, following a trail of footprints leading to the structure—it was more of an origami box than a tent. "One of my students is a fishing enthusiast."

Hearing Whit's voice, a husky man in a ratty fisherman's cap popped his head into the cold and exhaled smoke from his Swisher Sweet.

"Place is all yours till midnight," he said. "I'm grabbing myself a burger and boilermaker at Miller's."

A tiny infrared heater radiated just enough warmth to make the inside of the hut bearable. Whit situated them, pulling off his gloves and connecting a playlist of sultry standards—Dean Martin, Lou Rawls, Ella Fitzgerald, and others—to a wireless speaker. He rifled to the bottom of his backpack, wrenching out a bag of Jays potato chips, a plastic container of red pepper hummus, and two water bottles. He unzipped his parka and handed Tamsen a silver flask with the Juilliard logo emblazoned on the front.

"Cocktails and appetizers," he said.

She sniffed the warm, oaky smell that reminded her of Cormac and drew a burning sip of whiskey. Whit shuffled two folding camping stools side by side in front of a foot-diameter hole, then pulled a wool military blanket over their shoulders, bundling himself close to Tamsen. She felt his cold nose press into her cheek as he kissed her mouth, softly at first and then gaining determination, his cold, bare hands giving her a jolt as they jockeyed for a spot beneath her winter coat in the small of her back. Had it not been for the cramped space of the hut, the bulk of their outerwear, and the fact that they were basically hovering over twenty feet of frigid water on an ice cube, Tamsen would no longer be wearing clothes. He couldn't keep his hands off of her and she couldn't get enough.

"If we don't put in a line, we'll never eat," he said, pulling back to calm himself. He must have seen the corners of Tamsen's mouth turn down because he started to laugh.

"Sushi," she said. Whit laughed. She wondered whether he was kidding about catching their dinner. She'd seen the hideous carp that fishermen wrestled out of the water by the docks during the summertime.

"I'm good with chips," she said, drinking from the water bottle. The Jays chips were salty. She was suddenly so thirsty.

Tamsen watched as Whit baited a stubby pole and lowered a squirming minnow into the small dark pool at their feet.

"What would your fancy friends say if they knew you were ice fishing on New Year's Eve?"

Given that the Socialati were presently assembled for the bash at the Pullman Yacht Club, not even a quarter-mile up the harbor, Tamsen had already considered the question. "They'd assume I was on an Abercrombie and Kent expedition where a staff of ten uniformed minions held the rod and another ten dangled grapes over my mouth while administering a shiatsu treatment."

"Damn, I forgot the grapes," Whit said.

"I'll let it go, provided you deliver on the shiatsu," she replied, squeezing his knee.

She heard the sound of feet crunching through snow. Reflexively, Tamsen hid the flask between her legs, like she used to do at St. Christina football games when the principal approached the bleachers. She looked for a thick, blue coat and gold badge of the police. Instead, a delivery guy announced himself. He slid a cardboard deep-dish pizza box from a large insulated sleeve and handed Whit a receipt and a fistful of napkins. Tamsen clapped her hands together like a delighted child. She was both relieved that they wouldn't be having carp sashimi for dinner and thrilled with the ingenuity of Whit's planning. It was the simplest of meals, in the most unlikely setting, yet no Michelin-starred restaurant ever served anything that tasted even remotely as delicious as the deep-dish pie of tomato, garlic, and cheese. She smiled at the recognition of an old feeling. She had her hunger back. She wanted to eat.

Tamsen lost track of time until a popping noise broke through the sky. Fireworks blasted into the air from Navy Pier, illuminating the fishing shelter like lightning. Whit quickly packed up his Herschel bag and Tamsen finished the last drop of bottled water. As she folded the green military blanket, Tamsen noticed the spring bobber on the fishing line toggling seismically above the water. Whit quickly grabbed the short fishing pole from where he had wedged the rig and began reeling as the tip of the pole bowed with the weight of their fighting catch. He grabbed the line close to the mouth of a bug-eyed creature with a black spot on its dorsal fin. Whit lifted the fish, liberating it from the hook in its lower mandible.

"Round goby," Whit said. "Bottom feeder."

"What do you do with it?" Tamsen asked.

"They're an invasive species, so not much. They're natives of the Black and Caspian Seas."

"That's a long way from Lake Michigan," Tamsen said.

"They came by cargo ship—the ballast water." Whit held the creature, eye to eye. "Fishermen hate 'em. They'd have me toss the dude out on the ice, but it's not his fault he's here. Happy New Year, goby," he said, tossing the fish back into the hole in the ice.

"Moby the goby," Tamsen mused. "We caught him, so he's really not our white whale."

They stepped out into the subzero open air to the distant sound of car alarms and sirens while bright confetti lit up the darkness. Whit stood behind Tamsen with her body enveloped in his grasp and her head tucked perfectly beneath his chin, marveling at the spectacular bursts of color that launched the start of January.

"Any resolutions?" Whit asked.

Tamsen didn't even know where to start.

"I don't want to set myself up for failure," she laughed.

"Let's make wishes instead," he said. He reached in his pocket and pulled out the two cappuccino tokens the coat check girl at the conservatory had given him.

"But the lake is frozen," Tamsen said.

"Then think of these as time release," he said. "Throw yours as far as you can and when the ice melts in the spring, it will sink to the bottom of Lake Michigan, and your wish will come true."

"Unless it's swallowed by a goby," she added, throwing the coin in an arc as far as she could muscle.

"If a goby gobbles your wish, your wish will come true in spades," Whit said, hurling his token into the darkness.

They waited, listening for a soft thud. But Whit had propelled his wish far and when it landed, the soft snow silenced its fall.

A burst of fireworks lit up the sky above the Ferris wheel on the pier. The sky flashed orange, pink, and green, then sprayed silver bursts that crackled as they dissipated before touching the ground. Tamsen could no longer ignore the urgent signal her body was giving her after consuming three glasses of champagne, a couple shots of whiskey, and an entire bottle of water. She knew the only restroom in the vicinity was the one at the yacht club and using it would come at the risk of seeing someone she knew.

A part of her didn't care whether the Socialati spotted her with Whit; she could care less about their judgments and gossip. But she had to be discreet. One beady eye spotting her with Whit and Victor would hear within minutes. She wasn't breaking any rules, but Victor would be incensed if he thought she was seeing anyone. She'd asked for time to find clarity about their marriage, not to run around Chicago with a young boyfriend. Victor might mention her relationship with Whit to the kids, and Tamsen knew he would try to frighten them—to make them think she might abandon them.

The pressure in her bladder mounted and she squeezed her legs together the way Charlotte used to do in preschool when she was absorbed by a project at the finger-painting easel and refused to stop for a break to the bathroom. Tamsen knew the club had a side entrance; members often used it during the summertime when the yachts were moored in the dock. She would duck in and out, unnoticed.

"We need to make a pit stop," she told Whit, climbing onto the saddle. "Straight away, and please, pedal fast."

The yacht club was two levels. The first housed a small kitchen and a casual restaurant and bar. The second level was an immense, open room with a dance floor, bandstand, and nautical rope chandeliers. A vast wall of glass faced east toward the harbor—this is where the annual New Year's party was staged.

Whit leaned the bike against the white cedar siding between a blue dumpster and the building.

"Lead the way," he said as Tamsen entered through the side door, which had been wedged open by the staff, who had begun the job of post-party cleanup.

They slipped into a rear vestibule and down a long, carpeted hallway lined with black and white photographs of club members and their sailboats, chronicling countless regattas, including the "The Mac"—the oldest annual freshwater distance race in the world. It started every year in Chicago and finished at Mackinac Island in uppermost Michigan. Tamsen felt like a supercharged rebel, a stealthy imposter who belonged, yet didn't. She causally glanced around the corner at the restrooms. She could spot a number of partygoers in fur coats near the grand staircase, but they were a safe distance away and Tamsen knew she could slip by without being seen.

The thrill of the secrecy was almost as compelling as her persistent need to get into a stall as quickly as possible, which is why Tamsen only noticed the pair of silver satin Pedro Garcia heels on the other side of the partition too late. As she hastily lathered her hands, she heard the click of a latch behind her, sending a surge of adrenaline to every hair follicle on her body. The stall door opened, and to Tamsen's immediate relief, the modelesque young woman in a fitted, elastic, silver-bandage Herve Leger dress was not a member of the Socialati.

"Happy New Year," the woman giggled as she bathed her small hands under the automatic faucet. Tamsen looked down at her own dry hands and the veins that had become more prominent with middle age.

"Your bracelet is exquisite," Tamsen said, admiring the gold cuff she wore on her right wrist. Tamsen recognized the unique piece from a jewelry store window on Michigan Avenue.

"My boyfriend, he likes little surprises," she said, tossing a terrycloth hand towel into the basket under the floating marble vanity.

Tamsen recalled the last time her own husband had bought her something special. Theo had been a week old. Tamsen was in the kitchen with Aneta and Charlotte when Victor called down from upstairs that Theo had awakened for an afternoon feeding. Tamsen went to the nursery and found Theo sound asleep, a velvet box and a calligraphy note reading, "I love you, Mommy," staged beside the swaddled newborn.

The woman left and Tamsen surveyed her reflection. She smiled, thinking she looked out of place here, like a Yeti tailgating at a Bears game. She unfolded the cream turtleneck so that it concealed her mouth, thinking Whit would be amused by her disguise. She opened the restroom door a crack, plotting her swift exit and surveying the scene. Standing near the valet desk, the woman with the bracelet was engaged in a deep kiss, while her boyfriend's hand kneaded her flesh beneath the tight dress. She held still, her hands encircling his neck, as he pressed both palms into her perfect ass and then squeezed, his ravenous fingers exploring every angle of her roundness. His aggressiveness made Tamsen cringe—the way his hands groped the woman's body, so voraciously, so violently. Tamsen wanted to rescue her. She wanted to lift her onto Whit's fat tire bike and ferry her far, far away from here. A dull ache radiated from the floor of Tamsen's pelvis. She squeezed her legs together. The bike saddle, she thought.

The man's hair had a straight line across the base of his head—it was freshly trimmed, with a slight gloss of pomade to hold each strand in place. His tuxedo was fashionable, with a trendy double vent and fitted waist. When the man pulled his face off the woman, she recognized his profile. Victor.

Around the age of six, Tamsen had fallen out of a tree. On impact, all the wind had been knocked from her lungs and she had lain in the grass, under a sky scudded with thin clouds, thrashing her arms and legs and thinking she was going to die. Seeing Victor at the yacht club with the gorgeous woman in the bracelet shocked Tamsen. Her mind was consumed with the sight of Victor's groping hands, his head pressing into the soft skin of the young woman. As with the day in the tree, she could not breathe. It took Tamsen a moment to connect to the feeling. Her diaphragm tightened, cutting off her air supply. She gasped. Every hair on her skin stood stiff. From the pads of her fingers to the soft skin behind her ankles, a blast of panic flooded her limbs. It was not jealousy or betrayal she felt; it was terror.

Her mind took her to her bedroom on Astor Street. She could smell the tobacco scent of Victor's cologne burn in her nostrils. She saw the bookshelf beside her with a wedding photo in the silver frame, her and Victor. He smiled into the camera, but she was looking in another direction—she was laughing at something.

Tamsen tried to control her breathing, but the vision was all around her. The books were there, standing end to end—brown, red, and orange spines in perfect order. She could see them through the glass, but she couldn't touch them; she needed to touch them. Then into the nightmare came an element that terrified Tamsen enough that she needed every ounce of waning consciousness to suppress a rising, morbid scream. It was a figure behind the glass—a faceless specter.

Tamsen forced herself to feel the cool porcelain sink. She thought, *I'm here now, with Whit.* She drew in a strained breath and rushed from the bathroom, running with legs she could not feel, down the hall, past the sailboat photos, toward the service entrance. She extended her arm as she neared the door, grasping the steel knob and turning it, but the door would not move. She pushed her body against it again and again. She could hear Whit's muffled voice from the outside.

"They locked the surface bolt," he said.

She continued pushing, now feverishly slamming her shoulder into the metal door in an attempt to dislodge it.

"Tamsen, the bolt," she heard Whit say.

She looked down at the knob and saw a steel bolt—the staff must have secured it behind Whit. Tamsen unlatched it and stumbled outside, flinging herself into Whit's arms.

"What is it?" he said. "What's wrong?"

At first, she said nothing. She clung to Whit while she let the calm grow, allowing her terror to fade into him until any lingering fear of the scene that had momentarily taken hostage of her mind was cast out.

"I saw Victor in there," she said.

"You okay?" he asked.

She bent over, allowing blood to flow to her head.

"Gimme a sec," she said, drawing long inhales through her nose until she felt better. Until she was steady again.

"Maybe I should take you back to The Talisman?"

Whit's voice was comforting. She stood up slowly, feeling like herself again, and considered the information her brain had yet to process. For months, Tamsen had slept in a cheap hotel while Victor was out buying $25,000 baubles for a beautiful young woman.

Tamsen looked at Whit. "No, not The Talisman. Tonight, we're staying at the Corinthian."

Whit locked up the bike while Tamsen darted into the hotel. The five-star Hotel Corinthian had hosted a massive New Year's Eve event and the elevators were moving slowly on account of all the partygoers heading home. Tamsen hurried toward the tall black marble reception desk; she didn't want Whit to overhear the exorbitant room rates she'd surely be quoted. The bellman approached her, extending a complimentary bottle of Fiji water.

"May I have another for my friend?" Tamsen asked. Friend. She didn't know what else to call Whit.

A woman with a neat, chin-length brown bob tapped the keyboard at a furious speed while Tamsen waited.

"I regret that our standard and deluxe category rooms are completely sold out," the desk attendant said with diction and demeanor so far superior to Ron's that Tamsen figured the woman must have attended college for hospitality. "I am able to offer you one of our 46th-floor suites, however, at a rate of $3,400 this evening."

Tamsen gulped. The cost of the suite was more than eight times that of her room at The Talisman. But this would not come out of her hidden cash. This was going to come out of Victor's pocket. If he challenged her, she'd bring up the silver-dressed woman's bracelet.

"Tell me about the suite," Tamsen said as Whit joined her.

"It's 950 square feet with a king-sized bed and a full dining room with small butler's pantry. There's a soaking tub with bubble jets and a separate shower with steam and a rain head."

"A steam shower," Whit repeated. "Sounds over the top."

Tamsen debated. It was either this insane splurge or The Talisman. She couldn't justify the cost.

The attendant continued. "It's called the Writer's Suite. There's a complete library with first edition books signed by any author who has ever stayed at our hotel, as well as many other famous titles."

The Writer's Suite. It was a sign. Tamsen smiled.

"We'll take it."

1 2

Tamsen squinted into the sunlight, which had the disorienting intensity of an interrogation light. It formed a piercing sliver through the crack between the celadon silk drapes on the east window of the bedroom. She closed her eyes again, bringing her surroundings into mental focus: a plush cloud-top mattress, a feather pillow supporting her head, sateen sheets against her bare, contented body, the dull hum of a beverage refrigerator, and the rhythmic breathing beside her, in and out, in and out. Whit.

Tamsen lay still, wanting to roll from her side to face him. But if she moved, he might wake up. The last time she'd checked her phone for notifications was at 4:18 a.m., which was the exact minute they had finally untangled their bodies. She blushed and felt the slippery cotton under her limbs and the cool circulation of air skimming her bare skin. She spied her clothes in a trail where Whit had peeled them off, piece by piece, in the early hours of the morning. She suddenly wished that she had put on his Johnny Cash t-shirt before they'd finally gone to sleep. She knew her physique was fine enough when she was dressed, but there was no way to disguise the stretch marks on her abdomen and the slight paunch around her navel—the unavoidable imperfections of a naked, over-forty body that had carried two children.

Whit stirred. Tamsen held her breath. There was another moment of quiet and she heard the sheets rustle. His hand reached over and encircled her hip, pulling her close and laminating his chest to her back. He kissed her neck and ran his fingers lightly down the length of her thigh. Tamsen squirmed, then burst into laughter.

"Hold still," he whispered as his fingers continued to her waist. She could barely contain herself. "Are you ticklish?" he asked playfully, his voice gravelly from sleep.

The only people who knew this particular weakness were the ones who had grown up under her same roof on 113th Street.

"No," she replied, curling into a ball and suppressing an outburst.

In an instant, his fingers were under her arms, deep in her sides, beneath her chin. She squealed wildly as he managed to capture her knee between his thumb and forefinger. "I call this The Vise," Whit said, pretending to be ruthless. She struggled to wriggle free, pleading through flaying fits of hilarity for Whit to relent. The torture of being tickled was the only act that could force tears from Tamsen's eyelids. Not just tiny droplets that left a sentimental trail on her cheeks, but a full-blown, smeary deluge that squeezed from the four corners of her eyes and washed over her entire face.

He made a move for her feet and she jerked away with such force that her arm knocked the black silk shade from the reading sconce, sending it gracefully airborne onto the nightstand. It landed in a slop of melted ice cream and hot fudge, the remnants of the New Year's feast they'd ordered from room service before finally turning out the lights.

"Now you've done it," he teased.

Whit reached over her and delicately lifted the innocent projectile, leisurely raising it from the cut-glass chalice of sweet creamy soup. Tamsen dabbed her eyes with the backs of her hand. Her cheeks ached from laughing and her chest rose and fell while she tentatively regained her composure. She watched Whit float the malted vanilla bean–sodden shade over her exposed torso, where the gravity coaxed a heavy drop of liquid confection into a free fall toward her belly.

"Are you one of those guys who's into food?" she giggled.

He looked into her eyes, wordlessly daring her to stay still. He allowed the sweet beads of vanilla to drop in a dapple trail across her skin, then lowered his lips to her body and kissed them away, one by one, in a decadent, patient, adoring way. Like a sacrament.

Tamsen was alive again.

Afterward, they collapsed once more, side by side in unbounded exhaustion. Not one gusseted goose down pillow remained on the bed.

Tamsen's mind was scrubbed clean, momentarily void of self-judgment. She felt nothing but absolute presence. She closed her eyes. They lay in stillness on their backs, reconstituting their wits with their fingers meshed tightly together. Tamsen's toes found a point of contact on Whit's calf and felt the hairs on his leg matted with perspiration.

She put her hand between his legs and delicately ran her fingertips up and down.

"Just a little quid pro quo," she said and stopped. "For the tickling." He rolled toward her and grazed her shoulder with his lips, noticing the time on the bedside tablet. He groaned.

"What?" she asked.

"Will you be disappointed if I take off?" he asked.

"Before round number three?"

He kissed her. "Nothing sounds better, but I'm supposed to meet up with an old music friend. And by old, I mean, like eighty."

"That's sweet of you."

"Not really. He won't back off—flew in from Boston, so I can't exactly say no."

Tamsen wondered what the older man's agenda could be, but she didn't want to pry. Musicians often travelled most months of the year. He was probably in town for a performance. A skittish swarm of butterflies flapped their wings in her stomach at the thought of him leaving.

Whit poked her ribs playfully, causing her to yelp and recoil. Then he lazily swung his legs over the side of the extra-deep memory foam mattress and lumbered to the butler's pantry, humming a melody Tamsen did not recognize as he filled two tall glasses with cool water from the filtered tap. Tamsen reached to the floor for a crumpled sheet and pulled it over her body, partially concealing her figure from her clavicles to her knees.

"If you're cold, I can turn up the heat," Whit said. He meandered, naked, past the bookcase and pulled out a volume. "Herman Melville, yet another member of The Nucking Futs Society—he was president, I think."

"No, Tolstoy was president," Tamsen said. "Melville was social chair."

Whit laughed and tossed Moby Dick onto the bed. "What does the white whale represent, exactly—Moby Dick?"

She hadn't read the story in over two decades and felt a little like her seventeen-year-old self who'd been called on in Sister Rosemary's English class. Tamsen leafed the pages while he explored the suite.

"Well, it really depends on which character you're asking. Madness, evil, a great prize. The whale is an unstoppable force of nature, an enigma. I think the quest for the white whale is man's struggle against nature, really, against fate."

Whit pressed some of the buttons on the remote control. "This A/V system is too advanced for my grilled cheese sensibilities," he laughed.

Tamsen observed his body with detached scrutiny. He was da Vinci's Vitruvian Man, the perfectly proportioned specimen, standing akimbo with all anatomical points correlating to one another in reflective symmetry. "The length of the outspread arms is equal to the height of the man," she recalled from a coffee table book about the drawing. Tamsen told herself to memorize Whit, to catalogue every contour so she could revisit this moment whenever she doubted the reality of their night, or for when she questioned whether Whit was simply a fabrication of her desperate state.

He propped himself up on his elbow beside her. "You only cry when you're tickled."

"Crying is exhausting," she replied.

"I used to cry whenever I played *Metamorphosen*," he said. "I'd just sob."

"I don't know it," she said.

"Strauss. I want it played at my funeral."

"You need to work on your pillow talk," she said, cupping his cheek in her hand.

"Would you come?" he asked.

"This is the part where you light a cigarette," she replied.

"I'm serious, would you come to my funeral?"

She searched his eyes, as if she would find in their depths the origin of his terribly morose question. The mere suggestion of such a tragic event took her to a verdant cemetery lawn on a bright spring day, where a group of weeping relatives wearing dark sunglasses and black attire were gathered around a six-foot-deep hole in the ground.

"No," she said.

"I'm serious," he replied.

"I'd rather just send carnations," she said. She was keeping it light, but neither of them was smiling.

"Too bad. You'd love my Aunt Linda," he said.

"We probably graduated high school the same year," she shot back.

Tamsen brushed a clump of bangs off his forehead then traced her finger over his full brows.

Whit stared at her. "I start CBT this week," he said. Cognitive behavioral therapy—Tamsen had heard of it.

"That's great," she said, elevating her tone, relieved he'd changed the subject.

"My doctor recommended it, and my mom's all over me, too."

"Because she's your mom," Tamsen said. She had explored every possible therapy and diet when Theo was diagnosed.

"Everybody has an opinion on how to fix me—tinker with my meds, change what I eat, counseling. This guy I'm meeting, he wants to lock me in a padded cell with a cello."

"The exposure method," Tamsen laughed lightly and thought of being locked up with Victor. She flinched. No amount of the exposure technique could ever cure her of him. "It's worth a try," she said, wanting to encourage him.

"Yes," he said. "I think I'm getting closer."

Whit walked to the bathroom and started the shower. Tamsen stayed in bed with her hand where his body had been, replaying the mental tape of their night, registering images of him fastening the helmet strap beneath her chin, laughing with Lenny behind the piano, and baiting the fishing hook. Tamsen checked her emails from her phone: a reminder that she had a mammogram on Wednesday, and a notification of her upcoming appointment with Clay. There was also an email from the Leda Sparrow Financial Freedom people, urging her to purchase her ticket. They were offering a New Year, New You $150 upgrade to VIP level.

The message was brief. "Start the new year off right with the chance to mingle with Leda Sparrow in the Golden Osprey Lounge." Tamsen had moved between definitely not going and then definitely going to the seminar so many times that she didn't know where she stood. Leda Sparrow was likely all show and little substance, judging from her info-mercials; there were women crying in gratitude and auditoriums of people holding their hands up in the shape of birds and screaming. But if the seminar did have something of value to share—something that could help Tamsen smile like the women in Leda's shiny testimonials, to regain a shard of financial power, well . . .

Whit's voice from the shower broke through Tamsen's thoughts. He was singing the Robert McCrae tune, "You Can Have It All." Tamsen read the email again. A face to face meeting might get her personalized advice from Leda, but the total cost for the VIP ticket would be $650. It was too much. She was already anticipating the backlash from Victor, seeing the credit card bill with the Hotel Corinthian line item. What had she been thinking? He would ask her who she was with. She pushed the horrible thoughts away and tossed her phone aside, crawling from bed.

Tamsen opened the mechanical drapes, flooding the suite with late morning light and reminding herself that it couldn't be more than an hour till check-out time. She should order them breakfast, after the evening Whit had planned last night. She looked at the room service menu and rejected the least expensive item on the breakfast menu—a bakery basket of fresh croissants and brioche. The small print in the menu said that there was a 20% surcharge on all orders, not including an 18% gratuity, the hotel tax, the city tax. At least the tea in the butler's pantry was complimentary. She made them each a cup.

Whit emerged, dressed in last night's attire. His slicked back wet hair and flushed complexion gave Tamsen a glimpse of what he must have looked like when he was Theo's age, before the manic Vienna episode, at a time when he truly believed his prospects were limitless. He tossed her a fluffy Turkish cotton robe.

"That was seriously the best water pressure I've felt in my life," he said.

She interlaced her fingers behind his damp neck. "You deserve it," she said, kissing his minty mouth. "You deserve it all."

He took her hand and led her to the windows of their 46th floor view. They overlooked Michigan Avenue and the turbulent, gray lake beyond. They saw the lattice of arteries that were the streets, clogged with blue, black, red, and white car roofs that caught the glint of the noontime sun overhead. Tamsen felt the cold radiating off the spotless glass.

"Thar she blows!" he hollered, his forehead against the pane and his fingertip pressed against the window.

"Who?" she asked, tracking his sightline. He was pointing at the fat-tire bike leaned up against the No Parking sign where he'd locked it the night before.

"My bike," he said. "I've decided to call him Moby."

Tamsen walked him to the door, where Whit kissed her hard and then disappeared. She looked down at the street and watched him free Moby from the pole. He waved up in the direction of the 46th floor, even though Tamsen knew he couldn't really see her from the street. Then he blew a kiss in her direction and rode off. Tamsen heard the unsettling swish of the hotel bill sliding under the door of the suite and her heart quickened. She picked it up off the cold, marble entry floor and opened it. A giant pit sunk to the bottom of her stomach, crushing any butterflies that had previously occupied the space.

She unfolded the papers and saw the total amount: $4,120. The stranglehold of panic that gripped her chest made her lightheaded. She never should have put down the family credit card at the hotel registration desk the night before. Victor was going to explode when he saw the charge. She recalled the time she had put $2,000 on the card for a charitable donation to The Dexter School scholarship fund. She hadn't asked his permission first, so Victor reported the charge as fraudulent and told Tamsen that if she ever wanted to give away his money again, it would have to come out of her own pocket.

Her own pocket—what did that even mean? Any of the money she'd brought into their marriage had been absorbed long ago into the big pool of finances that Victor controlled from their home office. She conjured a mental picture of the deadbolted door and shivered.

Tamsen surveyed the Writer's Suite, trying to extract some modicum of pleasure from the sophisticated furnishings. She needed to appreciate every cent of this ill-conceived extravagance. The plum velvet sectional in the living area, the classic winter-white upholstered dining chairs around a chic, round Barbara Barry dining table, the high ceilings, the timeless molding details—none of these things erased her feeling of dread. The books, she thought. There was always value in her beloved books.

She walked across the plush, hand-knotted ivory carpet and stood in front of the Jacobean-stained armoire containing countless literary treasures. She ran the tips of her fingers over the still-rigid spines. There were classics mostly, but Chicago authors as well: Stuart Dybek, Rebecca Makkai, and Aleksandar Hemon. She was not surprised to see her former Beau Monde associate's name, Camille Sassi-Lehner, with a new book on the shelf. She wondered if Camille had done a reading at the hotel. Had Tamsen still been in publishing, she wouldn't have missed it. A little more than a year ago, she would have pulled the bound tomes out by the handful and sat down on the floor to examine each author's inscription. Then she would have voraciously devoured a paragraph from all the novels she loved, and maybe a few lines of some of the nonfiction books as well. So many magnificent hardbacks, and all Tamsen could think of was Victor and how he would punish her for her reckless night.

The sunlight through the east window captured the crystal on the

Cartier Tank watch he'd given her for her birthday when they were still dating. It cast a restless glimmering prism onto the ceiling. Tamsen heard a knock at the door.

"Housekeeping," beckoned a sweet voice.

"One minute," she replied, catching a glimpse of her puffy eyes and bedhead in a convex, starburst mirror.

Victor had something to show for the money he'd dropped on his date. Tamsen splurged on the Writer's Suite and would leave without even a bath. She walked into the butler's pantry and grabbed three tea bags from the mini bar. Keepsakes. As she dressed, she wondered what Victor's "corporate apartment" looked like. She had envisioned something as austere as The Talisman, but for all she knew, he might have taken up residence at The Four Seasons Hotel or one of the other five-star spots nearby. It seemed Victor was doing a lot for himself these days. A new luxury SUV, a sweetheart he showered with obscenely expensive gifts, and a big fat deadbolt on his office door to secure whatever dealings he didn't want Tamsen to see.

In the lobby, she maneuvered around an opulent seating area with two overstuffed sofas and freshly vacuumed Persian rug, stopping at the reception desk to pay down some of her massive bill with the $250 in cash she'd brought on her date with Whit. Far across the room, Tamsen saw a group of the elder WSC stateswomen gathering by the hostess stand at Le Verger, the hotel's opulent in-house restaurant. Le Verger was famous for their sumptuous brunches and house specialty, the crab cake Benedict. Tamsen turned her face away to avoid being recognized; she immediately felt like she was leaving the scene of a crime.

Under a crystal chandelier, she buried her nose in her phone, flexing her toes in her boots as she waited anxiously for the elevator to the street level. Her phone pinged. It was the Financial Future seminar again. Damn cookies. This time they'd sent a graphic of Leda Sparrow.

Her arms were spread wide and her head was tilted back as she smiled at the heavens, telling Tamsen that VIP tickets were going fast and if she didn't act now, she'd "miss the opportunity to reshape her future."

The elevator doors parted and there stood Cybill Hinton in a smart, Carolina Herrera dress with a black, mid-calf, collarless alpaca coat alongside her husband, who wore a conservative, gray pinstripe suit.

"Happy New Year, Tamsen," Cybill said. She seemed genuinely pleased with the chance encounter. "I have been meaning to call you."

All the blood rushed to Tamsen's face. She'd been caught in a walk of shame moment.

"Oh?" Tamsen said, remembering that she was still wearing last night's makeup.

Cybill pulled off her tan leather gloves.

"I know the word is out among *certain* WSC members that someone on the Board is vacating her spot." Tamsen hadn't heard. "I want to urge you to consider the opening," she said. "We're trying to reshape things. We need an infusion of youthful ingenuity, and I think you'd be a perfect addition."

Tamsen looked at Cybill, completely put together—the antithesis of Tamsen in her suede pants and ponytail. How could Cybill possibly think she was a suitable candidate for the WSC Board?

"I'm honored, Cybill," Tamsen managed. "I will definitely consider it."

"You've got some time," Cybill said. "We're still forming the nominating committee, but I'm a phone call away if you ever want to discuss the scope of the position. You could do a lot of good, Tamsen."

It somehow felt like this year was starting off on a different foot. Tamsen got into the elevator and looked down at her phone. She pulled up the Leda Sparrow email. Reshape. The WSC Board was a new shape. She'd do it. She'd buy the ticket and take the upgrade after all.

◆ ◆ ◆

Tamsen signed the registry in the lobby of Victor's building and clipped the identification badge to the strap of her handbag. Theo loved the badges. He liked to scan them at the entry terminals and watch the glass panels retract, allowing access to the elevator bank. It was "bring your child to work day" and Tamsen didn't plan to stay long. Just a quick hello to show Victor that she was trying. No one paid any attention to stay-at-home moms at this place, anyway.

"I want to put my face on the big copier," Theo said. It was one of the rituals the kids practiced any time they visited Summers & Peel. Tamsen had copies of Theo and Charlotte's scrunched faces dating back to the time they understood that they had to keep their eyes shut tight to avoid damaging their retinas.

The receptionist sat behind a curved, gray desk with clean lines and a floating walnut top. Behind her, a brushed-steel company logo was backlit and suspended against an orange suede wall. The floors were largescale, white glossy tiles. Two large heathered-felt rugs designated waiting areas to the left and right, each with a backdrop of a massive Hebru Brantley painting. Two anthracite Noguchi Freeform sofas with poppy-colored bolsters and eight coordinating white leather Herman Miller chairs were situated strategically, lending the arrangement to conversation. Tamsen appreciated the aesthetic, because she had executed it. It was nothing like the transitional décor of their brownstone on Astor; in recent years, Tamsen's taste had taken a turn toward a simpler style—less clutter meant less distraction.

In Victor's corner office, Charlotte and Theo raided his built-in snack bar while waiting for their father to finish up a meeting in an adjacent conference room. The wide selection ranged from popcorn to Oreo cookies, but Victor kept a supply of olives, parmesan cheese crisps, and pepperoni slices, all of which were allowed on Theo's ketogenic diet, on hand for special occasions like today.

"You guys are getting so big!" gushed Estelle, Victor's Executive Vice President of New Business. She carefully balanced her computer and a stack of periodicals in one hand, with a sugary soda, an apple fritter, and a media report in the other.

Estelle was the stereotypical French woman who could eat her weight in grass-fed butter and not gain a kilo. She was Tamsen's age and had worked for the firm since its inception. She was sharp, personable, tech-savvy, and impeccably organized. She set a business report on Victor's desk and kissed Tamsen on each cheek, and then once more, for good measure.

As Victor's right hand, Estelle easily worked ninety hours a week, commuting each day to Hilldale, an affluent Chicago suburb. The only time Tamsen saw Estelle's husband and kids was at the annual summer outing, when Summers & Peel rented out the largest amusement park within a hundred-mile radius. Estelle was unstoppable. She had a JD/MBA from Harvard, a pilot's license, and a black belt in karate. And for fun, she played competitive paddle tennis. The problems she deftly tackled on a daily basis involved decisions regarding billions of dollars, while the biggest issues Tamsen ever faced were whether to buy part-skim or whole milk string cheese, or how many tulip bulbs to plant in the parkway flowerbed. Tamsen felt entirely inferior every time she saw the woman.

"When can Sabrina sleep over?" Charlotte asked Estelle.

"And Pierre, too," Theo added.

Estelle looked at her watch. "You won't have to wait for a sleepover. Guess who'll be here in ten minutes for bring the children to work day?"

Theo cheered, and Charlotte went immediately to her backpack to pull out some sketches she'd been working on. Sabrina was an excellent artist and the girls loved spending time in the agency's art department. The assortment of Pantone markers, several in every conceivable color, was drool-worthy even to Tamsen.

"Daddy!" Theo jumped to his feet as Victor strolled in. Tamsen was glad Estelle was with them.

"I'll pick the kids up at 5:00, unless you're planning to take them to dinner," Tamsen said.

"There's something I'd like to discuss with you before you go," he replied, nodding to Estelle.

"Why don't I take Theo and Charlotte to reception and they can surprise *mes enfants*?" Estelle proposed. Tamsen suspected collusion.

Victor closed the eleven-foot walnut door to his office. "Sit down," he said.

Tamsen noticed a framed print ad on Victor's back wall, part of his menagerie of last year's award-winning concepts.

"Looks like you guys cashed in on one of my ideas," she remarked of a Thunderchicken ad with the tag line, *Gobble, Gobble*. "Does that mean I get a cut?"

"The concepts are always free, Tamsen. A monkey can come up with a tag line," he said as he checked his phone. "We make our money on the production; that's why Koop gets the big bucks."

He opened his *Daily Ad Deal* paper to the business section and tossed it across his desk so that it landed squarely in front of her with a slap. She read the headline, *Ms Majestic Narrows it Down*. Victor stood with his arms crossed, his eyes narrowed intently. Petra's company.

"I thought I told you to set something up for me," he fumed. "Everyone in this office knows she's your best friend. It's humiliating that I haven't been invited to pitch."

"I haven't spoken to Petra since before the holidays," Tamsen said.

"Do you have any idea how dismal business has been this year? Our accounts aren't spending a fraction of what they used to, and our revenues are the lowest they've been since 2007. If we don't land a big deal this quarter, people are going to lose their jobs."

"Petra's really busy. She doesn't even return my texts half the time." This was a lie.

"You don't get it, do you?" He bared his teeth. "Losing this deal will impact our children's financial future."

Tamsen turned her earring. Her nerves were choking her windpipe. She'd always assumed things were going well for Summers & Peel. Victor had never said anything to the contrary.

"We have one of those college savings accounts, right? And didn't you set up a trust for them a couple years ago? I signed all those papers."

"You mean our tax returns? The home refinancing stuff?" He laughed. "Not the same."

She felt like an idiot, as if she couldn't recognize a tax return. The truth was, she thought she'd looked the papers over. There were so many documents she'd signed in the chaos of Theo's diagnosis. She wasn't sleeping much at the time and it was enough to keep the mass of test reports and mountains of insurance claims in order. She'd never gone back to read any of the financial paperwork.

"Majestic hasn't selected an agency, at least not publicly. They're still in play. We need to nab them now, before they get swallowed up by some huge conglomerate."

Tamsen looked down at the article. Petra's name was in the first sentence. Tamsen's best friend was an international powerhouse. Tamsen envied how her best friend had Victor by the bollocks. They were always Tamsen and Petra. Twenty year-olds drinking pints and playing darts at the Whip & Carriage after classes. Tamsen noticed a line in the second paragraph, "account worth 100 million euros . . ."

"We can't afford to lose this, Tam," Victor said. "For Theo and Charlotte's sake."

For Theo and Charlotte. Tamsen stood up.

"I'll make the call."

◆ ◆ ◆

The day Tamsen met Hilly to fulfill a promise to the kids of a trip to the LEGO Store, Groundhog Day markdowns had mobilized hundreds of bargain hunters to swarm the indoor mall. A peppy, instrumental version of Whitney Houston's "It's Not Right, But It's Okay" provided a soundtrack to all the mayhem.

"A double espresso for me, and my friend wants a medium white mocha with skim and whipped cream," Tamsen said to the cash register attendant at the mall's coffee kiosk. The cashier tossed her head back and yelled the order to the barista, who was simultaneously steaming milk and combing her hair. Tamsen stepped back to have a clearer view of the LEGO Store, where she could observe Theo plunging his hands into bins of red and yellow mini blocks at the free play tables. Hilly saved a vacant bench closer to the store so the women could catch up without Tamsen worrying about Theo abandoning his construction project and leaving the store to ride the long escalators. Charlotte and Astrid waved to Tamsen from the floor above in the open atrium of the teeming building. Both girls had their phones and had been warned that their mothers thought they were responsible enough not to engage with strangers.

Tamsen didn't mind the drive to the suburban mall. It had long been her secret winter entertainment destination when Charlotte and Theo were younger. With an expansive food court, an indoor play area, and three toy stores under one roof, Tamsen considered the venue a boon for urban mothers who demanded ample parking, clean restrooms with changing stations, and at least two stores that sold high-end designer shoes.

"Did you bring hand sanitizer?" Hilly asked as she watched a girl walk by with a runny nose.

Tamsen produced a bottle of Purell. "I'm armed," she said, squeezing out a blob of the clear gel into Hilly's outstretched hand.

She was shocked when Hilly had agreed to join her on today's outing. Hilly had insisted they meet for a coffee to catch up, but never in a million years would Tamsen believe that Hilly would make the forty-five-minute commute to a mall. For one thing, Hilly shunned everything outside the Chicago city limits, calling even the nearest suburb "the country." She also refused to purchase anything for herself off the rack unless it came from Escada, Brunello Cucinelli, or Tom Ford on Oak Street. Department stores were far too plebeian for a woman of her means.

"Do anything special over the holiday?" Hilly asked, pursing her pink lips and looking around as if someone might recognize her. Tamsen thought of how far Whit had pitched his cappuccino token into the darkness over the frozen lake, and the way he'd playfully kicked snow onto her boots when her throw was less than half the distance.

"Pretty typical," Tamsen replied. Hilly spun the corrugated sleeve around her disposable coffee cup.

"Are you guys going to Aspen this year?" she asked. Tamsen tilted her head. The question was absurd, given the separation.

"Definitely not," she said. "What about you and Digby?"

"I wanted to ask you something," Hilly said, staring at her cup. Tamsen shook her head emphatically at Theo, who was holding up something that resembled a gun. He frowned but dismantled it anyway.

"What's up?" Tamsen asked.

"I need your word that our conversation will be kept in confidence." She took hold of Tamsen's upper arm. "You have to swear on Sister Magdalene's life." She was referring to the mother superior at St. Christina's.

"You have my word," Tamsen assured her, making the sign of the cross. "What's on your mind?"

"I have reason to believe that my husband might be seeing someone on the side," Hilly said.

"Are you sure?" asked Tamsen incredulously.

Hilly leaned in, her eyes widening. "So you haven't heard anything?" she asked.

"I don't know, he's always so attentive and adoring of you." After she said the words, she considered her own situation. By outward appearances, one would never suspect Victor of his true nature. She continued, "Has something happened that would make you think Digby's been unfaithful?"

A heavyset lady in slip-on shearling boots and a knit poncho meandered close to where the two women were seated. She hovered over an adjacent trashcan as she gnawed on a bulging tortilla that expelled bits of tomato and beans into the garbage with every voracious bite. Hilly eyed her and, with a grunt of distain, scooted closer to Tamsen.

"Digby is a creature of habit," she continued in the lowest voice she could manage over the din of chatter and piped-in adult contemporary music. "I've noticed he's been buying some new things for himself, and he's started working out with a personal trainer three times a week."

"I'm sure he's just trying to get in shape," Tamsen said.

Charlotte and Astrid walked up, giggling about a boy from choir on whom Astrid had a crush. Hilly immediately lit up and clapped her hands effervescently.

"How's the shopping, girls? I don't see any bags."

"Mom, can we get something to eat?" Charlotte asked. They'd planned to all have lunch together at Pickleman's. Hilly raised her eyebrows and looked expectantly at Tamsen. Tamsen knew she was not eager to sift through the forty-page menu with photographs of giant salads and burgers. "Food for the masses," Hilly called it, as if she had been raised in the French aristocracy.

"Why don't you two take some money and hit the food court?" Hilly proposed, quickly taking her wallet from her purse.

The girls squealed as Astrid grabbed the $50 Hilly thrust toward them and ran, rushing toward the pizza puff kiosk, to celebrate their independence. Hilly squared her shoulders to Tamsen, awaiting some further editorial comment.

"Hilly, if you're that worried, why not be direct? Tell Digby you're concerned," Tamsen suggested.

Hilly's eyes were beady. "I did ask him, and you know what he told me?" Her mouth was frozen in an open smile. "He said Victor inspired him, and everyone knows what Victor's been up to. You should have seen the woman he brought to the New Year's party."

Tamsen shook off the image of Victor groping the woman with the bracelet. She felt a wave of gratitude toward her friend. Hilly might have been a social climber and a fake, but at the end of the day, she was loyal.

"I think you're misjudging Digby," she said.

Hilly's hand flew to her mouth, but not before Tamsen saw that her lower lip was quivering.

"Hil," Tamsen said, putting her espresso on the floor. "What's the matter?"

"You don't understand."

"I do. Marriage is hard," Tamsen insisted. "It ebbs and flows. You guys have been together a long time, so you know that."

"He fucked the housekeeper," Hilly blurted, quickly checking that no one else had heard and then covering her face, sobbing into her hands. Tamsen opened her mouth, intending words of comfort, but nothing came out. She was stunned. She stroked Hilly's back. An old man in a blue tracksuit rode past them on a scooter. He noticed Hilly and made a sad face.

Hilly sat up and dabbed her eyes with the corner of her limited-edition cashmere Duo d'Etriers shawl. She opened her new Givenchy satchel and pulled out an orange bottle.

"Mommy's supplements," she said. "I'm so stressed." Hilly swallowed the pill with her eyes closed.

"What are you taking?" Tamsen asked.

Hilly straightened and stuck out her chest, pivoting in her seat. "So overwhelming to be around all these people."

Tamsen touched Hilly's hand. "Some of that stuff is really addictive."

"Digby fell right into Angeline's trap, stupid fool. She always pranced around the kitchen in these short shorts, tight t-shirts. 'I made eggs, Mr. Digby, here is your dry cleaning, Mr. Digby, can I suck your dick for you, Mr. Digby.'"

Tamsen knew the nanny as kind and hard-working. Angeline had watched Charlotte at the summer home on several occasions when Aneta was off and Tamsen needed to take Theo to a doctor's appointment. Angeline had refused to accept money for the babysitting because she was already being compensated by Hilly.

"Hilly," Tamsen said. "I am so sorry."

"Be sorry for Astrid. She doesn't know she has a half-sister on the way."

"At least Digby was honest about the affair."

"As if he could hide it. We have to foot the bill for this kid."

"I'm sure he regrets it," Tamsen said.

"We haven't had sex in months. Every time I think of being intimate with him, I think of that opportunistic home-wrecker and her twenty-three-year-old . . . young twat," Hilly exclaimed.

Tamsen listened as Hilly heaped all the blame on Angeline. If Hilly wanted to remain with Digby, it was just easier to make everything the nanny's fault.

"Do you need the name of a counselor?" Tamsen asked.

"We're seeing somebody," she sniffed. "I'm trying to therapy my way back into trusting him."

Tamsen couldn't even count the many times during their marriage she had wished she'd caught Victor cheating on her so that she could justify leaving him. Hilly didn't recognize that she was holding the golden ticket out of her troubled marriage.

"You could divorce him, you know," Tamsen said.

"And get an annulment?" Hilly huffed. "Not an option. Besides, I can't afford to leave him. I mean, how would I manage? You know that Frith woman, the one who was married to the finance mogul, got nothing when she and her husband split."

"Her name is Sally," Tamsen interjected.

Hilly continued. "Everyone said she was entitled to 50%, but you know these banking guys, they're clever as rats; they find loopholes and tropical islands where they bury the money. She's practically destitute. She's working at the new fitness club on Elston." Hilly's voice was high and pinched. "As a locker room valet! One day, penthouse of the Palmolive Building, the next, a dumpy two-bedroom in Ukrainian Village and filling the tampon machine."

Suddenly the mall felt very warm. Tamsen stripped off her mohair sweater and fanned herself with the paper sleeve of a stuffed pretzel. She looked at Hilly in her Zac Posen pantsuit and black Miu Miu shoes and imagined her wearing an off-the-rack polyester blouse, sucking on a loaded carnitas burrito with a shopping bag of returns on the floor beside her. She knew the fantasy was impossible, because Hilly would never allow herself to backslide after ascending the summit of Mount Socialati. Hilly and Tamsen's motivations were different, but Tamsen knew Hilly's fear of losing everything all too well.

Despite Charlotte's objection, Tamsen turned on jazz for the car ride home; Whit had introduced her to Miles Davis. "Birth of the Cool" had become Tamsen's serenity-now pill. Through the rear-view mirror, she noticed Theo in the backseat fiddling in his coat pockets.

"Whatcha got there, buddy?" she asked.

Charlotte turned in her seat to better evaluate the situation in the back. "He shoplifted something," she said.

Theo stared back at Tamsen in the mirror. "Nothing," he said.

"You know, your dad once told me that when he was little he used to shove anything in his pockets that would fit: bottle tops, marbles, crickets, rubber bands, even donut holes."

Theo smiled and looked out the window. "Really?"

"He said if it didn't belong to anybody and it wasn't nailed down, then as far as he was concerned, it belonged to him."

Theo slowly withdrew two fists full of LEGO blocks from his coat. "Do these belong to anybody? Or do they belong to everybody?" he asked.

"I think you know the answer to that question," she said warmly. "We can bring them back next time, okay? Along with a letter of apology to the store manager."

"Yeah," Theo smiled. "But I wanna tell Daddy I took them—and that I put them in my pockets."

"Mama," Charlotte said. "What were you and Aunt Hilly talking about at the mall?"

"Just mom stuff," Tamsen replied.

"Stuff about Astrid and me?" Charlotte pressed.

"No, not about you kids." Tamsen paused, trying to recall some aspect of the conversation she could reveal to Charlotte without having to lie about the entire discourse. "We talked about a lot of things," she said.

"Like what?" Charlotte pressed.

"Vacation spots, finances, work."

"You mean like money and jobs?" Charlotte asked.

"Yes, all those things," Tamsen said.

Charlotte twirled her hair the way she always did when she was ruminating on something. "Pierre and Sabrina take the bus to school."

"Cool," said Tamsen.

"Are you going to get a job?" Charlotte asked.

Tamsen blinked, considering the direction she could take the conversation.

"I had a great job before your dad and I decided to start a family, and I suppose I could go back. It might be fun, actually." Tamsen thought of Sally Frith and she knew she might not actually have a choice. She wished she had even one of Estelle's graduate degrees or an ounce of Petra's business savvy—anything to make herself more marketable. What had Victor said about middle-aged women? "Irrelevant."

"I like it when you pick us up from school," Charlotte said.

Tamsen reached over and squeezed her daughter's knee, the way her brothers and Whit did. "I like being your driver," she said. She was relevant for something.

CHAPTER

13

Tamsen stood second in line under a huge "Flight to Freedom" sign that hung above a long, white-skirted table. Someone with a Leda Sparrow canvas tote handed her a die-cut cardstock bookmark that was shaped like a bird and advertised *Migrating to Money*, Sparrow's new guide to financial independence. The hotel annex was chilly and Tamsen warmed her hands around a large jasmine tea while the woman in front of her insisted to the staff that she'd never received the parking pass she'd paid $40 for online. Tamsen thought of her misappropriated airline miles and her nerves lit like a sparkler. She pulled out her phone and did a quick search for the website that would accept miles in exchange for cash. The site she'd visited months ago was now defunct. Not a good sign. But the second website on the search list, Miles to Dough, directed her to a "miles to money" calculator. She punched in 675,000 and hit enter. In an instant, she felt she'd just won the lottery: $8,775. She settled herself. It could very well be a scam, but the number gave her hope—Cormac's miles could put The Fountain Fund into five-digit territory. It would truly be a massive savings, a huge safety net for Tamsen and the kids. Tamsen looked up and said a little prayer of "thanks, Dad" in her head. She would call the airline again tomorrow.

"And you are?" A stout woman with dollar-sign earrings wearing a name badge that read "Song" popped Tamsen's thought bubble.

"Kinney," Tamsen said, feeling deviously empowered for registering under her maiden name.

She had arrived at the downtown mega-hotel early because seating was general admission, and although her VIP status entitled Tamsen to a preferential section, she wanted to be close to the stage. By the size of the buzzing crowd, Tamsen guessed the seminar had sold out; she'd read online that the event capacity was one thousand. She imagined that the coordinators had merged the north and south ballrooms, which were separated by sliding walls. Tamsen knew from her research for a WSC holiday craft fair several years prior that other four-star hotels could have accommodated a crowd this size, but those spaces came with higher price tags.

The median age of the Sparrow event appeared to be around forty, but other than their years and gender, the individuals in line bore nothing physically in common. She hadn't seen so many women in one place since she'd taken Charlotte to see Nick Jonas in concert at the United Center two years earlier. There was an artsy-looking redhead with a nose ring, a patchwork skirt, and a beret, a petite African-American in a pant suit and black browline glasses, and two friends in high-waisted, stonewashed jeans who wore matching custom t-shirts with the words "Take me to your Leda!" across the front.

Song handed Tamsen a yellow lariat with an attached ID badge. "I see you upgraded to the VIP experience," she said, her voice laced with approval. "A few rules: put your phone on airplane mode, no body surfing, no pictures in Leda's Lounge, and no outside food or beverages permitted in the venue."

Tamsen looked down at her $5 drink, still three-quarters full.

"We have coffee for the VIPs during the lunch break, but you're welcome to purchase some now at The Sparrow's Nest if you'd like." She gestured to a stand with adjacent bistro tables where seminar staff in matching yellow aprons peddled $8 donuts to hungry attendees. Beside the makeshift café was a merchandise tent where hoodies, travel mugs, and books were on display for sale. Tamsen felt a burning surge of trepidation inside her ribcage. Parking, food, and propaganda—she began to question the authenticity of Leda Sparrow, a woman Victor ridiculed as "a hoax." It was a relief he didn't know she was here.

Song extended her hand for Tamsen to surrender the tea. Tamsen quickly took a final drink before reluctantly handing over the cup.

"You've never seen Leda, have you?" Song asked.

"No," replied Tamsen. "I've never done anything like this."

Song reached across the registrar beside her and rang a small brass chime. "We've got a hatchling!" she said as nearby attendees clapped and echoed, "hatchling!" while others made tweeting sounds. Tamsen tried to stifle her laughter at the complete absurdity of the scene.

Song affixed a red dot sticker to Tamsen's badge. "You can take a potty break at any time, but we ask that you use the aisles on the sides to enter and exit. This dot entitles hatchlings to 10% off all merchandise. Now, all I need is your business card and we'll get you entered for a personalized copy of Leda's new book, *Migrate to Money*."

Tamsen was too embarrassed to admit she didn't have a business card, but she didn't mind missing her shot at the book. She preferred her self-help to come from women like the Brontë sisters or Jane Austen.

"I don't have a job yet," Tamsen confessed. "Isn't the whole point of coming to this seminar to figure that part out?"

"You really are a hatchling," Song said, rolling her eyes. "Leda always says that if you want to soar to success, you have to fly like you're already there."

A woman in line behind Tamsen handed her a hot pink business card. It had the name "Sugar Pop Salon" imposed over an illustration of a bikini-clad woman and the words "Now Sugaring Chicago," with the woman's name, title, and website in the bottom corner.

"You've heard of sugaring, right?" she asked. Tamsen hadn't. "It's organic. Far fewer ingrowns than waxing. Just lemon-water and sugar." She popped a card into the mesh drum and walked away.

The scale of the hall was immense, and an elaborate network of lighting and wires was erected overhead. Rows upon rows of chairs expectantly faced an elaborate stage with eight oversized LCD monitors, a green couch, and oversized vases bursting with vibrant flowers. It looked like an altar in a megachurch. Beside a clear glass podium sat a small, round, white lacquer table on which a tall pitcher of water and a single drinking glass were set.

"Are you with the group from Aurora?" a lady with alopecia and bifocals asked Tamsen. She was easily the oldest person there, probably in her seventies.

"I'm not," Tamsen said, smiling politely, redirecting her attention to her phone. She had taken a seat with the other hatchlings.

"There's a huge contingent from Peoria," the woman said. "Two busloads. Must be a lot of entrepreneurs downstate," she added.

Tamsen nodded in agreement, but she didn't want to engage with the woman. She was not here to make friends; she was here to learn how to survive. Hilly's recent mention of Sally Frith made Tamsen realize how vulnerable a life of dependency had made her.

She looked toward the stage. A large-scale pastoral landscape was projected on a wide screen backdrop that hung from the ceiling. In the center, a digital countdown display indicated that the presentation would begin in exactly 19:04. Soft up-tempo music streamed from speakers overhead, and as the minutes ticked down, the song was drowned out by the anticipating chatter of excited attendees, who now occupied more that 80% of the chairs.

With one minute left on the clock, the overhead lights dimmed. The volume of the music began to build, with a synthesized hum of electronic instruments against an ascending top note that built into a shrill call to action. Tamsen quickly scanned the women around her, searching their faces, hoping to lock eyes with another woman who, like her, was uncomfortable with the unfolding spectacle. At thirty seconds, green laser light beams began to intersect the room from four corners, flashing wildly over the audience and ultimately coming to a geometric focal point at the center of the backdrop. Voices joined in unison to call down the final ten, nine, eight . . . three, two, one. Women jumped to their feet in a frenzy of approval as the backlit silhouette of Leda Sparrow emerged, her arms open wide, from a cloud of theatrical fog that threw Tamsen into a fit of coughing.

"Who is ready to take flight?" Sparrow hollered into a wireless headset in her British accent as the percussive music intensified. Women screamed, knotting their thumbs together over their heads and flapping their fingers to simulate a flying bird the way Tamsen and Charlotte did when they played shadow puppets.

The jumbotron behind the guru displayed a flock of sparrows flying in a synchronized spiral and then ascending into the brightness of the sun. Tamsen could feel the floor pulsing through the soles of her shoes and she realized that the entire room had kicked off their boots, sneakers, and heels and was jumping up and down in unison, led by Sparrow herself on the stage.

The Boss of Back to Work was fit and objectively attractive. She had straight, long, bleached-blonde hair and eyelash extensions that looked like fuzzy black caterpillars. She was not as tall as she appeared in her YouTube videos, and she definitely looked ten years older than she did in the promotional material Tamsen had seen online. Sparrow was dressed in conservative casual attire—a short-sleeved plum-colored sweater with a silk feather-print scarf and black gabardine slacks. Her straight white teeth had the uniformity of well-constructed veneers, and the size of the diamond on her right ring finger spoke to the bounteous volume of the $34.99 books she was selling.

For the first hour of the presentation, Sparrow spouted platitudes about mothers in business while sharing PowerPoint slides titled "Runny Noses as Resume Builders, Nappies and Networking, and PTYay!" The anticipation of enlightenment and the energy of the crowd kept Tamsen engaged, although the material Sparrow delivered was formulaic and riddled with corny puns. Tamsen felt bored and wired simultaneously. She kicked her shoes off under the chair in front of her, discreetly checking her phone to see how much longer till the lunch break.

"How many turtle doves are there in that holiday song?"

"Two," the audience said in unison.

"Yes. Please find yourselves a turtle dove for a simple exercise," Sparrow said, reaching toward the crowd with outstretched arms, her palms facing the ceiling. "And once you've coupled up, please exchange descriptions of three things you love to do. These things can be anything, from picking lint balls from your favorite jumper to balancing a $100,000 budget. Just be honest and share the first three things that come into your head. Then, ask each other questions about these tasks. Why you find them fulfilling? How often do you enjoy them? There are no right or wrong answers, so feel free to express yourselves openly."

Tamsen scouted right and left for a cohort, eyeing a stylish woman who had brought a leather crossbody briefcase to the event. Before she could signal her potential partner, Tamsen felt a tug on her sleeve. It was the older woman with the bifocals.

"Knitting, playing piano, and folding the perfect hospital corner," said the woman, who introduced herself as Beatrice. "Now, how about you?" she asked with a satisfied grin that revealed gold caps on her back teeth.

"Making Halloween costumes for my kids, gardening, and setting an incredible dinner table," Tamsen said, her countenance shifting at the thought of the red, white, and pink Valentine-themed dinner table she'd set for Whit and the kids the week before. There were felt placemats with cupid cutouts, pink votives and handmade doily valentines, silver heart confetti, and a centerpiece of red roses and photo clips displaying heart-shaped pictures of the kids.

"Sounds like someone belongs on Etsy!" bifocal Beatrice exclaimed.

"I need to make some real money," Tamsen replied.

"My husband was in hospice for six months before he died last spring," Beatrice said. "And in that time, I made two sweater vests, twenty scarves, and a dozen pairs of baby booties."

"I'm sorry about your husband," Tamsen said.

"Well, the upshot is I found what I'm meant to do with the rest of my life," Beatrice said.

"Knitting?" Tamsen asked.

"Being a caregiver. I'm not just good at it, I love it."

The seminar theatrics continued with a game of Sparrow Says, a version of Simon Says where those who were eliminated were excused to lunch, while the winner would be awarded a signed poster of Sparrow and a free sandwich. Tamsen deliberately disqualified herself immediately, making a beeline for the VIP lounge in hopes of refueling with a snack and some strong coffee.

Nothing about the lounge suggested Very Important. It was located in a carpeted conference room with three folding tables. The first was attended by a staffer who was peddling Sparrow's book. The second had a monitor running a video montage of Sparrow's worldwide presentations and a sign-up sheet for "The Flock"—Sparrow's $20,000 club membership that entitled participants to unlimited seminars for an entire year. The third table had an urn of coffee, some powdered creamer, a couple of pitchers of water, and two trays of a cookie assortment Tamsen had passed over at Costco. She picked up a jelly thumbprint and popped it in her mouth, scanning the room for Leda Sparrow. She spotted her, surrounded by a growing throng of VIPs near the video table.

"You've got to make your way to the top of the pecking order," Sparrow was telling one of her followers. Tamsen was moaning inside. Was there was no limit to the bird analogies? She had paid good money for her upgrade, so Tamsen decided to take Sparrow's advice and muscle past the other hens to where Sparrow was standing. She elbowed her way to the front, ignoring a scowl from one of the "Take Me to Your Leda" sisters, but she couldn't manage to penetrate the tight inner circle, many of whom Sparrow referred to by first name.

"I've been a full-time mom for eleven years and I'm worried about not being there for my kids if I go back to work," Tamsen blurted out from two arm-lengths back.

Leda Sparrow looked blankly at Tamsen and submitted to a selfie with one of the other hatchlings. Tamsen felt a sharp elbow poke in her side from an aggressive gunner who waved a Sharpie and an eight-by-ten headshot of Sparrow in the air. This was absolutely absurd. What a waste. Tamsen retreated.

"Is everything okay?" Song asked as Tamsen forcefully threw her Styrofoam coffee cup in the trash.

"I need to make money," Tamsen said. "And so far, all we've covered is how to turn dirty diapers into a resume objective."

Song reached for Tamsen's left hand, assessing Tamsen's marital status by staring at the finger she'd recently unburdened of her ring.

"I see," she said, a stern line forming between her eyebrows. "There is a chapter in Leda's new book that addresses your very dilemma. It's called *Chickens Can't Fly*."

Tamsen squeezed her fists. Was this woman joking?

"It seems to me this seminar is more about hawking books than it is about helping women," Tamsen said, snarkily applauding her own bird pun.

"The first half is just a warmup. The real return on your investment comes at the end," Song said.

Investment? Tamsen wanted to laugh; the only one profiting from the seminar was Sparrow herself. Still, Tamsen couldn't rationalize leaving. The only way she would be able to justify the $650 ticket was if she remained for the afternoon in hopes of gleaning even one scrap of useable advice.

The second half of Sparrow's presentation dragged. By 3:30 p.m., Tamsen had begun doing Kegel exercises to pass the time. Not only had Sparrow performed what amounted to an exorcism on a woman who said her preoccupation with coupon clipping was destroying her marriage, but she had also led the entire audience in a human wave, culminating in Sparrow shooting "Migrating to Money" Nerf balls into the crowd from a hand-held rocket launcher. Tamsen eyed the exit, lowered her head surreptitiously, and began gathering her belongings. "What's the hurry?" she heard Sparrow say. All eyes turned toward Tamsen. Her face burned. She kept her head down and pretended to rifle though her purse for a lipstick. Again, the voice came. "What's the hurry?"

Tamsen looked up and watched as Song gave Sparrow a calculating nod. Tamsen turned to Beatrice, whose mouth was open so wide, Tamsen could see her uvula. The fabric beneath Tamsen's armpits suddenly felt damp and it occurred to her that the warmth on her head wasn't just her nerves, but a harsh spotlight beaming down on her from above. Tamsen fumbled with her lariat and sat up. A staff member bounded over and handed Tamsen a cordless mic.

"Oh, I," Tamsen started, "I'm not good at this sort of thing."

"Please come up here," Sparrow beckoned with an outstretched arm. Tamsen was back in Catholic grade school, being called out by the nun for passing a note. A single cough emanated from the crowd. Tamsen knew it was pointless to argue. She rose, climbing the four steps to the stage.

"Make yourself comfortable, sit down," Sparrow said, in a whispery voice. Reluctantly, Tamsen abided.

Tamsen looked out over hundreds of expectant faces.

"Tamsen," Sparrow said, squinting as she read the name off Tamsen's badge. "I see you're a hatchling. Welcome."

The entire audience responded with chirps and, "Welcome, Tamsen."

Tamsen hesitantly brought the mic to her lips. "Thank you," she managed. She glanced behind her at the backdrop, which was now displaying an animated bird that glided against a sky of puffy clouds.

"Tell us about the career you chose," Sparrow invited.

"I was in publishing for ten years, then I had kids," she said. She wished she'd left off the second part. She wondered if the audience would think of her as a sellout.

"I see. And you're thinking of going back to work—to publishing?" she asked.

"Yes," Tamsen said.

"Because you choose publishing."

"I was good at it," Tamsen said.

"She was good at it." Sparrow said loudly to the audience. Murmurs of dissent arose.

"I was the youngest VP of marketing, I made a huge salary and a bonus, traveled all over the world," Tamsen said, trying to legitimize herself.

"You got lots of accolades, didn't you? Gold stars—the boss held you up as an example of dedication and hard work."

"They didn't want me to leave," Tamsen said.

Sparrow began to pace.

"And your boss, I bet your boss was a man." He was, but Tamsen viewed that fact as irrelevant. Tamsen wanted to tell Leda Sparrow to go to hell; she wanted to storm off the stage, but she couldn't bring herself to do something so audacious.

"Who was Tamsen's turtle dove this morning?" Sparrow asked.

Beatrice stood up and raised her hand. Another microphone materialized.

"Do you remember the three things that Tamsen loves to do?" Sparrow asked Beatrice.

"She loves dreaming up and making Halloween costumes for her two kids, Theo and Charlotte, she likes to work in her garden with her hands, and she likes to set a beautifully-themed dinner table."

"Sounds a lot like publishing to me," Sparrow said sarcastically, and the entire room burst into laughter. Tamsen felt ashamed. Her list made her seem like a dilettante. She put the mic close to her mouth.

"I suppose I should have mentioned my love of literature," Tamsen said.

Sparrow whirled around. "But you didn't, did you?"

"No," Tamsen acknowledged. This was turning into a "What Color is Your Parachute" moment.

"How will you honor yourself, Tamsen? What do you really want?"

There was a pause, and everyone was quiet, anticipating Tamsen's a-ha moment. Sparrow herself must have believed Tamsen was on the brink of a breakthrough because she raised her hands in the air, cuing the silent crowd by binding her thumbs in shadow bird fashion. One by one, participants joined the pantomimed flight until all Tamsen could see was a vast congregation of fluttering fingers.

"I'm not qualified for anything else." Tamsen knew it was the wrong answer. She wasn't even sure she was qualified for publishing any longer. She read the disappointment in the faces of Beatrice, the stone-washed jeans lady, and the artsy girl in the beret. Sparrow dropped her arms and the entire group followed. Now she wrung her hands while she paced. Sparrow stopped before her. This is the moment when the nuns at St. Christina's would ask, "Do you want the switch or the ruler?" But Sparrow's tone was soft with compassion.

"As long as you're addicted to the validation for competence, for what the world tells you you're good at, you'll never truly rise to the height of your fullest potential. Every single person here today has the wingspan of the elegant snow crane, but until one honors those sacred things that make them sing, they will not ascend." She addressed the room. "You may, like Tamsen here, enjoy the view from a treetop, or a telephone wire, but you will never know how it feels to touch the sky if you are addicted to external validation."

That was it? Another hackneyed bird analogy? Not a single action step or resource Tamsen could consult.

Bifocal Beatrice gave Tamsen a pinched "nice try" sort of smile as Tamsen returned to her seat.

Tamsen wished she could teleport to the nearest bar. She texted Clay and he said he'd be free by 6:00 p.m.

I'll bring liquor and Chinese.

She needed to decompress. She had come to see Sparrow for an answer, but her dream of unlocking the secret to a lucrative second career had instead been decimated. The money to build a new life with her children was swirling around a shallow basin and disappearing down the drain. Not only had this seminar been a complete waste of time, it had actually made her feel worse about her employment prospects and her ability to earn a significant paycheck.

Once again, the motivational music began to blare from the huge amps that flanked the stage, signaling the finale of the seminar. Song from registration appeared from the wings, pushing a wheeled brass drum packed with business cards. Sparrow proudly raised a copy of *Migrating to Money* overhead before parading it across the stage like a ring girl at a boxing match.

"I want to thank you all for coming to spend today with me," bellowed Sparrow as she closed her eyes and reached into the drum of cards.

"Come on, baby," shouted the cosmetics salesgirl two chairs down.

Sparrow drew a white card and let out a surprised laugh. "What do you know? Tamsen Kinney is our winner!" The volume of the music shot up and play money fell from the ceiling as Sparrow opened the book, scribbled something inside with a feather pen, and handed the book off to Song before waving farewell to her devotees. "Thank you for coming today, birds! Remember, you are only as financially free," the crowd joined the chant, "as you believe you should be!"

Dazed, Tamsen stood up amid the bewildering commotion. There must have been a mistake; she hadn't even entered the drawing. Surely Song from the registration table would recognize her as the one without business cards. She moved through the enthusiastic crowd, accepting high-fives from random strangers. Song extended the book to Tamsen, without hesitation.

"I'd like a refund instead of a book," Tamsen said.

"Leda believes the investment is part of the transformation. You can

read this or not," Song said. "But clearly Leda has a message for you."
Then Song wished Tamsen "good luck" and walked away.

Tamsen rushed up the icy steps of Clay's three-story walk-up salon,
holding a white sack of Chinese carryout and a six-pack of Tsingtao,
her breath crystalizing in the bitter cold air.

"This is new," Tamsen said, touching the seat of a sleek new Peloton
bike that pointed toward the frosty salon windows.

"I'm a cyclist now," Clay said.

"So, what's his name?" Tamsen asked.

"Isaac," Clay said, grinning shamelessly. "He teaches spin. And he's
got a PhD from the University of Chicago."

"Sounds like a step up from the oyster shucker."

"I want you to meet him. He said he'd give me guest passes to his
class."

"Uh, huh," she said dismissively.

"It would be good for you, sweetie," he said. "Exercise is a huge
stress reliever."

Tamsen sank into Clay's cushy love seat and gave him the play by
play on the seminar. She swirled her chop sticks in a steaming container
of egg drop soup. "Why do you think Sparrow gave me the book?"

"After humiliating you in front of hundreds of women, it's the least
she could do," Clay said.

"She must have sensed that I was onto her. That I wasn't buying
into the racket she's running," Tamsen said.

"The *New York Times* bestseller list, the Today Show. I'd say she's
the one who's onto something," he replied. "Let me see the book."

Clay flipped open the cover with the hand that wasn't holding an egg roll, tilting his head sideways to read the inscription on the title page. "Tamsen," Clay read with British affectation, "You are not beholden to the payroll of your past. Follow Your Bliss. Remember, if you can earn one dollar doing what you love, then you can earn ten, and if you can earn ten, then you can earn a hundred. A thousand . . ." Clay looked up. "It's not bad advice, actually."

Tamsen recalled a coffee-mug flower arrangement her mother had received when she was sick. It had a picture of a kitten dangling by one claw from a tree branch with the words, "Hang in there, baby!" printed below. In times of crisis, she thought, clichés become the advice of people who don't really know what else to say, and Leda Sparrow was a cliché. With wings.

"Cybill Hinton asked me to consider joining the Board at the WSC," Tamsen said.

Clay stopped chewing and raised an arched eyebrow. "It doesn't get much bigger than that."

"It's a massive time commitment and a lot of work," Tamsen said.

"Those matriarchs are fierce bitches, Tamsie. They don't just pick anybody to join their ranks," Clay said as he dunked a piece of orange chicken in hot mustard sauce.

He was right. She needed to remind herself that being invited to the Board was a tremendous honor. Their approval was recognition of all her work on various events over the years, but especially the effort she put into the Harvest Moon Ball. The nomination meant they valued her. Should she join, Tamsen would be the first member whose family didn't appear in *The Chicago Ancestral Register*, and definitely the only woman they'd ever accepted from "the Irish slum."

She took the last sip from her beer can and the taste of acrid bubbles cleansed her tongue. Victor would call her an unpaid servant, but at least Cybill and the Board appreciated her.

Tamsen crumpled the sides of the aluminum can. "I'm going to do it," she resolved.

Tamsen felt drained, but invigorated. She entered the house though the mudroom, and remembered it was payday—she paid Aneta in cash. She dropped her Financial Freedom swag bag on the bench and hung her coat on a peg beside Charlotte's teal Jansport backpack. She checked her phone quickly and saw three missed calls from Aneta; Tamsen had forgotten to switch off silent mode after the seminar. Aneta probably wanted to know whether to give Theo some extra time before bed—he was always lobbying for just thirty minutes more.

It was unusually chilly in the house, so Tamsen checked the thermostat on her way to the kitchen. The temp was set at seventy-three, but she imagined the radiant heated floors were struggling to keep up with the twenty-seven-degrees-below-zero outdoor wind chill. As she mounted the steps leading to the kitchen, Tamsen noticed a bottle of opened Glenlivet XXV on the island. Her reflexes ticked to hyperawareness mode and she advanced in slow motion, with knowing caution, scanning the room for evidence. She saw a black overcoat slung over one of the counter stools, its unmistakable burgundy satin lining peering out at her. There was a foreboding static charge in the air.

"Aneta?" she called evenly.

"I sent Aneta home." It was Victor.

Tamsen could sense the aura of his rage without even seeing his face. When he stepped in from the living room, his dark energy made him appear ten times his usual size. Tamsen stiffened. His ears seemed to pull back, tightening the skin around his narrow eyes. His hair was matted at the temples and he smelled of bitter alcohol and fermented sweat. She watched his chest rise and fall to the steady cadence of yet another ticking time bomb. He clinked a giant ice cube block in his half-full glass of Scotch. She noticed his feet were bare and his toes bit into the warm walnut floors.

Tamsen struggled to process the scene, her mind switching into its default practice—desperately sequencing her actions since her last encounter with Victor. Was he angry that she used Aneta on a night he expected her to be with the children? Had he found out about the cost of the Sparrow seminar? Impossible, she'd paid with cash. Then she remembered: Whit. The hotel bill. New Year's Eve.

Do this to get through this. The voice in her head was the whisper of a woman being strangled.

"I know it was a lot," she beseeched. "I was treating myself."

Victor cracked his neck and started to raise his arm. This time he's going to hit me, she thought. She pinched her eyes closed and shielded her face to protect it from his fist. She braced herself for the blow, but it didn't come. In a flash, she looked out from behind her raised arms and saw that Victor held something in his fists, the skin of his knuckles pulled white with bloodless tension. She heard the delicate sound of liquid dripping. It was far slower than her heartbeat.

Victor thrust his hand toward her.

"What is this?" he raged.

She stared at his grip with dumb astonishment. In his hand, Victor held a sopping wad of cash and gift cards. The Fountain Fund.

Tamsen stood in a state of abject paralysis and a sudden deceleration of time rendered her speechless. Victor's fat tongue passed over his lips, leaving them wet with saliva. He released a guttural roar as he flung her treasure against the wall with all his strength, sending a shower of plastic cards skidding across the floor, and hundreds of limp twenties, fifties, and hundred-dollar bills flying in every direction. Tamsen heard herself gasp.

He slammed down his drink. "The pipe to the fountain burst tonight and Aneta couldn't reach you, so she called me," he bellowed.

Theo. Charlotte. They would hear. Tamsen had to make him stop.

"Victor, if you let me explain . . ."

"Shut up," he yelled. "How much?"

"The painters were coming and I needed to hide some things." Her words flew out as fast as she could conceive an alibi.

"You thief!" he hollered, his skin bright red and bloated with fury. He grabbed the torn plastic bag containing the remainder of her savings and swung it violently, spraying all its contents like shrapnel into the air.

"I forgot the passcode for the safe." She was digging herself in deeper.

"How long have you been stealing from me?" he hissed.

"I can explain, Victor."

"I installed a camera on the patio," he said, pointing toward the computer monitor on the kitchen desk.

Tamsen looked and saw an infrared freeze frame of herself wearing lavender flannel pajama bottoms and ivory cotton bathrobe, kneeling on the bluestone with one hand in the copper trough, fortifying her savings with the cash-over she'd recently requested at Trader Joe's.

Victor took another swig of scotch. "Just look at you, you conniving snake, putting your stash in a fountain. Thousands of dollars," he slurred, his drunken incredulity dissolving into demonic laughter. "Right under my nose, like a fucking squirrel." He kicked a Costco card, slightly losing his balance as it skipped across the kitchen and came to a halt against the baseboard. "Cash, store credits, a Home Depot card? You're pathetic."

Tamsen looked in terror at her stash, scattered everywhere—her nest egg, her parachute, her "in case of emergency." Every penny she'd saved over twelve months, gone, exposed because she'd missed Aneta's call. Because while she was sitting in a new-age pep rally, listening to a pop culture icon deliver trite mantras to a room full of tragic losers, the pipe behind her beautiful fountain had burst. The pipe Whit had reminded her about in October. "Shut off the master valve before winter."

"Mommy . . ." Theo's faint voice called from upstairs. Victor cocked his head.

"I'll handle this," he said, turning toward the stairs.

"Victor, no, please," Tamsen pleaded, grabbing his arm. He shook her off violently. "You've been drinking, you'll scare him." She stayed on his heels as he stormed toward the front staircase. "Victor!" she quietly beseeched. "Let me." He ignored her.

Theo lay shuddering on his back, his covers pulled up under his nose. His teary eyes darting back and forth between his parents' faces.

"Are you cold, sweetheart?" Tamsen said, pulling a fleece blanket over his duvet.

"No," he said.

"It's late now. You should go to sleep, okay?" Tamsen managed.

"Daddy, why are you mad at Mommy?" Theo asked, his voice shaking.

Tamsen sat on the edge of the mattress and intercepted Victor's reply. "Daddy's just a little emotional. We were talking about some adult stuff."

Theo cautiously withdrew his arm from the covers, his small digits groping for the safety of his mother's hand.

Victor's right upper lip lifted in a snarl as he swayed and took a step closer to the bed, hovering over Theo's little form.

"Theo?" he said, his patronizing tone telling Tamsen that his next words were aimed at her.

Theo cowered. "What?"

"Your mother has done something very, very bad," Victor seethed.

In that instant, Tamsen thought she saw Theo's six-year-old body levitate above the mattress. The horror in his desperate eyes urgently pled to Tamsen: tell me it isn't true, say you didn't commit some unspeakable crime of which my father has accused you.

This was not how the separation book said it should go. This was not the benevolent transition she had pledged for her children. As much as she wanted to gently navigate Theo and Charlotte around the turbulence of the separation, as hard as she'd tried to minimize the damage they would suffer, Tamsen recognized that she was ultimately powerless to control anything but her own response to the carnage. Victor thought he'd won this battle, that he'd hurt her by condemning her to Theo, but maligning Tamsen came at a terrible cost to their son. Theo was afraid and the only thing Tamsen could do for him was pretend that she was not.

Theo began to sob with breathless convulsions. Victor cleared his throat. She knew he was uncomfortable when Theo went into an emotional state. They both feared that anything extreme could trigger a seizure. Tamsen clenched her jaw. The protective instinct that innately binds every mother to her child produced from her a glare so forceful that when he saw it, Victor took two steps back from the bed.

"Theo," she said with calming resolve. "Your father and I love you very much." She drew in a breath, praying that Victor would remain silent. "Sometimes adults have disagreements, and you need to know that these disagreements have nothing to do with you. They're not your fault, and they're not your responsibility to solve."

Tamsen heard the disturbing pop of Victor's neck. Her skin prickled.

"We do love you, Theo," he said as he staggered zigzag from the room. "And your mother will accept her consequences like a big girl."

Tamsen curled up beside Theo, remaining next to him long after he had drifted to sleep. She listened while Victor stumbled around the main level, collecting the entirety of her Fountain Fund, swearing and slamming the front door when he finally, thankfully, left the house.

CHAPTER

1 4

Tamsen sat in her car outside Dexter School. Drizzle spat down on her windshield, clouding her view of the street sign indicating that the open spot she'd found was a loading zone. She had heard of seasonal affective disorder; in fact, Victor had alleged his hypochondriac mother complained about it nine months of the year. But until now, Tamsen had never really believed it was a legitimate condition. The gray ceiling of clouds that characterized Chicago winter still hung low, despite the groundhog's prediction that this year's spring would come early. March plodded along, dragging Tamsen with it.

She looked at the time. The digits 9:45 a.m. glowed white from the dashboard clock. She had fifteen minutes before Theo's class talent show and the debut of the song he and Whit had been practicing for months. Pretending to be happy to see the other Dexter parents was a chore she simply couldn't undertake. So instead, she sat in the car, revisiting the words Whit had texted her the week before.

i miss u - not just the Abilify talking

Tamsen opened her photos and scrolled past the recent pictures of Charlotte wearing her new tap shoes and Theo holding up his first 100% spelling test. She found the day in December when she and

Whit had ridden the Holiday Train together and she'd gotten a shot of him making a snow angel outside the conservatory. Was that the day it had started between them? Or was it earlier, the day or the moment he appeared on his beat-up bike? She stared at the picture. The swell in her chest was still there, every time she looked at him, cheesing with his limbs outstretched and his pant leg scrunched above his boot, exposing his bare shin. She was relieved she would see him tonight—a concert at the Riviera. She reminded herself to search the band because she didn't recognize the name Thesaurus Rex when Whit had told her about the tickets.

"You hurry right ahead, beautiful," the shriveled school security guard said, waving her past the lobby desk without making her sign in. She fought to smile at him without Victor's vile remark about the blow job swimming around her. It was an association forever burned in her cortex.

Beyond the headmaster's office, Oliver Putnum was packing up pledge forms and a sign that read, "Dexter School Capital Campaign Fund: The Future Starts Now!"

"You're off the hook, Tamsen," he said. "Victor just wrote me a big check." Victor's early arrival didn't surprise Tamsen in the least. He not only wanted to make a big show of his dedicated child-rearing to Ms. Ellison, but he also wanted the other parents to glorify his commitment to the kids, regardless of the fact that in prior years, he had been a no-show for nearly every school skit, Halloween parade, and choir concert.

Tamsen scanned the lobby. There was no sign of any parent or faculty member, aside from Oliver. The sparseness was odd. Even in the primary grades, parents usually turned out in force for events like these, when they were allowed to surreptitiously measure their child's competency against that of all the others in the class. Who was the best behaved? Who showed signs of superior intelligence? Which child would present the most serious threat in the race for valedictorian and, ultimately, admission to the top Ivy League schools?

Still, Tamsen was glad to have a moment alone with the divorce lawyer. Every day, Petra's voice was in her head. *Talk to a lawyer, Tamsen—a good one.* And Oliver was the best. It couldn't hurt to speak with him. Just because she wanted a meeting didn't mean she was getting a divorce.

"Oliver, I was wondering if we could meet . . . confidentially," Tamsen suggested. "I have some questions for you about my separation."

Her friend's typically jovial apple cheeks deflated. He dropped his phone into his pant leg pocket and looked at Tamsen with a hardened expression she had never observed on him in social circles. His nostrils flared. "I'm sorry, Tamsen, but I'm afraid there's a conflict of interest."

"Conflict?" she asked. Maybe Oliver's firm had handled a human resources case for Summers & Peel?

"Victor has personally engaged our firm, so unless he signs a waiver, I'm duty-bound to serve as his, and only his, counsel." Tamsen heard a series of chimes over the school PA, indicating a top of the hour passing period for the middle schoolers. Her head fell back, and she closed her eyes. "I'm happy to give you some excellent referrals, if that helps," Oliver added, as if that would be enough to soften the blow of his newly-formed alliance.

"We were friends first," she said between her teeth. She was too tired to hide her anger. "Couldn't you have told him no?" Students spilled into the hallways adjacent to the lobby and Marni Fraser, a parent in Theo's class, trotted by with her bundled toddler in her arms.

"Hey, Tamsen," she smiled. "Theo was so sweet."

Was sweet? What did that mean? Tamsen grabbed the scribbled list of attorneys from Oliver's hand and hustled toward Theo's classroom, weaving her way down the hall, dodging two giggling pubescent girls who shared a pair of ear buds as they clandestinely viewed a video on an iPhone. She knew she had the correct date for the talent show; not only had she put it in her calendar, but Theo himself had also spoken of it two mornings ago, right after Victor's devastating outburst. Theo had wanted Whit to come and watch his guitar performance, but Tamsen said no. She had shuddered at the thought of Whit and Victor in the same room. Victor would detect their chemistry and potentially forbid Theo from taking future guitar lessons.

Tamsen noticed three of Charlotte's friends hurrying down the stairs toward the cafeteria, their lunchboxes in hand. Something didn't compute. She began to run—past the bulletin board display of Native American headdresses, beyond the folding tables exhibiting lumpy, glazed pinch pots, and between Michelle and Daniel Hornstrath, fellow first-grade parents who strode toward her, conspicuously carrying their daughter's ballet shoes and periwinkle-blue powder-puff tutu. Tamsen became possessed by a breathless frenzy that felt like she was sucking air through a flattened straw. No, she thought, it's not possible. She'd set her digital alarm clock at The Talisman. She'd double-checked the start time in the school newsletter.

Outside Theo's classroom, clumps of parents pulled on their coats and dispersed through the glass double doors leading to the back parking lot. Tamsen slowed her gait, feeling her heavy feet sink deep into the shit quicksand. There was no point in rushing because it was too late. She had already done the unthinkable—she'd missed Theo's performance.

Ms. Ellison stood outside the classroom, one hand on the doorknob, the other on Theo's shoulder. Tamsen heard the forced congeniality of a familiar synthetic laugh. It was Victor, all smiles, leaning against the wall with one hand as if he were holding it up. He turned his head and saw Tamsen, revealing a subtle shift in his casual disposition, a nearly imperceptible huff and a piercing glare of disgust.

"Mommy!" Theo said, tearing himself from his teacher's side. "Where were you?"

Tamsen panted. She couldn't get enough oxygen. Her lungs strained to expand. Had she not kneeled down to hug Theo, she might have collapsed. She wanted to shake her head, to clear the disorienting fuzz that clouded her brain, but she could feel Victor and the teacher staring down at her.

Theo's chest slowly rose and fell against her breast. His blue cotton sweater smelled of the honey-lavender fabric softener that Tamsen had told Aneta not to use on knits because it made them lose their shape. Dammit, Aneta. Charlotte had broken out in a rash on her arms recently. It was probably the fabric softener. Maybe not.

The chaos of Tamsen's thoughts would not subside. It occurred to her that though her heart broke for disappointing Theo, there was something far more insidious than guilt, rumbling like a distant storm in her mind—it was the awareness that she was somehow losing her grip. She had lost focus on nearly everything, yet she was acutely aware that she was unhinged.

"I am so sorry, buddy," she said. She looked up at Ms. Ellison, avoiding eye contact with Victor, who wore his satisfied gloat like a blue ribbon. "I thought it started at 10:00 a.m."

Ms. Ellison huffed, "It did."

Tamsen pulled out her phone. It read 11:12.

"Somebody forgot to spring forward," Ms. Ellison said. Tamsen could practically hear the sucking *tsk, tsk* sound coming from her pink tulip mouth. Victor put his hand on the teacher's shoulder and laughed with his whole body, as if she'd made the wittiest joke of all time.

"Tamsen has been under some stress lately," Victor said with his best attempt at sincerity.

Theo's lower lip quivered, and he blinked hard, pretending to have something in his eye.

"I didn't do the song," he sniffed. "I started but I made a mistake."

Tamsen stood up. "Please," she implored of the teacher, "can Theo try his song again?"

Ms. Ellison checked her watch and sighed.

"We are expecting a lama in five minutes," she complained.

"A llama?" Theo asked.

"Not that kind of llama, Theo," the teacher corrected. "And there goes the surprise," she said bitingly, as if it had been Tamsen who had revealed the identity of the surprise guest.

"Kimberly," Victor interjected with a tone of diplomacy. "I know this is really inconvenient, but if you'll indulge my wife—it really would mean a lot to Theo."

Tamsen bristled at how unapologetically he used the possessive moniker.

"Theo," the teacher said in a gooey voice. "Now that your mother is here, why don't you try to play us your song?"

A yellow washable marker grazed Tamsen's arm as the anarchy inside the classroom peaked. The children were riled by their parents' visit and the break in their routine. Their small faces were covered in powdered sugar from donut holes, their energy fueled by watered-down orange juice. Ms. Ellison attempted to restore calm by ringing a small bell on her desk. The ruckus continued as Theo tuned his guitar at the front of the room. Victor cupped his hands over his mouth and made a loud mooing sound, a distraction he used at home when Charlotte and Theo were squabbling, and the incredulous group momentarily paused to see whether there was indeed a farm animal in the room.

"Seats now," Ms. Ellison said, taking advantage of the lull. Tamsen watched as the young woman beamed at Victor, the good guy.

Theo shifted his weight from one foot to the other then locked eyes with Tamsen in the way he'd done this summer when he'd finally jumped off the diving board for the first time. They had been guests at the provincial Hunter's Glen Country Club and Theo had stood on the edge of the fiberglass plank at least two dozen times, cautiously peering down at the rippling blue surface, trying to measure the enormity of a nameless threat that lurked below. Time and time again, he mounted the board only to retreat back to the security of the dry concrete deck.

"Don't look down," she had told him. "Find me watching and imagine we are holding onto opposite ends of an invisible rope—a rope strong enough to pull an elephant from the deep end."

The classroom was quiet. Theo didn't break his stare from Tamsen as his fingers took their position on the frets and he began to strum. Tamsen wanted to be his protector, but the rope was thin and hanging on by only few fraying threads. She was grateful Theo couldn't see her hopelessness; he didn't know that this time, he was on his own.

Theo closed his eyes, the way his guitar teacher always did, and Tamsen noticed the wide rubber band that hung limply from his wrist. His clear, sweet voice did not waver as he played a verse and the chorus from *Skyscraper*. Demi Lovato.

The children erupted in a chorus of cheers and applause, celebrating their typically invisible classmate's hidden talent. Even Victor and Ms. Ellison seemed shocked by Theo's elegant command of the guitar. Tamsen knew that his budding self-possession was the real star of the show. Theo wasn't as fragile as before; in fact, he was strong and confident, and it was all because of Whit.

◆ ◆ ◆

When Tamsen arrived at the concert venue, Whit was waiting for her under the blinking Riviera marquis. His hair was freshly cut and his jacket hung loosely over his shoulders. Tamsen slid her arms into his coat, touching the ripple of his ribs beneath his fitted Henley.

"You feel nice," she said.

"My doc wants me working out. Endorphins, you know," he said, flexing.

"Well, you were a hero today. Theo's performance was incredible. You've changed him, Whit," she said.

"I don't have that kind of superpower. I just taught him the chords, Theo did the rest," Whit replied, bending to kiss her mouth.

The Riv was packed with bodies. Tamsen followed Whit to the line for twenty-one and over, where a three-hundred-pound bouncer with a leather spiked collar checked IDs before handing out neon-green wrist bands. Tamsen reluctantly slid her driver's license from her back pocket and turned it over, as if the brute wouldn't recognize her as clearly legal.

He scrutinized the date on her card and then looked at Whit before handing her a wrist band. "Have fun in there, young lady." He waited until Tamsen crossed in front of him before he gave her a knowing grin.

The floor of the venue was a packed sea of a thousand undulating bodies, whose arms swayed like anemones in the tide of a shrill synthesizer rhythm. Tamsen tried to imagine the old jazz-age movie theater at a time when it still had seats and patrons would actually dress up for a night of film under the gilded rotunda and steep balconies. The ladies and gents of turn-of-the-century Chicago society would be mortified if they saw their revered theater now, its walls painted purple and a squad of long-haired, tattooed rockers thrashing like tased inmates on the stage. The only thing that likely hadn't changed was the exorbitantly long line for the women's restroom.

The opening band wrapped up their set, and there was a brief lull in the deafening volume.

"Let's get to the front while everyone's at the bar," Whit suggested, grabbing hold of Tamsen's hand.

She would have been fine at the back of the theater where you could actually squeeze a dollar bill between the dancing twenty-year-olds, but she didn't want Whit to perceive her as rigid. Or old.

He navigated her through the crowd. There were girls in clingy tank tops with impenetrable layers of foundation and glitter in their cleavage, and boys in trucker caps with their skinny jean cuffs rolled at the ankle.

As they neared the stage, a pretty face with light wavy hair pulled back in a tortoise-shell barrette pushed blindly toward them. As she brushed against Whit, she did a double take and grasped his arm abruptly. He glanced down into her wide-set, glassy, ice-green eyes and Tamsen watched as a wave of recognition passed over his face. He let go of Tamsen's hand.

The girl squealed and threw herself at him. "Oh my god, Kyle!" Tamsen was struck by the unnatural sound of Whit's given name coming from her mouth. The only time she'd heard him referred to as Kyle was at the Pinnacle, and then it seemed formal. When the girl said it, it felt too familiar.

"No way, Lizzie!" Whit said. His arms seemed long enough to wrap twice around her size zero frame.

"I can't believe it!" she screeched again. The girl was so elated, Tamsen wondered whether she would bust out of her tight pink cropped top. "How long have you been back?" she yelled.

"Seven months," he replied as he diverted his eyes from the girl's abundant chest and gestured toward Tamsen. "Elizabeth, Tamsen," he said above the noise.

Tamsen extended her hand at the same time "Lizzie" went in for a hug, resulting in an awkward jumble of limbs between the girl from Kyle's past and the woman of Whit's present. Tamsen felt like a chaperone, suddenly obscured by a peachy-complexioned coed with ample collagen and huge boobs who insisted Whit take her number so that they could "hang out."

Lizzie pulled a flat aluminum stick from the pocket of her denim mini skirt. Tamsen thought it was a flash drive.

"You want a hit?" she asked.

Whit laughed. "What the hell is that?" he asked, taking it from her.

"Only the latest in vape technology," she smiled.

He turned it over in his hand. "Oil, right?" he said. Tamsen knew enough to understand they were talking about cannabis oil.

"No muss, no fuss," she bragged. "And it's got Bluetooth." She wagged her phone in the air, showing them its app.

"This is awesome!" he raved. "I love a tech-savvy party girl."

"Watch this," Lizzie said, dragging on one of the ends. A band of pink light on the tip illuminated as she inhaled deeply.

"It even matches your top!" Whit said, noticeably peering down at Lizzie's breasts. Tamsen wished she'd worn a pushup bra.

Lizzie extended the stick, offering Tamsen a try.

"Don't let me hold you two back," he said, holding his hands up with amused approval.

Tamsen hadn't smoked weed since the two times she had tried in college. But her experience with it hadn't been bad, not like the sleeping pill last year. In fact, she'd barely felt anything when she'd inhaled from a joint. She watched Whit leaning toward Lizzie. Hell, it was even legal now.

The vapor tickled on its way down her windpipe, and although she did her best to suppress the spasms, she couldn't stifle her immediate fit of coughing.

Lizzie raised her eyebrow to Whit. "You gotta cough to get off," she shouted over the piped-in alternative rock music. Tamsen did not like this girl, who made her feel like an amateur.

Lizzie disappeared to "fill her water bottle," something Tamsen figured was a code expression for the act of scoring more drugs. All the kids seemed wasted, the way they were hugging one another, staring blankly at the brightly colored stage lights, or moving dully through the mob like one of those round, robotic vacuums.

Whit groped for Tamsen's reluctant hand, guiding her laterally until he finally settled on a spot in the center of the floor, near a group of three flannel-bound hipsters. Around them an aroma cloud of marijuana hung as thick and pungent as skunk spray.

"You okay with the smell?" he said loudly into her ear. She felt belligerent over the enthusiastic reception he'd given his perky, blonde friend.

"Tell me about Lizzie," she said casually, as if she wasn't really threatened.

Whit opened his mouth to reply and the lights simultaneously went down in the theater, rousing the noisy crowd into a frenzied uproar. He positioned himself behind Tamsen, his hands firmly gripping her waist while the members of Thesaurus Rex trotted out onto the stage and took their positions in front of a backdrop of dimly lit, suspended light rods.

Tamsen was immediately taken by the sound of the punchy dance-rock fusion. They were close enough to the stage for her to notice the incredible number of percussive implements situated behind the lead guitar and bassist. Tamsen relaxed into the numbing of her appendages as her mind gradually disconnected from her body. The drummer crashed his cymbals together and Tamsen raised her arms involuntarily, moving in sync with the squiggly synthesizer, wishing she knew the lyrics to the refrain so she could sing along with the writhing frontman.

She tried to purge her mind of the Lizzie encounter, but Whit's delight in seeing the girl was undeniable. She tried to focus her attention on the motion of his hips against her, but she began to obsess about whether he was watching the band on the stage or scoping the mob for his ice-eyed friend. One of the hipsters discreetly tucked his chin and dragged on a joint. He noticed Tamsen watching him, and he obligingly extended her an offering of concert fellowship, passing her the spliff. *He must be too high to see my crow's feet*, she thought, and she accepted the toke.

The crowd began to jump up and down, cheering for the pyrotechnics show that accompanied their hit song, "Walk In Place." Tamsen recalled the Leda Sparrow experience, and how all those middle-aged women tried to cut loose in a similar fashion, only they looked awkward and silly, versus all these concert kids. The contrast was hilarious, and she burst into a fit of giggling. Whit laughed at her, feeding her amusement by busting out a dance move that reminded her of the New Kids on the Block music video for "The Right Stuff." But somewhere around the band's fourth song, things ceased to be funny.

Tamsen's breath quickened and the room around her began to shrink. She nervously scanned the opera boxes and balconies, turning her head from left to right, then looking upwards, evaluating the ceiling's structural integrity. She felt like there was an expanding hole in the center of her chest and it was rapidly filling with liquid paranoia. What if the balconies weren't secure? They might loosen with the heavy vibration of the music, crushing hundreds of innocent people who had come to see Thesaurus Rex. Or what if the pyrotechnics on stage set the curtain on fire and the theater exploded into a ravenous inferno? She frantically searched for the nearest exit. She turned to Whit.

"Bathroom," she said loudly.

"You want me to come with you?" he asked.

"I'm fine," she said, faking normalcy. He gave her the thumbs up.

She was calmed by the task of putting one foot in front of the other, but a cold, uncomfortable sweat oozed from her pores as she anxiously pressed her way between bodies toward the back of the venue.

In front of the lobby merchandise kiosk, Tamsen could breathe again. She looked at the ornate tile mosaics on the walls and felt a profound sense of compassion for laborers who must have spent months, perhaps even years, delicately placing each tiny tile in its precise spot.

The roadie behind the kiosk spoke to her, his words dribbling out at an unusually slow rate. "You okay, ma'am?" he inquired. "You want water or something?" Tamsen was transfixed by the profound message he wore on his sweatshirt: "Smile While You Still Have Teeth." She contemplated the powerful words. Their meaning was almost too overwhelming to wrap her head around. Smile. Teeth. Birth. Death. It was beautiful and tragic, like the love between Heathcliff and Catherine in *Wuthering Heights*.

"Ma'am," the roadie said again.

"I feel you," she replied with a toothy smile. She was sending him a message that she understood the truism on his chest.

Tamsen floated into the ladies' room. She lingered in front of the mirror, hearing music from Thesaurus Rex buzz through the walls. She felt like she was outside herself, but if she was outside, who was on the inside, sitting at the controls? Maybe her true self was a tiny being in a tall captain's chair at an instrument panel inside her own skull, operating every action and expression with the toggle of a lever or the push of a button. Of course, she thought, it all makes perfect sense. A tiny, benevolent mind commander who faithfully guides a corporal, directionless vessel.

Tamsen noticed an incessant vibration at her hip. She put her hand on top of her crossbody bag and the tiny commander in her head directed her to remove the wireless communication device. She followed orders, pulling out her phone in what felt like slow motion. She looked down at the glowing screen and saw a list of notifications. Six phone calls, and one Facetime attempt. They were all from Victor.

He was trying to ruin her evening off. The one night she allowed herself to disconnect, to forget the nightmare from which she could not extract herself, Victor insisted on reminding her that he was always hovering near. She didn't care—the weed had anesthetized her, taken the sting out of his incessant haranguing. What could he possibly want? Uh oh, maybe she had forgotten to stock the pantry with his favorite energy bars. Or was the powder room out of toilet paper? She laughed at the thought and decided to play at least one of his voicemails for her own disengaged amusement.

Within the first two seconds of hearing Victor's frantic tone, Tamsen's herbal Zen consciousness was obliterated. Something was gravely wrong. She knew from the way he said her name that it was one of the children, but the cell reception was poor, and Victor's voice kept cutting out.

"We're . . . hospital." He was crying. "They're running tests . . . procedure . . . call me . . ."

Tamsen wrestled with her murky thoughts. They were coming quickly now, but she couldn't manage to put them into a meaningful sequence. Someone is in the hospital. Children's Hospital. Theo or Charlotte. You are high. Who is in the hospital? You are high. Get to the hospital. Go now.

Tamsen threw open the restroom door and tore through the lobby toward the street. She looked down at her phone. So many apps. Where was the right icon? She was too stoned to try to locate it, and there was no time to waste.

"Please there be an empty cab. God, let there be an empty cab," she repeated, waving her arms furiously in front of the concert hall. She watched as a yellow taxi pulled a sluggish U-turn at the corner and circled back for her.

The air inside the cab was stifling. The mingled smell of rancid perfume and warm vinyl seats, combined with the odor floating from a pine-tree deodorizer dangling from the rear-view mirror, made her retch. She sat in the backseat while the passenger TV loudly looped a story about the skating rink in Millennium Park. She felt nauseated and deathly claustrophobic. How could she have been so irresponsible? Why didn't Whit tell her taking a hit was a bad idea? Whit. Shit. She pulled out her phone and texted him.

Had to leave

Tamsen would have elaborated, but she was so carsick from typing, she nearly vomited onto the stiff vinyl. She furiously pressed the automatic window opener, but the driver had the controls on child safety mode.

"I need air," she pleaded. Tamsen saw the glaring whites of the cab driver's eyes regard her skeptically as he casually lowered the glass a few millimeters. Putting her face close to the open window, she fruitlessly willed away the pot stupor that clouded her head. It's going to be okay, it's going to be okay. She forced herself to say it over and over.

At Children's Hospital, Tamsen rushed toward the general information desk. Even at midnight, the pediatric ward seemed optimistic. Suspended from the ceiling of the white marble atrium was a sprawling mobile. Its arms floated in a silent trajectory, dangling primary-colored geometric shapes in a wakeless orbit through space. An oversized aquarium, shaped like a giant cylinder, bubbled quietly at the center of a vacant waiting area.

"Tamsen Peel," she said as she registered her illegible signature in the log book.

The desk attendant put aside her Sudoku before entering something into the computer and scribbling the date on a visitor's badge.

"Your son is in 306. Take these elevators up to the green level," the desk attendant said.

Theo. Tamsen knew from experience that the green level was intensive care.

Victor sat in a chair at the foot of Theo's bed; his head leaned back against the wall behind him. His hair was disheveled, and he had fleshy pillows under the red rims of his eyes, yet he was impeccably dressed in tailored Italian trousers and a cashmere vest. He jerked to attention when Tamsen entered, rising to stand beside her at Theo's bed.

"Oh, God," Tamsen managed, throwing her hands to her mouth at the sight of Theo's pale, sleeping body. His head was wrapped in a thick swath of white bandages. A series of monitors hissed, chirped, and beeped in syncopation as a nurse attended to his IV drip.

"He was jumping on the bed in the guest room," Victor said. "He was singing."

"My bed, with the wooden headboard?" Tamsen gasped.

"He came downstairs and blood was pouring down the back of his head."

"Did he seize?" Tamsen asked.

"I called 911," Victor said.

Tamsen felt like she'd been slugged in the stomach. The sobering horror of seeing Theo hooked up to so many machines was terrifying, but that she was at a concert when the paramedics had been summoned was unforgiveable.

"Did they do an CT scan?" she asked urgently.

"They found a small subdural hematoma."

"Oh, no," Tamsen gasped.

Victor's voice quivered. "The neurosurgeon said his exam was good—his mental state is normal."

"But his epilepsy," Tamsen said.

"He's under observation. The doc said twenty-four hours, minimum."

Tamsen lifted Theo's frail hand and cupped it in her own, bending to kiss her son softly on his bandaged head.

"I love you, baby," she said.

"He's been sleeping for about an hour," Victor said with rare compassionate calm.

The nurse popped an empty syringe into her pocket. "He probably won't wake up anymore tonight. We've given him a mild sedative."

"What about his meds?" Tamsen asked.

"IV," the nurse replied.

The neurologist on call entered the room, a resident in tow.

"You're Theo's parents, correct?" she said flatly. They nodded. In this moment, Tamsen felt a huge sense of relief that Victor was by her side. Good or bad, having an "other" to help shoulder the burden alleviated tremendous pressure. It was a comfort.

"I'm Doctor Berkovits, the attending," she said, gesturing for Tamsen and Victor to step outside into the hallway. The doctor's humorless disposition was a stark contrast to the variety of cartoon character pins and buttons she wore on her white lab coat lapels, and to the bright green Crocs on her feet, which were loaded with Jibbitz charms.

Dr. Berkovits scanned a series of documents and then abruptly handed them to the resident.

"Theo is stable. We'll have a better handle on things tomorrow once we do a follow-up scan. If the subdural hematoma isn't progressing, we won't need to perform surgery," she said. "You were smart to call an ambulance when you did. Hematomas can be nothing, or they can cause major issues, especially given Theo's epilepsy."

She wrote on her tablet with an embellished stylus. A bright orange feather and two googly eyes jostled as she recorded her notes. The plume reminded Tamsen of Leda Sparrow and how she should have been with Theo and Charlotte the day of the seminar, rather than wasting her time on some ridiculous dream for her life.

After the doctor left, Victor and Tamsen returned to Theo's bedside. Victor traced the circumference of his face and recited a nursery refrain he used to say when the kids were toddlers. "The moon is round, the moon is round. It has two eyes, a nose, and it makes no sound. The moon is round."

As she watched him, Tamsen saw how supple Victor's body seemed in his clothes. His sincere voice was full of warmth and undeniable love. This was the warmhearted Victor, the compassionate twin to the hardened man who had displaced the husband she married. Once upon a time, Victor had exhibited this tenderness to her.

For a long while, they just watched Theo, saying nothing at all. The chorus of bleeps and hisses from the medical instruments brought back memories of torturous nights on the neuro unit when Tamsen had to force an exhausted Theo to stay awake so that the doctors could measure his brain activity.

Tamsen stood up to adjust Theo's pillow, and she saw Victor's eyes taking in the leggings and cropped sweater she'd worn to the concert. She held her breath and braced for an attack. But instead, Victor smiled lightly. It was an authentic smile. The same smile he'd given years ago, the time when he'd surprised her at her office during a stressful work week with a picnic lunch. The same smile he'd given her when they'd stood at the baptismal font at Charlotte's christening. The smile of solidarity when they'd decided, together, that they'd stay in the city to raise their family. Victor opened his mouth and started to ask her a question, but before the words were fully out, Theo mumbled something indiscernible and then fell quiet, and they both resumed their silent vigil.

Someone paged the attending physician over the loudspeaker in the hallway and a service cart jangled past the open door to Theo's room. A male nurse entered to check Theo's vital signs.

"I see the mother finally arrived," he said bitingly, inspecting the digital gauge showing Theo's blood oxygen level.

"Tamsen got here as quickly as she could," Victor said with a tone firm enough to put the nurse in his place.

"Sorry," the nurse said. "I didn't mean . . ."

"Good," Victor interrupted.

Tamsen tried to reconcile the man who called her despicable names, who would ignore her for days, who criticized her constantly, with the man who stood with her now in solidarity and love. She couldn't bring herself to look at him, but she allowed herself to cautiously appreciate his peace offering in the presence of their son.

The nurse piped up again. "If one of you wants to stay overnight, this chair reclines. You're welcome to use it."

"I'll stay," Victor said without looking at Tamsen. "You go home. Aneta texted—she cleaned up the blood, but Charlotte was pretty upset."

Tamsen kissed Theo again and then turned in her chair. "I'll be back here first thing," she said. Victor sniffed and nodded. Tamsen became uneasy as he followed her out into the florescent light of the hallway.

Victor's head was down. "Can I ask you something?"

"What is it?" Tamsen prepared herself for his justifiable inquisition—why hadn't she answered his calls or text messages? How come she smelled like she'd been at a Grateful Dead show?

He shuffled his foot on the speckled linoleum floor. "Neil Nevin is hosting an annual client outing at his estate in Forest Bluff in two weeks," he said. "The Thunderchicken people are going to be there, and I just thought, since they like you so much, that maybe you'd consider making an appearance."

Tamsen exhaled in relief. Victor just wanted something from her. Familiar territory.

"Victor, I honestly can't think about anything beyond this minute with Theo," she said.

"You're right," he answered. "It's just such a critical year for the company, revenue-wise, I mean."

"Let me sleep on it," she said. As if she could sleep.

"Thank you," he replied.

Thank you. Victor hadn't thanked her for anything in four years.

The house was dark and quiet. Aneta sat on the sofa, folding dish towels and chatting in Polish through her Bluetooth earpiece. As soon as she saw Tamsen, she disengaged from her conversation.

"I have been praying all night," Aneta said, gathering the Summers & Peel tote bag Tamsen had given her.

"Aneta, thank you so much for coming to sit with Charlotte on such short notice."

"Oh, I was already here," she explained. "Mr. Victor was getting ready to go out when Theo had the accident."

That explained Victor's outfit. "Of course," Tamsen said.

Tamsen peeked in on Charlotte, who was curled up on her side, fully dressed, snuggling Theo's favorite stuffed frog. She switched off the lava lamp that cast a blue hue across Charlotte's walls, and she tossed a wad of socks in her hamper. Tamsen noticed a framed family photograph beside Charlotte on the mattress and a series of silly photo-booth prints she and Theo had taken at their cousin's sweet sixteen party last summer. She carefully placed the pictures on Charlotte's dresser, pausing for a moment to look at the portrait of all four of them. A touch of melancholy caught Tamsen by surprise as she remembered that autumn day, three years ago, by the pond in Lincoln Park where the photo had been shot. The photographer had captured the precise moment Victor had unknowingly stepped in fresh goose poop. The incident had delighted the kids, who brought it up any time they spied any bird resembling a duck or a goose.

Tamsen slept in Theo's room that night. It was too disturbing to lie in the guest bed, the one on which Theo had struck his head. As Tamsen wearily crossed the threshold, she remembered the tumbler of water she had left on the counter downstairs. On her way to the kitchen, she noticed something curious—a light emanating from Victor's office, with the door gaping open. In his rush get to the hospital, he had not locked it. Tamsen lingered on the threshold. Maybe this was an olive branch, a prescient gesture from Victor's subconscious, or perhaps it was a deliberate oversight in the wake of Theo's accident. Tamsen put her toe through the door.

CHAPTER

1 5

The office was exactly as before. Victor's high-backed Eames chair was tucked behind his father's nineteenth-century mahogany library table, where stacks of papers were organized neatly into piles beside a leather cylinder intended for pens but filled instead with golf tees, and an antique banker table lamp with a green, translucent shade. Tamsen was, however, struck by the glaring addition of two new storage pieces: a pair of immense oak cabinets that she recognized from the estate of Victor's late mother. Ten feet tall, the cabinets nearly reached the ceiling, and each had a set of upper and lower doors. The gaudy storage pieces had been exiled to the couple's storage space because the ornate, inlaid brass embellishments clashed with the sleek design Tamsen had chosen for Victor's office millwork.

She walked to the cabinet closest to the door and tried to open it. It was locked. The second wardrobe was secured as well, but it had a small drawer built into the skirt at the base; when Tamsen pulled it out, she discovered two keys with faded tassel passementarie.

She unlocked the first cabinet easily with the rusty key. Her eyes scanned the boxes, which were neatly arranged from the first to the seventh shelf. In the lowermost position, Tamsen saw one of the flat, yellow, polka dot storage bins in which she kept Charlotte's winter hats and mittens during the warmer seasons. Victor must have borrowed it from the front closet. Tamsen removed the top and looked inside—the first thing she noticed was a purple plastic device with not one but two lobe-like fingers. The object looked more like an infant's bulbous teether than a sex toy. Nested beside it were a multitude of paramour delights: nipple clamps, hand cuffs, and even a lime-green, silicone caterpillar called a "Buttsy Bug," still in its blister pack, its face smiling up at Tamsen. She and Victor had never ventured into territory this racy; perhaps he curated this assortment for the New Year's Eve girl. She shook the next successive images from her mind. *Better her than me.* Tamsen opened a wrinkled brown paper sack that lay beside the toys. She pulled out two interlocking tubes of his-and-hers "Hot Mess" gel lubricant, as well as glow-in-the-dark condoms and a bottle containing all-natural "Myagra"—plant-based erection capsules. Victor never did like Big Pharma.

For a split second, Tamsen allowed herself the hope of believing the erotic playthings were the only reason Victor had locked the office door. Of course, he needed to secure the adult items so that the children wouldn't discover them. But upon closer examination of the remaining shelves, Tamsen's blood began to thin.

Victor had always had expensive taste. He had never been shy about hiding his wardrobe upgrades, but nothing could have prepared Tamsen for the vast wealth of shoes behind door number two. There must have been twenty pairs of pristine athletic sneakers mixed in with an assortment of ultra-luxe brands like Tod's, Valentino, and Lanvin, still smelling of factory-fresh rubber and neatly stored in their boxes. The shoes were all elevens, including a pair with the curious name on the sticker: *Air Jordan 3 Retro "Grateful."* Tamsen found it odd that Victor would purchase red gym shoes that he would never wear, but then again, she hadn't had any idea that he had a girlfriend. Maybe he was taking up basketball.

Victor had accumulated a bon vivant's share of exotic, dressy footwear that included designs by Gucci, Salvatore Ferragamo, Isaia, Mezlan, and a couple of brands she didn't even recognize. Tamsen peeked beneath the lid of every box and saw that each finely-crafted pair was constructed of a precious skin: alligator, caiman, and Victor's favorite—cordovan leather, aptly harvested from the rump quarters of a horse.

More than the dress shoes, Tamsen was nearly knocked over by a backdraft of shock when she opened a large, orange box with a brown bow. It was an incredible Hermès black matte crocodile *Sac à dépêches* briefcase. She ran her fingertips over the bumpy surface, feeling the flawless seams and the integrity of the craftsmanship. The lead time on a made-to-order piece like this was a minimum of twelve months— Tamsen's knees buckled with the knowledge that Victor had ordered this extravagance before their separation. He'd been planning this stockpile for a year and had successfully spent more than a year's tuition for Charlotte and Theo in footwear and the briefcase alone. To think, he had the audacity to complain to her about business being bad.

In the lower cabinet, she discovered two stacks of supple cashmere knits, woven of the softest baby Hircus goat fibers, in every texture and conceivable color. At the top of one pile, wrapped in gossamer paper, was a luscious navy Vicuña classic zip-up bomber-style sweater—the same one Hilly had purchased from Loro Piana for Digby last year. Tamsen had been with her when the refined saleswoman had rung it up at over $8,000. This one sweater handedly surpassed the entire value of her decimated Fountain Fund. How dare Victor attack her secrecy when he himself was hemorrhaging money all over The Magnificent Mile.

There were Moncler jackets in every conceivable color, a mink-lined trench coat, a coyote trapper hat, and silk ties—so many that Tamsen didn't bother looking at their brand names. She recognized the patterns; she knew they sold for hundreds of dollars each.

Tamsen kneeled to open the lower doors. They were misaligned and jammed from age, so she grabbed a polished silver letter opener from Victor's desktop and jimmied them apart. On the left, she found a large red leather jewelry box. She lifted the lid and beheld the spotless crystals of thirteen watch faces: Breitling, Omega, IWC, Blancpain, and Rolex, each nestled in its own suede-lined compartment. There were stainless ones, ones with blue faces, gold ones with Roman numerals, and some with leather straps. The coup d'état was a Patek Philippe with a bezel of small rectangular diamonds. Her stomach flipped; she was ill.

The second cabinet loomed, and her apprehension around seeing its contents was rooted in her wish to remain in denial about the extent of Victor's hoarding. Every article was purchased with the sole intent to take from her, to hurt her. Nevertheless, she needed to know the scope of his enterprise. She unlocked the cabinet and swung open the door. Suspended from a dowel rod in the upper half, Tamsen found hangers of never-worn suits. Herringbone, tweed, pinstripe, and hound-stooth—every fabric was represented. There were Brioni sport coats and Boglioli ones as well. At this point, not even the new Zegna tuxedo or the Kiton jacket riled her. However, one particular acquisition did grab her attention. She noticed a hunter-green garment bag wedged between a double-breasted Burberry blazer and a blue velvet Tom Ford smoking jacket. The zipper bag bore a distinguished gold logo: Marion Albert. On more than one occasion, Victor had pledged that when he amassed enough fuck-you money, he would spend $75,000 on one of the Savile Row tailor's custom suits. It was a single excess that even Victor considered extreme, but to him, a hand-stitched Supreme Bespoke Marion Albert suit was the ultimate "I won." Tamsen pulled the zipper

322 | LAURA HOLTZ

down and looked at the handcrafted masterpiece. She folded open the suit coat. Above the inside pocket, in gold thread, were the upper-case, embroidered letters: "VICTOR."

She tried to swallow but the muscles in her throat would not activate. For months, she had lived like a miser, curtailing all spending like some sort of upper-class martyr, St. Tamsen of Chicago. She'd attempted to demonstrate to Victor that she'd left him to escape his tyrannical behavior, that the separation was not the first step in a premeditated plot to take him to the proverbial cleaners. Standing before Victor's arsenal of apparel, however, it occurred to Tamsen that her husband wasn't simply preparing for battle, he was already waging a war. It was 4:00 a.m. and she had a throbbing weed hangover headache, Theo was in the hospital hooked up to five machines with his head swaddled in a bandage, and her husband was aggressively depleting their cash stores. The bony claw of dread wrapped itself around her ribcage and squeezed. To think that she had even considered for a split second that Victor's behavior at the hospital represented a change, that she should entertain reconnection, and that attending Neil Nevin's party with Victor might be an option. She felt like an idiot.

Tamsen sat slumped over and cross-legged on the floor and attempted to mentally calculate the sum total of all Victor's indulgences. But her brain was too overwhelmed for math. It was then that she noticed a banker's box sitting beside Victor's desk chair, its lid askew. She stood, moving slowly toward the vessel, as if it contained a waiting asp.

She hoisted the box to the embossed leather tabletop and scanned the orderly file tabs: "Accounts," "Banking," "Estate," "Funds," "Holdings" . . . Tamsen backed up to the "Funds" tab and pulled the thick folder. She needed to dispel the thought of Sally Frith—the one who was working long hours at the wellness club and rarely saw her children because her husband tied up their funds in secret offshore accounts and liquidated vast portions of their estate. Poor Sally—hers was a tale of a fallen member of the Socialati. A woman scorned, who once enjoyed the security of her husband's prosperity, and who was left to fend for herself without health insurance or a retirement plan. Tamsen could hear her pulse surging in her eardrums.

She leafed through document after document, ignorant of their relevance and confused by all the jargon. Midway through the bundle, she discovered a thick dossier fastened by a black binder clip. Her hand trembled as she lifted the cover page. Far beyond the net value of Victor's extravagant purchases, Tamsen read the two words that could determine her financial fate: Irrevocable Trust.

The white marble, mosaic bathroom tile beneath Tamsen was hard. Part of her didn't care, and the other part thought she deserved the discomfort of sitting on the guest bathroom floor until 8:00 a.m.—that's when the recording said the airline's special services office would open for business. Cormac's 675,000 miles were the only thing of value Tamsen could count as her own and she literally refused to rest until she knew they'd been restored to her account. She needed that money—$8,775. It was a running start, a deposit on an apartment, rent money. With a job, or even two, she would try to make it work. She didn't have a choice.

Her head bobbed with exhaustion, but she was ready, her hands on her phone, ten minutes before the alarm she'd set for 7:59 a.m. would sound. She punched in the 800 number like it was the nuclear code. She knew the sequence of numeric prompts well enough to get a live body on the line within thirty seconds.

"Good morning," the agent finally greeted her. "How can I help you today?"

"I am calling about my miles," Tamsen said. Suddenly her hands were slippery.

"I can see from your record that we received your documentation for the relocation of Mr. Peel's miles into your account." They were never Victor's miles, they belonged to my dead father, she wanted to tell the woman, but there was no point.

"So, you have everything you need?" Tamsen asked.

"Your case has been ele . . ."

"My case has been elevated, I know," Tamsen interrupted, her knees pulled tightly into her chest. "Please, I need to speak to someone who can help me resolve this today."

"I can get you to the right person, if you'll hold on," the woman said.

"No," Tamsen said, "I need you to stay with me—I am desperate. Can you do . . ." What was the term Whit had used? "Can you do a warm transfer?"

Tamsen did not see Victor that day. She arrived at the hospital with Charlotte about ten minutes after he'd texted her that he'd left. Theo seemed weak, but otherwise he was himself.

"I can't believe they make you eat that," Charlotte said to Theo of his runny eggs. "Mom, can we go to Cuddle Cakes and get Theo a breakfast bar?"

"When can I go home?" Theo begged. Tamsen kissed the top of his gauze-wrapped head.

"Not until Dr. Berkovits gives you the all-clear," Tamsen said. It was such a relief that the kids were having this conversation. Now if they'd only start squabbling, Tamsen would know everything was as it should be.

"Can I see your phone?" Theo asked his sister.

"No screens," Tamsen insisted. "Blocks and board games until the doctor says otherwise."

Charlotte opened her backpack and pulled out Jenga. "I brought Connect 4 too," she told him. She swung the tray between them and began to set up a tower. Tamsen's phone pinged. It was Whit, her joy. Her escape. She exhaled.

You okay?

Long story. More later.

"Guys, I need to make a quick call, okay? I'll be out in the hall."

"Sure," Charlotte said as she stacked the blocks on Theo's tray.

Tamsen fought the urge to call Whit. She wanted to hear his voice and explain why she disappeared at the concert. But right now, Tamsen needed to follow up with the last lawyer on the list Oliver had given her. She had already tried the three best firms: Bays Kreiter Mann, W.H. Drake and Associates, and one law practice that had a string of five surnames beginning with Shank. Victor had met with them all and in doing so, he'd made it impossible for Tamsen to hire any of them. The final firm on Oliver's list was small, and based on her Google search, it was run by a woman and located in Greenview, Tamsen's old neighborhood. The office of Iona Sullivan.

After a brief explanation of why she was calling, the receptionist transferred Tamsen directly to the managing partner.

"Iona here." The woman already sounded like a referee with a pack-a-day habit.

"My name is Tamsen Kinney Peel and I want to set up a consultation."

"P, E, E, L?" the woman asked. "Sounds familiar." Tamsen heard the tapping of fingers on a keyboard; she held her breath. "Your spouse is Victor Peel?"

Tamsen could barely squeak it out. "Yes."

"He's conflicted you out everywhere, hasn't he?" she said through a mouth full of what sounded like crunchy granola.

"How did you know?" Tamsen asked.

"Because we're usually the last place men call if they're covering every base," she said. "Sorry I can't help you."

Tamsen leaned against the wall and stared down at her feet. She'd been shut out.

"Me too," Tamsen said.

"Piece of advice," the woman said. "Stay out of court. You're going to lose tens, if not hundreds of thousands of dollars in this process if you can't mediate."

Tamsen's legs felt heavy. She did not have access to that kind of money. She recalled an article she'd read on Goop about an online divorce service started by a powerhouse female Hollywood divorce lawyer. It's Over Easy touted an uncomplicated divorce for as little as $750. Tamsen knew Victor would be amenable to the price—but would he ever be willing to entertain such a civilized way to split? Who was she kidding? There was no way.

A nurse pushing an empty wheelchair stopped and put her hand on Tamsen's shoulder.

"Are you all right, Mom?" the nurse asked. "Cuz you're looking a lot worse than Theo right now."

"It's nothing," Tamsen said. "I'm just tired." Her eyes followed the nurse until she disappeared into the room next to Theo's.

Petra would understand about trust funds, but the rules in Britain were different. And Tamsen didn't want to bother her again. Petra hadn't returned Tamsen's call from a week ago; she'd sent a text that she was in the midst of the biggest acquisition of her career. Tamsen's domestic problems could wait. But there had to be someone she could ask. Someone who knew something about money. Tamsen watched the nurse reemerge, wheeling a girl around Charlotte's age into the hallway.

The girl had a chin-length, curly black afro with a side part. Her eyes were wide-set and hazel, and she held a book in her lap. Tamsen wondered what ailment had landed her in the hospital, then she noticed the cast she wore on her left leg, the green wrapped plaster running all the way up to her thigh. The girl stared at Tamsen and smiled, revealing deep dimples as the nurse pushed her past.

"Hi," the girl said.

"Hi," returned Tamsen. The girl was wearing tartan flannel pajamas. Of course, Tamsen thought. He was a financial genius. She texted Victor.

What time does Neil's party start?

The Nevin Estate, inherited by Neil from his late Uncle Hamish, was situated on ten rolling, lakefront acres in the village of Forest Bluff, a suburb located an hour from the city. Tamsen likened it to the Pavillon de la Lanterne at Versailles, with its vast gate and carved limestone buck heads adorning the entry columns. The driveway was long and laid with loose brown pebbles that crunched as Tamsen pulled up in her Audi. Behind the main house was a newly restored reflection pool. It was flanked with stone containers, holding manicured boxwoods shaved to look like alternating cones and spheres. The expansive vista of Lake Michigan from the immense living room was juxtaposed against two atmospheric Sidney Richard Percy paintings that hung above the fireplaces at either end. Tamsen found all three views mesmerizing, but there was nothing like watching the motion of water to facilitate detachment.

"I'm glad you decided to come," Victor said, lifting a champagne flute from a passed tray and handing it to Tamsen. "Please spend some time with Eleanor Woodley. She's the one calling all the shots."

He said *please.*

"I will," Tamsen agreed. Victor saw Estelle and her husband at the bar and motioned hello.

"Estelle deserves a raise for her commitment to Summers & Peel. She makes us look good. And she's smart, too, I'll give her that. Making money is second nature to her."

Tamsen bit her tongue. *And she's smart, too?* Was he surprised by that fact? She was angry with Victor in that moment, but she itched with envy toward Estelle. There she was in her chic Brunello Cucinelli wrap dress, flanked by George Woodley and Koop, discussing the justice department's price-fixing probe with aplomb. Tamsen imagined hundred-dollar bills flying in her direction every time she opened her mouth. Estelle did not need a hack like Leda Sparrow to show her how to succeed; she was doing just fine on her own.

"Any word from Petra?" Victor asked.

"She's busy on a deal."

"What deal? Did you ask?"

"She can't discuss it, Victor," Tamsen replied.

He tilted his head. "Doesn't sound like much of a best friend to me," he said, and he walked away.

Tamsen scanned the room for Neil. He was speaking to George Woodley near the grand piano. Out of the corner of her eye, she saw Jacqueline approaching. What the hell was she doing at a Summers & Peel function? Tamsen tried to take evasive action, ducking behind a medieval suit of armor, but Jacqueline was on a crusade of her own.

"Has Cybill Hinton spoken to you about me?" Jacqueline asked. "Because my sources tell me she's on the WSC Board nominating committee." She petted her white fox fling; apparently animal skins were back for spring.

"I think the nominating committee is anonymous," Tamsen replied.

"Well, of course that's the case for most members, Tamsen, but for those of us whose ancestors were charter members—you know, part of *The Chicago Ancestral Register*—we're privy to certain things."

"I see," Tamsen said, looking at the axe in the knight's hand and contemplating its weight.

"Anyway, you and I have been friends for quite some time now, and I know I can count on your support should Cybill approach you about my qualifications for any possible . . . future . . . Board seats. She does seem to have some sort of fascination with you." Jacqueline set a pensive index finger on her lips and looked Tamsen up and down. "It's endearing, actually." The white tips of Jacqueline's French manicure were precise to the millimeter. Tamsen wondered if the salon charged extra for such talons.

"She hasn't asked me about you," Tamsen said.

"Just know that I think you'd be a solid choice for chairwoman for the next Harvest Moon affair," she said, stuffing her tongue under her lower lip and gliding away. Jacqueline stopped short of offering Tamsen the position. It was clear Jacqueline was looking for something reciprocal. *I'll scratch your back if you scratch my spiny scales.*

"Wow," Tamsen said under her breath. Hilly sauntered up with an exaggerated sway, and Jacqueline shook her head and promptly vanished. Tamsen didn't have the energy to discuss the pregnant nanny right now.

"I can't believe you came," Hilly gasped, sloshing her vodka drink. "Are you and Victor back together?" She was so intoxicated, she made the question sound like a tongue twister.

"Why is Jacqueline here?" Tamsen asked.

Hilly shook her head. "She's been dying to see this place, and Digby said something about doing billboards for Stephan's new real estate venture, so I guess that makes them clients?"

A server walked by and Tamsen placed her untouched flute on his tray. She wasn't sure how she was going to make it through the afternoon. She pinched the bridge of her nose. "My head is killing me," she said.

Hilly took Tamsen by the elbow and spoke into her ear. "My rescue clutch has anything and everything you need." Hilly was referring to the shimmery leather drug store she carried under her arm. "I'm out of my favorites, but two of the yellows will do the trick." Tamsen didn't bother answering. She'd had something over the counter in mind.

Tamsen looked at the lake. "Do you ever feel like you're nothing?" It was mostly a rhetorical question.

Hilly's eyes widened. "I'm Astrid's mom, and that's something," she said.

Tamsen looked at her. Her enlarged pupils were vacuous black holes, but there was depth in her answer. Working mothers were warriors, but mothers like Tamsen, who chose to stay home, volunteered at school, chauffeured their kids around, managed the sports, the meals, the medications—they too had value. Employed or not, being there for the little humans you were raising—that was something. That was everything.

"Yeah," Tamsen said. "And maybe that should be enough."

A number of guests milled around a table of exotic charcuterie, shoveling Turkish figs, truffle honey, peppery duck pâté, thinly sliced Italian prosciutto, and buttery triple cream cheese down their throats. None of the delicacies appealed to Tamsen; she had spent the past week subsisting on white wine, Theo's keto-friendly beef jerky, and occasional spoonfuls of almond butter. She meandered around the first level of the house, trying to distract herself by envisioning ways she could update the décor of Neil's mansion. The fringed gold and blue damask drapes would be the first thing to go; they weren't even suitable as play clothes for the von Trapp children. Next would be the furniture. She'd never seen anything as hideous as the tufted, burnt-orange settee that was situated between two gold and malachite rococo side tables in the music room. The house had great bones, but Uncle Hamish's fixtures should have been buried along with him.

"I know what you're thinking," she recognized Neil's Scottish accent. "How the hell can he expect to pass himself off as a straight man when his furniture looks like Liberace's fever dream?"

"It's great," she said, noticing an obscene, anatomically correct statue of a male Scottish wolf hound in the corner.

"Don't lie to me, Tamsen," he said. "We both know you have taste. How about helping a bloke out and becoming my decorator?"

Neil loved to joke with her. She was glad it was just the two of them in the garish room.

"Free advice . . . no more soldiers in metal suits," she told him. The voices in the adjacent rooms were muffled by the heavy tapestries on the walls. "Actually, Neil, I was wondering if I could ask you about a document." She took out her phone and scrolled to the photos she had taken of the contents of Victor's office. She pulled up the picture of the trust. "I agreed to this a number of years ago."

Neil squinted then zoomed in. "An irrevocable trust. What's your question?"

"Is there a way to reverse it?" she asked.

"Absolutely," he replied. "But only if Victor had a gun to your head when you signed it, which I suppose he didn't because his weapon of choice is his tongue. Or, if you were out of your mind when it was executed, which I suspect you weren't, given that I know you as perhaps the most reasonable person at this party." Tamsen was curious that Neil knew about Victor's arsenal of words. She wondered how Victor's verbal tactics looked when he exercised them at the office.

"There has to be some way," she said. "He didn't tell me that he was rendering all our assets untouchable when he did our estate planning."

Neil pursed his lips, then he scrolled down. "I'm afraid you're locked in."

Locked in—yes, that's exactly where Victor wanted her, a prisoner of their marriage. Tamsen's head spun. "Neil, Victor's been hiding a bunch of stuff from me, and I need someone to translate the fine print. I can't make sense of most of it."

Neil frowned. "I can't, Tamsen. You know I like to stay out of the fray, not to mention I work for the man." He handed her back the phone with genuine remorse. "I sincerely wish there was something I could do."

"Would you just have a look at the files? I took pictures of everything. No one has to know," she pleaded.

"I can give you the name of a good forensic accountant," Neil offered. Tamsen knew she could never afford such a thing.

Hilly shuffled in, stabilizing herself on a Victorian standing lamp whose beaded fringe shade shimmied as she seized the brass neck. "Anybody seen Digby?" she slurred.

"He was asking about my 1967 Maserati Mistral. Maybe he's gone out to the garage," Neil suggested. He noticed Hilly teetering and he put his hand out to steady her. "Maybe you'd like to sit down?" Neil suggested.

Tamsen looked at Neil with expressionless resignation. She understood why he didn't want to get involved in her personal life; it was enough to keep his own secret in a "family firm" in which the biggest client was trying to set him up with their pastor's daughter. "Get back to your guests," Tamsen said. "I got this."

Neil was still within earshot when Hilly remarked, "God, that sofa is ugly." She made a move to open her clutch bag and Tamsen took it from her, setting it on the ghastly settee.

"Let's walk this off," Tamsen said.

Tamsen led Hilly outside. It was a brisk fifty-five degrees, but the sun was bright in the clear sky and the play of its warmth on her bare arms against the cool lake air revived Tamsen's dull senses. They walked the garden path, past the barren grape vines, beyond the withered hollyhocks that had been tamed by jute twine and bamboo stakes. It was a shame that the dead stalks had not been properly cut back for winter; their flocked blossoms might have yielded hearty seedlings in a month or so, but at this point, the formerly vibrant plants were beyond saving.

"Is that the guest house?" Hilly asked, pointing past the groomed, clay tennis court toward the garage.

"Not unless the guests want to sleep in Neil's Bugatti Chiron," Tamsen replied. She steered Hilly in the direction of the lavish auxiliary building with its eight automatic garage doors and stately copper cupola and weather vane on top. Tamsen was beginning to feel anxious. Victor had seen very little of her since she arrived at the party, and she hadn't even spoken to Eleanor Woodley once.

The pea gravel surrounding the garage was deep and shifty and Hilly was having a tough time navigating it in her four-inch Saint Laurent Tribute sandals. She seemed to find this amusing because she laughed hysterically until they were able to find solid ground through an unlocked back door of the garage. Heat radiated from the floor and the air was comfortably warm. Tamsen switched on the lights. Unlike the house itself, the garage seemed contemporary, with crisp white walls and modern overhead fans. There were twelve cars parked in diagonals, each slightly turned as if the entire ensemble was posing for a foldout magazine cover. Tamsen recognized the red Jaguar coupe from Halloween; it was parked between a yellow Ford GT and a silver

Mercedes 300 SL that looked like it had never left its original showroom.

"Neil's a catch," Hilly said, touching the hood of a white Lamborghini Countach as she wove between the pristine sports cars. "We need to set him up with somebody we know so he'll have us over more often."

Tamsen looked at her watch. "We should really get back to the party," she said. She wanted to put her time in with Eleanor and then head back into the city. She urgently wanted to see Whit.

Plans tonight?

She was relieved when he responded immediately.

What do you have in mind?

I'd come to you.

Uhhhh . . .

Please.

"What about that girl from my dinner party? Does Neil like younger ones?" Hilly asked. "The event planner. McKinsey? McCormick? Tam, I could go for something salty. Pretzels."

Tamsen ignored Hilly and her tranquilizer-induced non-sequiturs. There was one car in Neil's garage that wasn't as glamourous as the others: a shiny black 1964 Austin FX4—an authentic London taxi. Tamsen's memories of climbing into the back of one of these, flipping down the two auxiliary seats, and tooling back to the dorm with Petra and three other friends after a night of pubbing in Leicester Square flooded her head with a transient dose of amusement. She had to get a closer look. The novelty of the car lifted Tamsen to a momentary place where doom could not reach—Tamsen's time in London.

"McCormick, I think that was it." Hilly was back on the girl from the party.

Tamsen nostalgically admired the lines, laughing to herself about the time Petra had thrown up in the driver's lap when she rode shotgun on their way back from a party in St. Johns Wood. She wondered if the taxi had a meter—probably. She took two steps around the side of the car and noticed a strange, furry lump on the ground. At first, she thought it was some sort of unusual dusting accoutrement for Neil's auto collection, but as she got closer, she recognized Jacqueline's fox fling. She jerked her head to her left and peered into the back seat.

Despite the glare caused by the overhead spotlights, Tamsen could still make out two figures on the floor in the back of the taxi. She saw an unmistakable French manicured hand frozen in stillness upon a mound of middle-aged, white, male ass. Was there some sort of thrill in being adulterous under the nose of one's spouse, she thought, or were Digby and Jacqueline so incredibly shameless that consequences were immaterial?

"Madison," Tamsen said, kicking the fur beneath the car. "Her name was Madison." She walked quickly toward Hilly, who had wandered over for a look at the taxi.

"Right, I knew it was one of those presidents," Hilly said.

"I need a drink," Tamsen blurted, attempting to intercept Hilly's path. "Let's get out of here."

"I've always thought these things looked like hearses," Hilly remarked. Tamsen knew if Hilly saw the passengers, the taxi might indeed become just that.

"They're going to wonder where we've disappeared to," Tamsen insisted.

"Let's get in?" she giggled conspiratorially, pressing past Tamsen.

Tamsen was desperate. "We can't touch the cars. Neil said. No touchy." She made a play for Hilly's arm, attempting to spin her around, but it was too late. Hilly spotted just the tip of the white fur mound peeking out from beneath the undercarriage.

"What's this?" she said, incredulously. A tiny piece of Tamsen wanted Hilly to know; the rest of her wanted to spare her friend the heartbreak.

Hilly shook free of Tamsen's grasp and slowly, like a stalking cougar, moved alongside the vehicle. Tamsen thought of faking a stroke; she considered body-checking Hilly, or even sitting on the hood of the neighboring Maybach in hopes that the car alarm would sound. But at this point, there was no stopping the chain reaction of shit show that was about to ensue.

Tamsen held her breath as Hilly pointed her toe and gently slid the fox fling out from under the car. A cackle that could have shattered a windshield escaped her. Tamsen watched in horror. Hilly stood beside the rear door, laid her hand on the chrome handle and opened it. There was a rustling from the back floor and Digby sat upright, turning toward Hilly. She took a single, wobbly step back, her hand over her mouth. Then Tamsen saw the flutter of Digby's limbs as he struggled to pull on his pants, accompanied by the frenzied flapping of Jacqueline's arms, hurriedly yanking the bodice of her dress up and over her perfect, never-nursed-a-day-in-her-life breasts. And before either of the cheaters could utter even a grunt, Hilly raised her shimmery rescue clutch above her head, yelled out a battle cry worthy of a bloody gladiator movie, and brought the purse down on top of Digby's head, sending dozens of yellow and white pills flying through the air like contraband confetti.

"I hate you," she bellowed from the depths of her decimated soul, and then she collapsed on the floor in a mess of tears.

Jacqueline glared at Tamsen, as if Tamsen had been the one under Digby. Digby, his hair drenched in well-earned perspiration, scrambled out of the London taxi and sat beside his blubbering wife.

"I don't suppose you intend to keep this quiet," Digby said to Tamsen, between breaths.

So many secrets, Tamsen thought. Victor, Neil, Digby, Hilly,

Jacqueline, the nanny, and even herself. Everyone had something.

Tamsen looked at the spray of pills that littered the garage floor. "It's best that we clean up after ourselves, don't you think?" Tamsen replied.

Jacqueline fluffed her hair, smoothed her dress, and marched stoically past Tamsen, out the back door.

Inside the mansion, the party was winding down and Tamsen was relieved to see Eleanor Woodley still present and being charmed by Neil, who sat beside her on a Chesterfield leather sofa with what appeared to be a collection of old photographs. Tamsen could sense Victor watching her from the bar on the opposite side of the room. His disapproval of her extended absence from the party was palpable. She knew the only way to regain his favor was to fulfill his wish; she would engage with Eleanor before she and the Thunderchicken team climbed into the obnoxious Hummer limousine that Summers & Peel had rented to whisk them to the small nearby airport where their private jet sat waiting.

Tamsen drifted past Neil's Rococo Steinway. She touched the swirling burled wood and wished Whit were here now—he would make the instrument sing louder than Koop's gratuitous howls or George Woodley's kindly southern guffaws. Whit could drown out all the background noise.

Tamsen heard Victor's voice as she neared the wing where the guests were assembled. She didn't feel like she owed Victor anything now. Her desire to make good on his request to connect with Eleanor Woodley was simply an exercise in self-preservation. The less he had to criticize, the less she had to deal with him and, ergo, the easier her entrapped life would be.

For a split second, Tamsen's mind flirted with the thought of being back home with him. She allowed her mind to graze the notion that she would again have to sleep with him in their four-poster bed. She felt the unpleasant claw reaching for her, so she stepped back, pressing her back into the wall around the corner from where the company was winding down the party on Neil's long sofa. Terror chemicals seeped into her bloodstream and a fuzzy vision of the bookcase started to materialize in front of her. She drew in a breath and tried to pull her consciousness back. She needed to get angry. She forced herself to focus on Victor's office—on the reserve of sport coats and sweaters, on all those shoes. She remembered the briefcase and the Marion Albert suit, and she could feel her terror submit to rage. The vision dissolved.

Tamsen closed her eyes. *Do this to get through this. Do this to get through this.*

"Come sit by me, Tamsen," Eleanor Woodley beckoned when she spotted Tamsen.

Tamsen took the open space on the sofa beside Eleanor and tried to appear interested in Neil's narrative around an old box of photographs.

"Tamsen, y'all would not believe the amount of history that surrounds this house. Sir Winston Churchill himself stood in this very room in 1929," she said. "Those were simpler times, no doubt about it."

Tamsen stared vacantly through the French doors at the lake. It was dolphin gray today, and calm. But it was still too early for sailing, she thought, unless the warm weather continued. Eleanor dug her hand into a bowl of fancy mixed nuts that sat atop coffee table books on art and horticulture. She crunched enthusiastically as Neil explained the history of the house. Victor stepped behind where Tamsen sat and she shivered, holding the assortment of his new watches in her mind.

"This is a shot of the famous Adler house built next door. You can't see it now because my uncle's father constructed a berm on the lot line and planted white pines from the street, all the way to where the beach grass begins," Neil said.

"A beautiful place like this, I can see why he wouldn't want to look at the neighbors," Eleanor remarked. She extended the bowl over her shoulder to Victor. He took several.

"I'm all for privacy," Victor chimed in. Tamsen tensed, thinking of the deadbolt on the office door. She had left the room exactly as she found it.

Neil got a playful look in his eye. He lowered his voice to an exaggerated whisper. "They were Catholic folk who commissioned the Adler house next door." He laughed heartily. "May as well have been pagans as far as the Nevins were concerned."

Tamsen thought she spotted a white cap on the horizon.

Eleanor puffed out her chest and leaned in. "The house across the street from us in Birmingham . . . it just sold to homosexuals." Tamsen's gaze flitted past Neil. She saw him look down. "I have nothing against the gays, but I don't exactly want them as neighbors. I mean, we have five young grandchildren who visit us." She popped a nut in her mouth. "I keep telling George, 'I just don't know what we're going to do.'"

Tamsen's back tensed. If there was a single character trait Tamsen couldn't stomach, it was prejudice.

"You could go over there and introduce yourselves," Tamsen said. Victor lay a hand on Tamsen's shoulder. She felt his fingers squeeze through the thin silk of her dress. But she couldn't stop. "There are several gay families at our children's school and they are incredible parents. Really, they're just like anyone else."

Eleanor cleared her throat and upgraded her southern drawl. She smoothed her Lilly Pulitzer dress, indicating in the politest manner that the discussion was officially over.

As if on cue, Koop swooped in. Tamsen could feel the pressure of Victor's knuckle relent.

"We need to put you in one of our Thunderchicken television spots, Eleanor. You have the most honest face," Koop gushed.

"It's a great idea," Victor concurred.

"From the mouth of a creative genius! I am flattered you think so, Koop! I would love to be in one of your productions!" she said. The conversation was saved.

Neil hid his smirk in a napkin, making a move for the kitchen. Koop whisked Eleanor to where Estelle was updating the other Thunderchicken execs on plans to sponsor several summer music festivals.

Tamsen turned to face Victor. It was there, the punishing glare. Piercing eyes, ears back. He chewed on walnuts, his mandible rotating in slow circles. Tamsen was too numb to feel his power. It didn't make her shrink; it didn't banish her to a corner of her mind where she pulled her knees in tight to her chest and covered her head. Not this time.

"Do you have even the slightest idea who you've offended? Twenty-one hundred stores, thirty-seven states, nine billion dollars in annual revenue." He popped a few nuts in his mouth. "If we lose this client, so help me. Years of work, countless hours at the office . . ." Victor's eyes were red. He had never laid into her in front of people, but she may have pushed him too far.

There was a loud cracking from Victor's mouth. He stopped short, grasping his jaw. Estelle appeared beside him.

"What is it?" she asked.

"I think I just lost a filling," Victor said.

Estelle locked eyes with Tamsen.

"Why don't you see about that tooth," she said. "Tamsen and I haven't had time to catch up."

The servers scurried through the living room, collecting crumpled cocktail napkins and half-empty stemware.

Estelle put her hand on Tamsen's wrist. "Let's go someplace we can talk."

There was a small orangery off the side of the southern end of the mansion where the gardeners maintained several Meyer lemon trees, among other topiaries, over the winter. The pitched roof and walls were mostly glass and there was a tiered fountain that quietly trickled in the center of the space.

"You've been going through so much," Estelle said, crossing her long legs on the teak bench where they sat. "You wear it in your body and on your face."

"I'm managing," Tamsen lied. She felt small and useless in the presence of such a self-possessed woman.

"Victor loves you, Tamsen," she said. "He is a difficult man sometimes, I know, but when he speaks about you, it is with such adoration. You are everything to him." Tamsen was surprised Victor ever spoke of her at all. "It's hard to be in a position of power, to be responsible for so many peoples' livelihoods. But I know Victor appreciates your patience—your tolerance of his schedule." It was true, Tamsen never complained about Victor's long hours or traveling. "He has not been the same since the two of you separated."

"It's been hard for both of us."

"You know, Hadrian and I took some time off after Pierre was born," she said. "I think I had become too demanding. I was used to people following my orders, and when things at home didn't meet my definition of perfection, I became very intolerant." She looked up at a copper ceiling fan that rotated slowly above them. "Thankfully, though, Hadrian gave me a second chance."

"I didn't know you two went through anything like that," Tamsen said. Suddenly, Estelle seemed more human.

"We had been together for twelve years. We had built a family and community of friends. I think we both valued that so much. We knew all each other's idiosyncrasies—how I like my eggs, how he can't stand it when the dishwasher isn't loaded a certain way." Estelle's already impeccable complexion glowed a little brighter as she spoke of her husband. "And, let's be honest, it wasn't as if either of us were going to meet someone better, that's just a fallacy. It's tough to be married, but it can be harder to be alone."

Tamsen looked at Estelle's wedding ring. It was a simple gold band, not a giant diamond that advertised her status. Maybe simplifying was the key. "How did you rebuild?" Tamsen asked.

"Well, it took time, and a lot of communication, but it was worth it. Somehow, overcoming our challenges made us stronger together."

Tamsen imagined the long conversations she and Victor used to have over Indian food. They'd talk about buying a house on the perfect street, about raising a family and sending their kids to the best schools where they would be nurtured and challenged. Those times were so far in the past. Victor had been kind then. He had turned into a different man.

Estelle slung an arrow. "I think ultimately, Hadrian and I knew the children would suffer if we gave up on our marriage. That fact alone compelled us to sort out our differences." The orangery began to feel claustrophobic. Tamsen's skin was hot. She wanted to jump into the fountain.

"I'm a facts and figures girl," Estelle continued. "And when I started looking at statistics and reading about the deleterious effects of divorce on children, I just couldn't walk away in good conscience."

Tamsen thought of Theo and Charlotte and how much they loved family outings to the Adler Planetarium, the Museum of Science and Industry, and the annual fishing derby in Lincoln Park. How they glowed on the nights Victor came home for dinner and the four of them ate in the warm light of the kitchen together.

"I don't know that compromise is going to solve things for Victor and me," Tamsen said.

"I can't put myself in your shoes, Tamsen. Every marriage is different, but I do know this: if you divorce Victor, I don't think he will ever recover."

"How do you mean?" Tamsen asked. Victor had the means. He'd have his choice of partners.

She reached out and took Tamsen's hand. "His family is his center, and if it's dismantled, he will be a rudderless ship."

"People eventually move on," Tamsen said. "He could remarry."

"Of course, he could," she said. "But do you really want some other woman raising Theo and Charlotte? Some flaky, twenty-something he met in a bar in the Viagra triangle who has her own agenda?" Tamsen thought of the girl in the silver dress with the bracelet. "An uneducated, alcoholic tart who would rather jet off to South Beach with Victor instead of sitting through one of Charlotte's ice-skating competitions or Theo's tennis matches?"

Tamsen hadn't considered the specifics of this. If Victor ever remarried, she would have no say in how this stranger might parent her children. She gulped audibly.

Estelle squeezed Tamsen's hand and fired a poison dart into her neck. "We have a French saying: *les enfants sont ce qu'on en faits*. Do you understand?"

Tamsen's high school French was enough. "Children are what they are made."

CHAPTER

16

Whit met Tamsen at the door of his apartment with a glass of the same Sancerre she ordered every time they met at the uninspired bar around the corner from The Talisman. He wore Levis and a white apron over a slightly wrinkled blue oxford shirt. After dragging her body up the three flights of stairs to reach the studio apartment he called home, she fell into him, leaning her cluttered head against the retreat of his steady chest.

The smell of rosemary and garlic saturated the air, and when he escorted her in, she noticed a small, round bistro table near the window. It was set with dishtowel placemats, mismatched plastic tumblers, and a pickle jar holding top-heavy yellow gerbera daisies. She pressed the rim of the wine glass to her lips, sniffed, and smiled at the orange Glade candle Whit had staged in the center of the dinner table for ambiance.

"It's not as nice as you do," he said. "But I don't entertain much." Tamsen walked to the white Corelle plates with a yellow filigree and butterfly border and ran her finger along the edge.

"Where did you get these?" she asked.

"Salvation Army, I think," he replied. "There or Ikea."

The plates were the ones she'd grown up with, the same ones her mother used in their kitchen on 113th Street. She was struck by the irony of her nostalgia; she had been brought back in time by her twenty-something boyfriend.

"Let me give you the tour," he teased, gesturing to an Amana countertop microwave from the 1980s. "This is where I prepare my 500-watt ramen and my instant oatmeal." He swept his arm to the right. "And here we have the living area, music room, master bedroom, and LP library."

Tamsen drew in a breath as she scanned the space; after months of imagining where Whit spent his time away from her, she was finally in his world—all 375 square feet of it.

He walked to a turntable that sat atop three red plastic milk crates crammed full of records. "This Pioneer belonged to my grandfather," he said. "The vinyl's all mine though. You ever been to Reckless?"

"I've driven past," Tamsen said of the store on Milwaukee Avenue. Record stores were a charming relic, but Victor had installed the latest smart streaming system in their house, so she had no reason to shop for music.

Whit set the needle down carefully and a prelude of dusty crackles and pops started from the speaker. The vibration of the upstairs neighbor's heavy steps was suddenly drowned out by the soul of a warm trumpet. The Sancerre began to soften the tension in her muscles. Tamsen bent to get a closer look at the photographs that were suspended by curio shop magnets on Whit's refrigerator. There was a picture of a man pulling a little boy in a red Radio Flyer wagon, and another of the same man wearing a gingham shirt in front of Sleeping Beauty's Disneyland castle while a boy in Mickey ears clutched his leg.

"Your dad?" Tamsen asked.

Whit yanked on the oven door and it released with a squeal. "That's him," he said. "The picture with the smoking-hot savage wearing floods with the blonde at the Grand Canyon, that's me and Mom. She still looks exactly the same."

Tamsen leaned in to examine the woman Whit called Mom. She had a vibrant grin and Whit's high cheek bones. She wore a fitted black t-shirt with wide-leg white denim slacks and glamourous round sunglasses. Whit, shielding the sun from his eyes the way Theo always did, appeared to be around ten in photograph. That put his mother in her mid-thirties, Tamsen guessed. She couldn't resist the urge to extrapolate Whit's mother's current age. She was roughly fifty-two, closer to Tamsen than Whit was. She looked like the type of woman Tamsen might speak to spontaneously in the checkout line at Whole Foods.

Whit peeked into the oven and then checked the timer on his phone. "My magnificent attempt at a roast needs another fifteen minutes," he said.

He took her hand and they moved to a clear space in front of his futon sofa. He pulled her in close and she was content to melt into his form, feeling absolute mental abandon with his arms around her ribcage. He held her up while they swayed together to the music that poured from his mismatched floor speakers. She saw Moby and Edmond Dantès propped up against the wall beneath Whit's collection of framed concert posters. There were reproductions of Johnny Cash at Strathspey Place, James Brown at the Apollo, David Byrne at Red Rocks, *Aida* at the Lyric Opera House, and Yo-Yo Ma at the New York Philharmonic.

There was a menagerie of instruments neatly organized at the far end of the studio: two guitars and a ukulele hung from wall hooks, an assortment of bongos and conga drums were against the wall, a rain stick was in the corner, and a clarinet sat beside a folding spectator chair—the kind Tamsen set up curbside every year at the St. Patrick's Day Parade. Whit's cello stood alone in a burgundy, hard-sided shell. Given that he refused to play, she imagined it as more of a sarcophagus than an instrument case. She understood his paralysis; they were comrades in that respect—two cellmates in a jail they could not escape. Their bodies moved back and forth, and Whit's hands traveled from her hips to her shoulders. He kissed her neck and she closed her eyes.

"You're tight," he said.

"Rough few days," she replied.

Whit let her go and wrestled with the futon until it submitted and assumed its form as a bed. He yanked off the mousy brown cover, revealing patterned, flannel sheets with cartoon penguins in exultant poses. There was one wearing earmuffs, another standing by an igloo, and two with their wingtips touching and hearts floating above their heads. The corners of her mouth curled up. It felt good to smile.

"They were a Christmas gift from my mother," Whit said. "Her version of a mood elevator."

Tamsen laughed. "They're certainly uplifting."

"Lie down, I'm giving you a back rub."

Whit pressed the heels of his hands into her sacrum, stretching the muscles on either side of her spine upwards and relieving the pressure in her lower back. He shifted forward, slowing digging his fingers deeply into the folds of her scapula. Tamsen winced.

"Too much?" he asked.

"It's the good kind of hurt," she said. Still, Whit lightened the pressure. She closed her eyes and nestled in. She was a million miles from anything. How lovely it would feel to be with Whit every night. "This is so nice."

Whit's phone timer jangled loudly from the speckled Formica countertop and he jumped up to pull the roast from the oven. Tamsen tugged on her shirt and fluffed the penguin-clad pillow. She imagined Whit's mother pushing a cart down the bedding aisle of a big box store or leafing through a linens catalogue, thinking of her son's reaction when he opened the gift of silly sheets. Tamsen knew the satisfaction that was the gratifying byproduct of caretaking. She felt it with her own children.

"Mind if I use your bathroom?" she asked, as Whit banged the foil pan on the coils of his enamel, four-burner stove. He couldn't hear her over the roaring exhaust fan.

Inside the tiny quarters Tamsen recognized the lingering freshness of a lemony cleaning solution. She noticed the empty Scrubbing Bubbles can in an unlined, plastic trash can beside the light blue toilet. Nevertheless, no amount of scouring could possibly return Whit's Neolithic Era–grout to its original color. The same could be said for the rust-stained sink.

Tamsen stared at her reflection in the medicine cabinet as she rinsed her hands and wondered what contents were stowed behind the hinged mirror. She grasped the corner, tempted to have a peek inside, but she hesitated. What would she be snooping for? A look at the medications he'd been prescribed? The color of his toothbrush? Even though she'd known him for nearly six months, she was curious to know him more. Being in his space changed the calculus of the two of them. She felt like he was a person she'd just met. He hadn't left out a towel, so she opened the white vanity cabinet below, revealing nothing but a couple rolls of toilet paper, a plunger, and an economy size box of condoms, large enough to protect the entire population of a horny third world country. The kitchen exhaust fan died out and Tamsen heard Whit's microwave beep three times.

When she emerged, Whit was setting out their plated dinner of carved pork, frozen peas and carrots, and quick rice.

"You make cooking look way easier than it actually is," Whit said, wiping his glistening forehead on the back of his sleeve.

"It just takes practice," she said. She found it endearing that he was oblivious to the way the Hawaiian Breeze perfumed candle was competing with the smell of seasonings.

"No, seriously, you are an incredible cook," he added.

"You don't need to flatter me to get laid tonight," she said, as he topped off her wine and poured himself a splash.

"Tamsen," he said, setting down his utensils. "Every time I pay you a compliment, you turn it into a joke."

"That's not—" she began.

"Let me finish," he interjected. He reached across the small table and took her hand. "I wish that you could see yourself the way I see you. Strong, incredibly beautiful, giving. You have everything going for yourself and you make me feel that way, too."

Tamsen quelled the urge to blurt out a self-deprecating one-liner. "Thank you," she managed instead. And somehow, through the act of accepting his admiration, she felt a twinge of special.

Whit leaned in. There was a serenity about him tonight. "There's something else I want to say, Tamsen," he said.

She bit into the salty meat, dabbing her lips with the square of flowered paper towel Whit had set out as a napkin. She braced herself, recalling the time she'd almost told him she loved him, under the glittering shower of fireworks on New Year's Eve. She knew how vulnerable he must feel in this moment. The words had seemed too charged with expectation that night, and she held off because she didn't want to frighten him. But things were different now. They had evolved.

Whit took her other hand. "I've been accepted to grad school. In Boston," he blurted.

The words ricocheted nonsensically inside Tamsen's skull. Warning signals and flashing lights blinked an alert of some sort of neurological malfunction. The trajectory of the conversation had suddenly veered perilously off course. Her mind grappled with the message, trying to translate the implications of his statement and process the jarring information. The record on the Pioneer turntable had ended and she heard the sound of the needle thumping against vinyl.

"Grad school?" she choked out, drawing her hands from him.

Whit nodded. "Yes," he said. His eyes scanned back and forth across her face like he was reading a book.

Tamsen folded her arms across her stomach. "Oh. Really?" she said, trying to be cool under the surge of her heartbeat.

"Whoa," Whit reached for her across the table. "All the air has gone out of the room."

The spinning record made a repetitive, low thumping noise.

"I didn't know you applied," she said. She couldn't look at him.

"It wasn't a sure thing, you know. They might not have taken me."

"Guitar or cello?" she asked. She wrung the paper towel in her lap.

"Composition," he said. "I got a full ride."

"That's great news," she said. She needed to remain upbeat. It was a tremendous achievement. He deserved to have it all, but what about the kids? Theo? Her? He should have said he was planning to leave Chicago. Maybe not at first, but at least by the conservatory, or New Year's Eve. She recalled him saying his old girlfriend was in Boston; she probably had something to do with this.

"When do you start?" she asked lightly, stabbing her fork into the mound of vegetables.

"Fall," he said.

"Do you have a place to live? I have some publishing contacts in Boston if you want to talk to somebody about neighborhoods," she offered. She had to keep talking, to keep up the energy of excitement for him or she would break into a thousand pieces. "The school has graduate housing," he replied. "My lease here is up at the end of the summer, so it all works out."

Yeah, it all works out great for you, the voice in her head hollered. She took a gulp from her wine glass. "Perfect," she said. She stared at the flickering, scented candle.

Whit leaned back in his chair and inhaled through his teeth, plunging his fingers into his hair. "It doesn't sound perfect when you say it," he said.

"I'm just surprised, that's all," she said. But the news was indeed suffocating. She felt herself being buried alive beneath a tonnage of cement.

"Tamsen, I've thought about this. We'll still see each other. I can gig in Chicago. You can come visit."

"For parents' weekend?" she half-joked.

He looked hard at her from under his clenched eyebrows. "We can make it work," he said.

She sat opposite him, but her consciousness drifted from her body and hovered above them. Whit, the luminous jewel she carried with her during these dark months, was at once plucked from her palm. He had been her antidote to misery, and he was leaving. Every cruel and defeating thought that had stealthily plagued Tamsen since they first met bubbled up from the depths of the swamp. What had she expected from this? Was he planning to stick around for the thyroid meltdown? For the hot flashes? And what about the kids—how was that supposed to work? She imagined herself in a tiny apartment, alternating weekends with Victor, Whit dipping into town now and then. Even in this state of despair, when she wanted to depend on his words of devotion, Tamsen knew this was a life of which Whit would quickly grow tired. She'd been insane to imagine a future together. The scholarship was a gift. She had to end it now.

Whit stood, walking to the old hi-fi. He flipped the expired record to the B-side. The renewed melody returned Tamsen to the moment.

"We have to stop seeing each other, Whit." She couldn't make eye contact with him.

"You're part of the reason I decided to go," he said. "What happened to 'supreme happiness?' I thought we'd forge ahead together."

"This new chapter doesn't have room for me. You think it will, but it doesn't."

"Is this about you, Tamsen?" he asked. "Have you changed your mind about being with a man who lives in a shitty apartment and rides a bike to get around?"

Tamsen dropped her fork and it landed with a clank in the cold, white rice. "We've always had a shelf life, I've just been ignoring the expiration date," she said. It felt better to get angry than to feel the despair that was threatening to crack her. "You are going on to better things," she said.

"Is it that hard to believe that I might actually want to be a part of your life?" he asked, his voice raised to a level the upstairs neighbor could certainly hear. "That the depth of my feelings for you transcends our birthdates and the balances in our bank accounts?"

She stared at refrigerator photos behind him. Magnets were worthless against the stainless steel Sub-Zero at the brownstone, but Victor hated when she used cellophane tape to hang the kids' artwork. Tamsen was puzzled by Whit's insistence that they stay the course—that they continue, despite his opportunity. That they could build something together.

"You still have options," she insisted. Her imagination saw him sitting in the student union, enjoying a discourse on jazz with a fellow musician over some exotic tea he'd picked up at a shop in Cambridge where they sold quirky infusers and loose-leaf varietals from all over the world. "I am a middle-aged housewife with two children and a life I signed up for before you even hit puberty. We're in different places, we have always been in different places," she said.

Like Edmond Dantès from the prison, Château d'If, Whit had escaped. He was swimming to freedom while she, like his dead cellmate and friend, the Abbé, was left behind to decompose. Tamsen wanted to punish Whit for being okay, for getting unstuck. She rose and the legs on her chair created a dull moan as they slid backward.

Whit's arms were limp at his sides. "So, that's it? 'Sorry to eat and run but I can't keep my miserable existence waiting.'"

She set her plate down beside his instant hot water kettle, leaning in to the counter so she wouldn't buckle in a heap on the floor.

His voice was hoarse. "I'm sorry, you didn't deserve that."

"I know I'm miserable, but thanks for driving the point home in case I might have forgotten for the last forty-five minutes," she said, grabbing her jacket from the back of the chair. "I should go."

Whit stood, reaching for her arm. "Please don't."

Tamsen saw her brothers' expressions, daring her not to cry. *Do this to get through this, do this to get through this*, she yelled at herself inside her mind.

"Congratulations on grad school," she said. "It really is fantastic. You know I want the best for you, Whit."

"I'll see you Wednesday, for Theo's lesson," he said, stepping aside to clear a path to the door.

"I'll have Aneta be there. I'll let you tell the kids about your plans before I do," she replied. She would sit Theo down after school, or maybe they'd take a walk.

"Aneta. I see." His mouth twitched downward and he swallowed. "This is not how tonight was supposed to go," he said.

"Someday you'll thank me for letting you go," she said.

"For the record, you are hurting me, Tamsen," he said. "And not in a good way."

She didn't hear the sound of him closing the door as she rushed down the stairs. She hardly noticed the ambulance siren as she ran toward her Audi, nor the distant clap of ominous thunder. But the cool evening air was a sympathetic caress on her skin. This really was best for him. She loved Whit too much to ever pull him down the way a drowning victim, in their desperation, overcomes the rescuer and causes both swimmers, the stronger and the weaker, to perish. One of them would be free, yet she felt a throb of grief in her chest knowing she had just abandoned her life vest.

Her windshield began to fog over and the horror of being confined to her aloneness tore her heart to tiny bleeding fragments. And then it came again, fuzzy at first—the terrifying image of her bookshelves with her treasured tomes: Hardy, Austen, Brontë, Dickens, Eliot—Victor's cologne, the silver frame, and the wedding picture. She couldn't contain the fear this time; she wasn't strong enough to summon the anger that could cast out the sensation of hurling into terrifying oblivion. The scene appeared again; it was a transparent specter behind the glass, stalking her, its hovering form blurry. She tried to make out its face, but the eyes were hollow, dark smudges. She clutched the steering wheel, panting now, and the specter disappeared, the bookcase fading behind it.

Tamsen's hand shook as she dumped the contents of her purse onto the passenger seat, grasping for her phone, desperately punching the illuminated glass for her list of contacts—for a lifeline. She dialed.

"You have reached the after-hours line for the Devi Group . . ."

Fariah had responded to Tamsen's emergency call immediately and moved another client to get Tamsen the 8:00 a.m. session. Even this early, the therapist was put together. A silk blouse, tight pencil skirt, and four-inch high heeled pumps. Fariah's glasses were new and the red, cat-eye frames made her look simultaneously sensual yet fiercely intelligent. She sat patiently, watching Tamsen, whose knee bounced up and down as she tried to find a suitable resting place for her hands.

"I can't sleep," Tamsen said. She had maybe caught an hour. She mostly lay awake thinking of her future. She needed a plan.

"Insomnia?" Fariah suggested.

"I guess." Tamsen rubbed her eyes. "I can't focus." Fariah was silent. "And it's causing me to get this vision."

"Tell me about the vision, Tamsen," Fariah coaxed. "Is it a memory?"

Tamsen shrank into the sofa, letting the overstuffed, plush cushions envelop her frame. She stared at the EKG lines on the rug. The heart attack rug, she thought.

"It's my bedroom. The bookshelf. I see it, but it's sideways and there's a ghost behind the glass. It's moving, but I can't really make it out."

"This ghost, does it frighten you?"

"It's not Casper. It wants to hurt me."

"It's hostile. How does it make you feel?" Fariah asked.

Tamsen wiped her hands on the jeans she wore from the night before and folded her arms across herself, gripping opposite elbows.

"Helpless. And disoriented. But it's really just because I've been so exhausted."

"You haven't mentioned these flashbacks before. When did they start?" Fariah picked up a yellow Moleskine journal from her side table, her pen poised.

"I've seen it off and on," Tamsen said. She wondered when the first time had been. "More since January. I didn't think they meant anything." She didn't want to discuss the visions. They were probably remnants of the thousands of nights she'd woken up in the brownstone and seen the same bookcase with all her classics and the same picture frame holding her wedding photo.

"This is my last session."

"Oh?" Fariah asked.

"Victor has secured all our money in a bulletproof trust. I can't access any of it." Even if she wanted to continue seeing Fariah, she'd have to start skimming again, and that was out of the question. Victor would be watching every penny now. "He's holding me hostage."

"So you feel like a prisoner," she reflected back.

Tamsen raised her voice, "That's what I just said to you."

"I can sense your agitation. I think it would be wise to talk about your life moving forward."

Yes, strategies. She wanted strategies.

"You went to that Sparrow seminar," Fariah began. "You've been contemplating going back to work."

"No. The seminar was a waste of time. She told me I was addicted to validation in my career." Tamsen looked out the window. "Even if I did go back, I'll never make any real money."

"If you get back into publishing?" Fariah asked.

"Yes," Tamsen said.

"So, there are no prospects for you?" Fariah asked.

"I'm tired of sleeping in a hotel room, separated from my children. They're all I have, and I refuse to abandon their upbringing to a stepmother." Tamsen drew her finger across the chenille armrest, creating a line in the fabric. "I've decided to go home."

"To Victor?" Fariah asked.

"I'll manage him."

"I'd like to explore this," Fariah said. Tamsen was signing onto a life sentence and Fariah was steady and calm as if she were going to peruse a menu. "Let's talk about what it looks like to be back in a marriage with a man like Victor."

"You don't need to be Carl Jung to figure it out, Fariah. It's not that complicated. If I move back in and follow Victor's rules, then I don't have to worry."

"Worry about . . . ?"

"I know a woman who divorced her husband and it ruined her. He hid all their money from her—said they were broke. Two years later, he's got a five-bedroom luxe co-op on Lakeshore Drive and not one, but two new Porsches. Meanwhile, she's folding gym towels in a locker room so she can pay the electric bill every month."

Tamsen's phone pinged. She had been religious about checking messages since Theo's close call.

"Everything okay?" Fariah asked.

"My friend, Clay—he wants me to go to a spin class this afternoon."

"I think that's a great idea," she said. "Exercise helps everything."

"His boyfriend is teaching," Tamsen added. She had no intention of taking the class, but she knew if she could use spinning as a diversion, then the appointment would expire, and she wouldn't have to endure Fariah's judgments.

The therapist let the tip of the sidearm on her frames rest between her lips. "About being Victor's wife, let's discuss what that entails more specifically. For example, you'll attend work functions, right?"

"Yes," Tamsen answered.

"And, of course, social events. Charity benefits, galas, holiday parties, Christmas, New Year's Eve . . ."

Tamsen's elbow jerked from the arm rest and she snapped her head up, looking vacantly toward Fariah.

"What was that, Tamsen?"

"Huh?" Tamsen felt dazed. It was the sleep deprivation.

"Your eyes were cast down, then I said 'New Year's Eve,' and you looked up like I had stunned you, and your arm twitched, like this."

She reenacted Tamsen's physical response.

A swell of perspiration broke through the surface of Tamsen's skin and the small room felt like the temperature had plunged thirty degrees. New Year's Eve. She would stop drinking altogether, she thought. If she stayed sober, not even getting a tiny bit buzzed off a glass of wine, it would be okay.

"Tamsen?" Fariah called softly. "Are you okay? Can I give you a blanket?"

Fariah rose and took the knit throw off the back of the loveseat, draping it over Tamsen's trembling shoulders.

"I must be getting the flu," she said.

Fariah handed Tamsen a cup of water and returned to her wingback chair. "We were talking about you and Victor, some of the things you'd do together," Fariah said.

"I don't know," Tamsen said. "Take vacations, I guess."

Fariah kept digging. "You typically get adjoining rooms, then? With the children?"

Tamsen remembered the last family vacation they'd taken to Riviera Maya. She'd secured the largest two-bedroom suite on the hotel property and was relieved when Charlotte's recurring nightmare about a man-eating shark necessitated that Tamsen sleep three consecutive nights in her daughter's bed.

"Yes, something like that," Tamsen said, shifting in her seat. Then there was the wedding this past summer for Victor's niece in St. Louis. Tamsen had told Victor she had food poisoning and insisted on sleeping on a rollaway so he "wouldn't catch anything" from her.

"Well, I suppose you will move back into the master bedroom then," Fariah said, watching Tamsen's hands. "Tamsen?" Fariah repeated. The therapist's voice was a distant tone. "Tamsen, what are you doing?"

Tamsen looked down. Her index finger was purple, strangled by a thread she had wrapped tightly, around and around, until blood ceased to flow beyond the first knuckle. Tamsen's insides began to quake and the whirring of the noise machine became deafening.

"Can you turn that fucking thing off?" she blurted, undoing the thread from her finger.

Fariah opened the door to the empty waiting room and pulled the plug on the noise machine from the wall. She swished back to the wingback chair.

"What happened with Victor, Tamsen?"

"I told you, he tied up all our money."

"I understand about the money, but what happened on New Year's Eve?" Fariah entreated.

Tamsen looked at the clock. "He's robbed me," she said. "And he spent tens of thousands of dollars on dildos and cashmere sweaters."

"What did he do to you?" Fariah insisted.

"He won," Tamsen said, standing.

"Tamsen, I think you're bumping up against some trauma memories," Fariah said.

"You think?" Tamsen was getting agitated. She pulled on her trench coat and nodded toward the clock. "Time's up."

"Tamsen, it would be good to address these," Fariah continued. "But for today, surround yourself with comforting people. Go to the spinning class with your friend."

"Why? Have I put on a few pounds since our last session?" she said, patting her flat belly.

"I'm serious," Fariah said. "Sometimes physical exertion allows our minds to release things we're holding onto. I think you need to move."

Now they were both standing. Tamsen's palpitating heart felt like it was going to explode. This meeting had been a waste of time. Her head pounded. She remembered she had Advil in the glove compartment.

She picked up her handbag and pulled out her wallet.

"How much do I owe you?" Tamsen asked.

"We covered a lot for one session. Strong feelings might come up after today." Fariah touched Tamsen's arm lightly. "I think it would be helpful if we kept our scheduled appointment."

"Tomorrow's not going to work for me," Tamsen replied, counting out her last bills.

Fariah's voice was a hair above a whisper. "Then let's find another time."

Tamsen already had one foot in the waiting area. "Maybe," she said. The absence of the white noise was stark; even Tamsen was struck at how the lack of auditory interference made the entire space feel as if it were holding its breath. The void allowed a clear path for Fariah's words to trail Tamsen as she flew out the waiting room door, into the hallway.

"I'll be here when you're ready."

"What can I do for you, sweetie?" Nicole asked Tamsen. "Some extra towels, shampoo, bottled water?"

Tamsen stood at the reception desk at The Talisman. She slid her and Victor's joint credit card across the granite top. "No, Nicole," Tamsen said. "I just want you to know that I'll be checking out for good tomorrow morning."

Nicole's shoulders fell. "I wish I would have known. I'd have baked you some cookies or something," she said. "You're my all-time favorite guest."

Tamsen had grown fond of Nicole as well. "We could have coffee sometime," Tamsen suggested.

"Any excuse to get out of here for a little while," Nicole laughed, but Tamsen's expression was flat. "Hey, you all right? You don't seem like yourself."

"I'm feeling sluggish, that's all," Tamsen said.

"I get like that too," Nicole said, lowering her voice. "You know what I do when I'm down? I lock myself in my bedroom and blast my girl J. Lo. She sets me right every time."

On another day, Tamsen might have laughed, but this morning she was willing to listen to any suggestions that didn't involve sitting on Fariah's couch and resurrecting the past. "J. Lo?" she said, signing the bill.

Nicole glanced over her shoulder. "I play her till the windows vibrate. I literally dance out my demons. It's such a release. You should try it."

It was the most absurd thing Tamsen had ever heard. "I'll keep it in mind," she said.

Tamsen threw her coat and bag down on the hotel bed. For the first time ever, she didn't even remove the bedspread. What did it matter if someone had sat naked on the cover? Bodily fluids, fingernail clippings, bed bugs—what difference did any of it make at this point?

Tamsen flipped open the top of her suitcase and began to empty the contents of the highboy at the foot of the bed. She grabbed a fistful of underwear, her Petit Bateau t-shirts, a pair of cropped, black yoga pants, and the velvet jeggings she'd worn with Whit that day at the conservatory. She opened the double doors on the closet and reached for her silky, cotton robe. Maybe she'd put it on and curl up in bed, order delivery, and binge-watch *Game of Thrones* for the next twenty-four hours. She eyed the untouched stack of books on the nightstand, and *The Count of Monte Cristo* with its dog-eared pages. The breakup left her raw, but it had been the right thing to do.

She spotted Whit's Christmas present to her—the blue bike helmet on the upper shelf. She took it down and turned the smooth plastic in her hands, smiling as she traced the sasquatch sticker with her index

finger. Whit must have thanked the kids a hundred times for Moby—
the reason he could now navigate the city streets in spite of the snowy
winter. She thought of his beloved Edmond Dantès, recalling the sensation of her legs dangling from the saddle and her hands encircling his
waist for support as he rode her to the falafel place on Halloween night.
Tamsen hadn't felt that free in decades. She remembered the reverence
with which Whit spoke of his dilapidated bike. "My counsel and my
therapist," he had called it. She wished she could access this deliverance
for herself, rescue in the form of an inanimate object.

Tamsen looked at the clock. Maybe she should meet Clay. If Nicole
could "dance out" her demons, and Whit said biking was like therapy,
then maybe Tamsen could run her problems over with a spin bike. Or,
at the very least, maybe she could chase them away. It wasn't even lunchtime yet—she still had time to make it to the class. Tamsen grabbed her
yoga pants and a tank top from the suitcase and headed down to the
hotel lobby, where Nicole was filling a wooden bowl with green apples.
Nicole smiled at seeing Tamsen with the workout gear. She raised her
fist in the air as Tamsen dashed toward the revolving door.

"J. Lo," Nicole yelled.

CHAPTER

1 7

The cycling studio reception area was congested with athletes in tights. White, glossy subway tile covered the walls and only a band of bright orange and the graphic of a wheel on an adjacent partition suggested that the place was anything other than a pathology lab.

A willowy, young desk attendant handed Tamsen a tablet. "You need to read and sign this waiver," she said. She was probably a model/actress on her off days.

"What size?" she asked.

"I'm a ten," Tamsen said, sliding out of her sneakers. Tamsen admired the perfection of the girl's seemingly effortless messy bun.

"Have you cycled with Isaac?" the attendant asked. A woman who appeared to be around Tamsen's age hustled by and Tamsen could see every defined sinew in the musculature of her back.

"I haven't worked out in months," Tamsen answered. She was beginning to regret her decision to come. She had heard about these spin classes and how some studios had huge metrics boards at the front of the room that displayed the bike numbers and wattages of all the riders.

"You do you, sweetie," the model chirped as she flashed her embellished gel nails. The pinky was extra-long and had a fake diamond

embedded in the tip. There was an electronic monitor on the wall
with the day's classes listed. Tamsen noticed the name of Issac's class,
"Psych-All."

"I'm a beginner," Tamsen said. Psych-All sounded advanced. She
hoped the party-nail receptionist would suggest she come back when
they were hosting an introductory ride.

Tamsen changed into her yoga gear and the stiff, cleated bike shoes.
She shoved her belongings into a cubby, then followed a hard-bodied
man wearing a yellow Tour de France jersey into the dimly-lit spin room.
Thirty-plus riders sat perched atop stationary bicycles, warming up their
legs to the low, hypnotic beat of a thumping reggae tune. A perfectly
chiseled African-American man with a small, silver hoop earring and a
wireless headset stood tinkering with the controls on his media tower,
his back to the riders.

Clay waved eagerly to Tamsen from the first row, pointing to the
empty bike beside him. There was no way in hell she was going to sit in
the very front. She gingerly climbed between bikes and up two risers to
the back row, where only one empty spot remained. She tried to unjam
the seat, which was stuck in its lowermost position.

"It's not working," a doughy man on the adjacent bike told her over
the increasingly loud music.

Clay hurriedly unclipped from his pedals to help Tamsen adjust her
bike. She felt like all eyes were on her—the novice. She pictured herself
in bed at The Talisman, where she should have stayed. She should be
there, warm and alone, transfixed—not by a book, not even by Dumas,
but by a band of fur-clad noblemen gratuitously spearing one another
on the screen.

"Here's your towel," Clay said, draping the white cloth beside her
hand. "And water," he added, indicating a plastic bottle he'd staged in
the cradle affixed to the frame.

The mirror at the front of the room reflected back the pedaling bodies and doubled the perceived size of the crowd. The geometric relief on the back wall was awash in color that transitioned from green, to robin's egg blue, to pink. The residual glow illuminated the riders' humorless faces as they stared ahead into space, giving the group a collective trancelike appearance that made Tamsen uneasy. It wasn't too late to bail, she thought. A futuristic synthesizer note emanated from the overhead speakers. She took a gulp of her water and the instructor secured the studio door. There was no getting out of here now.

"Welcome to your road," he said in a voice that could have doubled for James Earl Jones. "Welcome to your path—wind up your legs and let this journey take you where you need to go." He paused. "Now breathe with me."

For a minute, Isaac closed his eyes, and then slowly and audibly moved air in and out of his lungs. Tamsen watched in the mirror as all the riders, including Clay, followed his every command. She fiddled with the resistance wheel on the bike frame. It was set too tight and she was having difficulty moving her legs.

"My name is Isaac. I have a PhD in psychiatry from the University of Chicago. I'm also a black belt in mixed martial arts and a certified physical trainer." It was an impressive resume. Tamsen was terrified.

"Don't be intimidated. I promise, this might hurt, but the next sixty minutes will take you places you forgot you could go. Release your shoulders, and with them any preconceptions. Shake out your arms and unburden yourself of your fears. Let your hands rest on the bars in front of you and know your bike will support you. Most importantly, relax—you're going to thank me on the other side . . . let's ride!"

With that, he kicked up the rhythm and directed the group to follow his cadence. "One, two, one, two, one, two."

Tamsen focused on the reflection of all the knees bobbing up and down. She found the beat, but all the riders were leading with their right foot and she was on her left.

"Let's all pedal together, right, left, right, left," he commanded. He was definitely singling her out. Finally, she managed to align herself with her neighbors. Maybe he would focus on someone else now. Isaac tapped his controls and the lights emanated a steady blue aura.

"It requires a great deal of courage to accept the emotional challenge of my Psych-All class, but it also shows a tremendous self-advocacy, so good on you for making it today."

Tamsen thought she saw Isaac looking directly at her when he said "courage." She wondered what Clay had told the spin instructor about her. Did he know about Victor and what she'd been through the past months? She pedaled faster. She could feel her heart rate rising and she doubted she had the stamina to endure an hour-long workout.

"This first song is on a flat road," Isaac said. "And your job is to let that road carry you to the gate. When you reach that gate, you will make a pledge—not to me, not to the person next to you, but to yourself. You will promise to leave this room stronger." Isaac pumped his fist in the air. "You will honor your truth by advocating for that which has been lost in you. Can you see that gate?" Just what Tamsen needed, another guru.

The group hollered enthusiastically, "Yeah!"

Isaac put his hand behind his ear, pressing the group harder, "I can't hear you. Do you feel your power?" He was better than any televangelist Tamsen had ever seen.

The music suddenly seemed louder and the entire group yelled in unison, "Yes!"

"Then, to the gate!" Isaac commanded.

The second song was an easier tempo. The riders were told to add resistance and rise from the saddle into something called third position, with their hands out in front of them as they climbed an impossible mountain. Tamsen knew she was in over her head when she was the only one in the reflection who lagged behind the beat, struggling to emulate Isaac's beautifully lean legs, which were illuminated by his up-lit platform. She had to hand it to Clay, he definitely had good taste in men. Tamsen noticed that Issac's legs were hairless; she wondered whether he shaved them. Probably.

"I need you to focus this instant," Isaac ordered. The room fell into blackness, and although she couldn't make out the direction of his gaze, Tamsen was fairly certain Isaac was calling her out for not paying attention.

Clay yelled, "Come on!" from beside her. She would have whacked him, but she didn't want to get scolded again, or worse, lose her balance and fall from the bike onto the rubberized floor below.

Isaac cued another song. This time, Tamsen recognized the melody. It was Kesha's "Praying."

Tamsen stared forward into the reflection of her own eyes and realized she had caught up with the group. They were all moving in concert now, bobbing in syncopated motion like pistons—up and down, all on the right leg and then the left. She closed her eyes. Tamsen had made it through the gate.

She followed along as Isaac guided them through rolling hills and sharp descents, each song more compelling than the next. Tamsen barely noticed her exhaustion. The quick tempo segued into the slow cadence and Isaac introduced "Fight Song" by Rachel Platten. It was one of Charlotte's favorites, but Tamsen wasn't a fan. The singer spoke of taking back her life, something that Tamsen knew was impossible. But Isaac's voice was determined, and she found her mind strangely open. Her lungs were taxed, but she pressed on. The music boomed from the speakers, exciting something inside, urging her on and enveloping her entire body in electric vibration.

"This next tune is what I like to call your moving meditation. It is your time to reflect on what got you here, to this place. I ask that you take full responsibility for your present circumstances because you, and you alone, have crafted a life that has dropped you squarely where you are at this very moment. That family, those friends, that job, that lack of a job, your relationship—it's all your doing. You need look no further than the mirror in front of you—culpability is staring right back into your face. What agreements did you make? To what beliefs did you subscribe? And why did you do that to you?"

Tamsen was fixed on her image in the mirror and she saw herself—her gaunt cheeks, her matted hair, the circles beneath her eyes. I married Victor, I did that to me, she thought. I agreed to leave my job, I did that, too. I relinquished control of our finances. I let him berate me.

"Own it!" Isaac hollered at her.

I allowed him to cross lines over and over again, brutalizing me with his words. I agreed to stay. I agree to stay. Every day I agree to stay.

These affirmations of accountability agitated Tamsen. They were all just a repetition of the ideas that had occurred to her many nights while she lay awake under the Water Tower painting at The Talisman. The same ideas she'd explored in therapy. Admitting her missteps didn't yield relief, it simply crystallized the futility of her circumstances.

Then Isaac dismounted his bike. In her peripheral vision, Tamsen detected his perfect physique moving slowly in her direction.

"Please have a seat in the saddle and hydrate. You have been stripped down and I thank you for taking ownership of your situation. For taking complete responsibility." He stood squarely in front of her. "Now," he screamed, "what will you do about it?"

The music amplified to a deafening volume and the soundtrack cut to an anthem by Sia. Tamsen recognized it: a remix of "Titanium." She had listened to it often in the car, but she'd only dreamt of having titanium armor that could protect her from Victor's sadistic attacks.

Isaac was in front of her now, squatting in her face like a deranged drill sergeant. He reached for the frame of her bike and gave her resistance knob a slight turn, increasing the load on her legs.

"What happened to you?" he hollered. "What happened that made you this way?"

Tamsen huffed, struggling to propel the stationary bike up an impossible, nonexistent mountain. She heard an involuntary yelp escape her lungs. Her thoughts began to tick back.

"What happened?" Isaac yelled.

Tamsen felt a twinge. A pain between her legs, the sensation of saddle against her pelvic bones. She squeezed her eyes. The seat was steel with little cushion—rigid, hard. She was sore. The room disappeared. It was New Year's, she couldn't move—she had taken the sleeping pill so that she could rest, finally sleep. She'd drunk champagne. One glass? Two? She lay on her back in her bedroom. The ceiling and its recessed cans and the wash of light emanating from the bookcase beside the bed. Victor pressing down on her and the crown of her head ramming into the ebony headboard. Tamsen cried out—she thought she'd cried out. He withdrew, dragging her by the ankles down the mattress, pinning back her knees and then mounting her again, pushing harder into her hips. She thought of the children. Had he locked the door? Theo sometimes wandered in at night. Victor's fingers dug into the flesh of her sides, then they were on her chest, groping, pulling, while he hammered her again and again. It was so dark, she was weak, or perhaps too groggy to distinguish whether she was indeed asleep, or dreaming, or anesthetized. She looked at her books, each in its place, and noticed the silver picture frame—the one from their wedding in which the photographer had snapped the shutter at the precise moment Cormac had yelled to her, "I'm proud of you, Tamsen—you landed yourself a good one!"

Tamsen remembered now.

"Stop," she told him. "Stop, you're hurting me." She had spoken. She had cried out.

The limited clarity of that awful night split her skull open. He thrust into her and she wanted to vomit from the smell of his cologne. She looked at the bookcase and could see his reflection, his body pummeling her. And his face, his teeth bared and his eyes searing holes in his head. Victor was the specter.

She replayed the next morning, New Year's Day, the aperture of her mind expanding as Victor came into focus, sitting on the edge of the bed. He cracked his neck. But unlike before, she now saw her wounded body in the bed, how she reached down to feel the tender tissue between her legs and how she delicately touched the swollen marks on her breasts. She recalled the throbbing headache from the lump on her head and the stinging sensation of her nipples, like they been twisted in the teeth of greedy pliers.

Tamsen screamed on her bike. She screamed the rage she had been incapable of expressing that first morning of the New Year, while her limp body lay defeated on the Anichini sheets that bore the monogrammed initials of victim and Victor: "TPV". Tamsen gripped the handlebars. Her body shook, and she screamed again and again over the bellowing refrain of the melody.

Isaac spread his arms like wings. "Someone's going deep. We don't leave our comrades hanging!" Isaac flew his head back and howled. Other riders followed, passionately yelling along with her in solidarity.

When Victor had turned to look back at her that day, he'd worn the vile smirk of a triumphant conqueror. Disgust, dominion, triumph.

Tamsen became aware that her sweat-drenched yoga pants had

gathered behind her knees, how the little toe on her left foot felt jammed inside the tight upper corner of the cycling shoe, and that "Titanium" continued to wail from the speakers. In minutes, she'd traveled through a wormhole in her subconscious, back in time to confront her greatest shame. The lights flashed wildly and Tamsen let her body throb with the outward rush of every exhale. Isaac cued a new song, and a rising beat pulsated from the speakers, the bass gaining the strength of a locomotive as the cadence of the riders' legs slowed to meet it. The voice of a female artist hummed a foreboding warning. Isaac called out the song title, "Enough." This was the finale. Tamsen wiped her face and unclipped her shoes. Clay reached for her.

"It's not over," he said.

"Yes," Tamsen replied, "it is."

The taxi dropped Tamsen at the curb in front of Victor's building. She ignored the stiffness in her legs and the fact that her sweat-drenched raspberry tank top had not yet dried completely. She put the collar up on her trench coat and stormed the security desk.

"Tamsen Peel, here to see Victor Peel," she said, scribbling her name in the registry. "He is not expecting me."

The security guard picked up his phone and called the Summers & Peel receptionist, who gave Tamsen immediate clearance.

Estelle was waiting to meet Tamsen in the 46th floor lobby when she got off the elevator.

"Hello, Tamsen," she said, her smile dissolving as she looked her boss' wife up and down. She had never seen Tamsen in anything but full makeup and heels. "Victor is just finishing up a video conference with London."

"London?" It had to be Petra. Tamsen sidestepped Estelle. "Which conference room?"

Tamsen was propelled down the long hallway by an other-worldly force. She flew past the break room and the copy center. She even waved at the mailroom guy, who had run the company picnic dunking machine. Tamsen felt her old skin melting away; she was a seed cracking its hull and stepping out anew. With every stride, she invited in her fears. So, she'd have nothing. So, she'd have to reinvent herself. Make her way somehow. What mattered to her most were Charlotte and Theo. There were more important things than two parents sleeping in one house. She would demonstrate for them the most vital of principles: all lives and roles are precious. Every person deserves care and respect.

Estelle stayed close behind Tamsen, almost at a trot. Thankfully, the S&P conference rooms were like fishbowls and it wasn't difficult to locate Victor with his minions. Tamsen stood watching them through the glass as they chortled patronizingly. Victor caught sight of her and knocked his coffee cup with his elbow. He took in her yoga pants and unruly ponytail, and his eyes seemed to expand in his head, as if he were looking at a deranged maniac on a street corner and had only seconds to calculate an evasive move. Tamsen pushed open the heavy door, allowing her sticky fingertips to imprint smudges on the clear glass.

"Is everything all right?" he said, in a voice that was level but taut.

Tamsen noticed Neil Nevin. Unlike the other men at the table, he seemed at ease. "Nice touch, Neil," she said of his tartan bow tie.

Neil smiled.

"Tam?" Petra said, as Tamsen moved into the sightline of the video camera.

Tamsen plucked a grape from the fruit bowl in the center. "Hello, friend," she said.

Petra cocked her head slightly, seeking further clarity. "I was just telling Victor I have another trip to Chi-town on my calendar." There was a flutter of motion surrounding Petra as her associates gathered their things to disband. Tamsen was motionless, staring intently into the shiny lens of the camera.

"Great!" Tamsen said.

The ventilation system clicked off and the fan stopped spinning.

"Pet, you know you were wrong about that frog."

"Oh?" she asked.

"The story is a parable. It's a myth. At a certain point, the frog jumps out. Every time," Tamsen said.

Petra gave a practically indiscernible nod. Even in its subtlety, Tamsen knew she understood.

"That's a braveful frog," Petra grinned.

Victor's subordinates scrambled to leave the room, tripping on one another as they dashed for the door. Victor pressed the escape button on the video conference equipment and Petra's omniscient smile faded to black. Neil Nevin brushed passed Tamsen, looking back over his shoulder at her as if he had something to say, but Victor's swift hand on Neil's back shuttled him out with the rest of the men. Victor closed the door.

"What the hell has gotten into you?" Victor spat.

"Endorphins," Tamsen replied.

"If we don't land Ms Majestic—" he began.

"What, Victor? The entire business will fold? You'll have to cancel your golf club memberships and your ski trip to Chamonix this winter?"

Victor's lips curled back. "It's not just me who suffers, Miss Kinney."

"Then what?" Tamsen continued. "Will we have to sell the brownstone? Will Theo and Charlotte be forced to attend a public school because you can't afford to pay the tuition bills for Dexter?"

Victor fumed. "Summers & Peel is a company built on family values, Tamsen, and you better start behaving like a member of the goddamn family. Look at you, coming in here dressed like that, like some sort of two-bit . . ."

Tamsen's reflexes were faster than the word that never had a St. Christina's prayer of passing Victor's lips. With years of pain and humiliation channeled to her open hand, she swung her arm and slapped his cheek with enough force that his temporary crown was knocked from his mouth, and the mark of her hand on his face was the lesser of the impressions she made.

Her voice was cold and unwavering. "You will never speak to me like that again. You will never again look at me with your sadistic glare as if I am subhuman and worthless." She was shaking. Her mind was moving fast but steady. She borrowed The Count's words and said, "Woman is sacred; the woman one loves is holy."

Tamsen tore open her coat with an upwelling of pride.

"And you will never, never touch this again because you do not own me, and I am not yours to mistreat."

Victor rolled his head side to side, but his neck didn't crack. He searched Tamsen's stony face, then he let out a laugh. "Are you prepared to tell your children you're walking out on their father?"

"No more prepared than you are to admit that you raped their mother." Tamsen's countenance was cool. "Both these things are true, yet there is justice in only one."

She tied the belt of the trench coat, tugging it tightly around her waist, and floated away from him, out the door, down the long corridor, and into the lobby.

Neil Nevin appeared from around a corner.

"Do you have a minute?" he asked.

"Some other time, Neil. I need to get home to my kids," she said. She wanted to gather them close and hold them.

She stepped into the elevator and two women in pantsuits from the consulting firm one floor above chattered loudly.

"He dumped the party in my lap again, as if it wasn't a profound failure last year," the short brunette said. She imitated her nasal sounding boss. "'Two hundred people, a city venue, keep it under budget—make it memorable.' In two weeks we'd be lucky to book a sports bar and he wants memorable!"

"You're screwed," the tall one who smelled like gardenias commiserated.

"The stables on Orleans," Tamsen said.

"What?" gardenias asked.

"It's spring, so the stables don't stink. The paddock is covered, so weather isn't an issue. You can rent picnic tables, or buy them cause they're cheap, and Smoque BBQ offers a great catering package." Gardenias took notes.

The two women locked eyes in disbelief. "What about entertainment?" the short brunette asked.

"The party's a country western theme, you know . . . bandanas as napkins, white paper plates, hay bales for seating. Square Dance Chicago has callers—they bring music, so you don't need a band, and you should splurge on dessert. Hoosier Mama Pie Company does a killer pecan but sour cherry's a good bet, too."

Tamsen looked up at the floor numbers as they counted down: five . . . four . . . three. "Just make sure people wear boots," she added as the elevator lurched to a stop. "Because, well, horses."

The brunette grabbed Tamsen's arm. "Can I get your card?" she enquired.

Tamsen turned to her. "What?" she asked.

"Or do you have a website?" the other woman asked. "For your event firm?"

Tamsen looked down at herself. Sweaty yoga pants and teal running shoes with neon-green racing stripes, hair that must have looked like she hadn't bathed in a week, and these women thought she might have a firm—no, that she *did* have a firm. Tamsen straightened. Yes.

"I'm working on it," Tamsen said.

"Then here," one of the women said, "take mine." Tamsen looked down at the white card with its brown and blue logo and raised Helvetica type. She held it in her hands like a winning lottery ticket.

The elevator pinged. Tamsen let the women exit first. She stood there alone for a breath, and then rushed to a vacant enclave at the far end of the lobby. She collapsed onto a bench and stared ahead, waiting—and then it came. First as a tremor in her core, slow and foretelling, and then as a deluge. The tears rose like a cresting river, with the force of a thousand-year flood, saturated with the stinging salt of the countless hurts that she had harbored for far too long. Her swollen eyes burned, and her cheeks and palms were soaked as she mourned herself and all that had been destroyed. She let it all go; she let it all wash away.

Tamsen returned to the empty brownstone. Aneta would be home with the kids after tennis, but there was still time to shower before they returned. She laid her keys on the kitchen counter and walked to the patio doors, opening them wide to let the cool spring air expunge the lingering vanilla-tobacco scent of Victor. She knew the house would always carry the faint smell of him; he was in the walls and the wood and the fabric of the drapes. But there would someday come a time when he was no longer in her bones.

She went over to the computer, where Charlotte had created a new photo montage screen saver. There were silly bathtub pictures of Charlotte and Theo, others where the children were dressed in matching Christmas outfits, seated at the fireplace. There was a photo of Theo in his high chair, one with him on his Big Wheel, and one of the four of them standing on a windy beach with a crystal-blue ocean backdrop, their hair streaked from the sun and smiles gleaming against tanned skin. Tamsen heaved and the tears continued to come, spilling down her face as she watched the images of their family history click by. She cried not for the failure of her marriage, but for the tragic loss her children would endure; she couldn't shield them from that, she could only uphold her end of a pact to escort them with gentle benevolence into the inevitable new reality they would face—a fractured family.

She stepped under the rain showerhead in the guest suite and let the water pour over her body, taking with it all the sweat and the salt and the anguish of the day. She took a loofah and sweet lavender soap to her skin, cleansing herself of him the way she had done on New Year's Day. But there was no washing off the sense loss and disappointment that moored her to the fourteen years of memories that were as much Victor's as they were hers. She emerged from the shower and wiped the steam from the mirror, staring at her cloudy reflection. It had been the longest twenty-four hours of her life, Tamsen thought. But in the arc of one day, the sentence she thought she'd serve for the rest of her life had been reversed, and there was comfort in that alone.

Clay came as soon as she texted. He canceled his remaining appointments and arrived with two overflowing grocery bags. Tamsen, Theo, and Charlotte sat on the floor in front of the fireplace, playing Chutes and Ladders in their pajamas, while Clay spooned turkey chili into scalloped earthenware bowls. The island was set with a buffet of toppings: avocado chunks, shredded white cheddar, sour cream, scallions, and crispy tortilla strips.

"Mommy," Theo asked, pushing himself up from his elbows to cross-legged. "Where's rehap?"

Tamsen's brain didn't translate the word right away, but Clay's did. "You mean rehab, buddy?" Clay asked.

Charlotte slapped her hands on her knees, "Theo! I told you it was a secret."

"Rehab is short for rehabilitation," Tamsen said, wondering why Charlotte would be discussing such a thing with her brother. "People go to rehab to work on problems they can't handle by themselves."

"What problem does Aunt Hilly have?" Theo asked.

"I can't tell you anything," Charlotte shot.

Tamsen and Clay made knowing eye contact between the two open rooms. Astrid must have disclosed the news to Charlotte at their sleepover last week. Tamsen was relieved to hear the news; Hilly had not spoken to Tamsen, or anyone, since the night in Neil's garage. Pills had always been her brittle crutch. She needed help and Tamsen felt relieved she was finally getting it.

"I'm sure the Summers are dealing with Aunt Hilly's issues privately, so let's be respectful of that and just try to send good thoughts her way."

Clay's call to the table was well timed. "Dinner is served, rugrats."

Afterward, Theo went to his bedroom to grab his Martin. Clay had not yet heard him play and Theo was eager to garner praise from his favorite pseudo-uncle. He dragged Whit's hallmark stool up from the playroom and positioned his capo on the neck of the instrument, plucking a few strings to test the tuning, the way Whit had shown him. Theo beamed with pride when Clay gave him a standing ovation for "Hey Jude."

"Dude, you can sing, too!" Clay gushed. "That falsetto of yours is cash in the bank."

Theo shuffled his foot on the floor; he was still bashful about his voice. "Yeah, that's what my guitar teacher said. He told me I must have gotten it from Dad because Mom couldn't even carry a tune in her pocket."

Charlotte chimed in from where she was curled up like a cat in her favorite velvet chair. "Mom is even worse than Astrid," she said.

"Hey, take it easy," Tamsen defended. She didn't mind their humor at her expense. She felt sturdier now and it was good to laugh with them. "It's true, your father is an excellent tenor, but you got your incredible drawing and painting skills from me."

Charlotte tilted her head. "Yeah, you're right, Mom. We got the best of each of you."

Tamsen desperately hoped this was true. She quickly dispelled a vision of Victor at his most vindictive. She consciously turned her focus to sweet Theo, who confidently strummed his guitar, thanks to Whit.

Whit. Things still felt unfinished with him. She staved off a wave of sadness that the thought of him evoked.

With Charlotte and Theo tucked snugly in bed, Tamsen hugged Clay goodnight. She was too exhausted to recap her day, and he was a good enough friend to know there would be plenty of time to catch up some other time.

"I just wanted to make sure you were okay," he told her.

"Thank you for making me take Isaac's class," she said. "Something happened in there, I can't explain it."

"I pulled a hamstring, for one thing," Clay said, reaching to massage the back of his thigh.

And I pulled myself back to life, she said to herself.

Tamsen sat in bed with her laptop and a daunting stack of unread junk mail addressed to her. She was completely spent, but the events of the day had left her amped and she couldn't sleep. The tedious job of sifting through old mail, with the chance of coming across something important, made for mindless busywork. Tamsen disregarded notifications for cable

TV upgrades and impossibly annoying sweepstakes entries. She tossed aside an invitation to apply for a credit card, but then she reconsidered. She would need accounts of her own now, and a card under her name alone would help her bolster her credit score. She had Leda Sparrow to thank for that bit of knowledge.

A letter postmarked from February was caught between the pages of an Oriental Trading catalog. The return address read: "Airline Miles Processing Center." The miles, she thought.

Tamsen carefully tore the envelope's edge and slid out a note from the same agent to whom she had spoken months ago—the agent who had ensured that Tamsen's matter was taken care of, and not simply abandoned to the pool of wayward, unresolved issues. Tamsen recalled the first time she engaged with Whit, that day on the phone when she picked up his call and lost contact with the airline representative. She thought about her subsequent encounter with Whit on the patio, how he'd told her of his experience with the suicide hotline, which had been instrumental in the resolution of the airline miles fiasco. A warm transfer—someone to stay with her until she got where she needed to go.

Tamsen looked at her new mileage balance noted at the top of the page: 701,520 miles. It translated to $9,119.76—enough to hold them until she knew the direction her life would take.

Dear Ms. Peel,

We are pleased to inform you that the 675,000 miles bequeathed to you by your late father have been duly deposited in your airline mileage account. We apologize for the inconvenience and we would like to extend you a bonus 25,000 as a thank you for your patience and your ongoing loyalty.

Best Regards,

Constance Duncan

Customer Support Specialist

Two months had passed since Tamsen declared an end to the birds-nesting phase and moved back into the brownstone. Victor had taken a year's lease on a four-bedroom waterfront apartment not far from The Dexter School. On the mornings after the kids stayed with him, he'd begun walking them to class. His regular presence gave Ms. Ellison the chance to impart her wisdom; Tamsen had been forced to admit that the teacher's advice had been quite helpful in Theo's transition to his "second home." As soon as school let out for summer recess, Tamsen predicted the parent-teacher relationship would blossom into its full potential. Innocent and smart, Ms. Ellison did seem to care for their Theo. Victor could definitely do worse.

While Victor had stepped up his parenting, he had similarly ratcheted his offensive. He would deposit only enough money into the checking account to afford two days' worth of provisions at a time. He'd canceled Tamsen's gas card and would go ten days straight without responding to her text messages. Victor even went as far as giving Aneta a "leave of absence." Tamsen knew the only reason he hadn't cut her off completely was because someone needed to feed the kids and drive them to school. When Victor requested to chaperone Charlotte's year-end field trip—something he knew Tamsen looked forward to every May—she begrudgingly bowed out. He had already demonstrated that there would be tougher battles to fight. She needed to save her energy.

Tamsen walked through the archway of First Episcopal Church. The church stood grandly at the head of the Magnificent Mile, impeccable with its limestone barrel-vaulted ceilings and stained glass windows. The sanctuary was filled with spring foliage. Magnolia branches, pink tulips, and sweet-smelling jasmine adorned the altar, while deep crimson and blush ribbons hung from the lectern. It was exactly what John Knox had requested.

"She lived a dynamic life and she wanted to be celebrated," he had told Tamsen five days earlier on the phone when he'd asked her to put together the reception for hundreds following the service. It was Tamsen's idea to consult on the floral arrangements for the church. John had told Tamsen that Edith was always impressed with the parties she'd organized for the Women's Social Club and that in her last days, Edith had expressed that Tamsen was the woman she wanted for the job. John Knox certainly could have hired any professional company in the city, but Edith preferred someone she knew and liked, he'd said. Tamsen had been shocked and honored that Edith had chosen her, and she'd poured every minute of the last five days into planning and managing every last detail of Edith's sendoff.

The memorial service would be the last, bittersweet occasion to which Tamsen could volunteer her time for anyone or anything related to the WSC. She would no longer have the luxury of working simply for the joy of giving back. She had met with a free career counselor at Illinois University, who'd urged her to begin drafting a business plan.

He'd suggested she find a job while she established herself; some initial capital would be helpful, plus, he'd said, it can take years before a new company turns a profit. Years. Tamsen had been hopeful her elevator encounter would have led to something, but by the time she contacted the brunette woman from Victor's building, the consulting firm had already hired an outside event planner. She wasn't discouraged. She had set up interviews with two floral shops in the neighborhood and made a note to herself to call a temp agency as well.

The massive, carved wooden doors to the vestibule were open and warm sunshine flooded the worn, mosaic tile floor. Tamsen had situated Charlotte, in her navy Milly halter dress with a black cardigan, and Theo, wearing a smart black suit and a powder-blue oxford, on either side of the main entrance to the nave with the programs Tamsen had engraved on hundred-pound cotton stock.

Clay breezed in wearing sunglasses, a dark blue suit, and a lavender, pink, and green plaid silk tie.

"My man, Theo!" he said, high-fiving the boy.

"This is a serious occasion, you two," Tamsen said in a hushed voice as the deep groan of the church organ echoed through the sanctuary.

"Sounds like a scary monster movie," Clay joked. He held out his arms like Frankenstein and groaned, drawing laughs from the children.

"The attendees will start arriving in fifteen minutes," Tamsen explained. "I need you to greet the guests, hand out programs, and make sure there are plenty of tissues on hand."

"She was pretty old, Mom," Charlotte said. "Do you really think that many people will be crying?"

"Edith Knox leaves an incredible legacy," Tamsen said. "She made a difference in many lives. A generous spirit deserves a thoughtful good-bye—I think you'll see a lot of tears today."

"I brought tissues," Clay said, "and cheese sticks." He winked at Theo.

Tamsen heard a faint yelp. She saw a small box stowed in the corner of the vestibule with a bedazzled leash sitting on the floor beside it. She went over and lifted a corner of the angora blanket draped over the top.

"Dog," Tamsen said. Charlotte squealed and rushed to have a closer look. John must have left the Havanese while he went into the office to speak with the reverend.

"Mom," Charlotte was using her high-pitched pleading voice, "can we keep Dog since Mrs. Knox is in heaven?" Theo began jumping up and down.

"I'm sure Mr. Knox wants to take care of him."

The dog was the last thing Tamsen wanted to deal with in that moment.

"Here's the leash." She handed it to Charlotte and looked at Clay. "Take him for a walk so we know he's done his business. He goes back in the kennel for the service. The first three pews inside are for family and we are to sit behind them." Tamsen closed her eyes and held the bridge of her nose. She had a checklist of to-do items: donation table for contributions to Mothers Trust Foundation in memory of Edith, folding chairs, and the guest book. Thankfully, the altar flowers were all set.

"I'll see you guys in a bit," she said. "Clay is in charge, you two."

"Gotcha covered, boss," Clay said.

The reception was to be held in the annex immediately adjacent to the church sanctuary. Tamsen mandated a series of buffet stations to accommodate the enormous crowd of anyone who ever knew Edith or wanted to say they did. Tamsen had also brought in servers from the WSC to pass small bites to mourners who might not be as mobile, and who might be more comfortable at one of several ten-tops covered in blush-colored fabric near the exit.

The catering crew hurriedly banged silver chafing lids on top of steaming water baths for the lamb chops and the veal meatballs, and shuttled carts of hors d'oeuvre plates to the raw bar and dessert table.

"Guys, we need to cut out percussion, okay? The organist doesn't need accompaniment," Tamsen said. She directed placement of the thirty arrangements sent by friends and family so that they wouldn't obstruct the food presentation, then she pulled a few of the mature buds from the magnolia branches and sprinkled the petals across the white linen table cloth.

Nicole emerged from the kitchen, pushing a cart on which sat a giant ice sculpture, carved in the likeness of Edith herself. It bore a striking resemblance to the matriarch, with its regal forehead and slightly hooked Roman nose. The hairstyle was Edith's typical up-do, but Tamsen noticed the sculptor had made a few cosmetic modifications in the neck and chin area, giving Edith a bit of a lift.

"Where did this come from? And what am I supposed to do with it?" she asked Nicole, who'd called in sick to The Talisman to help Tamsen for the day, and to whom Tamsen would owe a kidney if they pulled this off.

"Your friend Mr. Knox said it was on his mother's list of final requests. He said you'd figure something out," Nicole added with a skeptical eye.

Tamsen scanned the room. "We'll have to make space for it."

"We could put the shrimp around her neck—they need to be chilled anyway," Nicole suggested.

"If we put a shrimp collar around the neck of the Grande Dame of the Socialati, Edith Knox will haunt us for all eternity. But I like how you're thinking, Nicole."

Tamsen stood back and beheld the five-hundred-pound frozen monstrosity: Edith Knox smirking at her from the great beyond and daring her to rise to the creative challenge. Tamsen's adrenaline surged.

She lived to solve problems like this and she would not disappoint Edith, even posthumously.

She turned to Nicole. "Set up a sixty-inch round with risers and linens. I want a coffee urn with paper cups. Call Alliance Bakery and tell Peter I need every last danish he's got in individual, white bakery bags and that I need them here in the next forty-five minutes."

Tamsen reached into her wallet and pulled out a $200 grocery store gift card. It was the last vestige of The Fountain Fund, the only bit of currency that had escaped Victor's raid when it had dropped from his hand and lodged in a snow bank the night of the burst pipe. Tamsen remembered the afternoon she had purchased it; it was the day she refilled Theo's prescription on her way home from her very first meeting with Fariah. She turned the card over in her hand and drew in a long breath, handing it to Nicole.

Tamsen waited for fear to take hold, but instead of the insidious panic to which she had grown accustomed, she felt relief. Despite the constant harassment, the threatening emails, the difficulty sleeping, and the uncertainty of her future, Tamsen let go of the gift card with the smallest notion that she was going to be okay.

"There's a grocery store on Elm. Send Miguel, tell him to buy every box of Cracker Jack in stock," she said as she zipped up her wallet and tossed her apricot pashmina over her shoulders.

"Where are you going?" Nicole asked. "The service starts in a half-hour."

"You're in charge. The caterer knows the routine. Just make sure the bartenders have enough blue cheese-stuffed olives. This is definitely a martini crowd," Tamsen said, and flew out the door.

Tamsen knew enough to wear her most comfortable heels on the day of an event on the chance she might need to run a last-minute errand, and that's exactly what she was doing: running. Past the Michigan

Avenue shops, whose window displays with beach balls and bare-legged mannequins promised the arrival of swimsuit season, and across intersections where pedestrians violated the *Don't Walk* signals to the irritation of honking taxi drivers. An unauthorized Chicago Cubs mascot in sunglasses did the Electric Slide for dollar bills on the corner near the future home of a 43,000 square-foot coffee behemoth. Tamsen waited till between songs and then she pulled out a fifty, making a deal with the cub, and shaking on it.

Tamsen jaywalked across the busy shopping street and pushed through the revolving door of her second stop—the Dolls Like Me store. She wove her way between parents who'd driven from adjacent states just to indulge their girls in the ultimate experience of pint-sized capitalism. It had been a year since Charlotte had outgrown her own Dolls Like Me dress-up doppelganger, Charlotte Jr., but Tamsen was intimately familiar with the line of "Pretty Like Me" clothes designed so daughters and dolls could dress alike for fancy occasions. Tamsen shoved past a mother in a John Deere hoodie to grab the object of her quest, but she was not quick enough. An eight-year-old with banana curls and Levi's seized the sparkling accessory just as Tamsen laid a hand on it. They faced one another like two adversaries on either end of a wishbone.

"I was here first," the girl said, tugging the accessory toward her.

"I really need this, honey," Tamsen replied, pulling back. She didn't have time to argue with a petulant third grader. The little girl scowled at her. Tamsen noticed the Dolls Like Me doll under the girl's arm. It wore a red gingham shirt and work boots. It was the rare "Girls on the Farm" edition. The woman in the green hoodie stepped in.

"Are you really going to try to rip that from my daughter's hands on her birthday?"

Tamsen had an idea.

"Have you heard of the Dolls Like Me utility tractor?" she asked, still clutching one half of the accessory.

"Don't mess with her like that," the mother said, putting her hands on her hips. "Everyone knows that tractor was discontinued."

"What if I said I had one available for trade?"

The girl looked at the accessory, squinted her eyes, and pondered the offer.

"With the heavy duty spare tire?" the little girl asked.

"And the optional front-end loader," Tamsen purred.

The service was nearly over and the sea of congregants stood for a final invocation. Scores of Chicago's most prestigious had turned out for the celebration of Edith's life. The general mood was more like a party than a funeral. Tamsen snuck up the side aisle, nodding to Cybill and her husband. Digby was there, accompanied by Hilly, to whom Tamsen had spoken twice since her release from inpatient rehab in Arizona. Hilly looked tanned and rested and she blew a kiss as Tamsen walked past. Neil himself was there too, seated on an interior aisle and donning his typical kilt, only this time with a black jacket. Tamsen spotted Victor standing with his hand on Charlotte's shoulder at the opposite side of the church. He may have only met Edith once, but he would never miss the opportunity to be seen amongst Chicago's highest caste. The networking possibilities were too good to miss.

Tamsen squeezed into the fourth row where Clay, cradling Dog, stood with Theo. They were behind the towering figure of Stephan Cole. How he and Jacqueline, who was wearing a wide black velvet hat with a veil over her eyes, had insinuated themselves into the family section, Tamsen had no clue. But it didn't surprise her in the least.

The organ bellowed out a final hymn, "Crown Him with Many Crowns," accompanied by a concert of strings and a blaring trumpet. The voices of the Socialati resounded through the vast chamber. Theo gripped his mother's hand as the last note from the organ pipes trailed off, and the pastor gestured from the pulpit for all to be seated.

"You're missing it," she thought she heard Theo say as a rumble of shifting feet boomed from the old oak floor planks, and the bodies of the congregation eased into the stiff creaking benches.

Tamsen hushed her son. Even seated, Tamsen could not see past the tall back of Stephan Cole's dark pinstriped suit. She heard a swish as he dropped his program to the floor. When he leaned forward to pick it up, the view of the splendid altar, with its sacred paraments and imposing cross, came into her view. More striking than the carved wood ornamentation, however, was the sight of an elegant young man seated at the front of the musical ensemble, cradling against his body the gently curved figure of a polished spruce instrument. Whit.

Tamsen froze. They had not seen or spoken to each other since the night at his apartment. Tamsen had thought of him many times. She had even started several texts: *How are you*, or *I hope you're doing well*. But the words seemed empty and impersonal. She simply didn't know what she could possibly say to thank him—to tell him how much she cared for, even loved him. At this point, it was best to move forward. She had such a singularity of purpose surrounding her own survival: the welfare of Theo and Charlotte. She was unable to glance back into the past, where she had left him.

She watched as Whit scanned the crowd, searching for the one pair of eyes who could appreciate the significance and the triumph of this moment. She knew he wanted her to see him, and then, for a micro-fraction of a second, they locked eyes. Then Stephan sat back upright, adjusting his posture in the uncomfortable pew. Tamsen felt her face flush. Her heartbeat quickened and she looked sideways at Clay, who gave her a weak smile. Whit had found his way back to the cello.

John Knox stood and made his way to the front of the sanctuary, where a large black and white photograph of his mother stood on an easel. He tugged lightly on his lapels.

"As many of you know, Mother was a great lover of and patron of the arts, more specifically the symphony. Last fall, we attended a function for the Women's Social Club of Chicago, where she recognized Kyle Whitman, a world-class cellist who she saw perform in Austria. Two days ago, I learned of an arrangement wherein Kyle promised my mother he would perform at her memorial. I am very grateful Mr. Whitman was able to be with us on such short notice."

Tamsen moved close to Theo, lifting him to her lap as she found a window of space through which she could see Whit between Stephan's arm and Jacqueline's hat. She rested her head against Theo and watched as Whit centered the cello between his legs and relaxed his shoulders, the same thoughtful way he did when their conversations delved into something meaningful, something personal. He straightened his posture, closed his eyes, and took a breath so full it expanded his ribcage and thrust his collarbones upwards. He raised his bow, immersing himself so intensely in the moment that his entire body became part of the cello, urging every note forward to its full expression. As he played, Tamsen pretended, just for a second, that he was playing only for her. She knew why Edith Knox requested him and why everyone here would recognize his brilliance. The virtuosity of Whit's sound was born of its humanity, the depths of which he was only able to reach by experiencing the torment of life for himself, of illness, of death.

When Whit was through, Theo looked up at her. "Is Whit a genius too, Mom?" he asked.

She kissed his forehead. "I'd say you two have that in common," she replied as the congregation erupted in applause. Dog barked with the flurry of excitement and Tamsen grabbed him from Clay, returning him to the kennel at their feet.

Nicole and Miguel opened the side doors of the nave and Tamsen rose, quickly moving ahead of the crowd. She had a party to throw.

The food stations were perfect: carved ham and roast beef with pretzel rolls and horseradish spread, an abundant raw bar with Kumamoto and Wellfleet oysters, crab claws, and enormous jumbo shrimp. Tamsen knew the Socialati kept a close eye on their figures, even if they did binge secretly on Belgian chocolates before bedtime; she had directed the caterer to construct an extensive bar with every varietal of chopped greens, manned by two staff members who tossed custom salads for guests who called out their favorite ingredients.

Cybill stood beside a tiered display of savory tarts and nibbled demurely on a lamb meatball. She motioned to Tamsen, who was occupied near the bar, filling crystal bowls with Edith's favorite, Brazil nuts.

"The Board is very sorry you've declined our invitation to serve, Tamsen," Cybill said.

"I love the work the WSC does, but the timing isn't right for me. Besides, I think there are other worthy contenders."

"I agree," Cybill said. "Still, I was hoping you'd say yes." Tamsen had considered it. With a decade of service from the lowest rung, it would have been thrilling to see what impact she could have had on the top. Nevertheless, she was a single mom now and she needed a paycheck.

Tamsen noticed John Knox directing Whit and the rest of the quartet toward a riser at the far end of the annex, where their music could be heard, but where it wouldn't overpower the conversations that were buzzing among the attendees. Whit spotted her looking his way, and Tamsen quickly turned back to Cybill.

"Is the word out yet, about the new Board member?" she asked.

"As soon as she accepts," Cybill said.

Nicole picked up stray paper napkins and cocktail forks as she replenished dolmades on the Mediterranean table.

"The caterer cannot keep up," she said. "These people are eating like it's tuna tartare Armageddon."

"How is my dessert station holding up?" Tamsen asked.

"I hope you don't mind, but I put Charlotte on it," Nicole said.

Charlotte stood in front of the dessert table, handing out caramel corn sundaes. The monument to Edith really was a piece of work, perhaps Tamsen's finest. The giant ice sculpture sat in the center, encircled at the neck by hundreds of impeccably round vanilla ice cream scoops, forming the perfect Holly Golightly pearl necklace. The brooch clasp under the sculpture's chin was a carefully placed edible arrangement of silver-sprayed white chocolate curls and the Dolls Like Me girl's jeweled tiara, which nested tightly around the ice Audrey Hepburn's high up-do, shimmering under a pin light Miguel had added for effect. The entire presentation was set on a borrowed robin's egg blue tablecloth with a white runner, and to the sides of it, Nicole had arranged baskets of white bags containing Danish pastries.

"The sunglasses definitely look more glamorous on the sculpture than they did on the dancing bear cub who loaned them to me," Tamsen remarked to John Knox.

"I'll have a sundae, please," John Knox said to Charlotte. "Sorry to spring this thing on you at the last second," he told Tamsen. "I wouldn't have blamed you if you had dumped it into the baptismal font."

Tamsen was surprised by his humor; John had always appeared so formal. "I have to admit, I had to think on my feet for this one," Tamsen said.

"The Cracker Jack is an excellent touch. Mom loved the scene where they tried to engrave the prize ring at Tiffany's," he said, then he quoted the film, *"Do they still really have prizes in Cracker Jack boxes?"*

"Oh, yes," Tamsen said, in her best Holly Golightly. They shared a laugh.

"Thank you for handling the party," John Knox said.

"Happy to do it," Tamsen replied. "Edith gave so much. She deserves a great farewell."

"I've told the caterer to bill me directly," John Knox said. Then he reached into his jacket, pulled out an envelope, and handed it to Tamsen. "But this is for you."

"Oh, no, John," Tamsen said. "I can't accept this."

"Mother would have insisted you be compensated for your work," he said.

Tamsen took the envelope, recognizing a check through the clear window. "I don't know what to say."

"You're a professional, Tamsen." He extended his hand. "In my line of work, we simply shake hands and say, 'it was a pleasure doing business with you.'"

John Knox's handshake lingered a millisecond beyond protocol and Tamsen thought she saw something personal in the flick of his eye, but the moment disappeared after he was pulled away by a woman in a white sari and bracelets that tinkled when she moved her arms.

Tamsen turned back to Charlotte. She could hear Whit's cello playing a classical piece in the background. The notes were cheerful. She wondered if he had already moved into some Back Bay apartment, out at night visiting music venues, or riding Edmond Dantès along the Charles.

"What did Mr. Knox give you, Mom?" Charlotte asked.

Tamsen lifted the flap on the envelope, peering in at the paycheck made out in her name for a sum that could have covered both her work and that of ten assistants.

She leaned into her daughter. "Mr. Knox paid us for our work today."

"Does that mean I can afford to go shopping?" she asked.

"Maybe, but first we're both setting up savings accounts because everyone needs to learn to look after themselves and their money," Tamsen said, kissing her daughter's cheek. Tamsen untucked the flap and peeked inside one more time. $20,000—it was equivalent to what Flare Events might have commanded. She ran her fingertip over the words "Pay to the Order of Tamsen Peel." Leda's book flashed in her mind. "If you can earn one dollar from your dream, then you can earn a hundred. If you can earn a hundred, you can earn a thousand." A lot more than a thousand.

A woman in a simple black cap-sleeve dress touched the back of Tamsen's arm. She was lean and muscular, and she didn't wear much makeup. Her skin was clear and radiant, and her smile revealed two rows of straight, white teeth. She was a natural beauty.

Sally Frith.

"Someone said you put this party together," she said, her shoulders back and her heart high. "I just wanted to tell you I think Edith would be pleased." Sally Frith didn't appear unhappy or indigent.

"Thank you for saying so," Tamsen replied. She hesitated, but she was moved by the courage Sally had demonstrated by coming to a memorial service where she would mingle among women with whom she used to shop and lunch. "I know you and your husband divorced and I admire your bravery. I'm sure it took a lot to start over."

"No doubt you've heard I'm working a job that isn't particularly glamourous," Sally said. "But I'm almost done with my yoga teacher training."

"I feel for you," Tamsen said with sincerity.

"Please don't take this the wrong way," Sally said. "I'm an educated, white woman in a free country. There are much better places for you to put your compassion."

Tamsen embraced her. She was absolutely right.

Hilly cradled a bite-sized salmon tartare cup in one hand and held a sparkling water with lime in the other. Astrid stood beside her with pale lips.

"Astrid, Charlotte would love some help at the dessert table," Tamsen said.

Hilly smiled at Tamsen. "Thanks, she's having a rough time with all the honesty at home."

"You look good, Hil."

"Doing better every day," Hilly said. Her voice sounded chipper, but Tamsen could detect the heaviness behind it.

"You sure?" she asked.

Hilly picked at the buffet. "Where did you find these incredible crab claws—are they even in season?"

She avoided Tamsen's eyes, but Tamsen didn't back off. "I know a good lawyer," Tamsen said. "She's from the neighborhood."

Hilly moved closer, her mouth drawing into the old, open-mouthed fly-catcher smile.

"Sometimes it's better to keep things status quo—let things settle," Hilly said quietly.

"Settle," Tamsen repeated, nodding her head with resignation. What more did Hilly need from Digby before she would finally leave?

"You and I may come from the same place, but I am not you, Tamsen." Hilly watched one of the Socialati breeze by, wearing an emerald bracelet that cost at least a half-million dollars. "You don't need this." She made a discreet sweeping gesture with her hand. "I do."

Tamsen thought of Fariah and the tolerable limit. Digby's behavior hadn't crossed the line for Hilly, and perhaps it never would. And that was okay.

Hilly began to twirl a piece of her hair. She looked down and cleared her throat. Tamsen noticed Jacqueline approaching with Stephan lumbering behind.

"Decent party, Tamsen," Jacqueline said while she folded some greens into her mouth. She was nudged by a passing senior citizen supporting himself with a three-wheeled walker. "But a bit crowded."

"Definitely too crowded," Hilly said, scowling. Jacqueline ignored the dig, but Tamsen was pleased. Absent the sedatives, Hilly had some of her vinegar back.

"I want to thank you for putting a word in with Cybill. My interview with the nominating committee could not have gone better." She plunged her fork into the salad on her plate.

"Yes, it could have," Hilly said flatly, sipping her fizzy water through the narrow stirring straw and eyeing Jacqueline like a crouching lioness who'd spotted prey. Tamsen felt a wave of euphoria because she knew exactly the direction the conversation was about to take.

Jacqueline looked back at Hilly as if she might feed Hilly to her pet dragon. "I thought we all agreed to play nice, Hilly. Especially given your fragile state of recovery."

It felt strangely satisfying for Tamsen to be the bystander in one of Jacqueline's verbal sparring matches, especially because Hilly was about to turn it into a street fight.

"You're so right, Jacqueline," Hilly said. "And in the spirit of playing nice, I want you to be the first to know that I have decided to accept the Board position offered to me by the WSC nominating committee this morning."

Jacqueline's upper lip twitched. From her mouth escaped a loud, high squeak, which sounded like she'd just stepped on a bat. Tamsen beamed with pride. Hilaria from the South Side was back.

"Does that mean you've been passed over?" Stephan interjected.

Jacqueline's attention turned, and she sank her venomous fangs into Tamsen's neck. "It means Tamsen is worthless."

Tamsen looked at the glass in Hilly's hand and she imagined tossing the water into Jacqueline's smug face. She smiled at the fantasy of Jacqueline slowly melting into a puddle on the ground, with nothing remaining but her dress and black hat at Tamsen's feet. Tamsen drew in a breath.

"You can question many things about me, Jacqueline. Why I would never endorse you for the Board, why I will never again give freely of my time and energy to one of your galas, or why I put cattail greens in that salad you can't shovel down your throat fast enough—but if you're going to talk about worth, consider why we're here." Tamsen nodded toward a beautiful eight-by-ten headshot of a young Edith Knox that sat on the table beside them. "You know, it's not too late for you to use your powers for good."

Jacqueline pivoted in her Nicholas Kirkwood slingbacks and marched off. Stephan raised his eyebrows and took a turn toward the bar.

The reception continued and the guests lingered, devouring the passed shot glasses of tangy gazpacho with crème fraiche and crispy tortilla cups with avocado and octopus ceviche. Tamsen spied Whit and the string quartet heading into the caterer's staging area for a break. She pulled Nicole aside.

"Nicole," Tamsen said with a flutter in her stomach, "run into the back and show the cellist where the caterer put the back stock of falafel."

Nicole was too busy to be perplexed by the dispatch. "You got it," she agreed.

Clay stood in the center of the melee, trapped by a former client who was apologizing profusely for migrating to a lesser salon in Lakeview. She was begging for Clay to take her back, along with her overly processed split ends. He rolled his eyes in Tamsen's direction and she swooped in for the save.

"What was that about?" Tamsen asked him.

"She was on the verge of showing me her roots," he replied, sweeping up two flutes of champagne from a passing silver tray. "To you and this incredible achievement."

"And to Isaac," Tamsen said.

Clay gave a passing waiter the once-over. "I told you—the best workout in the city."

"Thank you again for making me take his class," she said.

"Well, we broke up," Clay said.

Tamsen's face fell. "Oh, no. I thought Isaac was a keeper."

"Imagine having sex with someone who won't stop chanting 'get to the gate, get to the gate.' I couldn't take it anymore."

Tamsen searched the room for Neil Nevin, spotting him adjusting his black sash near a monstrous floral arrangement the mayor had sent.

"Come with me," she said, hooking his arm. "There's a prince I want you to meet."

Neil was unzipping his soft side bagpipe case.

"Edith and I first met in 2014 at St. Andrews. It was a big day because the Royal and Ancient Golf Club finally allowed women to become members," Neil said.

"I did her single-color process for that trip," Clay bragged.

"Are you going to play?" Tamsen asked, looking at the wind instrument.

"As soon as you want to clear the guests out, give me the signal." Neil laughed.

He reached into the side pocket of his bag and slid out a plastic

DVD case. On the front was a picture of a cowboy wearing nothing but a ten-gallon hat and mustache. His 'pistol' was hidden behind a piece of electrical tape. Neil held it out ceremoniously.

"Tamsen, I brought you a gift."

Victor hovered close to a group near a gallery of laminated photo boards displaying scenes of Edith in her personal and philanthropic triumphs. Tamsen figured the clique had to be John's business associates. Even though the Knox empire was solidly entrenched with their current advertising firm, Victor always stood downwind, hoping to catch a scent that might hint at some new business opportunity.

Armed with the new knowledge begotten of Neil's offering, Tamsen watched Victor from a new aspect. Now she was the one with the upper hand, and the elation of knowing that he had no clue how hard a hammer was about to come down on him gave her the sweetest satisfaction. She allowed her mind to soak in a mental bubble bath of euphoria before goading his attention by stacking the dirty plates elderly guests had left on the ten-tops. Victor couldn't resist—he came up behind her.

"You better get used to doing someone else's dishes," he growled, "because this is your future."

Tamsen crossed her arms, the vitality of her righteous rage burning as she stared at Victor without blinking.

"The funny thing is, I would have *licked* plates clean for money—if I had to. But that's not going to be necessary. We're moving ahead as planned, but under my terms now."

Victor's posture stiffened, and he smirked. "Terms," he huffed, "you don't know what you're talking about. My money will never go to anyone but my kids. You can't touch a dime."

"You love to boast about how Summers & Peel is a company built on the decency and values of moral America, but do your clients know that your production department uses software to make the babies in your Bummies diaper ads look chubbier?"

She was going to slowly savor every second of this discourse.

Victor threw his chin back and laughed, "Oh, Tamsen, Tamsen. Is that all you've got? You know clients allow us certain liberties."

"Liberties, as in exaggerating the effectiveness of Blizzard dandruff shampoo?"

"You really are stupid," he said, his ears drawing back.

"Okay," she chirped. "How about your golden boy—he's been moonlighting, you know?"

"I expect all my artists to moonlight, Koop included. They need a place to express themselves. Freedom of creativity improves our ads," Victor snarled.

"Well, then, it's no wonder you get such great work from Trent Queerantino."

"Who?" Victor asked.

"Koop. He directs all his 'art' under the name Trent Queerantino."

"What the hell are you talking about?"

"One hundred and twenty-seven films. Gay, Straight, Fetish, BDSM, Scat. He's quite prolific," she said, smiling sweetly.

Victor's eyes grew wider than Tamsen ever thought possible. She knew in his mind he was connecting two large dots: Thunderchicken and porn. He quaked a little and finally opened his mouth to say something.

"I don't believe it," he said.

She waved her hand. "No matter, you can search it later. Right now, I'd like to discuss how things are going to go."

"What do you want?" Victor said, smacking his dry mouth. His attempt to call forth his evil mask was short-circuited by a slight twitch in his right cheek.

"One, I will send you a link to a site that outlines the simple steps to a low-cost, hassle-free dissolution of marriage."

"Go ahead with your penny-pinching strategies, I'm hiring the biggest shark in the city," Victor fumed.

"You'll work with It's Over Easy or I'll send Thunderchicken the canon of Koop's films," she countered.

Tamsen spotted Nicole with Charlotte and Theo, who waved from near the chocolate fountain. "Two, we will only speak positively of each other to our children. We will never involve them in any of our disputes, nor will we discuss with them any matters pertaining to our divorce." There, she'd said it.

"You wouldn't dare expose Koop," Victor put his hands in his pockets and his eyes dodged around the room. "We'd lose Thunderchicken. You'd be on the street."

"You're wrong, Victor. I'd happily say goodbye to all of it. You see . . ." She looked around her at the beautifully appointed tables and the impeccably dressed mourners, her eyes coming to rest on the dripping visage of Edith's melting bust. "I have nothing to lose," she said.

His mouth was agape.

"Third," she said, "I'll be pulling together a set of documents to initiate the termination of the irrevocable trust you established in an effort to starve me of the assets to which I am entitled."

"You're not entitled to shit," he said.

"Actually, we live in an equitable distribution state," Tamsen retorted, "so, technically, I believe I am entitled to at least half our shit."

"I'm not terminating any trust. It's ironclad," he scoffed, the shine of perspiration glazing his forehead.

"Eleanor is going to love *Duncock*. And didn't she say she wanted to star in one of Koop's productions?"

"I will fight you, Tamsen."

"Think about it," Tamsen's voice was level. "Do this my way, Summers & Peel lives on, and we amicably part ways. It's a win, win." Her voice jumped to a cheery lilt. "We're both Victors!"

Victor left, and John Knox gestured a summons. The woman with whom he spoke had her back to Tamsen, but her stature was vaguely familiar. A pale blue, calf-length coat hung over her shoulders and she carried a distinctive taupe leather bag. For a second, Tamsen was confused. Context was playing tricks with her mind. But the woman turned, and it wasn't an illusion—Tamsen saw the unmistakable brown face of a woman who could captivate an entire room with her glow. It was Petra.

"You've met the new President of my latest acquisition, have you not?" John said.

Tamsen put her arms around her friend.

"President?"

"I've just landed. I came to pay my respects. Plus, we hit the ground running tomorrow," Petra said in an appropriately subdued tone.

"So, this is why you were here at Christmastime?" Tamsen asked.

"The buyout of Ms Majestic was just announced. US expansion starts as soon as we work out some logistics," she said.

Tamsen could hardly contain her joy. She hoped this meant she would see more of her best friend than she had since college.

"You were talking to Victor," Petra said. "Is there anything I can do?"

Tamsen watched as John stood with Nicole and Miguel—shaking their hands, commending them for their good work. The reception had been a flawless success and Tamsen had relished every second of the preparation, right down to the Cracker Jack. But she could not have done it without help. John opened his suit coat and handed each of them an envelope. Tamsen touched her dress pocket where she had put her own check.

"I have things with Victor under control," Tamsen replied, "but there is one thing I'd like."

"Name it," Petra said.

"I know I'm fairly new to this, but I have experience with caterers and florists and rental companies." A smile curled across Petra's cheeks. "I don't have a huge staff yet," Tamsen said, looking at Nicole and Miguel. "But I'm well-connected."

"What can I do for you?" Petra asked.

"I want a shot at your US corporate events. The Ms Majestic business is the perfect size for me. We can grow together."

Petra squinted quizzically, as if she questioned whether this was the same broken woman from their rendezvous at the small restaurant over the holidays. "There's talk of a kickoff meeting in Palm Springs. I can help you get a foot in the door with the corporate events team, but the rest is up to you."

Tamsen made a conscious effort to appear cool, but if she'd truly expressed her inner sentiments, she would have been screaming with mad elation. Her mind was already alive with décor possibilities: a chic but updated mid-century modern vibe—a neon Ms Magestic logo at the entrance, pink flamingo lawn ornaments or blow-up palm trees as take-home swag. And that was just the start.

◆ ◆ ◆

The afternoon dwindled and so did the seemingly endless supply of provisions. Only family and personnel remained. Edith's great-grand-children, nieces, and nephews played chase games in their crinoline and dress slacks, hiding under the folding tables and sneaking sips of half-drunk whiskey sours and watered-down old-fashions. These were the Socialati of the future, only vaguely aware of the rules that would ultimately dictate their behavior as conditioned adults. Tamsen surveyed the assemblage of heirs as they tumbled about thoughtlessly, chasing poor Dog, who by now was certainly missing the throne of his departed master's lap. She wondered which of the new generation inherited Edith's character, her generosity. Maybe they all held the potential to be authentic, uninhibited, even eccentric.

Nicole directed the servers to strip the wine-stained linens off the tall cocktail tables and dismantle the food stations from which the day's delicacies had been devoured.

"We've got it from here, Tamsen," Nicole assured her.

"You are underemployed at the hotel," she said. "You know that, right?"

"I heard people talking about how good today was," Nicole said. "I think you and me make a good team." She re-tied the strings of her white apron. "If you need me, I will be waiting for your call."

Tamsen had to pause to process all that had transpired. She stood in disbelief of her circumstances: in her pocket she held a check for doing something that was second nature to her, her best friend had just handed her the chance to compete for a huge contract, and—the tiara on the ice sculpture, as it were—she knew Victor would be compliant with her, at least enough that she didn't have to worry about how she would manage.

Tamsen gathered her handbag and wandered into the sanctuary to pick up the pashmina she had left behind. The nave was empty except for an elderly homeless man, who sat hunched forward in a middle pew, and for Whit, who waited for her, playing softly to the audience of one. He lifted his bow.

"Please, don't stop playing because of me," she told him.

"I started because of you," he said, and he played a quick upbeat riff. He rested his bow across his lap.

He saw Tamsen noticing his knee bouncing up and down and he stopped. She coughed lightly, thinking about what to say next. They both spoke at the same time.

"How've you . . . ?" he began.

"Did you . . . ?" she started to ask.

The homeless man lifted his head and raised his finger in the air, proclaiming something indiscernible.

"Can we take a walk?" she asked.

They crossed Michigan Avenue, not touching, but in stride, as shadows filled the street and the remaining sunlight was chased up the sides of the buildings. She handed him her shoes when they reached the crosswalk at Oak Street Beach, and he tucked them gingerly inside his backpack. The cool sand was a relief against the achy soles of her feet. A yellow lab raced wildly across the beach and launched himself into the lake to retrieve a dirty tennis ball that bobbed merrily on the surface.

They walked to the frigid water's edge and Whit skipped a flat stone across the glassy surface in the waning daylight. The scudded clouds appeared to be uplit, the softest pinkish-periwinkle.

"I like seeing you in action," he said.

"Same," she told him over the whir of the Lakeshore Drive traffic, watching as he cocked then snapped his wrist, sending another rock spinning across the water. A distant sailboat crept toward the harbor, hoping to beat the sun to the finish line of twilight.

"What was Edith's end of her bargain with you?" Tamsen asked.

Whit threw his chin back, following the soft, white line of chalk a jet had left to dissipate against the deepening azure.

"She saw me perform in Vienna, right? But the night she came was . . . that night . . . she was actually there." He shook his head. "I still can't get over it." He tossed another rock and it skimmed and jumped, finally disappearing under water. "She offered me an outrageous amount of cash to play again—the cello. I told her I couldn't. Then she asked me if I had a cause." He stared at the flat water. "I got to thinking that if some good could come of my epic break with reality, helping somebody else with my same variety of madness could be really cool, or meaningful, I guess." He looked at Tamsen. "She had her lawyer draft a real contract." Tamsen knew Edith's estate lawyer; she and Victor used the same firm. She'd seen Whit speaking with the attorney at the reception. "The donation went to suicide prevention." He snapped his finger, joking, "But I probably should have taken the money."

"You definitely should have taken the money," Tamsen laughed.

Whit brushed the sand from his hands and buried them in his pockets. "Have you reconsidered things? Thought about me, Tamsen?" he asked, drudging the sand with the toe of his black leather shoe. She still felt her heart dilate when he said her name out loud.

"I think I've mostly been jealous of you . . . your freedom," she admitted. He raised his head and his dark brows lifted. She looked out over the glassy water and envisioned the land that was beyond. "My marriage is over. I'm filing for divorce." The word had not mellowed; it still tasted bitter on her tongue.

"Maybe that's why you seem different," he said.

Tamsen saw a young couple on the pedestrian beach walk. They grinned as they sauntered, the sides of their two bodies fused together. The girl held a red rose loosely in her free hand. Tamsen's mind sounded the shrill warning bell signaling impending catastrophe. She might be different, but she knew she was far from better.

She encircled Whit's waist with her arm and he immediately reciprocated the gesture, placing his around her as they strode slowly up the shoreline.

"Do you believe in Providence?" she asked.

"Like the Count? That depends," he replied. "If Providence is on my side, then yes, I'm a devout follower."

"We are an unlikely duo, you and I." She could see Hilly and Digby's posh building from the beach, and their unit, with its grand balcony overlooking the lake.

"Not really," Whit said. "We've both suffered . . . a lot."

"So, you think it's that, as opposed to fate, that brought us together?" she asked.

"No doctor, or treatment, or even million-dollar promise from an eccentric octogenarian was enough to displace the darkness. You did that—call it whatever you want."

"A warm transfer," Tamsen said.

Whit stopped and turned her shoulders to face him. His irises were their dark amber and his nostrils flared delicately as he exhaled. A light wisp of her hair blew in front of her face, catching in her lashes, and he softly swept it away with the same calloused fingertips that gave his cello its voice.

He drew her body close and kissed her mouth decisively, as if the act was the indelible signature of an immortal treaty. When he pulled back, his breath warmed her parted lips before it diffused into the atmosphere of lake air.

The lump at the back of her throat was born of the truth she saw: that she had, in turn, been his warm transfer. Safe passage was made, their conveyances complete.

Now they looked ahead. Whit to the east, and Tamsen here, on terra firma. Her future had been a dull wasteland—scorched earth. And somehow, out of the devastation, a tiny cotyledon was gaining vitality, its pale green tentacle uncoiling a broad leaf to the sun.

"I'm still hoping my New Year's wish comes true," he said.

Tamsen took in the vast expanse of water, a slanted moon brightening in the fading blue sky. A fresh memory of New Year's Eve replaced the old—she was with Whit, on the back of his fat tire bike, awed by the view of their shimmering city, eating pizza under blankets in a cramped hut, and casting dreams out over a frozen lake under a rain of fireworks.

"Mine did," Tamsen said. She squeezed his hand.

"I'll keep waiting," he said.

Tamsen thought of all that lay ahead. Theo and Charlotte would enroll in summer camp at the park district, there would be gardening and walks on the lake. She had a business to start, a life to rebirth.

"I don't know how this works," she said.

He drew her hand to his chest and pressed it close to his heart.

"This knows," he said.

"Not yet," she said.

"So, where does that leave us?" he asked.

She looked up at him and a tear sprang from the corner of her eye. She felt it roll down her cheek, but she didn't wipe it away. Her hand remained in Whit's.

"Somewhere," she said, "between *wait* and *hope*."

DISCUSSION PROMPTS

Compare the manners in which Tamsen and Fariah express their feminine identity through their clothing. What factors do or do not influence the way you express your sexuality? Where is the line between femininity and sexuality?

Tamsen and Whit develop a relationship with more than fifteen years between them. With what age difference would you be comfortable? Would you ever enter into a relationship with someone vastly older or younger than you?

Was it wrong for Tamsen to enter into a relationship with her son's guitar teacher? What are your feelings surrounding the ultimate outcome of their romance?

What do the airline miles and the Fountain Fund represent to Tamsen? Is money power in your relationships? How does power express itself in your romantic relationships?

Tamsen has a psychological breakthrough in a spin class. Have you ever had a breakthrough while exercising?

Edith is a nonconformist. How do you conform to gain acceptance? What have you done to resist conformity?

What would you advise a friend who was in a marriage similar to that of Tamsen and Victor?

The are several examples of sexual objectification in this book: Victor's objectification of Tamsen, the gay man at Clay's holiday party who tells Tamsen, "I would totally fuck you if I wasn't into guys," and the elf who slut shames Charlotte. Does Tamsen objectify Whit? What does the word objectification mean to you?

Whit tells Tamsen that a warm transfer is "when a person stays on the line with you during the call transfer, you know, to make sure you don't get disconnected." What are the metaphorical warm transfers in this book? Who has been a warm transfer for you?